SWELTERING PASSIONS . . .
FORBIDDEN LOVE

She reached out a hand for his, and he took it.
"I appreciate this, Abel, more than I can say. It's
been two months since I've had a man to advise
me."

He knew, then, that she wanted him in her bed.
He ought to have realized it all along. He wanted
her, too, but didn't know if this was the time. He
did know that if he made a suggestion, she would
draw back and make believe she had been outraged. Oddly, he didn't have any idea what to
say. It had been such a long time since he had
tried to make love to any girl but Nancy—he had
honestly forgotten the slave girl, Blossom—that
he wasn't sure he would know what to say or how
to make himself clear.

He found that it wasn't necessary. Serena's soft
hand, rising from his, brushed against a pants leg
and slowly was drawn back to herself.

"I beg your pardon," she said.

"Not at all."

In dry, hesitating voices, the invitation had
been made and accepted. He found himself glancing outside this room and toward the carpeted
stairs.

THE
BLACKBIRDER
Lionel Webb

WILDSIDE PRESS

To G.E.
With the best of good wishes

Published by arrangement with the author by
Wildside Press LLC.
www.wildsidebooks.com

Published by arrangement with the author.

"He (Livingston) is a man of splendid abilities, but utterly corrupt. He shines and stinks like rotten mackerel by moonlight."

—John Randolph

Book One (1862-1865)

1

The black man's voice was raised. "But I'm free, and you can't do this!"

"You're not free now," the ringleader said harshly. "Be quiet, boy, or this will be even rougher on you."

The black man's hands had been tied tightly with gritty gray rope. He had been forced to sit bareback on a dark full-grown horse that moved restlessly under him. One end of the rope was around his neck. The other end was being tied around a cypress tree by a hard-breathing man in the saddle on a white mare. Strong sun shone full on their faces. The black man's voice was a little higher now, his speech no longer as precise. "I a free men." He insisted. "I free!"

The ringleader snorted. "You're free to die, boy. That's the free you are. Brave men aren't fighting over at Shiloh so that a nigger can keep on—. Drat it, aren't you ready with that rope?"

"Will be in a second, Ch———."

"Don't use any names!"

"Okay now," the second man said and pulled his horse back, although still in touching distance of the full-grown horse that the black man had been forced to ride.

The ringleader nodded. "Anything you want to say? Get it off your chest now, boy. Admit your sin. Tell the truth and shame the devil."

The black man, hardly able to make out the face of his tormentor on account of the strong sunlight, threw his head back. "You're not just out to throw a scare into me like some of you fools have done with different black free men, and then send 'em packing. You mean to go through with it. I can tell."

"If there isn't anything you want to say—."

The black man suddenly started to curse. He called the

9

ringleader every name he could think of, his voice not losing pitch or volume. His mahogany skin glowed with anger, and his full head of crinkly hair almost seemed coiled to strike in venom. He didn't repeat himself.

The ringleader's thick lips tightened. He turned toward the second man, but didn't look directly at him just then. A newcomer in white with a wide white hat and riding a chestnut quarter horse, had suddenly entered the clearing. After a quick glimpse of what was happening he spurred the chestnut forward.

"What do you think you're doing here?" the newcomer demanded.

The ringleader snapped, "Abel, you keep out of this."

"You expect me to let you kill somebody and go the other way? Is that what you want?"

"Get away from here and leave us to do our work!"

"If you're so brave you should be fighting for Jeff Davis and not going around killing a free nigra."

"I do what I please."

The newcomer shook his head. He was five feet eight and in his thirties, but his small-featured face looked determined. Sparks seemed to surge out of the narrow eyes, and his nostrils looked as thin as the tips of ice tongs. His lips were slim. The face gave the impression most of the time of a man who had been born playing poker and had never got out of the habit. It didn't give that impression now.

He turned to the other man. "Cut him down right away."

The other man actually started to move forward, but the black didn't seem to have heard what was happening. He hadn't stopped cursing since Abel had come upon them; his voice remained high.

The second man, his chunky body stiffening, now spurred his horse forward. With a hard, sun-reddened hand, he slapped the rump of the horse on which the black man was sitting. The horse moved away, but the black man straightened in the air, held in place by the rope. It was over in seconds. The black man's lips were distorted,

10

and his mouth opened uselessly for air that would never come. There was a scream that suddenly halted, and a gurgling sound rose from the black man's throat. His sturdy legs moved uselessly in the hot, still air.

The ringleader spat. "He's free now, the nigger bastard."

Abel said tonelessly, "I hope you both feel proud of yourselves."

"At least that scum won't be desecrating others while our boys are fighting at Shiloh and Bull Run and where-all else."

Abel didn't put up an argument. There was no point to it any longer. He turned the horse around deftly.

"It's time to get you out of my sight, Chad. You're making me sick to my toenails."

He rode slowly. The lengthening shadow of the dead black man dangling from a rope on the cypress tree was at his right. He looked away from it.

The second man suddenly said, "That free nigger is crapping in his pants."

"Well, what did you expect from those scum?" the leader snapped. "Even when they're dead they don't give you anything but trouble."

2

The man on the chestnut kept up an even pace as he rode past the levees and onto the Bermuda grass-fringed land. His sharp eyes took in the presence of the young black stockminder who was sitting on a patch of Bermuda grass while half the Fairlawn Plantation mules grazed negligently. The boy didn't see him, and Abel wouldn't divert the boy's attention from the job of animal tending.

He rode down the rutted lane, glancing only idly at the old house used for ginning cotton and the old stable that faced it. The mansion would come into sight at the first

11

turn, and he left the quarter horse at the stable before moving onwards. The two story white-painted house gleamed in the sunlight. China and pecan trees had been set around it like a paper heart around a box of toffee candies.

He walked swiftly, pausing to make sure that no activity whatsoever was coming from the double row of canvas-topped quarters on the other side of the mansion unless it was in his view as he moved. He suddenly frowned. A pickaninny was running back and forth in front of one of the frame houses playing a child's game. Abel smiled, shrugged, and walked on. He moved more slowly, out of habit, as if he still needed to clear his way gingerly between the flocks of hens and chickens that had always seemed to find themselves in front of the mansion. He didn't need to do it any longer. Not since the war had got under way. Not since a few weeks after the shelling of Sumter in North Carolina.

One of the woman house slaves was fussing with flowers in a fat red vase when he walked into the dim reception room.

"Where's the mistress?"

The house slave didn't look around. "In her room, Mistuh Abel."

He wondered if any of Chad Goldthwait's house slaves treated Chad in such a cavalier fashion, but he was smiling as he walked up the gleaming steps. It was impossible to tell from his manner that he wasn't particularly looking forward to the next few minutes of his existence. He knocked swiftly on the door.

"You might as well come in."

He was in a wide room with flowers on the mantel, a statue against the far wall, and long mirrors. Most of the furniture was covered with chintz. There was a miniature model piano that played mechanically, which had been imported from Vienna after heaven-alone-knew-how-much haggling. The writing desk, the plainest piece of furniture in his wife's boudoir, was more like a chest of drawers than a desk. The room had cost over a thousand

12

dollars for furnishings that were probably worth less than a tenth of that money, now. Abel didn't begrudge the expense to make his wife feel more at ease in her southern home, but he never felt that so much beauty had been really worth it.

"Is there something you want to tell me, dear?" She was smiling lightly.

"Some news I thought would interest you."

"If you say so, then of course it will. What my lord and master has to say is of great interest to me, as always."

He wasn't aware of any sarcasm in the British accent with its seven year overlay of southern drawl that made her voice attractive to other plantation owners during social evenings. Nancy van der Meer Debenker smiled at her husband of twelve years. She was five feet three, with tawny hair falling gracefully to thin shoulders. She wore a dark cotton dress with white lacework at the throat and sleeves. Her eyes were wide. At the moment she swayed back and forth where she stood.

"Very well, then. You remember Tuck."

"Tuck who?"

"I don't know if he ever had a last name."

"Then he must be what you call a nigra." She was smiling even wider, now. "Black as a sump hole."

"Serena Pollard's boy."

"Not a boy, a free nigra. Serena set him free."

"She set him free and then kept him with her."

"Well, if Serena Pollard wants to set a nigra free and keep him as a servant, that's up to her."

"Not really. Tuck was the only other person who lived on her land."

"It's a small piece of land, Abel."

"Small, but she could have used two-three hands. Instead she sells the other hands, sets Tuck free, and lives with him and nobody else. You know what they were up to. The whole state of Louisiana probably knows what they were up to. Certainly all of Festin knows."

"I'm sure every loud mouth in the town of Festin has got his ideas about that." Nancy's sweet tone belied her futile anger. "It's nobody's never-mind except Serena's and her Tuck's."

"The town doesn't think so, like I tell you. Chad Goldthwait certainly doesn't think so."

"Chad Goldthwait." Her lips were shut tightly, and a white line rimmed them momentarily. Then she nearly smiled. "Not that I've got any dislike for a business friend of yours, my lord and master. Oh, no. Far from it."

"Chad was so sore about Serena and Tuck that he took one of his men along and taught Tuck how to dance in the air."

Nancy's smile had become fixed in place. "Hanged him, you mean? That—. Chad Goldthwait hanged a free man?"

"It took place in a cypress patch, not far from our grounds. That's why I have to warn you—."

Nancy's good manners hadn't deserted her. The smile stayed frozen, but without amusement. "Do you have any real idea why he did it?"

Abel pursed his thin lips briefly, then started, "I've come to tell you—."

"Just one minute, if my lord and my master pleases. Do you know why Chad Goldthwait really did that unspeakable thing?"

Abel waited.

"I'll tell you why: it's because Serena Pollard isn't one of your la-di-da hypocrites! She wanted something and got it and didn't care who knew or what they thought of it."

Abel quirked his brows. "Are you finished?"

"If Serena had said that she only needed one hand to tend her six acres and had kept Tuck in slavery, then there might have been rumors about what went on, true. But nobody would have known anything. It's the knowing that Chad Goldthwait couldn't stand—Chad and all the rest of 'em with their hymn singing on Sundays, and the black slave gals they bed down during the balance of the week. A bunch of dirty, smarmy hypoc—. What are you doing?"

Abel Debenker narrowed his eyes very slightly as he moved toward the writing desk. The top drawer had been opened a quarter of an inch. He pulled it open further and

14

glanced inside. There was a bottle the size of a memorandum book. Inside it was a brown liquid. Abel Debenker pulled the cork, gave one sniff, and put the cork back.

Nancy was saying quietly, "A gentleman wouldn't do any such thing."

"A lady wouldn't drink in secret, my dear." He looked into the drawer again, and the corners of his lips were pulled down in disapproval. "At least you ought to drink out of a glass."

"I take a little nip now and then so as to make the Southland look even rosier."

"Who do you buy it from? Is it Jethro?"

"Jethro? That very large nigra, you mean? No, certainly not."

"Good. He's liable to put poison in one of your bottles sometime. He doesn't like his owners much."

"I do declare, Abel, you're funning." She grinned at him. "We could lock the door and take a little time together."

"Some other time very soon, dear."

"I know. You hate the smell of liquor on a lady's breath. In that case, I'll be glad to wash out my mouth."

"A little later, my dear, if you still want to."

She flushed prettily, from the cheekbones upwards.

"I came to tell you to be very careful during the next few days, Nancy, and to keep your eyes on Kermit whenever he goes outside the house. You see, the trouble took place—."

"It was a lynching!"

"The lynching took place not far from our property, and the nigras always seem to find out what's happened in the neighborhood."

Now her voice was lowered. "Do you expect trouble?"

"I always do, my dear, but now I've got reason to think we may have some very soon."

"I'll watch out for Kermit," she promised grimly. The only moment of communication came when talking about their boy.

"And now, my dear, if you'll excuse me," he said.

15

"But, of course, I will excuse my lord and my master, whom I worship."

3

"Pardon me a moment, Mr. Debenker, but I can't let the bitches get away with this."

The overseer spurred his horse out to the road repair unit where two burly women had stopped loading a dirt cart and were quarrelling. A third person, a younger and prettier gal, was whispering to each in turn. The young girl turned away first when the overseer came close. He let his rawhide whip crackle in the air above the heads of the burly women, but spoke sharply to the pretty one. He turned to ride away at last. The young gal leaned forward again.

"That Blossom is the worst nigger gal I ever saw," Dolph Morin said, wiping his face with a handkerchief as he returned to Abel, who was on his chestnut. "Let her go work with anyone and she puts her at somebody else's throat and you can't pin the goods on Blossom. She's never responsible for what happens except as she makes it happen."

Abel Debenker looked across at the lissome gal in oversize road-mending clothes. She seemed to sense his gaze, turning around to smile. Abel wet his lips briefly. If he had been hooked up with a white gal as purposeful as Blossom, he might have owned several neighboring plantations.

"The job will take two hours, Mr. Debenker," the overseer said, wiping his straggly mustache. "It has to be done, sir. Otherwise, if we have the niggers carry cotton to the gin over a bad road you'll have ten bales of filthy cotton from the gin before the end of the day."

Abel cocked his head to one side and did some swift calculating. "Five hours, I'd say. Most of a whole working

16

day, Dolph. You're right, though. It probably is necessary. However, that's not what I came to talk about."

"Sir?"

Abel drew down the rim of his white hat to protect himself from the sun. The noises around him made it hard to catch Morin's complete attention. A cart full of dirt was dumped across the roadfill when he started to talk. He could hear shovelling and hoeing. Wood was being cut down and pulled across mud and Bermuda grass.

"Have you had any unusual difficulties with the nigras today?"

"No worse than ever."

"Any rebelliousness?"

"No more than—. No, sir."

"Good. If there's any change in that situation, I want you to let me know immediately. Is that clear?"

"Yes, sir." It was a signal between them to repeat what had just been said. "I'm to let you know immediately if there's any unusual rebelliousness among the niggers."

"Thank you."

"Excuse me, Mr. Debenker, but has—has anything happened?"

"There's been a lynching near this property."

"Yes, I see." Morin had been an overseer too long not to recognize possible danger. "I certainly haven't had any trouble at all so far, except for the nigger bitch, Blossom."

"Good." Abel looked past his overseer and shook his head slowly. "She's at it again, egging on the others to fight. Put her with an old man, a very old man, and a young one."

"Yes, Mr. Debenker." The overseer spurred his horse once more and rode into the field.

Abel turned his chestnut around for the trip back to the mansion.

Blossom cried when she was put to work with Moses, but it didn't do any good. The old man must have been a hundred years old if he was a day and couldn't lift a piece of wood to save his life.

17

"I let him rest," she told the buckra, when he asked why the old man was laying down in a patch of shade. "I tell him to be easy as he not do any work."

The buckra yelled at Moses a little and sent him off.

"*You* haven't been doing any work, you little bitch," the buckra said. "I'll fix that."

He put her to work with Jethro. That was bad. Here she was next to the best-looking buck in the world, but she was dressed awfully. For road work she had to wear one of those dirty gray dresses with a cord drawn tight around her, but at a point above the hips. And she had to wear those strap-wrapped blanket pieces and heavy shoes. At least she didn't have to wear a handkerchief over her head to keep the sun off, like the other gals; she wore the cap that Jethro had given her at the last planting time.

"I he'p you with the wood," she said loudly.

When the buckra couldn't hear, she gave an impish giggle and sat down to watch him. His muscles moved wonderfully. He wasn't working much faster than old Moses.

"You feeling good?" she asked lightly.

He nodded, but suddenly put his hands down to his sides and clenched his fists. She gazed up at Jethro's slim face over the strapping body, lazily, as she'd done many times in the past. He didn't seem to notice her this time.

"You know what happen today? A lynching happen."

"How do you be sure?"

"Old Elijah see the body."

"Elijah is old as the stable house. He sees, but don't know what it is."

"I believe him."

She grinned, knowing how to make herself important to this buck.

"Blossom make sure."

"How?"

She winked. "Blossom ask, that's how. All you have to do is ask, and it come to you."

"Who do you ask? The buckra?"

"No, not him. I ask somebody who really knows."

"The masta? You ask the masta himself?"

18

"When I ask 'bout different things, he tell me. Why shouldn't he tell a nigger gal, now?"

Abel spent half an hour in his small, neat, white-walled study after a scanty supper—imagine the Debenker's plantation serving hardly enough at a meal! He pored over his books for purposes of comparison and wouldn't have been surprised if the war's conclusion saw his land worth as little as thirty dollars an acre. And that was likely to be a good price, no matter who won.

Offhand, he didn't think too much of the C.S.A.'s chances. Robert E. Lee might be a good soldier in charge of the C.S.A. forces, but the South was hurting. By 1862, less than a year after the secession, there was talk about a regiment of free nigras being formed in South Carolina to fight Abe Lincoln's men. It was impossible to think highly of a sovereign state that had to fall back on nigras to defend its peculiar institution.

Abel hurried up to his nine year old son's room, and joined Nancy in the ritual of saying goodnight to a lad who wanted to stay awake. Nancy was almost like the girl he had married in '55, warm and charming and generous. Abel stayed close to her at one point, long enough to make sure that there wasn't any smell of liquor on her breath. She must have washed out her mouth with attar of roses before coming up to the lad's room.

Afterwards, he left her without a word and walked out to the wide white porch. He was looking out at the banana-yellow Louisiana moon when he heard a shout that was more like a scream. He had drawn his thin lips down in irritation until he heard the sudden flick of leather against some surface and another cry of pain. Moving swiftly, he hurried off the porch and over toward the double row of frame one story cabins that faced each other, as if resignedly, on the other side of the mansion.

He stopped, his head cocked to one side, so that he could tell where the sound came from if he heard it again. It did come. He was able to identify the scream as having been made by a female. In his eagerness he looked furiously at one cabin after another, and only modified the glower when his eyes lighted on the small scruffy church building at the foot of this impromptu street of slave cabins. And again there was the whick of leather and a resonant scream of terror.

"Mr. Debenker!" The overseer, Dolph Morin, was standing at his side. In one hard sun-browned hand he carried a club with dried bloodstains at the tip.

"You haven't been flogging any of the gals," Abel Debenker said quickly. "Do you know who has?"

"No, but I mean to find out." He rushed toward the first cabin at the left. Abel put a hand over his nostrils before rushing into the cabin that faced it.

"Call out when you find whoever's doing it, and I'll do the same," he shouted.

He hurried past the projecting posts. There was a clay fireplace rising to a split-stick chimney, plastered with mud. There was a mud wall down the middle of the area to separate one family from the other. On an oar-shaped wedge of dirty hay, a buck was raising his body and lowering it. Underneath him a gal looked up and smiled vaguely at the master, then raised a hand in greeting. Abel hurried out. Breath surged from his nostrils and lips. He hadn't been inside a canvas-topped slave cabin for six years or so. The smells hadn't changed, or the liking for fireplaces, the matting for beds, the wooden blocks that were used as tables and closets. Very little seemed to change in five or six years.

In the next cabin he found a boy and a gal lazing around, but they got to their feet hurriedly after one fearful glance. In the other division, a man was lying on the floor. In one brown hand he held an opened bottle. The smell of cheapjack whiskey almost overpowered every other odor in this cabin. Abel, stepping out gratefully, saw the overseer on his way out of the third cabin in the row he was searching. Dolph Morin's straggly mustache twitched at both ends in pleasure at the hunt, wherever it might take him.

There was another whick-and-scream, almost like one

20

sound, as Morin plunged into the next cabin. Abel, his head cocked once more, felt himself nodding. He took half a dozen steps toward an area behind the next slave cabin, and then went on tiptoe even though he hadn't made any noise. Nothing but a pair of small vegetable gardens was in sight when he looked to his left. At the right, however, he found the answer.

There was an upturned can at the center of a vegetable patch. The slave gal, Blossom, was standing over it. She wore a coarse cotton dress that showed slim hips and breasts like young fruit just before coming into season. Abel felt his palms itch at the sight of her, from just below the thumbs to just below eight fingers. There was a smile on her face, almost hiding the high cheekbones. It made her face look very much like a child's. Abel wished his shoulders hadn't suddenly ached, and that he hadn't recently seen a black buck and his gal making love on dirty hay in one of the cabins.

As he watched, Blossom raised a fishhead's length of thong which she probably wore when she did road work. With one bare foot on the upturned can, she hit the thong against it and called out loudly as if in pain. Then she smiled again and looked up. Her features suddenly lost their life. The smile died, and a tiny pulse vanished from her temples. She wasn't nervous, however, only waiting for his response.

"Why?" he demanded.

"To see you again, masta. I know you come if Blossom hope to see you."

"What I ought to do is beat you until my arms get tired."

Her eyes were downcast. "You the masta, you do what you want with Blossom."

Breath was hard to come by, what with the memories and angers that were part of him now. This slave gal had never in seven years said anything that didn't take place in the present, maybe because she wouldn't let herself think about a future. There was less fear in the slave gal then in her mistress, who had turned into a secret drinker in

21

headlong flight from the present and dread of the morrow. No man could spend all his free time with a woman afraid.

As he watched, Blossom suddenly came closer to him and stretched out her hand. The black hand touched Abel in the lean midsection and started to move down, like that of a sightless person feeling her way. Part of his body rose.

"No," he said in a whisper.

As he turned, Morin was coming out of a cabin, his heavy feet hammering against mud that yielded. Abel walked in his direction.

"Haven't found anything yet, Mr. Debenker."

"The trouble seems to be over. Why not go back to your place?"

"I might as well finish my inspection," Morin said. "You deal with niggers, you have to break in on them unexpected-like every once in a while and catch 'em by surprise. They have to know you might be almost anywhere. It keeps 'em from stealing the horses and mules, or your eyeteeth for that matter."

Abel nodded. He knew very well that Dolph Morin was a good and efficient overseer, holding on to the keys that might unlock stable doors, not using the whip unless he felt he had to, not demanding that a slave gal go to bed with him, making sure that the slave food was at least palatable to nigras. Thoughtful. Considerate. A hard worker.

"Finish your visits, then, and get a good night's sleep," Abel ordered. "The plowing starts soon enough, and we all have to be on our toes."

"Yes, sir."

The overseer rushed into another cabin, taking his pleasure in the hunt for its own sake. Abel turned and walked to where Blossom waited. The black gal had straightened herself and was smiling. She had pinched her cheeks to make them seem softer, and by the moon's light it was possible to see fingerprints on the brown skin. He didn't speak, but turned from her and started to walk across his land. At no time did he look back to see if she was following or pause to hear barefoot steps behind him. It wasn't necessary.

22

The walk took him to the old sugar house down the newly repaired road. The door of this out-of-use building opened at the touch. His grandfather, Lyon, had spent forty-seven thousand dollars to build and equip a sugar house, but his slaves had destroyed the work systematically. Lyon had lost thirty-six thousand dollars on his first sugar crop and thirty-two thousand on his second. At two percent interest on his outstanding loans, he had lost a total of one hundred and thirty-eight thousand dollars. He hadn't recovered until he switched back to planting king cotton, sold off seven of his field hands, sent three house slaves into the field, and whipped one troublemaker to death.

Abel stood in the darkness, but moonlight through the opened and dirty window showed him as much as he wanted to see of the equipment. Brass fixtures had been looted by different slaves over the years, and only some rusty pipes were left. The boiling pans had vanished along with brass fixtures. Pickaninnies sometimes played in the wide trough where fluid sugar had been cooled and crystalized. Its only users nowadays, aside from the pickaninnies, were the occasional whites who took slave gals over here from time to time. Abel hadn't used it in years.

He didn't hear the wooden door open at Blossom's touch, but she was in the sugar house when he turned.

"Lie down and wait for me," he ordered.

Carefully he pulled off his white shirt and pants and shoes and socks. His underclothing took time and care to take off, and he put the whole business down on the floor in a small pile. There was no clean area to be found.

She was waiting for him, one leg raised and dark arms outstretched. He joined her. Not a word was spoken. He had never in his life used a woman with brutality or for his pleasure alone, and certainly he wouldn't do it this time. The gal started to breathe hard and to rake his back with crack-nailed fingers, pretending that she was eager for his attentions. Abel was calm and purposeful without hiding his desires. He eased his weight across her and went in at last, moving almost rhythmically. At one point Blossom

23

stopped the overdone ecstasies, and her eyes looked directly at him with something in them that he had never seen before. Was it gratitude? Warmth? He looked away from the sight of emotion directed at him from a slave gal. Blossom closed her eyes tightly although she wasn't in pain. The cruel child's smile was on her beautiful face once again. When it was over for him, he kissed her on the top of the head and then raised himself out of her and away.

His clothes were in an untidy heap. He struggled with the underpiece first and then put on pants and socks and shoes, then the shirt and jacket. He drew out a C.S.A. five dollar bill of the State of Louisiana from an inner jacket pocket. Blossom lay on the floor, a leg raised in readiness in case the master wanted her once more when he was dressed; the position told more about her relations with men of all colors than he wanted to know. Abel folded the bill in half, reached over, and tamped it firmly into her right hand. Then he left without looking back.

Late as it was, he ordered Hester to prepare a tub for him downstairs and washed and soaped his private parts thoroughly. With a glass of fresh water he rinsed his mouth. Then he dried himself, avoiding any look at his figure in a mirror. He put on a dark robe with the white piping he insisted on, then told Hester to take the clothes he had been wearing and wash them thoroughly and to throw out the underpiece only after it had been washed; she wasn't to use any part of it for a clothes rag until then. He hurried off to his room and went to bed.

Blossom hurried into the cabin that Jethro shared, next to last in the slave quarters. She was prepared to wake him up, but it wasn't necessary. Jethro's housemates, two boys she had never particularly liked, were fast asleep in each other's arms. Jethro was sitting on the floor, wide awake.

"The boy is lynch, all right, Jethro. Masta tell Blossom he do it himself."

Jethro's thin-featured face was working angrily in the moonlight. He started to get up.

24

"I kill," he muttered. "I kill."

"No." Blossom took his shaking hands in hers. "Do that, and somebody kill you."

"I don't be here any more. I run away."

"You live in the swamps and go hungry, you run away. Foolishness!"

"What I do, then? I do nothing? Masta takes the rope to one of ours, and I do nothin'. Is that what you want?"

"No, but you get even at the right time and in the right way. We all do, every Black in the quarters."

She spoke swiftly and very much to the point.

4

"Of course, there hasn't been any trouble." Chad Goldthwait rumbled, settling his heft into one of the gold-lined chairs that his wife favored in her dining room. "The niggers didn't like the idea that one of their own was carrying on with a white woman any better than we liked it. The niggers were on our side."

Abel let out a deep breath, then glanced at his wife. Nancy didn't seem to have stirred. She was wearing a shade of gray that brought out the tawny red of her hair, and her free hand reached for the dropsical wine glass at her right. She must have taken a number of drinks even before letting herself be brought to dinner at the Goldthwait plantation on Sunday night, the twenty-third of February; it was the day after the George Washington birthday celebration, and the Goldthwaits had called it a Union Deathday dinner; to refuse them would almost have seemed unpatriotic.

"It doesn't make sense to get into a feud with a neighbor, much as you'd like to."

"Certainly not, O my lord and my master," she had said muzzily in her thickest English accent. "We are all living in an outpost of 'empah'."

They sat with other planters and their wives in the brightly lighted dining room with its hundreds of disguised lanterns mounted far over their heads. The furnishings were of the best, but the food was of low quality because of the blockade by Union forces. Abel knew enough to eat only the garnishings and not the tough and wiry old chicken. Nancy didn't seem to have eaten at all.

"We have plenty of troubles, Lord knows, without worrying about free niggers," Tom Holman said. He was a tall, whey-faced planter who generally kept his own council. "Loan prices are going up to two and a half percent from what I have been told. Drawing a profit in spite of two point five interest isn't too easy."

"Every planter is being squeezed," Abel agreed, pinking his thin postrils with a forefinger. "Look at the entire situation. Your expected work quota from a field hand is ten bales for every crop. Now that should bring in some two hundred dollars, those ten bales. Your field hand ought to produce that much income for the plantation every year."

Chad Goldthwait put in quickly, "If he doesn't make believe he's sick as a dog, the lying coon!"

"Has the situation changed? In several ways. Two hundred dollars nowadays isn't what it used to be. Abe Lincoln's money could be trusted, but nobody is very sure about Jeff Davis and his bills from the sovereign state of Georgia or Alabama or what-not. The sovereign state of confusion, if you ask me! What good is a currency without centralized responsibility? None at all."

A gray-haired man at the other end of the table gave a wintry smile. "You always did have a level business head, Abel."

"Yes, Jarvis, and necessity has taught me what you left out during our talk when I took over the plantation."

Lawyer Jarvis Whitcomb, who owned sixty acres in addition to his law practice, was smiling as he wiped his dry lips vigorously with a gold-colored cloth napkin initialled *CG* in lace script.

"Just as importantly," Abel said, reaching for one of the Cuban cigars he had brought with him, as other planters

26

had done; cigars weren't easy to import into Jeff Davis' Confederate States, "the number of non-field hands has picked up. I myself have two gardeners these days when I used to have only one. Let a house nigra get sick and it's necessary that somebody be ready to take that nigra's place at a moment's notice, which actually means having two nigras for the work of one. I'm not talking about children, although one of my couples has six of them, and the woman can't work shortly before she gives birth. Further, I think all nigra women arrange their pregnancies so as not to have to work when the crop is in the ground. I can't say that I really blame them, all things considered."

"I do," Goldthwait said furiously. "Lazy good-for-nothings, every one of 'em."

The black man who was clearing away dishes drew in his breath sharply.

"Except Sambo over there," Goldthwait said, almost genially for him. "We as good as grew up together, and he knows that if he doesn't get the work done, it's back to the fields for him and twenty lashes besides. Don't you, Sambo?"

"Yes, sah," the black man said, after a pause.

Abel had looked away swiftly from the black man, unable to bear the expression on those mahogany features.

"We were talking about added expenses," he said mildly. "A nigra needs new clothes once a year, and there are medical expenses during the year. You have to give food once a week; at the very least, mess-pork, and corn meal, flour, molasses, and salt. Flour has gone up by fifteen percent in price during the last year alone. There is an occasional runaway who doesn't do any work at all while he's at large."

"And there's theft," Goldthwait snapped. "A nigger steals whatever he can get his hands on without being caught at it. Another thirty dollars in merchandise goes down the plank that way every year."

"Fifteen to thirty per house slave," Abel said consideringly. "And then there are the expenses of other types: an overseer and maybe some assistants, a carpenter and white menials to handle the jobs we can't risk our property to do. Considering everything together, I'd say that our basic expenses have risen eighteen percent since the war."

"Not more than fourteen percent," Charles Passy said carefully. He was the owner of a huge plantation and occasionally got into New Orleans for what he called business reasons.

"Fourteen for you because you can economize on some purchases by quantity buying at discounts." Abel was shaking his head fiercely. "In the case of a smaller planter —myself, for instance, with four hundred acres for pecan groves, cypresses, and timberland along with cotton—in my own case I'd say that not only have costs gone up, but that earnings haven't risen accordingly. And if they had risen, you see, we would only be paid in Jeff Davis' currency."

Lawyer Whitcomb suddenly cleared his throat. "I am beginning to think that old Abe Lincoln was trying to help the planters, in his fashion."

"How?" It was Passy, his mouth open in surprise.

"By abolishing slavery."

Chad Goldthwait looked annoyed. "Jarvis, I always thought of you as a man of business! If each field hand earns two hundred dollars a year for the plantation in round figures, and you have forty slaves, then the income is eight thousand dollars a year."

"Yes, but not if the money is useless in itself, and not if war-caused expenses swallow your profits." Whitcomb leaned forward in a spry manner. "We could have dropped the slave money and said that it was for 'humanitarian' purposes. Meanwhile the niggers work for a salary and know they won't get it unless they do the work."

Goldthwait sighed at this reasoning with an idiot. "You don't know niggers very well, Jarvis. They believe from the bottom of their hearts that every white man owes them food and a roof over their shiftless heads whether they want to work or not. Take slavery away from them, and instead of working like honest people they'll cluster 'round

28

New Orleans and Natchez with their hands out to beg for money."

"They wouldn't beg for Jeff Davis' money, which is the position that we're in."

Chad Goldthwait's wife, a slim woman with dyed blonde hair, rose to her feet nervously.

"And now if the ladies will follow me, we can let the gentlemen argue about affairs of state. Girls, I think this is going to be a long evening—and Chad, dear, I want you to watch yourself, now. I don't want you to have palpitations from arguing too much."

Chad Goldthwait shook his large head slowly, amused in spite of himself. It was Lorna Goldthwait's idea that her husband gave too much of his energy to others and was far too generous. It might have been true, for all that Abel could know, but he'd never seen it like that himself.

The women stood. Nancy, though, gripped the edge of the table before raising herself. Abel was putting out a hand to help her, hoping to hide it from the others, when there was a commotion at the far door.

Sam, the black house slave, came running in and said quickly and loudly, "Let's all be kind to the woman, the wild wom——."

He was pushed to one side as the door opened quickly. A woman in a lavender cotton dress stood in the doorway, a dark-haired snapping-eyed woman of no more than thirty-five. There was fury in the long jaw, and hopelessness in the angry eyes.

"Aren't you men all proud of yourselves?" she demanded, fists on hips. "You killed a free man, you found him, and hanged him. And why? Because he was helping me, that's why."

One of the planters snickered.

Serena Pollard whirled on him. "Yes, he was helping me! He was a decent and gentle person, and if there really is such a place as hell you should all fry in it."

Goldthwait, taking charge, said, "Now, Serena, we can understand that you might be upset. But it isn't very nice

29

for a Southern lady to come charging into somebody else's home when a dinner is going on, and to cause all sorts of difficulties about some nigger or other who you didn't even own. Why not take a little drink of wine in the ladies' salon, Serena? Do you all the good in the world."

Serena Pollard said carefully, "I came here to tell you all just exactly what I think of you. Is that clear, all of you fine ladies and gentlemen?"

The woman's breath was coming with great difficulty now. She hadn't used up her energies. Her right hand was moving to the lavender cotton dress and away from it, as if she was nerving herself to reach for something inside. Abel, his eyes on that hand, jumped to his feet and stepped towards her.

"You, Chad Goldthwait, I know you're the one who's mainly responsible and I want you to have something to remember me and my man Tuck with. I want you to have something out of—this!"

She reached into a dress pocket, letting two fingers swoop inside. She brought out a dusky-brown matchlock revolver no bigger than her palm. As everybody in the room watched, Serena Polland pivoted to point that revolver at Goldthwait. Abel Debenker moved instantly, reaching for the wrist of her right hand and pointing it upwards to the high ceiling. A shot was fired. There was a noise like a horse's neigh, and a toothpick-sized hole appeared in the ceiling. A fine powder of singed dust drifted down toward the planters. Abel eased the matchlock from the woman's suddenly nerveless hand. She stood in place, swaying back and forth in silent grief.

"Let me and Nancy take you home," he said carefully. "You'll accomplish nothing else here. You won't change one opinion. You won't cause one flicker of regret in anybody's mind."

The men breathed deeply in relief, almost like one. Only then, with all danger out of the way, did Mrs. Tom Holman suddenly call out.

"I know I'm going to swoon," the woman gasped, her face papery white. She had been standing at Nancy's side, but Nancy slipped away and went over to Serena Pollard. She was walking quickly, but not with the assurance that she might have had without so many drinks inside her.

Abel held the matchlock by its sanded brown butt as he turned to look at Chad Goldthwait. The planter had been rubbing his jowls, but stopped himself in midmotion. Abel's small features expanded briefly in a smile. Goldthwait drew back. Abel dropped the small revolver into his pocket, having taken out the rubber-tipped bullets, and turned back. He walked to the door first, Nancy and Serena following. The women walked arm in arm. An unkind thought raced into Abel's mind as he watched them at the moment he was opening the heavy door, but he dismissed it.

A burst of talk exploded in the ornate dining room when he was out of the room with the two women. They were in a candlelit passage with a hunting scene—his overseer would have enjoyed that—painted on one entire wall. A portrait of some previous Goldthwaith, doube chin and all, faced it.

The black man, Sam, the slave who was supposed to know his place, swiftly opened the outer door for them. Now he leaned forward, whispering to Abel, "I send one of the boys out to drive the lady's buggy."

"Yes." And he found himself adding, "Thank you."

As they walked into the warm night, they could hear Goldthwait's voice raised to a roar.

"Sam? . . . Where is that good-for-nothing black bastard? . . . I'll whip you to within an inch of your life, you dirty coon bast——."

Abel led the way to his carriage, Nancy following with Serena. The older woman shaded her eyes as she stepped into Abel's carriage and settled herself on the white upholstery. Abel gave orders to old Moses, who was driving, and settled back to a point where he'd be able to look outside.

"You should never have stayed in town after your husband died," he said. "You certainly shouldn't have remained by yourself for even a day."

31

"I didn't want to go anywhere else."

"Then you should have paid for some relative to be brought out here and stay with you."

"I wasn't living alone for the last few years."

"You've been an outcast as far as society is concerned."

"I was happy."

Personal feelings, emotions, were forbiddedn territory. "You'll have to arrange for some relative to stay with you if you want to keep the land. I don't know if you expect to get slaves who'll work it for you. They're hard to find."

"Yes, I understand."

She was sitting between Nancy and Abel, and for a moment their eyes met. It was Abel who looked away and out the opened window. Dark as it was he could see a grove of oaks that sagged with moss under the honey-colored February sky. The countryside rose in twisting ridges under coarse and warm grass. Thickets sprang up every few feet, looking like old gray ladies fanning themselves with spiky leaves. There was a mound of rock with a wooden cross over it where somebody unknown had been buried. Part of Abel loved the land, while a different part wondered why it wasn't being put to good use with cotton or sugar cane or the trees cut for timber.

As the carriage topped a rise, the horses pulled back very slightly. Moses cracked the whip over their heads as Serena Pollard's house and land appeared in sight. Abel and Nancy took the woman into her home and spent enough time with her to feel sure that she'd soon be fast asleep. The field hand who'd driven her buggy back was using a horse-card on the fractious beast when Abel caught his attention.

"We'll drop you off at the Goldthwait plantation," Abel told him. "Ride with my driver."

The trip didn't take too long. He became aware of Nancy sitting opposite him at the far end, but looking almost as if she had never seen him before. The line of her cheeks and the silhouette of her breasts reminded him that he had married a good-looking girl.

32

"Just when I decide you're—ah, unusual, you do something generous," she said softly. "You behaved nicely to Serena."

"We've known each other for a long time."

"You were very confident that she wouldn't shoot you with that little-bitty gun."

"She hasn't got any grudge against me."

"I'd always had my suspicions about you and Serena."

"They weren't justified."

"At any rate, you did behave generously."

"Not at all. If Serena had hurt or killed Goldthwait, she'd have to face trial, and Chad's wife would be in a desperately bad situation. The plantation would go downhill as a result, for a while at least, and the South can't afford to lose good crops."

"Well, I'm sorry I accused you of being generous. I'll try not to do it anymore."

He made a face.

"If anything else had happened, that would have been bad business," she agreed, nodding again and again. "That's perfectly clear. Think about business details long enough, and human beings disappear and don't amount to more than dirt under a thumbnail. I certainly envy you that calm and detached point of view."

"I did the best I could."

The eternal senseless smile had returned. "As ever, mighty lord and master. As ever."

Certainly, he had missed a chance to make things up with his wife; if only for a little; if only for half an hour during the night. They didn't talk again during that ride. When they arrived back at the mansion, Abel walked off to make sure that the horses were being attended to at the stable in spite of the lateness of the hour. Nancy's door was closed when he returned. He tightened his lips angrily and moved forward. Useless. The door was locked against him.

5

Dolph Morin was on his feet before dawn on the first Monday in March, the fifth. He dressed himself in heavy boots, brown pants, and brown shirt. He wore a brown hat with a floppy brim. Not his favorite color by any means, but the overseer was convinced that Abel Debenker didn't like any of the workers getting dressed in white. Morin was ready to work. With a cowbell in one hand and a rawhide whip in the other, he left his little cabin and walked down toward the slave quarters. He rang the bell as he walked, calling, "Up, up, up . . . , get ready to work, you lazy buggers! . . . up, up, up."

No response.

The overseer drew a deep breath and rang the bell again. He was doing it loudly enough to wake the dead. His own ears were tingling.

From one of the canvas-topped cabins he sensed himself being watched, feeling eyes on him at every motion he made. That was his first certainty that today, the first day of plowing, was going to be difficult. His hunting instincts aroused, Morin set the bell down and rubbed his straggly mustache with a thumbnail before rushing into the next to last slave cabin on the right side. Jethro, the biggest buck of them all, was lying on the earthen floor in his half of the cabin. His eyes were wide open.

Morin gave a peremptory flick of the whip.

"Come on out!"

No response.

Morin looked at Jethro and then at the two boys who shared the cabin with him. Their eyes were wide open, too, but they didn't move, either.

"How many strokes do you want, Jethro?"

"Don't care."

Morin came closer, raising the whip.

Jethro shouted, "You whup me, I can't work, you can't sell me."

"Then the master have you killed."

The whip cracked down across Jethro's thighs. The big slave called out, but didn't move.

"Maybe you need a good lesson."

Jethro said nothing, but his lips were pursed, and he had made a pair of fists. He was prepared for a whipping. Morin knew the value of surprise, though. He whirled around and struck the whip solidly against the backside of one of the other boys in the cabin. The boy let out a squeak that was more feminine than Morin had expected, and it told Morin that what he had guessed about those two was the truth.

"Get up and out," Morin ordered, bringing down the whip on the other boy. "Out to work."

The boy cried, but didn't move.

"All right, you," Morin shouted, turning to the other, "if you don't get your black ass out there to work right away, I whup your boy friend till he can't move. Is that clear? It's up to you, now. Do you get out there or not?"

The boy whose life had been threatened called, "Let him do what he want, but you stay here."

"No, I won't." The other boy hurried out of the cabin.

Morin said, "You might as well go, too, or I'll whup him senseless 'til you're outside."

The other boy, shamed, and turning away, walked outside slowly to prepare his own breakfast and to wait for the wagon that would take him and the other hands out to the cotton field to begin the plowing. Morin was alone in the cabin with Jethro. He wouldn't have admitted it to himself, but he was glad he'd only needed to use the whip twice so far. He believed that he never wanted to hurt good merchandise.

Jethro turned his head. Morin raised his whip hand and sent the rawhide crashing down for the third time.

"I'll be back," he said, and rushed out of the cabin to see if anybody else had been stirred into getting up at last. There was no movement outside. The church building at

35

the far left looked even scruffier from the outside than before. The overseer found himself staring up at two of the projecting roofs as if he expected somebody would be standing there with a gun; another hunter, perhaps.

He whirled as soon as he heard footsteps at one side, then made himself smile. It was Abel Debenker, probably roused before dawn by the sound of whipcracks. Mr. Debenker could hear from a mile away if any of his property was being damaged. Abel Debenker rubbed a hand across his thin features, pale under the white-rimmed hat. His eyes were on the overseer, asking questions without the use of speech.

"Those goddamn lazy niggers won't work," Morin said. "They won't get up and go into the fields."

Abel nodded slowly, not surprised. Large chunks of his life were spent in waiting for trouble from the nigras. The possibility of trouble guided his first question in the morning, his last question at night, his first steps when he returned from a visit to town, or a dinner at some other planter's house. Rest was for northerners, safe in their beds in New York City or Boston.

"What have you done about it?"

"Used the whip on a few of 'em. So far, I've got those boyfriends out." He pointed to the pair of slaves waiting moodily, without moving. "No wonder neither of 'em has ever given a gal a little bundle."

"Have you done anything else?"

"No, sir. I was going to call you."

An idea had come to Abel even as he asked the question, but he took a moment to check it in his mind. He faced a broad expanse of level land back of the slave quarters and sloping down to the swamp. Wide-open ditches were dry at their mouths, a good sign for the start of planting. If the levees didn't flood during the next month, he'd get a decent crop.

Abel turned back. "There's food in each cabin, Morin. Get it out and drop it into the cisterns."

Morin nodded approvingly. The game was going to be

36

flushed out. Then he cleared his throat briefly. "These boys' food, too, Mr. Debenker?"

"Certainly. Otherwise they'll be killed for it."

Morin nodded, going from one cabin to another as Abel Debenker watched, pausing only to drop cloth-covered food parcels into one of the three cisterns in the center of the double row of slave cabins. Abel was aware of sullen and hating faces in each cabin, their owners glaring out at him in the darkness. He stopped Morin, who had shoved the last food parcel into one of the cisterns.

"Don't go inside any of the cabins, but tell the nigras that there won't be any further punishments if they come out now."

"Leave it to me, sir."

The men and women rose sullenly, their eyes on the cisterns that contained their week's food. Blossom was the first slave among the holdouts to come running, almost smiling in her eagerness. Then she inclined her head respectfully toward Debenker and Morin. The overseer glared at her, good as she looked to him. The hunter recognized dangerous game.

"On line," he said, as others straggled out sullenly.

Blossom said brightly, "Yes, buckra, I on line." She was wetting her lips. The dark, glinting eyes shone like those of a mischievous child.

The prime field hands made the second line, twenty-four of them. Six smaller men were on line in front of them, one standing in front of every sixth man on the second line. Each of the smaller men carried a dogwhip in one bronzed hand.

Debenker approached the boy at the farthest end. "How long have you been a driver?"

"Since last crop, master."

"That is long enough for a boy who won't do what he's told. Get on line with the field hands."

The driver looked sick.

"You! Debenker gestured at one of the hands, thinner than most of them. "You're the new driver for these boys.

37

Your job is to make sure that every hand in your group is working. Otherwise you get a taste of that whip of the buckra's. Take that small whip from the boy whose job you've got now, and you can whip any of your boys up to six times to keep them working. No more than six lashes. Is that clear?"

As if it was a cue, Dolph Morin responded to those words once again. "Make sure your boys work, and give each boy up to six lashes if he don't."

The new driver was grinning savagely at the hand whose place he had taken. It wasn't unusual for drivers to be found strangled in a swamp, and Abel had previously risked naming several small Blacks as drivers. Usually, though, there was a certain justice involved. A driver wasn't harmed by the others if he whipped some boy who genuinely wasn't working at the time. Let him use the dog-whip to satisfy a grudge of his own, and he wasn't likely to live for another week. During this last year, Abel had been fortunate with drivers. He felt sure that a small nigra was likely to be more careful than a big bruiser. He didn't fool himself that he had been anything more than lucky in the matter, however.

As punishment for taking part in the near-rebellion, Abel changed jobs between another hand and a driver. Then he gestured Morin over to one side. The overseer waited until he had divided the men into the three mule carts, which took them to the field. He knew as well as Abel did that without such a precaution the niggers would overload one or two of the carts and claim that they couldn't be driven out to the field because the cart had broken down. When he was finished, he hurried over to join Abel near one of the vegetable gardens behind the cabins.

"They're to have the usual lunch. Call the cook and have her take all the food out of the cistern and prepare lunch evenly out of the whole mess."

Morin winced.

Abel said, "Another reminder of what they did this morning won't cause any harm."

38

"Are you planning to get rid of any of 'em after this?"

"Not till the crop is in."

"They'll be a little harder to handle if you ask me, Mr. Debenker. Of course I can do it, but I have to warn you about it all the same."

"Thank you, Morin."

"It's all in knowing how to take care of niggers, Mr. Debenker, if I do say so myself." Morin cleared his throat. "I'd suggest that you might want to get rid of Blossom right away."

"I'll bear that in mind," A'el said flatly.

"It wouldn't surprise me if she was back of this whole thing. She can twist a buck by the nose and make him do whatever she wants, but she herself doesn't get whupped no matter what happens."

Abel brushed that aside with a gesture. "Now I want you to send the stockminder into town for Rafe Carstairs. I want him to bring half a dozen guards with shotguns out here for the next six days. I'll settle the price with him during the week."

"Yes, Mr. Debenker."

Morin touched two fingers to his cap and turned to shout for the stockminder. Abel Debenker watched him briefly. A decent man and thoroughly honest, but without any stomach for dealing with nigras except by whipping them reluctantly and hoping that everything would work out. Not the best possible overseer by any manner of means. He'd not only have to shop for a few slaves after the cotton was in, but hire a new overseer as well. A plantation man's work never seemed to get done.

The last of the mule carts hauled sixteen blacks out to the cotton field. The sun was rising in the sky at last. A new day had started.

6

Plowing time had become a little more difficult for Nancy than it used to be. Nowadays, for instance, if a plow broke down, Abel insisted that it be fixed so it could be used again, and the whole process was bad for his temper. He was learning how to fix some equipment, but he gritted his teeth whenever it had to be done. Kermit, on the other hand, enjoyed trying to help his father.

Planting time wasn't so easy for her, either. Abel was usually finding it harder to control himself during those few months from April to August. That was the season when Blacks worked harder then ever at pretending that they were sick and couldn't go out to the field. The sobbing and whipcracking as they tried to keep from doing any work was fearful. Sometimes Abel would agree to have one of the Blacks severely whipped as a lesson to the others. He always spent the night afterwards deeply engrossed in ledgers.

It was bad, but there was always the secret bottle and the secret taunt to sustain her.

As for her feelings about Abel, she didn't actually know what they were, these days. She supposed she was fond of him for having fathered her child and being decent to the lad. Otherwise, (the truth, now!) she didn't often think about him anymore. He was there, and sometimes she had to do him a service. That was all.

Most of her time was taken up with the boy. Kermit was growing up nicely. At the moment he had Abel's small features, and Nancy's tawny red hair, cropped short. It always surprised her to think of him as a nine year old person with distinct likes and dislikes. Sometimes it seemed to her that he was very well aware of her own fears. When there was trouble with the slaves Kermit would come to her and they'd sit together, consoling each other in silence. Nancy supposed it was the war giving them all such a difficult time this year. The cotton was being grown, but it was harder to sell. The Blacks, seeming to know that freedom was one of the war's issues, were much more above themselves then they used to be, and always tense. Nothing was quite the same as it had been, before the war.

Abel didn't talk about it to her very often. One night at supper he'd said, "Robert E. Lee knows how to handle his soldiers." He sounded approving. It seemed that he thought of the commander of the Confederate forces as another slave owner who could only be tested by how much work he'd got out of those who were under him. Later in the year, he'd made some remark about another battle. "Imagine all the waste of what happens at a place like Antietam. People spend their whole working lives trying to build, to improve—and along comes a mad dog like this McClellan and tears everything to pieces."

It had even become unusual these days for Nancy to go out visiting. Before the war she used to make all her visits on Tuesdays, but it was impossible to keep to any plans nowadays. Not until a Thursday in late August was she able to get a carriage with old Moses to drive. She set out to visit Serena Pollard.

Nancy left Moses to see to the horses' comfort in the stable and walked up the short knoll to the main house. She suddenly sensed movement behind plain white curtains and knew she was being observed, but not until she had topped the small knoll did she realize that somebody was waiting for her at the door. She was used to wariness in human beings and wasn't surprised. A gray-haired, broad-shouldered white man with a gray mustache not much bigger than a crewel needle was waiting for her.

"What are you here for?" he asked in a high voice, looking behind her to see if anybody else was in sight.

"To visit Mrs. Pollard."

From the sitting room Serena Pollard's voice called, "Let my friend come in, Hubert."

Hubert stepped to one side. Nancy wiped dirt off her

41

boots and walked into the reception room. Serena was sitting at the far side of a sturdy oak table in a matching chair. She put a gray-backed blotter between two pages of a book by Artemus Ward, then closed it, and moved the coal-oil lamp closer to the center of the table. The light danced above her graying hair, wreathing her still attractive figure in a warm glow. Nancy stepped past a throw rug, which almost looked as if it had been made of grass, and sat down. The man called Hubert joined them awkwardly, looking as if he straddled a horse.

"Are you well?" Nancy asked.

"Oh, yes."

"Are you getting out a crop?"

"No, of course not." She almost smiled. "Hubert is a second cousin, and I certainly wouldn't ask him to work my acres. We've put up some vegetables, though, and that ought to help keep the table heavy for awhile."

"The war should be over soon, and help should be much easier to come by," Nancy said. "Then everything will get back to the way it used to be."

"Not to the way it used to be," Serena said, glancing at her neat, dark hair in a wedge of mirror above the mantel. "Never that."

"This war is a sin and a shame," Hubert said irritably in a Mississippi accent. He had been warming himself in front of the Mexican fireplace at the far end of the room. "Old Abe Lincoln has got no authority to keep any state from quitting the union if it wants to. He's going against the Constitution of the United States, Lincoln is. That man is a criminal."

It was an argument that Hubert seemed to have learned by rote, expressing his quarrel with the northern states in four brief sentences. His interpretation of a document was the only issue in the war. Abel may have had a narrow point of view, too, but he wasn't interested in paper unless it had something to do with his income.

She leaned forward. "Have you been having any trouble, Serena?"

"Not these days." Again the sad smile. "Now that Tuck

42

is gone I'm left pretty much alone by everybody except the young children. But, of course, Hubert is good enough to come into town with me when I go shopping, or otherwise I might not be left alone there."

Nancy smiled gratefully at Cousin Hubert, using that helpless-woman smile she had learned so well since becoming the mistress of Abel Debenker's plantation. Hubert looked gratified, and she wondered if he was flexing his muscles.

The women spoke for awhile longer. Nancy knew all the gossip that was worth knowing in the parish, it seemed. Serena had been out of touch. As she was getting up to leave, Serena stood, too, and asked timidly, "How is Abel?"

"Very well."

"Does he expect to get out a good crop this year, in spite of everything?"

"He does."

"I hope he's right. I understand he tried to stop those lunatic fools from doing what they did to my Tuck. I'm not surprised at that. He's always been considerate and decent."

That was the moment when Nancy knew beyond question that Serena Pollard and Abel had once been very close to each other indeed. She supposed she ought to have been angry, but the feeling wouldn't come. She wished with all her heart that it wasn't necessary to be sorry for this woman with her genteel poverty and cruel memories.

"My dear," she said, and surprised herself by embracing Serena Pollard. Serena returned that embrace with all her strength, and the two women clung to each other as if for life.

"Daddy wants me to bring you out to see the loading," Nancy told her son, "and that's exactly what I'm doing whether you like it or not."

Kermit sulked. He had been dressed in a shirt and a small cravat, short pants, and button shoes. The small

43

male with Abel's features and her own color hair was possessed by a will of his own. She had to take him by the hand. Old Moses drove them in the buggy. Kermit wasn't permitted to drive, of course, although she let him sit next to Moses. Kermit revelled in the companionship of the old black man, who drove away from the mansion carefully as if he was still afraid to run over the chickens that hadn't been in front of the mansion since the start of the war. Come to think of it, Nancy had noticed the same response from Abel on horseback.

In front of the cotton gin house, the buggy stopped. The house doors were wide open, front and back. Slaves, male and female, young and old, were carrying cotton bales under the September morning sun. It took three or four grunting slaves to move a bale out to one of the mule carts in front of the house. The overseer, Mr. Morin, was urging them on with shouts and an uncoiled whip.

Abel, who had been watching, turned at the sound of the buggy. His eyes passed over Nancy as if she didn't exist, but he grinned at sight of Kermit. He hurried over in time to see his son jump out and into an onion-shaped pile of mud. He laughed.

"Your shoes," Nancy said in protest, and then glanced rebukingly at her husband. "It's not funny."

"Your pardon, my dear," Abel said courteously and touched his son on the shoulder. "Next time he'll wear boots when he comes out."

"No next time," Kermit said softly.

She didn't think Abel had heard him.

"Forty-eight bales were produced this week, son," Abel said proudly. "And we had to work hard to get those out, but we did it. Do you know why we're putting them on those carts?"

Kermit was sloshing his shoes around in the mud, as if trying to get as dirty as possible. He didn't look up at his father.

"We're loading up those bales to take the cotton to market, son," Abel said expansively. "We take them to the

44

river bank every Saturday, get them on the boat, and sell our cotton bales in New Orleans."

The boy said nothing.

"Forty-eight bales aren't as much as we could produce, I'm sure," Abel went on. "We've made fifty-two in a week, and I think we could go up to fifty-five. However, I suspect things may get better after this crop."

Dolph Morin, out of Nancy's sight, was shouting, "Why in hell don't you move your ass, Blossom? Hurry or I'll give you a taste of this if you don't do your share—you hear?"

There was a whipcrack in midair. Nancy, eyes shut tight, sensed that her son was looking in her direction and opened them in time to put a finger to her lips so that he wouldn't call out.

She said quietly, "Nobody was hurt, dear, I'm sure."

The child let out a dry sob.

"Stop that!" Abel commanded.

Kermit took a long breath.

"I want you to listen to me." Abel hunkered down until he was almost face-to-face with his son. "Everybody has to do things in this life that he doesn't like to do. No one lays a whip to a nigra because he hates him, but only because work has got to be done, and the nigra isn't doing it. There's nothing personal to it. A lot of the things we have to do make me pretty unhappy, son, but in this world they're necessary."

"No," Kermit said softly.

"Oh, yes, they are, son. Sometime in the future, all this land is going to be your property—quiet, I say!—and maybe even a few more acres if I can make a few deals around here. The ginning capacity may go as high as a hundred bales a week, maybe even two hundred. You'll need over a hundred nigras to run this land whether slavery is the law or it's not. Otherwise, you won't get your cotton out and you'll go hungry. The sooner you make a start at learning all this, the better off you'll be. Is that clear?"

45

The boy didn't move, but antagonism was as plain from him as odors from the slave cabins.

Abel got up at last, his own face expressionless. Kermit turned to get into the carriage, but Abel pulled him back.

"I want to go home."

"You stay," Abel Debenker snapped. "You stay and you keep looking until the last cart is loaded."

Supper was a quiet meal for the family. Kermit wouldn't talk to anyone. He seemed more angry at his mother because she had done nothing to get him away from the loading area.

Nancy drank steadily from a clouded water glass, wondering why the liquor wasn't nearly as strong as it used to be. Abel, who had returned from the market with an armful of four-sheet issues of the *Festin Chronicle*, probably wanted the meal to be over so that he could lock himself into his study and find out how the war was going. Kermit was finished first, having eaten even more quickly than usual. He got up from the round mahogany supper table, the cut flowers shivering in their vase at the center.

They heard his small, angry steps up the wooden stairs. Abel wiped his pursed lips with a cloth napkin that was much more expensive than the wartime dinner of chicken parts with vegetables.

"That child doesn't understand; hating me on account of the nigras."

"Children are strange."

"Not that strange. If you haven't spoken to him, I'm sure your actions have spoken to him. He must see how leery you are of our nigras."

"I can't help that."

He glanced at the clouded glass and back to her. She knew the words that were unspoken on his lips: "I hope he doesn't grow up to be a drunkard on account of you, as well."

Nancy finished the contents of the glass and sat back. She felt only warm inside, not particularly happy.

Abel was on his feet at last. "It's been a long and

46

difficult week and it would be nice to have a little pleasure at the end of it. I'll see you in an hour, my dear. Please wait up for me."

" 'In an hour.' How businesslike, O lord and master. And do you know the number of times you will take?"

"What do you mean?"

"Have you decided how many times to be inside me and gain your pleasure?"

He blinked, letting himself show slight surprise and nothing more. Then he shrugged.

"Two times, I think. Perhaps three."

He turned and left the room.

Nancy went up to her boudoir and sat down at the writing desk. Her eyes went to the knob of the first drawer, but she looked away. The cut buttercups seemed almost alive in their vase on the mantel, the Aphrodite sparkling against the far wall, the miniature piano gleaming wickedly at everything else. Only the mistress of the plantation wasn't quite alive.

She waited half an hour and then went to her bedroom. Automatically, she turned the lock on, as she had been doing every night for years. She took off the dark-red dress with its frog-shaped sleeves and knee length hem. A very popular style in Paris some two years ago, she had been told. She dressed in a pinkish wrapper and went to the mirror to look critically at her hair. A washing wouldn't hurt it. Tomorrow night. She didn't want to do it now.

At five minutes to the hour she heard the doorknob being rattled back and forth.

"Nancy!"

"Yes, dear?"

"Are you going to let me in?"

"Dear, I have a very bad—well, headache."

"Nonsense! Do I have to break this door down?"

"Oh, you wouldn't want to hurt yourself, Abel!"

He drew back, and then she heard his shoulder crash against the stout door. It held firmly.

47

"Honey, I'll see you very soon, I promise." She was kneading her hands to keep from opening the door. Part of her did indeed want him tonight, now. If not for his behavior toward Kermit this afternoon, she wouldn't have hesitated. Not until the last few months had she ever kept him out of her bedroom when he wanted to be with her.

"No. You'll see me right away."

"Please don't try to break the door down. You can't, and you'll only hurt yourself."

Again his steps pulled back, and he crashed a shoulder against the door. This time, she heard him suddenly hiss between clenched teeth from the sudden pain.

"Please don't, dear. Please."

For the third time his steps pulled back. Nancy hurried to the door and unlocked it and opened it, but stood in the entrance.

"I'm not letting you in, mind, but I don't want you to hurt yourself, either. Now please be a good——."

But his arms encircled her and he was putting pressure against her, now. The door gave way in spite of her, it seemed. She pulled back, and he was in the room and his lips were on her and his hands were on the pink wrapper. There was a series of hammer blows from inside her own temples.

"Let's hurry," she whispered.

"Yes, yes." He was swiftly taking off his blue-striped white pants when she saw a lone key on a chain come tumbling out of a pocket. She recognized its shape, and her neck became crimson.

Abel smiled at her. "I had a duplicate made, just as a last resort."

"But you would rather have impressed me by bruising your shoulders than use it," she said, wide-eyed and delighted. "I declare, I never will understand men."

They were in bed together very soon afterwards, and it was a time for them both to remember past pleasures and to taste them again. And again.

At rest now, they lay back and smiled at each other. Shyly, she reached out a hand to him.

48

"We've been very happy together, you and I, Abel, at times. And we still could be happy, in some other country."

"We're here, though, because my source of income is here," he said, sitting up on one elbow. "We have to draw out all the happiness we can."

"Yes, *if* we can."

"Nothing to worry about, Nancy. I'm in control of this place and everything on it."

"How long can you control people with nothing to look forward to and no lives of their own?"

"As long as necessary, my dear," he said contentedly, and then turned to her. "But if you want to be out of control for the next few minutes, I won't mind."

"Not again, dear. I'm getting tired and—oh, all right, all right—oh, that's good, you're always so good, yes, yes, *yes!*"

7

Father was the first one out of the carriage, of course. He reached up a hand toward Kermit, but the boy shook his head sullenly and jumped down.

"Take my hand now," Abel said authoritatively. "If you get lost, Mother will give holy hell to both of us."

Kermit didn't smile back. He hadn't wanted to go into town for this trip. Mother hadn't wanted him to go, either. But Father had won out again, as he always did when he put his foot firmly down.

They were on the square block built around a brick courthouse in the town of Festin. Thirty-some houses clustered on the block, and several stores. There was a saddler's, with a drawing of a saddle on a big sign. A law office was nearby. A doctor. There was a schoolhouse and a hotel.

Father, in his usual whites, with a new black-ribboned

49

hat, and a dead cigar in his mouth, strode along as if he owned Festin and everybody in it. He stopped for a few moments talk with Lawyer Jarvis Whitcomb, who had been walking very slowly out of his office.

"I'm going home for the day," the old man said. "Feeling poorly."

"The weather and the war news put together are enough to make anyone feel poorly," Father said. "We'll miss you downside."

"Give my regards around," Lawyer Whitcomb said, and mustered a smile for Kermit. "You're gettin' to be a big lad."

"I'm takin' him to his first buy-session," Father said, smiling down at him. "One day he might have to do some buying himself and he may as well know what it's like."

Lawyer Whitcomb excused himself as a spasm passed across his wrinkled face.

A group of woodcarts, each with a cord of pine in them, had been placed at a point beyond the courthouse square. A black man was putting the nose bag on one tired horse, his gestures brusque. The horse whickered in complaint, but soon was gobbling its food.

Father, sparing a glance in that direction, said crisply, "Nigras can't handle horses at all. If that rascal belonged to me, I'd keep him in the fields."

Kermit smiled at the black man, meeting his eyes after a moment. The black man turned away, then looked back and ventured a grim smile.

As they walked along, Father stopped to talk with another friend of his. This was Mr. Holman, a plantation owner. He was a tall man who didn't usually talk much, and his face looked exactly the color of scrambled eggs.

After a few polite words to Kermit, Mr. Holman said, "Just paid eight hundred for a nigger woman."

"Young?"

"Thirty, I s'pose."

"Aren't there any papers?"

"Oh, you know what papers are like. A blackbirder can

50

put any lies he wants to on paper. No, this gal is thirty and with a three year old."

"Boy or gal?"

"Boy."

"The way prices are going these days, eight hundred isn't too high."

"The way prices for niggers are going these days, it's a sin and a shame," Mr. Holman said regretfully. "Well, I won't keep you, Abel."

Twenty feet past the end of the courthouse square, Kermit saw a group of men clustered around a duckboard platform. A black man stood on the platform. He didn't wear any clothes. There were chains on his hands and chains on his feet, and twin chains connected the manacles. The black man glowered and then looked off as if into the distance. Kermit wondered if the black man wasn't looking directly at him, accusing him. He squeezed his father's hand for comfort, but the pressure wasn't returned. There was a white man on the platform, too; a small white man who looked smilingly out over the crowd. He raised a thick hand with a stick in it toward the Black, but didn't look directly at him after that.

"Strong as a mule and a ten-bale-a-day worker, gentlemen," he was shouting, as Daddy eased Kermit into the crowd. "The sort of nigger who inspires other niggers to work, too. Look at them muscles, gentlemen, look at 'em."

Kermit couldn't see over anybody's head, which was a blessing. A smaller boy was in the crowd, though, and he smiled and waved before coming over to talk.

"Have you bought any niggers yet?"

Kermit shook his head.

"My daddy let me pick out a nursemaid for the young 'uns and now I think he wants another one. Don't you get to pick any niggers?"

Again Kermit shook his head.

"Well, if you do, only pick gals—young gals." The aggressive child, who had been smiling, made a gesture of distaste at Kermit's response. He turned away.

51

"As powerful a nigger as you'll ever see," the white man on the platform was shouting.

Father asked, "How old?"

"Twenty."

"Have you got certification to say so?"

"Absolutely, Mr.—ah, Debenker, yes. Good to see you, sir. Yes, we do have the papers. Would you like to come down here and see this nigger close up? A better buy you won't have."

To Kermit's embarrassment he found himself with Father as the center of attention, now. A path was cleared for them. He walked, as quickly as he could manage, at his father's side as they moved closer to the black man.

"Tell him to open his mouth so I can see the teeth."

The black man did it, but wasn't in Father's sight. The white man hit the Black with the stick across the shoulder blades. The black man gasped, but then stooped over. His mouth was wide open.

"As you see, ladies and gentlemen, the boy can be persuaded," the white man roared.

A few people in the audience rewarded him with snickers. There was a woman standing nearby, and at the black man's sudden closeness she let out a sound that Kermit had never before heard from a woman. A man standing at her side looked irritably at her.

"Two teeth missing and one looks like it's rotting," Father said. "Where were the teeth lost?"

"In two fights, Mr. Debenker, when he was very young. It's all in the papers."

Father looked away from the black man's teeth, and the black man straightened up.

"Any illnesses? Croup? Chicken pox? Measles?"

"The usual illnesses of childhood, Mr. Debenker, all of them conquered by this in-dom-itable boy here. And all explained in his papers, I might add."

"Can he have young 'uns?"

"Three already, Mr. Debenker, and all of them are boys who'll grow up as big and strong as he is."

52

"Nobody can be sure of that until the pickaninnies are grown."

"Well, perhaps. Is there anything else you'd like to know 'bout this here bargain, Mr. Debenker?"

"Yes, I—." Father suddenly turned and looked down at his son. "Is there anything else *you* think we ought to find out, Kermit?"

There was a chortle or two among the men in the audience. It didn't seem as if that aggressive child who had talked to him a few moments ago was the only one who was made much of at this kind of place. All the same, Kermit shook his head too swiftly.

Father, who knew the truth, said, "There is something, Kermit. Speak up, then."

For the second time, he shook his head.

The dealer rubbed both hands together. "Not to hold up our business, I think it's time we started the bidding on this wonderful property right here." Lightly the stick thumped against the black man's broad back. "I'll start the bidding at—."

"One moment." Father leaned down. "If there's something you want me to ask, son, let me know what it is. Whisper it in my ear, if you like."

Father leaned over until his right ear was in front of Kermit, seeming almost as big as Kermit's face.

Kermit whispered, "His name, father. If he's coming to our place, it would be decent to know his name."

Father straightened up. The look on his face wasn't like any that Kermit had seen in a long time. There wasn't any expression at all on it, but the nostrils were shaking as if they were alive all by themselves.

"Go on with the bidding," he said.

"Bidding starts at a thousand," the dealer said. "If no acceptable bid is put in, I reserve the right to withdraw the merchandise from consideration."

"One two five oh," somebody called.

"Come on now, gentlemen, you don't expect any merchandise like this to go for such a price as you're naming."

53

The bidding didn't take long. Father bought for two three two five. The black man was pushed to one side, and another black man was pushed out to the platform. Father bought this one, too. And a third. And a fourth. And a fifth. And one more, as well.

"Eleven thousand and seventy-five," the dealer said, adding up Father's account. "In United States money, by your leave, Mr. Debenker."

"Louisiana money is legal tender and should be acceptable as such, under pain of arrest."

The last four words hadn't been lost on the dealer. He said calmly, "I'm willing to accept jewelry or other valuables. Between gentlemen, a compromise is possible. Compromise is the life of horse trading and nigger trading, as my old daddy used to tell me."

"You won't get jewels either, Elkahan Melville. Our deal is off. I will not do business with a traitor, a Union-loving blackbirder, of all things."

"Suh, I remind you that we are all blackbirders." Elkahan Melville snapped, and threw his head back. "Bring out the first nigger. We'll start the auction again and hope to do business with a southern gentleman, this time."

Father was on the way out, Kermit at his side. There was a ruckus from the platform, and Kermit heard one of the white men grunt, "Coon bastard!" He whirled around, wide-eyed, causing Father to stop, if only briefly. The black man had suddenly dug in his heels, not wanting to return to the humiliation of midplatform. Elkahan Melville raised the stick and thumped it down across the bronze shoulder blades with all his might. Kermit, watching, gasped and called out. Father turned to see what was happening. The black man called out a pain-filled oath, but made no move. One of the dealer's assistants reached the platform, rawhide whip in hand. As the stick-thumping forced the chained black man to bend over, the rawhide whip descended across the broad back. There was an exclamation mark of blood across his back now. He let out a bellow and charged brutishly, head down, for the assistant with the whip. It was Elkahan Mel-

54

ville who brought the stick down now, again and yet again. Each blow was solid, each was rewarded by a grunt of pain and a dart of fresh blood.

Kermit looked up hopefully at Father. He knew very well that Father hated to have a black man beaten, and would go to almost any lengths to keep that from happening. Father was surely going to call out, to jump up on the stage if necessary, to prevent somebody treating another human being so badly. Father wouldn't let this happen.

But Father stood in place while the blows hammered against the black man. He didn't watch, though he made no move to stop what was happening.

Slowly, helplessly, the big black man had to move to the center of the duckboard platform. There was a terrible look in his eyes for Elkahan Melville, and it moved to everybody else in sight.

"The head hasn't been touched as you can plainly see," Melville roared. He reached into his pocket for a thin white cotton glove, put it on, then ran it up and down the black man's head at front and back. The black man didn't call out. Melville showed the white glove to the audience. There were no blood flecks on it.

Father waited until he was drawing off the glove and then said, "You'll have to get less for that one now, Melville. Nobody will pay my price. Indeed, I won't pay it myself, now."

"Suh, you haven't been asked."

"But I tell you what I will do. I'll pay two oh oh in Southern Rights Bank Bills. As for the balance, it goes toward a medical examination for the nigra before a legal transfer is made. I want to be sure that there hasn't been damage in any vital area."

"A ten-bale nigger paid for with Jeff Davis' shinplasters!" Elkahan Melville drew his head back so that his protests would carry further.

Father's voice had to be quieter, of course, but every word was clear to the audience. "I'm going to insist on medical examinations for the others, too, before the papers are signed. There isn't any way of knowing how badly

55

you might treat your nigras when no customers are nearby."

Elkahan Melville asked, almost quietly, "And do you intend to pay for six niggers with S.R.B.B.'s, suh? Is that your plan?"

Father pursed his lips. "Well, I understand that you do considerable business in Virginia, Melville. I'm willing to make half of the total payment in Corporation of Richmond notes. Trade them before long and you should realize a decent amount of goods or services as a result."

"Very well, suh." Elkahan Melville bowed his head as if crushed by the workings of fate. "If you will kindly speak with Mr. Rogers, my assistant, the transaction will be arranged subject to a proper fee for the medical examinations."

The assistant gestured for Father to join him, and Kermit had to follow. The discussion concerned how soon the money was to be paid and how soon the examinations were going to be made and how much was to be paid for them. Father was perfectly at ease, relaxed in spite of everything that had happened. When the dealing was finished, Kermit was aware of being looked down at in mild amusement. His father was waiting for a comment from him and for signs of admiration. Kermit was supposed to say that it had all been very clever and that Melville had been defeated by shrewd bargaining.

But it hadn't been accomplished on account of the whipping, only because his father would get a little more money for himself this way. It didn't have anything to do with decency and good feelings or with caring. His father didn't really care, or had certainly behaved that way. When had his father suddenly stopped caring? Had Abel Debenker awakened one morning, years ago, and decided that he'd never again care who did what to whom?

Kermit didn't speak to his father at all for the rest of that day, and for most of the week as well.

56

8

The plow gang, some twenty-two plows drawn by weary mules with whipcord lines attached to sweat-rimmed steel collars, was at work on this March afternoon. The land was being plowed in five foot beds at the rate of sixteen acres a day. Last year, as Abel's notes had confirmed only this morning, the plow gang had managed nineteen to the day. A plowman was starting down an area between two of last year's cotton rows when Abel gestured Dolph Morin over to him.

"Can't you do any better with the new nigras?"

"The new ones complain a lot," the overseer said, "especially that coon bastard, Ned. No wonder he's been whipped so often by others. I've had to give him a few tastes of the leather myself, for cause."

"Be careful," Abel said automatically. "Next time let me know in advance before you take the hide to him. But why are those nigras so tired?"

"They're always tired."

Two more furrows had been set down beside the one that Abel had been watching. The young gal doing the job was yawning as she moved slowly.

Morin said, "I almost wish we hadn't got rid of Shem and Pheeter. They were quick workers, for niggers."

"They were a pair of birdies," Abel said snappishly. "Birdies don't have children and they're troublemakers. I got a decent price for 'em, and as you say, they're willing to work sometimes. All the same, the new hands should be doing at least as good."

"Well, I'll keep at 'em, sir."

"Try to get more than eighteen acres per diem, Morin. I mean that."

The overseer touched the brim of his hat respectfully

and rode away. Abel, on his chestnut quarter horse, looked after the overseer in annoyance. He hated to fire any man only because he was angry, and he had previously made up his mind to get rid of the overseer; if the per diem didn't pick up, he'd have a good reason.

He rode to the stable and left his chestnut quarter horse to be taken care of, making a mental note to have the outside of the stable painted again. Nancy was waiting for him at the round mahogany table, prepared for a quick bite of lunch. Kermit wasn't in sight; the boy had been very persnickety for the last month or so, but young ones often did get that way at the age of ten. He ate swiftly, preoccupied. Nancy broke into his thoughts.

". . . in Boston, I think," she was saying, when he looked up. "Imagine being able to cut a dress with paper patterns instead of—."

"Yes, of course." He lapsed back into his preoccupations while the vegetable salad dish was taken away, and warm coffee with a dollop of cream was put on the table in front of him. His father and grandfather had taken coffee from the same cup and listened to their wives yammer and wondered what the future could hold for a slave state. Now that everything was slowly changing, now that the long-dreaded confrontation was taking place, there was no letdown of worry or firmness of purpose brought on by the knowledge that at least the waiting was' over. There was nothing but greater tiredness and ever more watchful attitudes to head off trouble. He tasted the coffee, and then drank.

". . . they all seemed so tired," Nancy said.

"Tired?" He was alert, now. "Who did?"

"The nigra gals, like I was telling you. I had to go over to the slave quarters to help Elihu and Sunshine with their youngest, who's been very sick, you know. All the gals were stumbling around and yawning. They certainly are supposed to get enough sleep. I can't think what would make 'em so tired."

"That's interesting." The coffee finished, he leaned over

58

and kissed her on the flushed forehead. "You're a very helpful wife."

"Glad to be of help, O Great One. Will you be seeing me tonight, do you think?"

"Not tonight, dear, but we'll make up for that."

Nancy looked after him with a bemused air, convinced that he had only been pleased by her good temper. He liked her, though, and she told herself for the millionth time that she would never understand men in general, or her spouse in particular.

A letter from London was waiting in his small study, and he opened it swiftly. Then he smiled. It had been dictated by one of his former slaves, Shep, who had bought himself freedom and settled in London, where he worked for Coy and Goldband, a northern-based firm that was dealing in military supplies. Shep wrote that he was married now and working harder than he ever had done at the Debenker plantation, but that he was enjoying it much more. He was grateful for every opportunity and sent his best regards to Abel, his good wife, and the infant who he supposed was practically grown-up by now.

Abel put the note away, a grim little smile on his face. He wondered if he'd let any slave buy himself freedom in these days of shortages and war.

At nine o'clock in the evening he was on the wide, white porch of the mansion, looking out over his land. The moon was at the quarter. He knew without being able to see much in front of him that one or more people were walking along the newly repaired road. He could feel it, somehow, on his property. He moved swiftly and quietly along the road, nobody in sight. Wasn't he being a damn fool? If a few nigras wanted to use the old sugar house for their lovemaking, say, that was up to them as long as they worked a day's nineteen acres. But they weren't getting the work done as they were supposed to.

The old sugar house came in sight at last, its front door open. He waited, indecisive for once. He was about to turn away with a resigned shrug when he saw the men. Six

59

men were coming toward the sugar house from the general direction of town, six men he had never seen before. Each of them was dressed in a gray Confederate soldier's uniform.

Abel moved forward without being seen by them. Then he heard a familiar voice, lowered. "Five bucks apiece," his overseer was saying to the men.

"That's more'n we can pay," the oldest man said in a high Georgia voice. "If you make it three apiece we'll be glad to go in."

"I bet you will, but the others are inside right now and havin' theirselves a good time, they paid five apiece, and if you want to go inside, gentlemen, you'll have to pay five bucks C.S.A. apiece, too. There are some high yaller nigger gals in there that'll knock your eyes out and do other things to you, too."

"We'll go up to four, but not a dollar higher than that."

"Five, gentlemen." Morin looked around from side to side, a fox looking for the sportsman. "Make up your minds fast, gentlemen. It's my hide if I get caught at this."

Abel Debenker said loudly and clearly, "Kiss your hide goodbye, Morin."

The overseer drew back as Abel stepped into the clearing. Morin's slitted eyes glared in hatred, his horny hands moving in and out.

Abel said to the soldiers, "I'll thank you to get your colleagues out of my sugar house and leave these grounds with them immediately."

The spokesman for the six soldiers nodded and walked through the door with the others. There was a sudden sound of threshing along the floor. One of the people inside, getting up, bumped against a piece of disused machinery and let out an oath. A number of women groaned, some of them sad, and others sounding as if they had been delivered from evil. The sullen men left silently, eyes averted from Abel Debenker and the overseer.

Abel told Morin, "Send 'em back to their cabins."

Widened eyes examined him unbelievingly. "Am I still on the payroll?"

60

"Do what you're told, for once."

Morin glowered at his employer, but walked into the sugar house, facing Abel with every move. He must have felt hunted now, fair game to be struck with a bullet as he slinked off.

"Back to your cabins, gals, and hurry. Now!"

There was some complaining, and then the seven gals walked to the door. Four were wearing their only dresses proudly, and two others looked away. Blossom, the last to leave, wasn't dressed at all. Abel watched the play of moonlight on the dark nipples. His thin lips were moist, but he couldn't remember having licked them. Blossom moved off with the others, Abel watching in spite of himself. He saw her look back directly at him, brows raised to ask if he wanted her to wait. A moment passed before he shook his head.

Morin's dry chuckle turned his attention to the overseer. "The gals get some of the money and extra grub, and I have an arrangement with the sutler at Camp McHarry —had, I suppose I should say, now. I've been planning to tell you about this, so you could take charge. After all, it's profitable, and this is your land. I just wanted to make sure everything would go off without a hitch."

"Nothing is profitable to me if the gals are too tired to get their work done the next morning." Abel raised a hand firmly to forestall any interruption. "I pay you three dollars for every working day and I'm willing to keep you on 'till the end of this month."

"That's right gentlemanly of you." Morin's smile was acid-etched. "No need. I've got a small stake by this time and maybe you'll find out how well you can get on without an overseer."

Abel asked bluntly, "Do you want to make some more money for a stake?"

"How?"

"I'll pay two dollars for every acre above twenty that the nigras can plow per day during this month."

"Twenty is a lot of acres, and they haven't reached it as yet."

61

"Twenty, or no extra. Is that clear?"

"Well, I guess I'll need a grubstake after all." And then, automatically repeating the deal, triggered by Abel's last three words, he said, "Two dollars extra for every acre above twenty per day."

Abel walked back to the mansion, trying to get the sight of Blossom in the nude out of his mind. He shook his head fiercely, then surprised himself by reaching into a pocket for a key. He smiled and hurried upstairs.

Gently, he knocked on Nancy's bedroom door.

"Think you'd like to spend some time with me?"

Nancy's voice through the door was muffled by sleep. "Abel, dear, have you really got time for me? It doesn't help your business at all."

"I'll make the time, now."

"Oh, I'd hate to think of you being tuckered out tomorrow morning."

"Open up, or I'll batter this door to pieces."

"Abel, you wouldn't!"

"Worse yet, I'll use my key instead."

"Please don't do that, Abel dear."

Her footsteps were at the door and in a moment it was open and Abel was inside the room.

9

"Just the hands," the slave, Ned, told the other big black. "Only the hands. The one who wins gets the gal for hisself."

"More better," Jethro said, waiting contemptuously with open hands, "the winner kills the loser."

"Right."

Jethro glanced to his right at Blossom, who smiled. There was an avid gleam in her eyes as she looked from one protector to the other. It had taken awhile to force

62

both boys at each other, but now the biggest and handsomest bucks were going to kill for her favors. She had never looked more fulfilled or felt more beautiful. This moment she'd never forget.

Ned, the slave who'd only been here for three full moons or so, caught the look Jethro cast at her, and suddenly said, "You get 'way from here, Bloss."

"No, I stay. On this side of sugar house, the side we standing, nobody see."

"Get out and go to the church," Ned snapped. "One white bastard there. You missing, he look for you. He look for us, you say we asleep."

"I be there very soon," Jethro said. "Go to the church, Blossom."

"No!"

"Get away, or I give you a good whupping later on, lazy nigger gal."

"You not to call me that!" She flared, then turned as if to go. Half a dozen feet away she looked back, but Ned and Jethro hadn't moved as they waited for her to get out of sight and over to the church at the far end of the slave quarters.

The Reverend Clack was finishing his speech when she got to the battered old building and sat on a wooden bench at the end of the row. The master himself was in church at the far door. A white man was always supposed to be in a public section when a lot of black folks got together.

"Know your place," the Reverend Clack was booming. "Be loyal and humble, for a proper place awaits the loyal and humble in heaven. The good Lord will protect niggers who know their place, the good Lord will give them eternal salvation. Amen, brothers and sisters. Bless you all and please leave very quiet."

One of Sunshine's six children, the second gal, impishly kicked Blossom on a shin as Blossom was walking out hurriedly. Blossom raised a hand, turning to slap the life out of her. Sunshine pushed the child away and shouted

63

for Elihu to come over and teach a bad nigger not to be bad to young 'uns.

Elihu looked warily at Blossom, his eyes half-lidded and hands raised in caution. Sunshine's horsey face darkened even more then nature had intended. She gave a grunt and shifted her weight to one foot as she reached up a hard hand toward Blossom's hair. She had to hold the back of Blossom's head and pull.

The master had turned just as Sunshine drew up her hands. Instead of hitting back, Blossom shouted for the help she didn't need, her ears hurting with the sound of her voice when she was partly bent over. As she shouted, she wondered if there would be any help.

The master's voice could be heard above her now, firm and strong. "Let go, Sunshine! Now!"

Blossom waited a moment after the hand had been raised from her head. She wasn't in pain at all, but had coldly decided to make believe that she was.

"You're not hurt," the master said.

Blossom moved her head warily from side to side.

"There's to be no fighting in the church or anyplace else," the master said sharply. "If there's any complaint, come to the buckra or to me and we'll settle it. Is that clear?"

"Yes, masta." Blossom nidded eagerly, but looked into the distance toward the sugar house. There was no sign of Jethro coming to the church, as he had promised to do when he had won his fight.

"Now, what was this argument all about?" the master demanded.

Blossom looked sullen. "I ain't talk."

Sunshine's lips parted in a grim smile, showing her prominent teeth. "Blossom try to hurt my youngest."

"No!" Blossom glared at the older woman and then turned to the master. "She got no youngest. None of the kids hers. She and her man get babies from slaves in the swamps and swear to raise 'em up proper. They got no kids. They been foolin' you, masta. All these years and

64

they been fooling you." She caught herself just short of grinning as she looked at the older woman.

The master's narrow eyes swivelled to Sunshine who was impassive. Elihu looked away, his face drawn, his head down.

"It couldn't be forever," he said sadly.

"Elihu, be quiet!"

He was. Sunshine turned to the master and knew from one look at his face that he believed what Blossom had said. And then Sunshine, of all the slaves on this land, suddenly put her head down until it was slmost parallel with her chest and raised her frayed dress hem to her eyes and cried bitterly in admission of guilt.

Ned knew that he was being hit harder and harder and that there was no chance to win this fight to the death. He had won every fight he'd ever had with a black man and knew that his luck, if it was luck, had run out. A punch snapped his jaw back and another one hurt him hard against one side. Ned stood swaying, his skull pounding furiously. There was a noise inside him that he'd never heard before. He opened his mouth as if to let it out, and blood streamed down a side of his mouth onto his chin and along one of the stalks of his neck.

"Fight, why don't you?" he shouted when Jethro drew back for a moment. "Fight, you black bastard nigger! Fight!"

The pain was very bad, now. The back of his skull felt as if it was close to the sun. The right side of his body was stiff, as though it had been paralyzed. He couldn't take a breath through his mouth because blood came out, and when he tried, he swallowed some of the blood that was coming up from all over his body. His nose wasn't any good to him either, now, so it had probably been broken. That was when he decided to take a step backwards and turn away. He would be proving that he knew he had lost the fight, and then Jethro would let him alone. His feet didn't move, it seemed. He was still facing Jethro, who was hitting out faster than before. He couldn't keep track of all the punches, all the new pains; and he couldn't move.

Jethro shouted, "White bastard is what you are! White mothafuckin' bastard!"

In spite of his agony, Ned suddenly wanted to stop the fight and embrace the man who had at least half-killed him. He and Jethro shouldn't be enemies. He knew that, now. He managed to raise his arms, opening the fists in a gesture of love, a gesture of peace. He was moving closer to his new-found brother. Jethro pulled back, raised a fist and slammed it with all his might into Ned's heart.

Ned suddenly stepped back, one foot behind the other. He swivelled and slowly dropped to the clayey Louisiana earth. His eyes were wide open and hands remained out-stretched as life departed. His friend had sent him out to the only freedom that he would ever know.

"It's true, isn't it?" Abel Debenker asked calmly, look-ing at the two slaves in front of him. "You've never had children."

Elihu talked quickly. "We try, masta, we try all the time and we can't."

Sunshine said, "Quiet, Elihu!"

Abel swayed back and forth on his feet. He had di-rected them to leave the church, and had sent Blossom on her way with the others. Blossom had looked disappointed at first, but had rushed off in the direction of the sugar house. Abel supposed she was meeting one of the bucks over there, and shrugged it off as best he could. He sup-posed that either Ned or Jethro would be waiting for her, and perhaps both. Now he stood under the warm Louisi-ana sun, white hat on his head and hands on hips. A choice had to be made quickly, and he didn't want to hear the couple in front of him apologizing.

Elihu started, "Masta, we want the kids to be brung up in a good place, to b'long to a good man."

"Elihu, quiet!" Sunshine looked directly at Abel De-benker, and then her eyes rested on his string tie and she talked to that. "Me and Elihu want to be together, but if

66

niggers don't have young 'uns, they can't stay together. We did this so we could be with each other."

Abel nodded, almost grateful for the straight-from-the-shoulder talk. Sunshine had cried because she was desolate, and not to impress her masta; now she told the truth about what she felt. She had the best instincts of a white man of business, and Abel didn't know of any higher compliment.

"Yes," he said. Other words trembled on his lips: "I understand, it was a natural thing to do," or, in a more businesslike way: "You've done well in recruiting new workers." The words didn't come. If he used them, he would be treating these nigras as if they had more humaneness than he had ever before wanted to admit. He would be losing something that was valuable to him in the way of business. At the thought of that one word, business, he didn't hesitate any longer.

Sunshine, sensing that the decision had been made, raised her eyes to look directly at him. Elihu was looking down at his bare feet.

"Never mind," Abel said quickly. "Never mind."

Without another word he walked off to join his family in the carriage, on the way to church in Festin. It was Sunday, after all. The best people in the parish would be at church.

Three days afterwards, a quartet of Rafe Carstairs' bloodhounds were scouring the swamps near Abel Debenker's land. One of the dogs suddenly stopped and began sniffing close to the ground. Carstairs, who had been watching intently, turned to the free nigger who worked for him and ordered the boy to dig.

The body of the slave, Ned, which Carstairs had been hired to look for, appeared just before the shovel's work was done. The nude body had been disfigured even further by a pair of shovel-made scars, but other marks had been stamped on it before the digging. Bray welts were on the face and neck and stomach. The lips were battered. Several teeth had been knocked out, their bloody stumps gap-

67

ing in the sunlight behind the mashed thick lips. The hard-bitten Carstairs didn't flinch at the sight, but after a moment he turned to the free nigger.

"Put him in the bag and carry him in."

The assistant nodded grimly and went to work, Carstairs held the large sack wide open at the mouth while the free Negro struggled to put the body inside. His other assistant was controlling the four bloodhounds with profanity and tight leashes.

Carstairs sniffed. Somebody, another nigger, must have hidden Ned on the Debenker grounds after the murder and waited until the fall of night. Then he had lifted the body and carried it back of the mansion past a broad expanse of level land that sloped down to this cypress swamp, managing to get past half a dozen wide-open ditched that blocked the way here. Only a very strong stud would have been able to do it. Carstairs ran a hard hand across his unshaven cheeks and watched his nigger tie the sack with rope across it and across its mouth.

"Let's take this package where it belongs," he said.

The free man sighed and turned his back, then knelt and put both arms around the filled sack and raised it as he raised himself.

"I think we might find some business of a different kind over at the Debenker place," Carstairs added with a contented smile. "Look careful, now! I don't want you to bring the merchandise back even more damaged than it is."

Abel came out to meet Carstairs under a cypress tree in the shadow of the mansion house. He never wanted to let Carstairs inside the mansion. Now he faced an expectant Rafe Carstairs who had sent his free Negro to bring the body somewhere else on the grounds.

"Only a big stud could'a done this," Carstairs said. "One of your niggers has been taking away your property, and I think you ought to teach him a lesson."

Abel said, "I'm sure you do think so."

Carstairs threw his head back and laughed. "I get

68

through with that buck nigger, and he'll be very mild from then on. What's more, he'll probably do you twenty bales a day after I get finished, and kiss your ass besides."

It was probably the truth. Abel had seen two slaves of Chad Goldthwait's who had come back after Rafe Carstairs took them to his place. The slave man had been terrified of even the slightest unexpected noise. Every other word from his lips had been "Masta . . . masta . . ." He had been hysterically anxious for approval and had worked so hard that he dropped dead in the fields a month later.

The woman slave of Chad Goldthwait's had been very quiet and had always looked down at her shoes when she was spoken to. She cried at nights and in the early mornings, though, and large circles appeared under her eyes. She was dead in a month.

Chad Goldthwait had talked to the slavebreaker about the deaths of his two slaves. Carstairs had shrugged it off, looking from Goldthwait to Abel, who had come along with him.

"There isn't a mark on those two and you know it," he'd said. "Can't help it if your slaves are weak."

Chad angrily swore that he'd never use the slavebreaker again, but in a few months there had been a near-uprising at his place and he'd had three boys and a gal brought over to Carstairs. This time he had sold the slaves as soon as they returned, no marks on them. The other slaves had been terrified at first at the example of what might happen, but the terror hadn't lasted long. It seemed as if an uprising was always possible at Chad Goldthwait's plantation. The quick-tempered Goldthwait was a fool.

"Well now, Debenker," Rafe Carstairs said, hitching up his pants. "Do I take your biggest stud with me or don't I? Let him get away with murder, and your niggers will be killing each other right and left in no time."

Abel had made up his mind without being conscious of it. "That won't be necessary. Here's what I owe you, come to think of it."

Rafe Carstairs looked down at the notes that Abel had

69

deftly drawn out of his back pocket. He was scowling. "Gahdam shinplasters!"

He spat and hurried off.

Abel's new overseer was in the fields, watching a crew at their four-furrowing. The men worked quietly and determinedly behind their rickety-looking plows. There was one woman in the crew, Sunshine, and she worked as well as any of the men. The new overseer joined Abel as soon as Abel dismounted from the chestnut. Lucas Tinsley was a tall, pleasant looking man, rumored to be a secret drinker and a womanizer with the slave gals. On some days, though, as many as nineteen bales were completed, and that was worth any other problems he might cause.

"Where has the body been put?"

"In the sugar house, Mr. Debenker." Tinsley faced him long enough to speak and then moved his head so that he could keep both eyes on the crew. "Do you want to have him buried in the slave plot?"

"He hadn't been here long enough to make any friends and he didn't have any relatives here," Abel said. "Besides, the slave plot takes up too much space already, it seems to me. No, I think that cremation will do."

"It'll be taken care of as soon as the work is over. There ought to be a service, too."

"Put off the service until after work. When the service is done, I'm afraid I've got an unpleasant job for you."

"I'll take care of it, Mr. Debenker, whatever it is," Lucas Tinsley promised, and then wondered why he was looking forward to it. . . .

The ceremony was held at the old church and was brief, but to the point. The Reverend Clack had been sent for and had preached to the assembled sixty-one slaves that Ned's eternal reward would have been greater if he had been humble and obedient. The speech hadn't taken more than five minutes. The service was over. Most of the slaves stood outside the battered old church building, weak on their feet after a day in the fields.

Lucas Tinsley shouted, "Get into a circle, all of you! Do it now!"

70

In one hand he carried a rawhide whip, uncoiling it so that its tip cut a path in the soil as the Negroes watched.

"Jethro, stand aside and go over to the red tree."

Half a dozen slaves moved away from Jethro, who was still. He looked to his right and left, then walked forward at a measured pace. He halted in front of a tree that was past the cistern at the far left.

"Strip," Tinsley ordered.

Jethro took off his tattered shirt and frayed pants. For a moment he stood naked under the sun, muscles rippling under his brown skin.

Lucas Tinsley ordered, "Tie him, Elihu, and make it tight, or you'll be next."

Elihu fetched the rope and did the chore swiftly, not looking at any faces. He tied Jethro's wrists together with baling rope and then looped it over the nearest branch of the red tree. The knot was tied above the wrists. Elihu stepped back.

Tinsley ordered, "The legs, too, and hurry."

Elihu fetched more rope from the gin house. He tied the fresh rope twice around Jethro's sturdy legs and behind the knees, then made a granny knot against the other side of the tree. Jethro had to keep one cheek against the bark stained red with the blood of other slaves who had been whipped at this tree.

"Twenty lashes," Tinsley called out. "You know what they're for, Jethro, and I'm gonna carve my initials right into your ass."

The whip sang in the dry evening air and landed across Jethro's buttocks. The black man didn't call out, but the semicircle of watching slaves seemed to call out almost as one. A gal gasped and looked away.

Tinsley must have sensed that. "You're all to watch, every one of you."

He waited without turning to them, and then resumed. The whip cracked again and once more, flashing across the buttocks and inflicting slashes. Drops of blood flowed down to the clay-like earth. Again the whip sang and cracked, sang and cracked. Jethro didn't call out, but

71

started to gasp for breath. Tinsley smashed two whipcracks across the black man's broad back and another that
missed the tip of the spine. For the last whipcrack, Tinsley
hit out across the legs and just over the knees. A wave of
disappointment washed over him when the task was done.
He had worked up a pleasurable glow at doing this distasteful task for Mr. Debenker. Honesty compelled him to
admit that he had enjoyed giving the twenty lashes that
had been promised.

He turned to Elihu and said, "Salt him."

Elihu nodded sadly. He went for a bucket and half-
filled it with water, then added strong brine that was kept
in the stable near the cotton wagons. He swirled the contents around with a stick, taking a long time over it. At
Tinsley's abrupt gesture, he dashed the contents of the
bucket against Jethro's broad bleeding back. The
brine-and-water did what the whiplashes hadn't done. As
the mixture struck him, Jethro let out a pain-filled gasp
that hung in the warm air. One of the slave gals sobbed
quietly.

"Get him down from there," Tinsley ordered Elihu,
"and see that he's in the fields tomorrow morning. I expect
a full day's work out of him."

Lucas Tinsley coiled the red-tipped whip and strode
away to the overseer cabin on a level above the slave
quarters. With the door locked, in the shabby room that
he lived in, he took out a bottle and uncorked it, sniffed,
and reached for a glass. He put the glass aside and took
three strong pulls from the bottle. He wiped his lips irritably with the back of a hand. Impossible to know what got
into him that he actually enjoyed whipping another human
being. It was wrong and indecent, but something took possession of him at a time like that and he couldn't seem to
stop himself.

He would take a few more pulls at the whiskey bottle,
he knew, and then probably walk down to the slave quarters and gesture at one of the gals to come up to his cabin
with him. Blossom, most likely. He wouldn't treat the gal
very well—he'd know it, but the gal wouldn't; niggers

didn't ever feel much—and then he'd make it up to her by giving her some easy work for the next few days. That was how it always happened with him. The overseer took another pull at the whiskey bottle and then another. He spent the whole night alone in his cabin.

Abel Debenker spent most of that night in his small, neat, white-walled study, poring over ledgers. The price of meal had gone up to four dollars and thirty cents the barrel and it must have taken him a full hour of research to find a supplier who wouldn't charge him that much. He went to bed by himself in his own room at half past twelve. Not a thought had entered his head all night unless it concerned business figures and business facts.

10

Abel, in his best dark clothes, got out of the carriage first and then turned to help Nancy. His wife gathered her black dress around her and walked up to the open door of the small house. Kermit, having been helped out of the carriage against his will, followed his father. As soon as they crossed the threshold of the small, comfortable house, they could hear the widow Whitcomb crying. Abel led the way to the living room, with its home-sewn mottoes on the walls and its painting of Jeff Davis over the hearth. Jarvis Whitcomb's widow looked up tearfully. It was the second Sunday of November, 1864, and the old lawyer had passed away two nights ago after more than a year's suffering from a wasting disease.

Abel kissed Lavinia Whitcomb on both cheeks, then made way for Nancy to take her hand. Nancy looked down carefully at the other woman, imagining herself as a widow in some years' time. Kermit, who had started to grow like a weed at the age of eleven, tried to take Lavinia Whitcomb's hand, too, but found himself showered with wet kisses instead.

73

"Abel, it's good to see at least one young man here," Charles Passy said. The wealthiest plantation owner in the parish was smiling at him as they shook hands.

"I've missed the battles of Vicksburg and Gettysburg and Chancellorsville," Abel agreed. He had refused to go into the army when others had volunteered in bursts of patriotism. Tom Holman had come back with crutches and a stump instead of his left foot. Others hadn't come back at all. "And I wasn't in Atlanta to welcome Sherman."

"You seem to speak, sir, from a lack of patriotism."

"Perhaps. By the way, is it true that Jeff Davis sent a peace proposal to Horace Greeley in New York City? Greeley's only a newspaper editor, and I didn't have any idea that he was causing so much agony to the South."

"The story about a peace offer is so much lies, sir," Charles Passy said frostily. "Yankee lies."

Chad Goldthwait and his solicitous wife were the last to arrive. Goldthwait, approaching Abel, looked slimmer than he used to, and even his thick lips seemed paler. He had spent three months in C.S.A. and then bought himself out of the obligation and hurried back to his plantation. There was a rumor that he had taken part in the bloody massacre of nigra troops at Fort Pillow, but he never talked about that or anything else that might have happened to him in the service of the army of the Confederate States.

"Sad occasion," he said, sitting down in the chair that his wife had pulled up for him. And, more quietly, "What's going to happen to his sixty acres?"

"Mrs. Whitcomb plans to continue working them," Abel said, having heard that from Nancy.

"Hmf!" Goldthwait said, annoyed. "Maybe 'Beast' Butler and his troops will leave her alone on their way to New Orleans."

"Well, I'd expect them to reach this area fairly soon," Abel said, after a pause to smile gently at Nancy, who went into the kitchen to join some of the other ladies; his wife's shape was still prime, Abel told himself. "Something has to be done."

74

"How can Butler be stopped from destroying our land?"

"Offer his associates money to stay out. Yankees will take it."

"Money isn't as strong as it used to be. What's more, it didn't buy us what we wanted when we were in the Union. The Lord knows how many senators we bribed to persuade Washington to reopen the slave trading routes. Hell, what would have been the harm in it? There are plenty of nigger chiefs in Africa who are willing to sell out their enemies and even their kinfolk for wads of cloth and other fancies! But we couldn't stir 'em up in Washington. You remember all that trouble we had."

"Offer United States money to Butler's men."

"That isn't worth as much as it ought to. I've been saying."

"Offer gems, then. They'll keep their value, and Butler and his assistant beasts must know that."

"Can we afford it?"

"We can't afford not to."

"But, Abel, hang it, who's gonna make the offer?"

"We might ask Elkahan Melville to talk to some of Butler's officers and sound them out. Melville travels all over the South, and the blackbirding business hasn't been very solid lately. He'll be glad to do it for a small consideration."

"Every man in this room is a blackbirder," one of the men said, reminding Abel of the comment he'd heard Melville himself make at a slave auction a year and a half ago.

Abel looked away, irritated.

The Reverend Mr. MacCubbin had walked to the center of the room, and everybody became quiet. Abel found a chair beside Nancy and bowed his head to listen to the long recital of Jarvis Whitcomb's virtues. The recital over, he and his family joined the others on the way to the family burial plot. The coffin was deposited into a wagon by four slaves, and the sad procession got under way. The ceremony was brief. The coffin was put into the earth to rest on pinewood from one of the old lawyer's trees. Every man at the ceremony approached the coffin in turn and

75

threw a shovelful of dirt into the hole so that it spattered across the plain coffin.

There was a distinct air of relief at the house afterwards when the mourners returned for a collation that had been prepared by the women. Abel thanked the ladies for a portion of warmed-over chicken and lukewarm root beer, then went over to join some of the men who were almost certainly talking business. Their faces looked downcast enough for that.

"My workers are running off," Dale Olson complained. He ran a sugar mill near Festin. "There's no way to get them to stay around."

Abel asked attentively, "And you need to have the sugar processed quickly? How much do you pay your workers?"

"I've never gone highter than thirty-five." Olson, a cadaverous man who had lost two sons at Chickamauga, looked interested. "What are you suggesting?"

"A business proposition. I'm between cotton crops right now, and my timber lands are useless on account of the war. I'm suggesting, if the conditions are right, that I provide the workers from my plantation."

"I don't want slave niggers in my mill."

"If you need the work done, you'll use 'em," Abel said. "I presume there's no field work involved and, the hours aren't more than ten a day."

"Yes, that's right."

"Then I think that forty a week per hand will be satisfactory."

"I could certainly get a better price than that."

"Sure, but you can't get nigras who won't try to run off and take every advantage and might even do you and the equipment some harm. My nigras are well-treated, and that makes a difference."

"I might consider it, but not at forty a week."

"The price has gone up to forty-five," Abel said, having done some figuring in his head. "But for that money I provide meals for my hands and transportation back and forth. What's more, I arrange to get the nigras to your place at the time you designate."

"A nigra doesn't bring you more than two hundred a crop, and now they'll be earning you two hundred a month. That's ridiculous!"

"It's good business, and I think you ought to consider the price of forty-five per week per hand in United States money," Abel said smoothly. "I'll give myself the pleasure of calling upon you this Wednesday afternoon at one o'clock, if that suits your convenience, sir; for the decision."

"I suppose I had better agree," Olson said with a mournful smile, "before you raise the price to fifty dollars per hand and want the money in pirate doubloons."

Abel grinned and turned away to Chad Goldthwait, whose wife was ushering him out of the place.

"Hope to see you again on a happier occasion," Goldthwait said, offering a hand. "As for thet other matter, I suggest a Wednesday meeting to determine a price offering and assessments for each business establishment in the area. Is one o'clock suitable? At my place?"

"Make it at three, if you don't mind," Abel said.

The Debenkers arrived at home late in the afternoon. Kermit was permitted to change his clothes and join some of his pickaninny friends at play. Abel walked out to see if the whites he had hired to paint the stable were doing a good job of it and decided that they were. He'd had to hire poor whites to perform dozens of chores on his grounds rather than risk the lives of his nigras.

He found Nancy in the boudoir, where she had changed into a brighter blue silk dress with puffed sleeves. She was sitting at the mechanical piano and pensively resting her fingers on half a dozen keys, with no response whatever; the piano hadn't been playing for several months, and it was impossible to fix it or buy a new one. She looked up in fright as he opened the door, her jaw dropping.

"What's wrong, Nancy? Who or what are you afraid of, all of a sudden?"

77

"I thought it might be—well, something else."

He knew about one fear of hers, a fear that lived inside her all the time. "One of the nigras with a hatchet? Is that who you were expecting?"

"I suppose so."

"Do you imagine all our nigras are just waiting outside the doors to strike us down?"

"Yes, Abel, yes. From the first moment we came here I've imagined that. You were shaken at the idea yourself at one time."

"Perhaps, but I've given it some care and thought and decided that nothing like that is going to happen. With careful management, there's no reason why it should."

"The Mulqueen plantation has had plenty of trouble."

"That rebellion took place ten years ago because Jed Mulqueen was the fool of the world."

"Chad Goldthwait and his Lorna are always talking about the chances of a rebellion."

"Chad has no brains when it comes to managing the nigras, either. I can remember our being at his place one night. He practically pats his butler on the head and calls him a good nigger who knows his place and then a little later he talks like he's going to whip the daylights out of him. That was the time Serena Pollard burst in and behaved as if she wanted to kill every planter in the parish—remember? No, that's a foolish way to handle nigras."

"And you think that your slaves love you . . . , O Great One?"

"They know that I'm a fair man and that I'll keep my word."

"If hiring somebody like that man Tinsley is a sign of fairness—."

"It's what the slaves think of me that you're talking about, not what they think of my overseer." Leave it to a woman to pepper any conversation with side issues that didn't really matter. "I don't think we'll ever settle this."

"Abel, don't you feel that the war will settle this whole matter of dealing with slaves?"

"Yes, I do think so."

78

To pick up a *Festin Chronicle* was to see one item of bad news after another: Lincoln winning re-election over McClellan, Sherman smashing Atlanta to pieces like a mad child. There were still some fools who felt sure that if C.S.A. naval forces invented a nine man ship that could sail underwater, then southern brains would win the war. Those fools wouldn't let them realize that it wasn't brains, but equipment that mattered, and munitions didn't have to be manufactured or shipped or used by men with brains.

"So you do think we'll lose?" Nancy asked quietly.

"I think we've lost."

"And then what?"

"We'll have to get the cotton out with free labor." Abel eased thumb and forefinger along the sides of his slim nostrils. "The changeover is going to be hard."

"Do you think—well—."

A grim smile came easily to his lips these days. "Are you worried that a free nigra will suddenly rise up and take his revenge upon you and me for having treated him decently for nine years? Is that it?"

She nodded.

"It won't happen. Now let's talk about some other things, if you please. Let's *do* some other things, and as soon as possible."

"I'm serious," she said, as if lovemaking was an activity for children. "Will you be glad when slavery is finally abolished?"

He pulled his head back in surprise. He knew what sort of answer his wife wanted, but he was inclined to tell the truth.

"It'll be a challenge and very different," he said. "We might be surprised to see that nigras work very well when they don't have to."

"I didn't mean the business side of slavery, but the human side."

He shook his head with fierceness, not wanting to talk about that. His wife, he decided, hadn't often looked prettier than she did now. The red hair, as full of highlights as he had ever remembered it, fell to her shoulders attrac-

79

tively. Her skin had become whiter with advancing years. The body, hidden under a blue dress, was even firmer and yet more pliable. The breasts, almost hidden by a huge bow knot, were as firm and as much like ivory to the touch as they had ever been.

His hands came around her at the waist, but she drew back.

"Not now, dear, please not now."

"Now, now, now!"

"Why?" She was more in the mood to argue than make love. The funeral of Jarvis Whitcomb had made her want to ask questions, to probe character, to be gently melancholy.

"Why?" he echoed, drawing out his hands. "Does there have to be a reason?"

"Of course, there does. We've just come from a funeral, a melancholy occasion. A man you liked, a man who helped you when you needed help, that man is dead—and all you want to do is make love. You won't answer me about your feelings toward slavery, but you can answer me about your feelings toward this. Why, Abel? Why do you want to make love now of all times?"

The words came without his knowing it. "Because I'm not dead," he whispered. "I will be someday, but I'm not dead now. I want to prove that I'm not dead now. Don't you want to prove it, too, about yourself?"

There was a shadow behind her eyes that he didn't remember ever having seen.

"Yes, I suppose I do," she whispered in turn. Then, a little more loudly, "Make sure that Kermit isn't in the house."

He was beside her in five minutes. It was a time of sweetness for them both, a time in which they gave and took freely, exploring each other as if never before, renewing their vows of love without a word spoken. When it was over, he knew that he was alive. Spent and tired and sweetly melancholy, but blessedly alive.

11

A crop was planted early the next year, in March of '65. Toward the middle of the month a flood came, and Abel's future was decided.

His lands weren't near the Mississippi overflow, but constant rains swelled the backwater from the swamp area towards his land. Abel and Tinsley put the slaves out to imprison the overflow of sluggish warm water on the back levee. It didn't work. They retreated to the next levee almost two hundred yards farther up. Desperately they tried to raise the levee so it could check the waters. Everybody worked as much as eighteen hours a day and only rested in shifts. There wasn't any slacking at a difficult time like this, however, and no complaints that Abel heard or even sensed. The slaves were glad to find themselves at some vital work, backbreaking though it might be.

The rains stopped on March nineteenth, the waters beginning to retreat sluggishly. Abel, watching the water on a humid afternoon, looked tense.

"How many acres do you estimate we can work with?" he asked his overseer, who was nearby.

"Three hundred, perhaps," Lucas Tinsley said. His pleasant features were rimmed with sweat.

"I'd make it at two hundred and fifty, myself. Two five oh hundred acres." Abel shuddered. "How many bales do you think we're likely to get to the acre?"

"I'd say a bale, where we usually get a bale and a half."

"I'd say a quarter of a bale." Abel shuddered. "We might just as well send the nigras into the army now that they're subject to draft call. I'm damned if I see what good they're doing us out here, unless—I think I've got an idea."

Lucas Tinsley looked interested. Mr. Debenker's depression was over, luckily, and his brains were on the job once again.

"Suppose the nigras drill into the furrows so as to massage the seeds and then tamp the seeds in place by rubbing the flats of their hoes along the sides of the seed furrows."

Lucas Tinsley pursed his lips. "It surely to the good Lord isn't going to do any harm to try."

Abel watched his overseer run over to the first crew and give them instructions with an excited tone of voice. There was no harm in letting Tinsley think that a small miracle might happen. He still didn't expect more than a quarter of a bale per acre from this crop.

A conversation with Chad Goldthwait gave him hope from another quarter entirely. Most of the parish planters were in the habit of having a drink at Chad's place on Thursday evenings, mostly to talk about the war news. When Abel got to the place on this particular Thursday, Tom Holman was already talking about a piece of news in the *Festin Chronicle*, the four-page paper spread over the stump of his left leg.

"If Abe Lincoln is meeting with a peace commission on a ship off Virginia, then the war is over, and we've lost," Holman was saying. "Let's get used to it, we've had the stuffing kicked out of us."

Goldthwait, who never talked about his brief army career, looked down at his thick body and said nothing.

"We might as well register at the nigger Freedmen's Bureau for advice and education, 'cause we're gonna need it every bit as bad as our niggers."

Abel, looking around him, said, "A few people couldn't make it this evening, I see."

The change of subject didn't soothe any of the bitterness from the planters in Goldthwait's airless and crowded study.

"They're not here because they aren't in the parish any longer." Goldthwait turned on his heels in a burst of anger, an oversized ex-military type after a shortened term of service, and now slanging those who wouldn't do the

82

job he couldn't handle. "They've turned tail and run off like rabbits."

"What do you mean?"

"Vic Jobelin and Giraud Duval suddenly packed up everything they could carry and ran off, abandoning their plantations."

Abel felt himself making a fishmouth and settled back with a hand over his pursed lips. He drew the hand down slowly, looking very much in possession of himself.

"Nearly fifteen hundred acres of workable land," he said.

"The flood got to those lands, too, so they don't amount to that much."

"Not for this crop, but for the next and the crops after that."

Tom Holman folded the four page *Festin Chronicle* over his leg stump, as carefully as if it had been one of the prewar editions of many pages and much social news.

"Are you suggesting what I think?"

"Almost certainly. A few of us ought to take over the plantations and divide the land. It can farm very well after this crop."

"Perhaps." Goldthwait agreed, running a heavy thumb and forefinger along his lower lip. "But we might consider taking our time about the claims."

"Why?"

"Let the niggers on the property find out that the land isn't gonna produce food for 'em, and then they'll get out of there."

"How about the old ones who don't know what to do? They'll sit there and starve to death."

"That's their lookout if they happen to be stupid."

"No, it's our lookout," Abel said decisively. "If there are nigras on those lands, then we take 'em over right away and feed them. I won't have close to two hundred nigras going around at starvation's door on our account."

"We didn't abandon the nigger bastards," Goldthwait said acidly.

83

Tom Holman pointed out, "The feeding costs are likely to be pretty big."

"I'll advance them, if necessary, and take a larger share out of the next cotton crop on those lands."

Goldthwait gave a lizard grin. "Suppose the rest of us decide to cut up the lands ourselves? Then you'll be shivering in the cold with over two hundred starving nigras."

"In that case," Abel started to say, and then shook his head fiercely. "No. We've been friends for a long time, out of necessity as it happens, and I think we're going to need each other in the next half a dozen years as never before. I'd suggest we stay friends."

"On your terms," Goldthwait sneered.

"On everybody's terms," Tom Holman put in, changing colors swiftly. "How do we divide the land? Offhand, it seems to me that Duval's west quarter and Vic Jobelin's north ought to be given to——."

Abel said easily, "Chad, get us a map."

Arrangements were made swiftly and fairly. It was decided that the claim should be filed by Jarvis Whitcomb's successor, a younger man named Peter Quendale. While the discussion was going on, the Reverend Mr. MacCubbin walked into Chad Goldthwait's study. The fair-featured clergyman, who had presided at the Whitcomb funeral, had only recently taken to joining the others for their Thursday evening sociables, as he called it. As soon as the subject of the talk became clear to him, he interrupted.

"How long do you think the courts will amount to anything? How long do you think claims will be honored at all?"

Charles Passy, who had taken no part in the acquisition talk, drew himself up stiffly. "Forever, sir. One way or another, on the field of battle or away from it, southern justice and southern ideals will prevail."

Chad Goldthwait, in the heat of argument, said swiftly, "The west of Vic Jobelin's land certainly ought to come to

84

me. It's as good as adjacent to my land, so who's got a better right to it?"

He looked up with the others, frowning. Abel Debenker had suddenly let out a short, sharp, cruel burst of laughter.

12

Blossom said eagerly, "You ask him, you see what he say."

Jethro snapped, "I ask him, he say No. He say, 'Slave, you do what I tell.' He the masta. We do what he want, all the time."

Blossom edged a little closer to the big buck. They were in the bare old sugar house, both prone on the floor. Moonlight through a dirty window gave Blossom's high cheekbones a disarming gleam. Her face wore the innocent childlike look that it assumed when she wanted him to make trouble.

"He not say No," she insisted. "He need us."

"He sell us if we don't do what he say."

"You a fool! The slaves be free soon, he need us."

Jethro shook his head angrily. "You never know. Gal has big mouth all the time."

Blossom grinned, smiled, and touched him here and there. She reached for his tool and held it almost thoughtfully in a surprisingly smooth hand.

"I tell you how big a mouth," she said softly. "I show you how big if you go to masta and tell him like I say."

"I don't know," Jethro said awkwardly. "You always want me to do things and I always do 'em and then I get the whip and you wait around and go on saying I do other things. My ass still hurts from last whipping. That's not right."

"You do this one thing now. Our time is a-comin', I tell you! The other whites from far away are a-givin' our whites a bad time. We get after 'em while we can."

"I dunno."

"Don't you want me to show you what a big mouth can do? A big mouth and a big hand."

"I—dunno."

She made a fist of his right hand, opened it and then drew the length of her tongue in to warm the opening. The other hand stroked Jethro's tool and she knew that it was rising.

"All right," he said tautly, his breath coming as if from a distance. "You show me. I talk to the masta."

Blossom smiled in the darkness. Jethro felt himself kissed on his thick lips, then on the side of his neck. He raised his head so that he could see what she was doing. She kissed his chest and bellybutton while her free hand worked to knead his tool so that it would be bigger. Lightly her tongue touched his dark springy hair. She paused, then, her head raised briefly with the tongue extended. Then the head sank down, her tongue on his tool and licking the top of it before her lips enclosed it.

"That's the way, honey. Oh, that's the way. . . . You sure do know your way. . . . Yes, that's how. . . . I ready, now. . . . I *ready*—."

13

Abel was watching a hoe gang cut down grass and weeds under a driver's laconic supervision. The pace was slow, and he found himself surprisingly unconcerned. Only a few days ago, word had reached Festin that Robert E. Lee had surrendered to the hated Ulysses Grant at a courthouse up in Virginia. It was impossible to know if his life would go on at its accustomed pace for long, just as the Reverend Mr. MacCubbin had suggested to all the planters at a Thursday evening sociable in Chad Goldthwait's study just a short while ago.

As he put spurs to the chestnut, he heard a deep voice he knew well.

"Masta, masta!"

He turned. Jethro was hurrying towards him, touching the top of his head deferentially while he moved. The big slave didn't wear a kerchief on his head to shield him from the cruel April sun, let alone a hat. He gestured at the slave not to run, but Jethro moved more quickly than usual.

"Masta, us boys and gals been talkin'," he began.

Abel cocked his head thoughtfully. "Tell me what you want, Jethro. Don't play games."

"We all have a patch of land where we grow food," Jethro said. "We want we should grow cotton instead." He touched his forehead in deference. "If masta say it good."

Abel tried to look thoughtful. He knew perfectly well that if the slaves were growing cotton there would be a considerable rise in theft from the cash crop of the plantation.

Carefully, he asked, "If you don't grow food, how will you get greens to eat?"

"We sell cotton with masta's, we use money to buy. In town, masta."

"Well now, let me see." Abel was calm, knowing that he had to delay any apparent decision, just as if it was all very important, just as if he remained a man of power. He was duelling with words, not knowing whether or not the duel was worth undertaking or the scars worth causing. "This year's cotton crop will amount to very little on account of the flooding. You know that, don't you?"

"Yes, masta. The boys, the gals, we all know."

"As for the next crop, well, let's see how the ground lays by that time."

"It's good to grow cotton on the next crop, then? Masta say it's good?"

"We'll see when the next crop is put down." The tone is reasonable, a verbal foil doing its damage almost without notice. "We'll do the best we can, all of us. I've always

87

treated you and the others as well as possible, Jethro. I'll keep doing that."

(The fight is done. The guisarme is withdrawn; the halberd is returned to its sheath. And now remains only the salute to the fallen foe.)

There was a mulish I-told-you-so look on the slave's narrow features. He was silently winning an argument with someone who wasn't close by.

"One more point, Jethro," Abel Debenker said carefully, "you shouldn't let a gal tell you what to say or when to say it."

Jethro looked away, humiliated.

"Blossom's a pretty gal, but she's not thinking of what's best for you."

The duel was finished.

14

"Masta not let us plant cotton," Blossom whispered, "then we go."

The slaves were in the rickety old church during a Sunday sermon. At the back of the church, the *buckra* stood with hands at his sides while the Reverend Clack talked about how important it was for a good nigger to be humble to his masters, as the Lord had wanted. The Reverend Clack's sermon made it possible for Blossom to whisper to Jethro on one side of her and Sunshine on the other.

"We all go," she whispered stubbornly. "All of us."

"Go where?" That was Sunshine, skeptical and practical as always.

"Away. We good as free now. We good as free." ·

"Who say so?"

"The war done, we free." Blossom smiled. "We free, we go."

"And do what?" Sunshine asked, whispering angrily behind a raised hand. "We all hungry by nighttime. The soldiers catch us and bring us back."

"But we all free very soon. The fighting finishes, and we all free."

"Who say so?"

"I know it true, stupid Sunshine. I know it."

"Does anybody tell you?"

"Nobody have to. I feel it, stupid Sunshine. We all as good as free."

" 'As good as' ain't good enough."

"What 'bout the old ones?" Sunshine asked irritably. "They can't go. They stay behind, they starve to death."

"It's best we think 'bout us and nobody else," Blossom snapped. "We leave here, we all go to first levee. We do it quiet, go there by different ways. From then, we on our own."

Jethro said, "Maybe."

The Reverend Clack's sermon came to a finish at last. There was little hymn singing, not like on one of those Sundays when the slaves occasionally turned a service into a noisy and pleasurable change after a week of tortured dullness. The songs were sung. The slaves started to walk out.

Blossom glowered, looking out the door.

"What bad?" Jethro asked.

"Buckra stand there, looks for gals."

"Bastard!"

"Let him pick somebody else to warm him," Blossom murmured. "He a no-good. First he gets rough, then he say he a no-good. Why he don't do it the opposite way for once, and save a nigger gal some welts."

Sunshine, back of her, whispered, "Quiet, Blossom, he can hear."

"Let him," Blossom said fiercely.

But she made no other remark as the slaves walked to the end of the aisle and out of the scruffy building at the foot of the slave cabins. It was one of those Sundays when the Reverend Clack took it into his head to stand at the

89

fly-specked door and shake hands with every slave and speak briefly. The Reverend Clack was a free nigger, so he didn't have to do that unless he wanted to or he felt that the Sunday sermon hadn't gone over too well.

He gave Blossom's hand an extra squeeze. "Good-day and bless you, sister."

Blossom returned her widest smile and said, as if guilelessly, "Fuck you, Reverend."

Reverend Clack blinked, the smile crumbling at its edges, and probably decided he must have heard wrong. He let Blossom's hand go and took Jethro's paw afterwards.

"Good-day and bless you, brother."

Jethro said, "Fuck you, Reverend." He sounded mild and patient, a slave resigned to his lot in life.

Reverend Clack looked disturbed and didn't smile again until Sunshine approached him. The smile refused to fade even though Sunshine said absolutely nothing, and wouldn't let Clack take her hand.

Blossom hadn't gone more than ten steps before she heard the sound of mocking laughter at her right. She turned slowly, well aware whom she'd see. It was the buckra, his pale eyes widened by drink and his body swaying back and forth.

"That was very funny, Blossom," Lucas Tinsley said. He wasn't smiling. "Don't you know that your masta sends the Reverend Clack out here to give you as much sense as one nigger can give another?"

Blossom's eyes were lowered. She was aware of Jethro having paused a few steps behind her. With a hand out of the buckra's sight, she gestured for Jethro to move on.

"I sorry, buckra."

"Yes, you should be. That was a contemptible thing to do to a man of God, even if he's a nigger. I want to talk to you about it, Blossom, in my cabin."

In spite of herself, she was surprised. "Now, buckra?"

"Yes, do it now." He looked stern and disapproving, as if he was giving an order in the field. "And if you don't get back to the hoe gang until tomorrow morning, don't be

90

surprised. You've been a bad nigger gal, so come to my cabin. If you do, I promise it'll go easier on you than it might, otherwise."

And he turned and led the way past the slave quarters to the rise and toward his cabin. Blossom didn't hesitate to follow. Anything else meant that all the slaves would be chased by bloodhounds and sheriff deputies if there was an escape. A slavebreaker in town took charge of those searchers for runaways and didn't treat slaves well if he found 'em alive. One more time, any prospect of choice had been taken away from her. If she didn't spur most of the other slaves, they'd wait around until they died--except for maybe five or six who might take out on their own. No, there wasn't any help for what had to be done, now.

"I comin', buckra," she said softly.

15

Abel arrived at Chad Goldthwait's place half an hour early for the week's so-called men's sociable on a Thursday evening in April. He wasn't surprised to find nearly every planter in the parish crowded into Chad's small study with most of the chairs removed. And he wasn't surprised to see shock and dismay on so many grim faces.

Tom Holman, cradling a drink in one hand just above his leg stump as he sat on one of the few chairs in the room, said quietly, "Who would have expected to feel sorry that Abe Lincoln is dead? The Lord only knows what Andrew Johnson will spring on us."

"Whatever he tries, he'll get back with interest," Chad said, his temper rising at the notion. He was filling glasses for the new arrivals, never letting Negro servants into the study during these weekly get-togethers.

"Never mind Lincoln and his passing," one planter said restlessly, as Abel took a filled glass from his host's thick hands. "We've got more to worry about than that."

"Yes, Goldthwait agreed promptly. "I'm not the only one losing niggers right and left. Rafe Carstairs tells me he's got so many coons to hunt that he can't hardly keep track of the numbers."

"We've all had some runaways," Abel said. "Five of my boys took off, two of them prime workers."

Goldthwait was sourly amused. "I thought you were such a good owner that the coons wouldn't leave you no matter what happened."

"I wish I'd only lost five," Tom Holman muttered. "About half of my fifty field hands are over the hill right now."

"Twenty hands here," said another planter.

Charles Passy put in quietly, "I've lost sixty hands."

Goldthwait snapped, "I told Rafe Carstairs that we'd form a party and clean out the swamp areas and send every coon we find up to meet his maker."

Abel said, "They've probably gone far from the swamps now, and a long line of killings isn't going to help get out a crop."

"There isn't any chance of getting out a crop this year, good or bad. To me, the whole year seems like a total loss. Forget it."

Abel shook his head fiercely. "I went to the jail house to ask the sheriff if he'd loan me some prisoners for the harvest, but there aren't enough to make any real difference or be any use. They aren't what you'd call able-bodied."

Half admiringly, Chad Goldthwait said, "You *would* think of something like that, Abel! You never give up."

"When it means losing everything otherwise, I won't give up."

"The only thing to do," Charles Passy said, "is to tell my hands that they're free and pay them a salary to handle my crop."

"Maybe you can afford that," Tom Holman said laconically. "We can't."

"If you think I can easily afford it, you're mistaken," the wealthiest planter in the parish pointed out. "Loan rates have gone past three percent and there's a chance I may have to dispose of part of my lands if I can't raise money from a factor in New Orleans."

Abel asked promptly, "Have you decided on a price? Well, let us know when you do. If more of us have to sell our accounts receivable, then the price should be uniform."

"Certainly. I don't think that arable land is able to fetch more than thirty-five dollars an acre. Not at a time like this."

Abel winced.

"We all seem to be virtually wiped out," Barton Manders snapped. He was a tall man with a sunburnt face and a luxuriant mustache. "Most of us have been flooded, our niggers won't condescend to stay if they don't get paid, and our expenses have gone past the ceiling. That seems like the end of it. We're finished."

A planter said hotly, "My daddy and granddaddy didn't work themselves into their graves raising cotton so I can quit and give up when there's bad trouble."

"What are you planning to do?" Abel asked promptly.

"I don't know. Dammit, nobody else does, either."

Manders said bitterly, "You might become a steamboat pilot, but the Yankees will probably take the Mississippi away and put it down in the middle of New York City."

Abel suddenly thumped a fist into his palm. "I won't give up! I don't care what you others insist on doing, but I won't give up."

"Well, you had better care," Manders said crisply. "What hurts one of us hurts us all. It's time you understood that, Abel. You may have got a late start as a planter, through no fault of your own, but you've been one of us long enough to know the score."

"Yes, I have and I do." Abel turned on them all. "And I know that we can't give up. We can't afford to put our nigras on a payroll, not after all we've been through in the last few years. Later on, well, it might not be a bad thing, but we have to——." He suddenly blinked, and then shut his eyes tightly for a long time before opening them again. "Yes, I think we have to."

93

Goldthwait asked swiftly, "Have you got an idea?"

Abel nodded, looking around to make sure that the Reverend Mr. MacCubbin wasn't in this study. He was sickened by what had come into his mind, the only idea that might work out. He knew that his lifelong dislike of slavery as an institution had to go into the discard for a little while longer. Had his whole life until now been leading up to the moment when he had to decide to tell the planters this one idea at this particular time? It was an idea that went against every principle of decency that he had ever felt he stood for. It was proof that the system of slave labor, that peculiar institution, had destroyed him as a human being almost in the same way it had destroyed black people. The world in which Abel Debenker lived had smashed him to pieces.

"Well?" Goldthwait asked crisply, ready to lose his temper. "Aren't you going to tell us this great once-in-a-lifetime idea of yours?"

The life he had lived until this day determined his course of action now. Abel Debenker leaned forward and began to talk.

Book Two (1855-1861)

1

Local residents will be pleased to hear that
Abel Debenker, who left the U.S. at the age
of five is returning after an absence of twenty
years in Great Britain. Accompanying him
will be his wife, Nancy, and their two year
old son, Kermit.
That the occasion which brings Mr. Debenker back to his native country is a sad
one cannot be denied. Readers of our obitu-
ary page will recall the recent death of Lyon
Debenker the Second, owner of Fairlawn.

—Social notes, *Festin Chronicle*,
May 7, 1855

"Your father did want me to make his own position
very clear," said lawyer Jarvis Whitcomb, holding on to
the seat rest as the carriage bucked and swayed like a
horse in a story of the Wild West. "He had to run the
plantation as a business, and he did so, but—."

"I can understand that," Abel said carefully. He had
been working for the last three years at an insurer's group,
in London, and his understanding of business disciplines
was pretty thorough. He sat rigidly, his thin-featured face
dripping with sweat. His baby son, Kermit, was on his lap
and making sounds of pleasure, riding and swaying as if
his father's knee was the horse. Nancy, in muslin, with a
pink hat that was even more out of place than Abel's
warm British clothes, tried to look comfortable.

"There's one major question, of course," Whitcomb
said, planting a hard palm down to keep his gray hair
from waving, because of the speedy carriage ride. "That is
simply whether you plan to hold on or to sell."

Abel and Nancy smiled at each other. He couldn't

95

imagine his tawny-haired twenty-three year old wife as the mistress of a southern plantation. He tried to imagine his son standing familiarly among a group of Negro playmates. His mind couldn't deal with either notion and the images didn't appear.

He had enough business sense, though, to say, "I haven't decided as yet."

Whitcomb looked sideways at him. The lawyer was a ruddy-faced man in his fifties who didn't look as if he'd ever known a day's illness in his life. "I would think that the time to make up your mind is before the plantation goes into the ground. Fairlawn has got potential, indeed, but it can only be realized by someone who knows what is involved."

"That's almost certainly true, but I plan to look around first."

"Of course you should, but being a plantation owner is hardly an occupation you can be expected to learn overnight." The lawyer took a deep breath. "If you do feel that you want to sell Fairlawn, I trust you'll keep in mind that a syndicate of your neighbors, of your father's friends, will be pleased to take it off your hands at a decent price. Times haven't been as good as I wish they had been for my clients. I have a sixty acre place not too far from here, and I'm in a position to know about cotton planting in addition to keeping up a law practice. But I'm sure that a satisfactory arrangement can be—. Here we are."

Abel supposed that he ought to have been tensed up, but he was very much at ease. The carriage moved slowly up a rutted road. There was an old disused house with dust-specked windows, stable with horses whickering in the hot sun. And here was a courtyard that seemed filled with turkeys and chickens prancing around. The mansion house seemed to consist of windows and broad porches. He had been born here, but it meant nothing to him.

He helped Nancy down. His wife tried to keep as much dirt off her shoes as possible. She smiled, but her nostrils were slightly crinkled with distaste.

Lawyer Whitcomb descended also. "One other point,

96

Abel— I'm sure you'll pardon the familiarity from somebody who dandled you on his knee—is that your father was very clear about not wanting you to become the master of Fairlawn, as I tried to say to you in the course of the carriage ride. That is the truth, as I'm sure you know. He told me that he had often mentioned it to you, and had sent you away to keep you from taking over the plantation after his death."

Abel nodded reluctantly. His father had come to see him three times while he was growing up in England, and had written to him once a month until just before he died. "The slave business is a bad one, but, alas, I cannot earn my living in any other fashion. . . . Men aren't supposed to use their fellow humans as chattels, as things . . . , slavery destroys the slaves themselves and the masters as well." Words of kindness and compassion in a crabbed handwriting on rice paper that smelled of greasy chicken. Love of humankind expressed by the owner of a suburb of hell.

"I'm well aware of my father's sentiments and I'll take them into consideration. And now I'd like to see the plantation and settle in for a short stay, I assume."

"Of course, Abel. Please follow me."

The next few minutes were confusing, even by the standards of the father of a young son. Abel was taken through most of the house, aware of the smell of cooking meat more than anything else. Furniture was made of wicker and wood, and had lasted dozens of years longer than anybody could have expected. Hunting prints in sepia lined some of the walls, along with paintings of his ancestors. He'd carried a miniature of the painting of his mother for a long time, having mislaid it shortly after getting married. Now, looking at the picture in full size, she seemed only another ancestor. There was a room off to one side for the master of the house to work with ledgers and other papers. That was the only room that put Abel at ease.

"Your good wife and your son are upstairs in the lady's boudoir, inspecting it," Jarvis Whitcomb said, as Abel's

97

attention was caught by a ledger entry. "Do you care to meet the overseer?"

"I have to learn enough to be sure I get a fair price if I choose to sell," Abel said, not looking up. "What is 'Hgsh Su'?"

"Hogsheads of sugar," the lawyer said promptly. "Your grandfather lost considerable money trying to grow and market sugar, so your father bought it from others."

"The price doesn't seem unreasonable at ninety-three dollars per," Abel said. "In England right now, a hundred and five is closer to the mark."

The lawyer led the way out to the back porch, facing what looked like two rows of tents with their sides and projecting roofs. There was a proper building down the far end of that double row, scruffy though it looked.

"The slave quarters," Jarvis Whitcomb said crisply in response to Abel's stare. "Niggers don't need the same conveniences we do."

"But—no walls?"

"Do you know what it would cost to build walls on those quarters? And the niggers wouldn't appreciate it at all. It wouldn't make any difference to them."

"How many black people does the property have?"

"Ninety-five at the moment, but only thirty-five are field hands and only twenty-one of those are what we call prime field hands."

"I've been told that every slave works an acre and a half of ground." Actually, he had read it in a newly published book called King Cotton while on the ship to New Orleans. "If that's the case, and considering that there are four hundred acres to farm, the plantation must be earning a comfortable income."

"Figures have been known to lie, Abel, as I'm sure you must be aware. . . . Here is somebody to explain. I took the liberty of sending a message to ask him to join us."

A man on horseback appeared on the way to the house. He halted the animal, dismounted without hitching the beast, smiled vaguely, and started to walk up to the porch.

98

Abel, watching the sturdily built man who needed a shave and smelled of horse dung, resolved that he'd never again meet a field worker anywhere but out of the house. A cypress tree less than a hundred yards away would do for that purpose, if it ever again became necessary.

"This is the plantation overseer, Felix Bygraves," Whitcomb said. "I think I can take my leave of you now, Abel. Mr. Bygraves will give you any details you might want to know about plantation business."

"I want to know everything."

"Yes, I understand that much by now." The lawyer looked annoyed; clients were supposed to put themselves in his hands, not think independently. "Your servant, sir."

"And yours . . ."

Bygraves talked about the plantation as if it were a beehive, and that no man without years of apprenticeship could hope to master its ins and outs. As for the black folk, the overseer talked about them as if they were so many cattle and not worth a moment of anybody's consideration.

"I want to look around and see how the plantation runs, Mr. Bygraves."

"Very well, sir. Are you a horseman?"

"I've hunted in Britain."

"That will make it a little easier, then. I'd suggest you change into plain clothes as much like mine as you can manage. We'll go over to the stable and get you a horse, and then I can show you the property."

Abel agreed to the sensible suggestion. He hurried up to the room he'd be sharing with Nancy and opened his largest suitcase. He was in a pair of sturdy gray pants and a shirt to match when he walked over to his wife's boudoir and knocked on the door. Nancy opened it, and she and Kermit then stepped out into the musty hall.

"That room hasn't been used for such a long time that I'll have to have it redone if we had any plans to stay here."

"Don't do anything much," he said quietly. "I plan to

99

be out of here and to get us back to London by July. I talk about being undecided, because it's necessary to drive the price up."

"How long will it take you to sell the place?"

"Longer than I'd prefer," Abel said. "I've decided to hobble the sale to a certain extent."

"What do you mean?"

"In this benighted country of mine, Nancy, black folk are considered so much property, and they've got a considerable value depending upon age and work capacities. There are ninety-five slaves here, and I'm going to free every last one of them before I put Fairlawn on the market."

Nancy smiled and nodded approvingly. Kermit watched his mother's response, and then gave a wide and happy smile of approval.

2

Half a dozen tired-faced black men and women, being watched by a black man with a dogwhip in one hand, were using what looked like cardboard plows to push the warm earth away from the tops of the tender young cotton plants in the field. Other gangs were at the same work in the distance. The men wore handkerchiefs on their heads; the women wore shapeless hats, dirty clothes partly covered by wraparound canvas, and no shoes.

"If I can get the plowing and planting finished by the middle of this month," Bygraves said, "I'm sure the crop will be a good one."

Abel, on a dark horse for this inspection trip, had been adding figures in his head. "Twenty-two thousand dollars is what the crop will earn."

"I'm not very good at figures, and there are a lot of expenses, you know, Mr. Debenker."

"Even if the final profit is only eleven thousand dollars

100

for a season, that is still enormous. And the managing of a plantation is purely a business problem."

His eyes rested idly on a rawhide thong draped around the horn of Bygraves' saddle, half an inch wide and a quarter of an inch thick. Bygraves, certain that Abel Debenker's attention was on the whip, gave a rueful shrug.

"I don't use this very often, Mr. Debenker, believe me. If you whup your property it doesn't work too good for you afterwards. Unless, like I say, the whupping is necessary."

Abel looked up, his eyes gleaming. "There are timberlands, too, Mr. Bygraves—aren't there?"

"Only 'bout a hundred acres."

"I'd like to see those."

"Of course."

The stands of trees looked well cared for, Abel agreed when he saw them, but the timber money wasn't likely to be as good as the earnings from king cotton.

"Your father and grandfather wanted a second crop in case cotton goes down in price, or the crop were to get flooded, which is also a possibility," Bygraves said softly. "That's only good business."

"Yes, I suppose so." Abel pondered. "There are swamp lands which don't belong to anybody, and it would seem to me that if there are trees on those lands they might be taken to market."

"It's been done on occasion, Mr. Debenker, but the wood pulp isn't of good quality, and there are complaints from the dealers."

"Then the timber isn't really very profitable, but is helpful in case some disaster strikes the cotton crop, as you say. Yes, of course. I think there's something called a gin, isn't there?"

"Bless you, Mr. Debenker, a gin isn't a disease." Bygraves threw his head back and laughed uncontrollably, but not for long. He suddenly coughed. The tips of his ears seemed dusky. "Come, sir, and I'll show you the way the gin works as best I can."

He was taken to a tidy looking house he hadn't seen

101

until that moment, a house by the road and with front and back doors kept wide open. They dismounted and walked inside. There was an odor on top of the horse dung emanating from Bygraves that reminded Abel of licorice candy. Bygraves explained the workings of the gin machinery to process the cotton. Abel stared, fascinated, and asked about the frequency of repairs and the cost of repair parts.

Bygraves was warily answering a question in a satisfactory manner when both men heard a horse whicker in fright. The overseer whirled around angrily and ran to his own horse, mounted it, and rode to the stable. By the time Abel followed, the overseer had dismounted and hurried inside and emerged more slowly. He was pulling a large Negro youngster by the ear. The Negro didn't call out, but his gleaming teeth were gritted.

Bygraves let go of the young Negro and cuffed him. "Why, you stupid bastard, a horse is valuable and necessary. What in hell makes you stupid niggers want to destroy horses, anyhow? You're all like that."

The Negro said carefully, "I jus' combing——."

"I heard the horse sound scared, and so did your new master."

The young Negro straightened and touched a hand to his forehead. He couldn't have been much younger than Abel, his features almost as thin as Abel's, and his body big and muscular.

"This is your new master, Jethro, and I'm going to ask him to have you whipped for what you did to that horse."

Jethro looked at Abel Debenker, without pleading. Abel found himself appreciating that.

"Never mind," he said to Bygraves. To Jethro he said, "Don't let it happen again." It was the first time he had spoken to a Negro in twenty years, and he wished that the words hadn't been an order. He had told himself that he would be very kind to the black folk when he came back to Fairlawn and to Festin. It hadn't worked out like that.

"No, masta," the young Negro said obediently.

Abel squirmed in his boots. "You can call me 'mister'

102

instead of the other thing. Now, Bygraves, I want to see—."

As he turned, he became aware of the slave's response. Near-violence and solemn threats hadn't disturbed him, but the new master's single request seemed to have made his face paler. He put both hands down tightly at his sides and tried to draw a deep breath, which wouldn't come.

Abel asked sharply, "Are you sick?"

"No, I fine, m—, m—."

Bygraves ordered swiftly, "Back into the stable, boy, or I'll blacken the ground with you."

"Yes, buckra," Jethro said automatically. And to Abel, "Thank you, masta—I mean m—."

"That's all right." Abel was mounting his black horse when he saw the young Negro girl. She had apparently run over from a distant field. Her ragged dress didn't hide the good sixteen year old figure and seemed to accent high cheekbones and bloodless lips. Very attractive to any man who liked the type.

"Get back to work, Blossom," Bygraves snapped, reaching for the whip, "or you get a taste of this."

"Yes, buckra," the child said instantly.

But she was looking all the time from Abel's thin features to Jethro's and back again, her eyes growing rounder with every swivel of the head, or so it seemed. Then she covered her lips as if to hide laughter. She turned and ran.

"What in hell was that girl doing?" Abel asked, irritated as he settled himself on the horse.

"Blossom is such a mischief maker that it's impossible to guess," the overseer said, rubbing his unshaven cheeks. "About your little problem with Jethro, Mr. Debenker. I'd advise you against treating the niggers as if they was even a little human. If you ride with me to the work, you'll find out what I mean."

"In that case, I think I'd rather look around the whole property and get the feel of it before I go back to examine the ledgers," Abel said. "I've never come close to a twenty-two thousand dollar income in my life, and I want to get some notion of what it feels like."

103

3

His circuit of the fields didn't tell him anything new or change his impressions. When he returned to the overseer, he saw that the man was in front of his own house on a level above the slave cabins, and that he was talking angrily to the pretty little colored girl Abel had previously seen.

"What's this?" Abel asked.

A number of slaves in the cabin area were looking up at them.

As Abel dismounted, the Negro girl started to talk quickly, but Bygraves said, "quiet, Blossom, or I'll raise some welts on your pretty face."

The young girl drew back, a look of terror on her face, dark hands planted over her cheeks.

Bygraves said to Abel, "I want to know where her mammy is, and if she's escaped. Blossom had better tell me, or Blossom will be ugly for as long as she lives."

Blossom put both hands to her eyes and started to sob. Abel saw the small space between two fingers through which she looked out at him, while her body was apparently racked by sobbing. The girl was prepared to take any advantage of indecision. The only skill she had ever learned was that of surviving, which was her vocation and avocation and trade and profession

"Buckra, I dunno where—."

"Don't lie, Blossom. You and your mammy get along pretty good, and if she was going to try and escape she certainly would tell you. Now I'm not going to repeat this, Blossom. Where is she?"

Bygraves, without looking to one side, answered the question on Abel's lips. "The old nigger woman is a cook and worth about three thousand dollars the way prices are going, nowadays."

Abel said nothing. Three thousand was almost the salary he earned for a year at his good job in London. And here somebody was trying to steal that much money from the plantation! Of course, it was a criminal act, no matter how much he sympathized with the cook, in principle. Three thousand dollars wasn't easy to come by.

"Put your hands down, Blossom," the overseer said coldly, "so I can see where to whip you."

"No, no, marse buckra, please don't whip Blossom, please!"

Bygraves pulled one of the girl's shaking hands down to her side, then the other. He took a step back to raise the whip. Blossom allowed herself one frenzied look at Abel's impassive face and then shouted, "I no tell 'gainst my own mammy, I no tell."

But she had moved herself so that her back was towards the field slaves, who were watching avidly. Bygraves didn't strike her, but his face, which the slaves could now see, looked more ferocious.

Abel watched, mesmerized, as the black girl's lips mounted the words, "First levee . . . first levee and then the swamp . . . first levee."

Bygraves nodded briefly while raising his voice. "I'll settle with you afterwards, Blossom. Now get back to your quarters, and hurry."

The whip cracked as she moved, not touching her, but the girl shrieked as if she'd been horribly scarred. The slaves at their quarters were out of sight when Bygraves turned to glare at them.

Abel asked quietly, "What happens now?"

"I'll go down to the first levee to look for the woman and see if she's waiting for others to join her," Bygraves said. "If I don't find her, I'll go into the swamp areas. But it shouldn't take long."

"And what happens to Blossom's mother when you get her back?"

"She's due for a visit to Rafe Carstairs, who teaches slaves to obey, just like you'd teach a dog "

"No," Abel said decisively. "None of that."

105

"Then she has to be sold. It's bad business for other niggers to see that one of them could try to escape and not be severely punished. You can understand that."

"Yes, I suppose so. Is there any way to make sure that the woman is sold to a kind—uh, owner?"

"No, there isn't, Mr. Debenker. You'll have an insurrection on your hands, though, if she isn't sold right away."

With a nod, he accepted the judgment of the more experienced man. "And what happens to Blossom? Does she get sold, too?"

"Blossom's a bigger troublemaker at sixteen than her mammy at thirty, but Blossom usually sees to it that somebody else is caught for what she does. In this case, she has to get a reward."

"Money, you mean?"

"No, she's got some of that, as many slaves do. You'd be surprised how much money drifts into their hands with the help of men who buy with what they manage to steal. In Blossom's case, though, I'll wait a month until this ruckus has been forgotten, and then I'll get her a kitchen job."

"But if she's a troublemaker, she won't last long at it."

"Oh, she'll lose the job quickly enough, Mr. Debenker, but things have to be done that way. It's the system, you see. All part of the system."

4

"How good to see you," said Anne Jobelin, embracing Nancy from her place on the reception line in the long hall. "You can freshen yourself in an upstairs room, dear. Gentlemen downstairs," she added with a smile at Abel.

"Your servants, ma'am," Abel said for both of them and shook hands firmly with the host.

"I gather you enjoy owning a plantation," Victor Jo-

106

belin said after the greetings. "It's September, and you must have pretty much made up your mind about it in five months."

"Not yet, sir." Why did Abel look sideways at Nancy in the bright blue taverner silk gown? "It takes time to make these decisions and find the best price for your land."

"I hope to see you for many parties to come." Jobelin said shrewdly. "Your servant, sir."

Abel walked with his wife over to the staircase and smiled at her. "Remember our pact."

She stuck out her tongue at him. "You beast!"

He walked downstairs, chuckling, and spent two minutes in the gents' dressing room. A house slave, who'd probably seen his best years in field service, brushed Abel's jacket carefully. A youngster, who couldn't work too many hours in the fields, was offering to shine his shoes, but he refused that. A planter named Duval was in the dressing room with him, having his hair barbered and giving precise instructions to the black man who was doing the work.

Nancy descended the stairs gracefully almost as soon as he reached the first floor at the other end of the reception line. She had rarely looked so pretty to him as in these last few months, with the red hair glowing as never before in his recollection. This southern climate was supposed to be harsh on a woman, but her lips were still full and warm, the eyes sparkled with love, the figure was full with large, comfortable breasts hidden at the moment behind blue silk. He felt himself change as he looked at this vision coming towards him.

"Now we carry out the pact," he said easily, "and find a room that isn't being used, and we use it."

She flushed. "You weren't serious when you suggested that at home! I wasn't serious when I agreed."

"We'll blow out the candles." He was touching her gently in the little hollows where even the slightest of touches was certain to rouse her.

She took a step away from him, but said in almost a child's voice, "Somebody might come in."

"I'll stand against the door."

"You're a beast," she said automatically. "Besides, we have to go into the ballroom."

"Very well, for now, but we stay together and look for a side room for ourselves "

The ballroom, so-called, was lined with gardenias and honeysuckle. A double door was open, leading to the porch. Abel started to take his wife in that direction, but Nancy tapped him urgently on the wrist.

"Over there," she whispered, "you beast."

There was a door against the east end of the room. It was half open. Abel and Nancy nooded and smiled at others, pausing for small talk that they themselves couldn't quite follow. The door led to a small room that was probably used to keep household equipment, but they had to open and close another door to get into it.

"There's enough room," Abel whispered.

"I suppose so, but what a dreadful place to put a tool room, so near to—."

"Forget that!"

"All right, beastie!" She leaned over and bit him on the ear. "We haven't done anything like this since heaven kn——."

"Sh!"

He reached for her in the darkness. There was a tingle of soft silk against his fingers and palms. Silk and harsh woollen material and projecting buttons all seemed to meet. Their mouths were set against each other now, and her teeth suddenly raked his tongue as he found her at long last. They moved back and forth as one of his hands went from the breasts to the comfortable rear of his wife and he held her by the buttocks and pushed himself deep into her and then part way out and again deep into her.

"Oh, it's good, good," she whispered

"Yes," he said huskily, and in the darkness they found

each other's lips again and each gasped into the other's breath.

Abel eased himself out of her and then heard a sudden deep intake of breath that didn't have anything to do with passion.

"Oh, my Lord!" Nancy gasped. "I dropped my gown a moment too soon and there's a little of it on my gown."

"Are you sure?"

"Of course. I'm going up to the ladies' dressing room and see if I can get it off."

He stepped to one side, letting her out of the pitch-dark room. He heard her running into the ballroom and then saw her walk swiftly out of it and into the hall. She held both hands in front of her as she moved.

Abel checked the buttons of his pants and looked down at the material. For good measure, he touched his pants at the crotch area and even along the thighs. There was no trace of liquid. He had wiped his dingus on a handkerchief and returned it to a back pocket after folding it several times. He was ready now, and he hoped that a moment's foolishness wouldn't cause him to have to take his wife home.

The ballroom had become quieter. A group of field hands on the porch, visible with difficulty through the opened doors, were singing for the guests' pleasure. A very pretty dark-haired woman in green suddenly turned to the man beside her and whispered, "Sh, Ben! The darkies are singing!"

"They aren't disturbing me," the man snapped.

"But, Ben—."

"Any time Ben Polland wants to talk, no nigra is gonna stop him," the man said. "And no wife, either. I hope that's understood, Serena."

"Yes," the attractive woman said quietly and resignedly, looking away from Abel's probing eyes. "I suppose so."

"Good." The man turned to Abel. "I'm Ben Pollard and

109

I know who you are. Image of old Lyon Debenker, I must say, but more calm."

Abel shook hands and said very quietly that he was glad to meet him. Pollard turned to introduce him to another planter that Abel had previously met. The appearance conscious Duval sauntered by, and half a dozen men were soon talking over the soft hum of Negro folk music.

> *In de nighttime by de fire,*
> *Keep you warm and softly singin'* . . . .

"I'd almost rather invest in the Pennsylvania Rock Oil Company," Duval was saying petulantly. "That good friend of ours in Washington, Franklin Pierce, removes the governor of Kansas because he's against slavery—. Yes, fine, but he should back up his feelings and allow slave shipments into the country. Not a halfway, namby-pamby situation like that fool Northern Congress has got us into now."

"I heard of a slaver that was caught off New Orleans," Pollard said irritably. "Two hundred nigras on board, prime merchandise, and simply useless."

"A million dollars," Tom Holman said. The usually taciturn, whey-faced planter had walked over swiftly to join them; Holman always moved as if he was on the run. "Imagine a million dollars going overboard."

"At five thousand the slave, it would be just that," Pollard agreed. "But prices aren't that high these days."

Victor Jobelin, the host, had come over with a finger to his thick lips. Now he paused, head cocked to one side. "If Lower California comes in as a slave state, that's what'll happen."

"Two hundred nigras," Pollard said wistfully. "And just think of all the forged papers that had been worked out for that batch."

"It's a shame about the ship and the crew," Holman put in after a pause. "Building and outfitting a slaver and manning it costs a fortune."

"Oh, the government couldn't hold any of 'em," Pollard

110

said. "The nigras were scrapped as soon as the Yankee ship hove into sight All of 'em dropped over in their chains; prime merchandise."

"The Mississippi is almost a million dollars richer," Jobelin said philosophically. "Too bad."

The singers paused and began to sing once more.

Come, where my love lies dreaming. . . .

Abel had been looking toward the door from the reception room, surprised that Nancy hadn't returned yet. There was a pause, the other door was flung open briefly, and then she did come in. Her hands were folded over part of the dress, but her face seemed controlled. He hurried over to join her.

"The stain shows," she said quietly. "Ever so lightly, but it does show."

"We'll leave in a few minutes, Nancy."

"Why the delay?"

"It shouldn't look as if we're being rude if we go now."

"I'll have to walk with my hands in front of me."

"Just give me another few minutes. The men over there are talking business, and I figure I might learn something."

"But you certainly don't plan to—." Her face, which had been white with irritation, suddenly became gray with anger. "Yes, I see. I think I really do see, now. I'll stay as long as you want to, of course. Of course, Abel dear."

The last word had been said sarcastically, which was unusual for her. He reached out a hand, but she turned away from him and walked toward the house slave who was carrying a tray of punch glasses. It was impossible to talk to a woman in her mood. Wisely, perhaps, Abel didn't try. The damage had already been done.

A number of other planters joined those who were talking about business affairs. Abel listened avidly until Jobelin repeated himself. When he looked at Nancy again, he saw that she had stopped another house slave with a tray of punch glasses and was drinking one while she held

111

another with her free hand; she didn't seem to care any longer about the telltale stain. She had got through half a dozen glasses when he hurried over to her.

"It's time we were going home," he said firmly.

"So soon, O great one? I was just starting to enjoy myself."

"It's time we were going home."

"Very well." She put down the second glass as soon as it was empty, rather than reaching for another to take its place. "You speak and I obey. For I am but clay in your hands, O my noble lord."

"Nancy, stop this!"

He got home with her at last, not realizing that she had discovered a tactic that got under his skin and that she'd use it again and again until it did nothing more than irritate him. It seemed like a small event to have changed the course of a happy marriage.

5

"A baby," Blossom said in her high youthful voice, eyes narrowing wickedly. "My mammy say if I don't bleed for six Sundays, then it means I have a baby."

Jethro scowled. He was sitting on the earthen floor in a corner of his quarters, eyes on the nearest cistern between the two rows of cabins, and nowhere else.

"A baby is yours," Blossom said, standing over him and leaning in his direction. "Yours and nobody else's."

"How I can tell a baby is mine? It might be the buckra's. You go to see him whenever he wants."

"Might be, but not, not, not." Blossom stamped a foot. "A baby that's yours is a quarter white and you know it."

Jethro suddenly looked towards her. "You talk like that and you get us both sold."

"It's true and I tell everybody "

"Don't." Jethro made his large hands into fists.

112

She started out of the cabin.

"Where are you goin', gal?"

"If I can't tell nobody, I gonna kill the baby."

He didn't follow her outside to the area between the rows of cabins, but she was stopped by Sunshine. The horse-faced slave, only a few years older than Blossom, stood with arms akimbo as she blocked the way.

"You not gonna kill no baby," Sunshine said sternly.

"My baby, so I kill it."

Sunshine drew out both arms in a gesture that was pleading and demanding at the same time. "You have the baby, and I raise it, Blossom. I promise. You won't have no trouble with it."

"I don't want the baby, I don't want the hurting." Blossom shook her head contemptuously. "You want a baby, you go to that foolish Elihu of yours, and let him give you a baby. Don't you come to me. I do nothin' for you."

Sunshine's horsey face twisted as if in pain and she turned away. Blossom gave a mischievous little smile and looked back to Jethro's cabin; he wasn't in sight and hadn't followed. She shrugged elaborately, then walked to the grassy area behind the slave quarters and out of sight of the mansion house.

She stopped, made fists, thrust her head forward, and started to run barefoot through the hip-high Bermuda grass. Back and forth she ran until she was out of breath. Then she started to twist her body around to one side and the other. Her youthful, unlined face was flushed, sweat drops lining the high cheekbones. The sun hammered at her as she tried to use her body to the utmost. She couldn't remember ever having done anything as difficult as this.

Again she started to run, but her legs wouldn't move quickly enough. She was making a turn when she nearly fell against another slave. It was one of the older hands, Moses, who wouldn't be able to work in the fields much longer.

"What you doin', gal?" Moses demanded.

"Leave . . . 'love."

113

"You try to kill yourself," Moses said hurriedly "You stop this!"

Blossom broke away from his grip and tried to run, but her legs wouldn't carry her any further. She felt herself fall, and turned her body around so that she would fall on her stomach. She rolled around on the earth. A pain that wasn't like any that she had ever known took sudden possession of her. She wanted to sob, but didn't have the strength. She was too bone-weary to die. For once, she desperately hoped she'd be let alone, not even noticed. Old Moses was calling for help.

That was when she started to soil herself. She had never known that there could be so much filth inside her. The flow wouldn't ever stop! Somebody was over her head and looking down, but it wasn't Jethro. She saw the horse face without recognizing Sunshine. In a sudden shout of disgust, which didn't come out the way she had hoped, she felt her eyes closing in spite of herself. She may have been going to sleep, but the agony was even stronger than it had been. She felt somebody rip at her one scanty dress and then she knew nothing any more. It was growing dark when she opened her eyes. Shep, one of the field slaves, was standing over her and looking down. When he realized that her eyes had opened, he bent over.

"Just wait till you feel better," Shep said.

There was a bad smell in the air, or what was left when a bad smell was mostly gone. She hated it and didn't want to be near it.

"I stay here long?" Her voice was a frog's croak.

"Long as you want. You want to try, I take you to cabin."

She looked up keenly at Shep, who was a hawk-nosed boy with burning eyes. She had gone to Shep's half-cabin once in a while, and had found him the only boy who didn't ever say that she was the gal he liked best and that he was crazy about her. Shep was more clear-eyed than the others. Blossom would have hitched up with him, maybe, but she didn't really think that Shep cared two pins about her.

114

"I be all right?"

He nodded. "Only trouble is that you might not be able to help bale the crop."

"Too bad, like hell!"

She looked down at herself. The one dress she owned was ripped down the front. There were dollops of red and yellow-gray in front of it and in the back, too. She knew she had been powerfully sick.

"A baby?"

"No baby for you, Blossom, not ever."

She knew she wouldn't be such a wanted slave if she couldn't have babies like Sunshine probably would. No help for it. She'd have to keep her own place some other way, probably by learning how to get just what she wanted out of Jethro. Jethro was strong enough to protect her, and he could be led very easily. Everything depended on that. She almost wished she hadn't got in trouble a while ago and lost the good kitchen job that she'd had when the new masta came, at plowing time. There was no help for that.

She looked up. "When we go?"

"Soon as you think you can make it," Shep said.

"I want to go."

Shep lifted her under the armpits, raising her slowly to her feet. She let out a gasp that couldn't be controlled, and looked to one side. Shep was helping her, but he had turned his face away.

"Why you do this?" Blossom asked.

"I tell Sunshine I will."

"You don't like me."

"I don't like the smell."

"I can't help it."

"I know," Shep said heavily. "Now we move ass over to the cabins."

It was endless. She couldn't walk. Her feet didn't want to carry her. She had to lean on Shep, almost to walk on Shep. They were on hip-high grass that smelled warm in the early evening. Somewhere a bird croaked. Chickens could be heard making little clucking sounds near the mansion. There was the smell of flour in the perfumed air, and Blossom couldn't understand that. She tried to fix all her faculties on that one odor, but the pain lived inside her just the same. Her cabin was fifth from the left. Shep helped her over to it, and the three old mammies who shared it with her came over, and two of them took her by the hand. Carefully they helped her down to the straw that served as her bed.

She tried to say, "Thanks, the first time she had ever said it to any of those old mammies. The word didn't come. She looked from one to the other and tried to smile her gratitude, but they weren't looking at her. They could remember too many fights with Blossom, too many times when Blossom had got them into trouble, and not suffered any penalties herself. Blossom tried to say, "To hell with you!" Those words wouldn't come, either.

She knew that she was in too much pain to sleep, and didn't suppose that she would ever sleep again. As soon as she moved so that she was lying on her back, though, her eyes were shut, and she slept.

6

Abel stood at the rear of the stuffy old slave church on Sunday, the twenty-first of December, and watched the ceremony. Elihu agreed to consider Sunshine as his wife until he died and to have many children by her and to obey his masters at all time. Sunshine said the same about Elihu as her husband, about her children-to-be, and her masters. They kissed shyly. A cheer went up from the assembled slaves and an aisle was formed for the bride and groom. As they reached the door, Abel heard the horse-faced woman say quietly, "Don't trip, Elihu. I don't want to lose you, now."

The slaves were still cheering as the couple walked slowly to the cabin which was going to be theirs alone for the next few days. By Wednesday or Thursday, the other couple who shared that cabin would move back in to join them. The marriage customs were severely ritualized among slaves, as Abel found out when he'd willingly given his permission for the horse-faced Sunshine to marry her long-time boy friend.

The clergyman said a few more words to the others, and then thet slaves drifted out of the scruffy old church. Abel, who had been the first to leave, found himself looking behind him. The clergyman, a small man who wore glasses with silver rims, stood at the door and watched. His lips were crinkled at the corners. He had been cheering the couple on towards the cabin at first, along with the slaves, but his behavior was restrained when he saw Abel watching him.

Elihu and Sunshine were out of sight now, but any number of bawdy remarks were being called out by the boys before they could be hushed by their gals. One or two youngsters capered around, not sure what was being celebrated, but glad to join in. In less than a minute, there was no one at the church except the clergyman, who smiled uncertainly at Abel and hurried back inside. Abel, looking through the open unpainted door while making a turn to leave, saw the clergyman reach for a Bible and some note sheets, then put them into a string bag and tie it swiftly. He pattered to the door with the bag under his arm, then smiled uncertainly when he saw that Abel was facing him. Abel wasn't sure himself just why he wanted to talk to this black man in the clergyman's collar. Words seemed to drift out from between his lips almost of their own free will.

"You're free, aren't you?"

"I am, suh, and an ordained clergyman as well." Tiredly, he opened the string bag. "I'll be glad to show you my papers, suh. I carry them everywhere, as the law insists a free black man must do."

"No, that's all right." Abel supposed he looked like a poker player showing serene unconcern. "I was wondering why you do this work."

117

"I am an ordained minister, suh. Clack is the name. I have a vocation to spread the word of God."

"Being a free black man in the South can't be very easy."

The Reverend Clack took off his silver-rimmed glasses briefly and looked down at them. "My fifth pair this year, suh. The others have been crushed or broken by drunks and so-called deputies of the law and soldiers who think that a nigra is getting above himself if he wears glasses or shoes, though I haven't lost many pairs of shoes. I don't suppose you'd care to try and guess how many times I've had to take out a Bible from this string bag and read a passage from it, because some white man doesn't believe that a nigra is able to read. Worse yet, how many times I've had to write almost anything, with some foul drunkard's breath over my shoulder, saying something like, 'Never thought I'd see a coon as is able to write.' " The Reverend Clack looked directly at Abel. "No offense meant, suh."

"Or taken." Politeness with a black man, except for offhanded casual friendliness, was making him ill at ease. "Why do you stay?"

"The South is my home, suh, and I have to spread the word of God."

"But what you're telling your people isn't the word of God, and you must know it." Abel wanted to be somewhere else, but his feet wouldn't take him and his lips wouldn't close. "God doesn't only want his people to be humble when they're under such stress."

The Reverend Clack shrugged. "Ah, suh, you tell me that I betray my vocation. But who is to say that, truly? If I preach anything like the true Word, if I say to my brothers and sisters that they are human being like their white masters, that they should rise up against oppression like the tribes of Israel, then I will be put into prison. The flocks to whom I preach, this one and others, will be without anyone to perform marriages or officiate at burials. My people may have become heathens, but the church has to keep up the best contact with them that is possible. Per-

118

haps, suh, they won't be heathens forever." Again the furious blinking. "No offense intended, suh."

"And none taken." The little ceremony, with its oriental politeness, was aided by quick smiles. "You think that all Blacks will someday be free, Reverend?"

"I hope so, suh. I pray so."

"How do you expect it to come about?"

"I don't know that, suh. The Lord God works in mysterious ways, His wonders to perform." A ritual of quotation, this time, the charmed words to keep away thought and hold off despair.

"What would the upshot be, Reverend Clack, if the slaves on any given plantation were suddenly free? Suppose their master waited until Christmas week, say, a week after next, when there's no work to be done, and called his slaves together, and said to them, 'From this moment onwards, you are free.' "

"It would be meaningless, suh, and perhaps worse than that."

"Do me the courtesy to explain."

"Of course, suh. This master would have to sign a number of forms and go to the sheriff's office and swear out a dee-position that he was freeing his slaves of his own free will and desire and that he was in a healthy and vigorous frame of mind. That is difficult, suh. Various obstacles might be put in his way. Hearings would be necessary, and those could go on and on for many years and at a large cost to the planter."

"Is there any way to avoid that?"

"Of course there is. He might make out bill of sale papers for every slave, indicating that the slave had bought himself free and that it had all been a business transaction. A man may perform some act of decency in the South only if he can prove that it has added to his wealth."

"Do you foresee any other difficulties, Reverend? I gather that you do, as you're not impressed by the working of the laws here."

"Indeed, yes. The plantation owner would have to alienate his family. For instance, cotton could no longer be

119

grown on the land at a profit, which would be pointed out to him. If there are male children, they'd not have any substantive inheritance. The family would lose its local friends, and no daughter could really count on making a good marriage, if she'd expected to do that."

"All of those reasons are very sound, but in this particular case most of them wouldn't matter."

"There could be one more reason, suh," the Reverend Clack said gravely. "I hate to say this, but I think it ought to be made clear."

"Go on."

"Some of my people aren't as—worldly—as others. I don't know why that is, suh, because their experiences in life have been about the same. You'd think that if you take twenty men and women and turn them into slaves and let them do similar work, they'll be as alike as peas in a pod. It's not so. As a result, I think that some freedmen and women, perhaps even most of them, would lose their freedom papers, and others would have them stolen or torn up by slavecatchers. They'd be sold back into slavery again by owners who might not be so decent, so Christian, as their current owner. What I am saying, suh, although it breaks my old heart to hear myself, is that not every slave could be freed. Not in the South as we see it presently."

"Yes, I understand." Abel, both hands in the pockets of his Sunday-best pants, nodded slowly. "I appreciate your help, Reverend Clack. You've cleared up a few points to be kept in mind."

He pulled his right hand out of his pocket and started to extend it toward the man as a friendly gesture. Clack, although he knew what was intended, pulled back as if the hand had been a snake. He looked to his right and left and even back of him as if wanting to make sure that the white man's gesture of friendship hadn't been seen or encouraged. Abel returned the hand to his pocket and drew back in turn, as if crossing a line that nobody could see. A boundary had been put down between himself and Clack, himself and the slaves.

"There will be something extra in your envelope this

week," Abel said, inclining his head with distant politeness.

The Reverend Clack raised a hand in acknowledgment, almost but not quite like one of the slaves. Abel turned and walked back to escort his family to church in town, where they listened to a sermon about the ultimate goodness of God.

7

It had been a hard day. Abel had decided to join Chad Goldthwait and some other planters at a slave auction in Festin. He knew perfectly well that he wasn't going to buy, but he hadn't realized how strongly he'd feel about what he saw.

The men on the block were handled and talked about like merchandise. Jokes were made concerning them. Property values were discussed. A good-looking black girl was put on the block and whistled at and became the subject for gutter remarks. She was being sold as a companion for young children, but every man at the auction was thinking of other uses for her. The bidding was slack, so the auctioneer gestured for the gal to strip. The men whistled and called out even more mockingly than before. Some men insisted on pinching the gal here and there. One owner touched her breasts and pressed them, but decided against buying because the breasts didn't get bigger at his touch.

"Don't need no more cold black bitches at my place," the man had drawled. "Got enough of them, already."

Abel had looked along with the others—how could any man look away from a beautiful female? After it was over, though, he excused himself and walked to the end of the crowd and stooped over and threw up half his insides.

But he didn't seem nearly as upset as Nancy when they saw each other again just before dinner. She looked cool,

121

with the white ribbon to hold her hair up and the white dress, but her lips quirked at the corners and for once there was no life in her eyes.

"Is anything wrong?" he asked.

"Only that my carriage ran over a chicken near the stable as I was coming back from my visits." She was trying to hide her distress at the recollection. "I want you to promise that you'll be careful when you're riding on the grounds, dear. Please promise to take extra care not to do anything like that."

"Of course, I'll be careful," he said, and meant it. "You've had a difficult day."

Dinner consisted of pea soup and creamed chicken—which Nancy couldn't eat—with hot corn bread and warm butter. There was black coffee to follow. Only Kermit's presence was lacking to make Abel contented at the moment. His almost three year old son wasn't allowed to eat at the table, because he didn't know too much about good manners, but Abel hoped his wife would change her mind about that before '56.

Not until they were sitting in what she called the morning room, with its wicker furniture and wall mottoes in three colors, did she apologize for her thoughtlessness and ask belatedly about his day. He told her, and she winced.

"When are you planning to free our slaves?" she asked. "We have to sell the place and go back home."

"I haven't received the money for the recent crop, you know. Nineteen thousand five hundred dollars." There had been some spoilage, and the steamboat fees had taken him unawares, so that the total returns hadn't been as great as he'd hoped.

"The check can be mailed to us in London," Nancy pointed out.

"Yes, but I—I haven't found a buyer as yet, you know, dear. I've got to sell the place before we can do anything else whatsoever."

"Do you now? La-di-bloody-da!" The nonsense words of local young belles came as easily to her lips as the inter-

122

polated British expression. "It doesn't seem to me as if you've been looking very hard."

"I've put advertisements into newspapers."

"Two of them, yes."

"They didn't bring any serious results, so I've decided to look into other channels."

"Such as?"

"Nancy, you know I've talked with some neighbors, who say that they'd be interested in buying Fairlawn."

"Three times you've talked with some people, including Jarvis Whitcomb. But that was before the crop had to be sent out to market across the darkies' backs."

"I've been busy, dear. Can't we please change the subject?"

She wasn't looking at him anymore. Her eyes stared straight ahead at the opposite wall where an embroidered, framed motto hung.

"Everything will come out all right, I promise, Nancy. Why, we'll have almost twenty thousand dollars more when we leave here. Think of it! Even if we let Fairlawn rot, we'd have as much money as I would earn in five years in England, without living expenses. We'll be very well off."

"*If* we ever go back."

"What does that mean?"

Now that she was looking directly at him, he wished she wouldn't. "I happened to see Mr. Whitcomb when I was in town today. Lawyer Whitcomb, Abel. I said to him that I hoped arrangements were being made to sell Fairlawn quickly, so that you and I could get back to where we belonged. Jarvis Whitcomb looked at me very coolly and said that he and some others had been very interested in buying, but it seemed impossible."

"Nonsense!"

"Mr. Whitcomb said that when you declined to deduct levee repair costs from the purchase price it was agreed to do what you wished, but then you wanted to be paid for added work to the cotton gin machinery. Lawyer Whitcomb said he didn't doubt from your tone that if the

123

buyers had agreed to that particular demand, another and even more outrageous one would have been put in its place. Jarvis Whitcomb has formed the conclusion that you aren't interested in selling."

"The old fool is wrong," Abel said quickly and mechanically. "I won't sell out for a pittance, that's true. I won't let myself be cheated. But I certainly am interested in getting the best possible price for this property. If Mr. Whitcomb says anything else, he's wrong."

"I told him that you had also promised me that you'd set our slaves free, momentarily. Mr. Whitcomb smiled and said that a lady like myself shouldn't take too seriously what she might have read in a novel. I suppose he meant Mrs. Harriet Beecher Stowe's book, but I haven't looked through it yet. I simply know what's right and wrong, and I know what you've promised me that you'll do."

"What I've promised to do, Nancy, will be done as soon as possible, and when it is convenient to all concerned," he said briskly, then got to his feet. "You'll pardon me, but I've got some bookkeeping to see to."

She said bitterly to his back, "This is all wrong, Abel."

He didn't make any response or look around. Quickly he walked into his office and sat down at the desk, where he felt at ease. The small office had been repainted white, and he'd hired some of the poor whites in town to build him a new desk with thick pigeonholes and a substantial rest for ledgers. He could put his hands on whatever record he wanted in minutes. At the moment, though, there wasn't any work for him to do, and he sat restlessly.

He bounded up and walked to the small mirror against one wall and looked at his face. The thin nostrils had become reddened at the tips with sun, as had his thin cheeks and almost flat chin. He decided to wear a hat at all times during the day when he wasn't in the house, and wondered if he'd be comfortable in white. He couldn't say just how it happened, but he had an itch to dress in white clothes and even in white shoes. It was as if he wanted to be able to

124

say to himself that he was different, somehow, from all the others.

He was nodding determinedly to himself when he suddenly heard something move against the floor over his head, something that must have been very heavy. His first thought at hearing the noise was that one or more of the slaves had come into the mansion and were ready to harm master and mistress. He reached into a drawer for his Flobert miniature percussion pistol, gripping it by the ivory handle, and pulling back the hammer so that the trigger unfolded into position. Then he rushed swiftly to the back stairs, skipping every other step as he ran up. On the second floor he saw Nancy's black, pebbled-leather trunk on wheels being shifted from their bedroom. One of the house slaves was pushing it from behind and along the hall, while the burly cook opened the boudoir door and shouted back to the house slave that he should be very careful. Nancy, grim-faced as she left the room that he had shared with her, looked directly at him.

"What are you doing?" he demanded.

She lifted a hand to her perfectly formed lips, then used her other hand to point to the slaves. The trunk was being wheeled into the boudoir, leaving them to face each other in the wide hallway.

"I demand to know what you think you're doing."

Nancy waited until the trunk was being put into the bedroom on the other side of the boudoir. The slaves were dismissed by Abel with only a gesture. Man and wife confronted each other.

"There isn't anything to explain," Nancy said civilly. "I feel that I'll be more comfortable with an entire room to myself."

"And it hasn't got anything to do with our conversation? You're not leaving me alone because I didn't agree to do just what you wanted?"

"Certainly not." Was there sarcasm in her tone? "You are the master of my house, the lord and master of all that he surveys. Would a small person like myself even dare to

125

trifle with the desires of her lord and master? Certainly not, Abel. You may rest assured about that."

He said from between clenched teeth, "I'll free the slaves as soon as possible, Nancy. I've told you that."

"Of course you have, O lord and master."

"Stop it!" Her sarcasm was driving him to say more than he had intended. "If I let the slaves free tomorrow, they'd be back in chains within a week. They couldn't take care of themselves."

"But that wouldn't be your fault," she persisted. "You'd have cleared your conscience."

"Listen, Nancy, my slaves are better treated than those of anybody in this area, or at least as well-treated as any others. I don't allow anybody to take advantage of them. You know that it's true."

She said quietly, "That's not enough, Abel."

"All right, then, is this enough? When I'm finished at Fairlawn, we'll be wealthy. We'll have enough money so we won't have to worry for as long as we live. We'll be able to go back to England, you and I and the boy, and live like persons of leisure, as if we were born to the purple. I won't have to take orders again from stupid people who don't know my business nearly as well as I do. You won't have to supervise dull little parties for people you're indifferent to, in order to help me get ahead in a job where I'll never amount to much. Do you understand all that, Nancy? Do you?"

She nodded, but only once. "Let's take the twenty thousand dollars and book passage as soon as you set the Negroes free."

"Our nigras will be free soon enough," he said, hardly noticing that he had taken Reverend Clack's term as his own, as well as the term of that boorish husband of the lovely Serena creature at the Jobelin ball. "Don't you realize that money has got to be worked for, and that twenty thousand is nothing in comparison to what we could come back with? Another season, only one, and we might have another twenty or perhaps more, and all in addition to the money from the sale of the land. One more crop, Nancy, could bring us to London knowing that we're worth over one hundred thousand dollars? More than twenty thousand *pounds,* Nancy, not dollars."

"And in two more years we could be worth almost a hundred and fifty thousand, and after three years, and four years, and so on. But we can't get the years back, Abel, don't you understand? You have to destroy people to get that money, and it isn't worth doing."

"Is it worth your son's future, Nancy? Kermit will be able to use that money to make a good marriage for himself in British society, and he won't ever have to put up with some of the things that have driven us crazy. Doesn't your son mean anything to you? Don't you care about the future, Nancy? Don't you care at all?"

She said, so quietly he hardly made out the words, "Yes, I care very much about Kermit." More loudly, she asked, "Are you saying that you do all this only for your son's sake?"

"For all our sakes, Nancy. Mine, yours, and his."

He was satisfied now, having produced the one argument to which she had to pay attention, to consider, to answer with silence. She couldn't attack him now. He was a good family man doing a distasteful job to benefit their child. No woman could argue with that, not one woman who had ever been born.

She took a step toward the boudoir, edging away from him. Her breasts, pointed in spite of the heavy layers of material over them, heaved under the white dress. Her red hair in its constricting ribbon gleamed angrily. She said nothing. It was understood, then. He allowed himself to smile, making the smile generous and unforced. He had been questioned, and he had explained. There couldn't be a dispute any more.

"As long as we understand each other," he said, and he reached for her hands. He touched icy-cold skin before the hands were drawn down and away. "I hope perhaps we'll have a drink together."

127

"Not tonight. I've got a headache."

He couldn't help saying, "You didn't argue like some-body who's got a headache."

"Very well then, dear." A wicked smile stretched those perfect lips. "If you prefer it, I am expecting to have a headache, and I'd rather drink by myself."

She closed the door behind her as she walked into the bedroom. He stayed long enough to hear her push a chair towards the door and set it against the knob.

"I don't want to come in," he shouted, then rushed out and went to the room where he slept alone.

8

The shout could be heard all along the grounds of Fair-lawn, it seemed to Abel. He was awakened after midnight at the start of Christmas week. The shout had come from the slave quarters, of course. He raised himself slowly, but managed to run to the window and look out. The roofs of two buildings in the slave quarters had come down, taking the projecting tent poles with them. In front of the quarters on this windless night, a quartet of slaves laughed uproariously.

It was Sunshine, the slave whose marriage ceremony he had attended, who had shouted angrily. The woman stood near one of the wrecked cabins and shook a fist at the quartet, whose members laughed at her. The woman might get beaten after awhile, it occurred to Abel. Better to pre-vent the trouble from happening. He reached for one of his new white suits, putting on the pants and a shirt over his night wear. At the last minute he decided against tak-ing the jacket, but did put on his new wide-brimmed white hat. He couldn't help thinking that it was a symbol of au-thority to wear a hat. As he hurried into the hallway he could hear his young son in frightened tears. He passed

128

the child's room, and saw Nancy pause to look out at him with hatred.

He was outside at last, warm air hitting him almost as if it had been a physical presence. After taking no more than sixty steps, he saw Sunshine shaking a fist at the idlers more vigorously than before.

She was saying nastily, "You all ought to be ashamed of yourself, and me expecting a child."

That sent the others into fresh gales of laughter. Her husband, Elihu, started forward, but the horse-faced Sunshine held him in place with a palm.

"I take care of this slum stuff," Sunshine said. And, her voice raised, "Me and my darlin' child take care of you all."

There was fresh laughter. From the other end of the slave quarters, two cabin roofs started to sway on their projecting poles. There was a shout of laughter from the original quartet and from three other blacks at the opposite end. A number of slaves were in sight now, some of them pulling out little relics from their quarters, good luck charms and various lucky pieces. One boy carried a comb. As Abel watched unbelievingly, the slaves threw away most of those items onto a mound. Other slaves started a small fire. There was the sound of paper being torn into strips, and it surprised Abel because he'd never known that any of his slaves used paper except for toilet purposes; then he realized that the slaves were destroying their own toilet paper. Two children started to laugh hysterically. An old man got up from a rocker and nodded benignly as the slaves, Moses and Tuck and Shep, reached for the chair and added it to the fire.

Abel moved forward, but the smell of horse dirt suddenly drew his attention to one side. Felix Bygraves, his overseer, was standing over to one side arms akimbo, as he watched what was happening. By the fire's light, he still looked as if he needed a shave.

Abel poked the sturdily built overseer in the ribs. "Are you going to help me stop this or not?"

"That isn't necessary, Mr. Debenker. The niggers will

129

clean up and put the cabins back into working order as soon as the holiday is over."

"How do you know that?"

"They always do. Niggers always do that."

"Do they always do *this*, too?"

"Only during Christmas and New Year's weeks, Mr. Debenker."

Abel took note of his overseer's calmness and of the fact that there wasn't a whip in the man's hands. His own voice became lower, more calm.

"Are you telling me that this destruction is a tradition?"

"Yes, Mr. Debenker, it's the start of two weeks celebration for them." Bygraves shrugged massively. "What else would you expect from a group of niggers, anyhow?"

"Why do they have to destroy things?"

"I don't know, Mr. Debenker, and I can't put myself inside a nigger's head. But all this is only the start."

"What else happens?"

Two more cabin roofs came plummeting down to the earth. The bonfire had grown brighter.

Bygraves chuckled. "Afterwards, they start to make babies."

Abel found that the words, "Is this a bad joke?" wouldn't leave his lips. He stood with fallen jaw and widened eyes.

"Why?" he asked hoarsely, at last.

"Because they want to celebrate or go back to nature." Bygraves shrugged. "I guess that's the sort of thing they did in Africa."

"Either that, or they'd blow up because they aren't free," Abel said quietly. "They've got to have some way to release all their hatred."

"Maybe so," the overseer agreed. "I've never given it any thought, really." He winked, one conspirator to another, the self-assured Cassius to the uneasy Brutus. "But don't you fret, sir! Things get a lot quieter around here after awhile when the baby-making starts."

Abel walked slowly back to the house, opened and closed the door behind him and walked upstairs. Nancy,

130

the wailing Kermit in her arms, waited for him in the hall-way. Her eyes seemed riveted to his thin lips, and he wished he hadn't told himself how attractive she looked. Not on a night when lust wouldn't be satisfied.

"It's not an insurrection," he said drily. "It's the Christmas holiday."

"What are you saying?"

"The nigras don't do any work this week or next, so they celebrate in any primitive way they can think of."

She hugged the child closer to herself. "How can you let yourself be any part of this?"

"Only for awhile, dammit," he snapped. He took a deep breath. "There'll be plenty of kids born as a result of these two weeks of hoorahing and that'll add to the wealth of the plantation and the money we get to take home with us."

Wearily, he went back to bed.

He went out to inspect the ruins of the slave quarters before deciding whether or not to spend the day after Christmas in town. The slaves must have been carousing all night long. Most of them were asleep, sprawled on the tops of their fallen roofs. Some men slept with women in their arms. The aged slept by themselves. As Abel looked around, one old slave, Obadiah, opened his eyes and glared directly at him and cursed and shook a fist. Abel turned away.

Bygraves, who had waked up an hour later than usual, smiled and looked comfortable as he joined Abel. "Nothing wrong, Mr. Debenker. Nor do I expect anything."

"Will you be on the watch for trouble? In that case, I'll go into town."

He took the carriage and drove by himself, as he expected the other plantation owners would be doing, too. He was right about all the owners he ran into except Chad Goldthwait, whose carriage was being driven by an angry-looking black man whose lips were pursed.

"My niggers are hell-roaring around," Chad said, "so nothing can get done."

131

Chad was leaving the doctor's, to whom his wife had insisted he go for a minor complaint. Abel ran into the whey-faced Tom Holman, striding around energetically near the schoolhouse on the court square. Jarvis Whitcomb was coming out of his law office when Abel passed in front of the building, and introduced him to a withdrawn young assistant, Mr. Peter Quendale. Charles Passy, the wealthiest plantation owner in the parish, was on his way out of the courthouse when Abel nearly bumped into him. In the hotel taproom he had a drink with the dandified Giraud Duval, and found it necessary to tell the man indirectly that he didn't have any sexual interest in other men. For a moment he felt sorry for any young male slave who was bought by Giraud Duval.

It had been a very pleasant social afternoon until he realized that he didn't want to be treated as if he was one of them. He wasn't a slavemaster, a blackbirder. Other men who had made lifetime careers out of exploiting the Blacks were all that and worse, but not Abel Debenker. Not Lyon Debenker's son.

His business didn't take long, involving the purchase of some supplies from a dealer who was a quadroon. He was welcomed to the food supplier's cluttered office, sat down ceremoniously, took half a dozen cigars for himself, and transacted the business in less than fifteen minutes.

Back at Fairlawn, he found that the slaves had awakened. The soul, walnut odor of cheap whiskey hung in the cool air. Abel, disturbed, sought out the overseer. He found Bygraves in his cabin, after knocking twice and then opening the door. A young slave gal was in the overseer's bed. Bygraves, who had been touching the gal's thick lips as he smiled down at her, suddenly turned around awkwardly.

"Get dressed and come outside," Abel said quickly.

Bygraves appeared in front of the cabin in less than five minutes. He was dressed neatly, but the smell of horse still clung to his clothes.

"Where do the nigras get rotgut whiskey?"

"Plenty of traders give 'em the stuff, sir."

132

"In exchange for what?"

"For part of their own crops, and anything else they can get their hands on, Mr. Debenker. You should know by this time how much thieving goes on around here."

"Does the whiskey selling go on all year long?"

"Yes, sir. The selling and buying—and the drinking."

"But it only comes out in the open during Christmas and New Year's." Abel pursed his lips. "You'll have to keep an eye out for any fights. Nigras probably don't take their liquor too well, if you can call that stuff they're drinking liquor. Any fights could result in maiming or killing a prime field hand."

"I'll keep an eye out for it, sir, as much as a human being possibly can." Bygraves glanced at the closed door of his cabin. "Will there be anything else?"

"Not right now. Go back inside to your friend."

Abel managed to sleep through the next night.

On Wednesday morning, he took Nancy and Kermit for a ride along Fairlawn. They stopped for a picnic near a cypress stand, then drove into town. Nancy bought some silks and muslins for herself, then ordered a dress from Paris, while Abel watched his young son play with some friends his own age.

When Nancy returned to the carriage, Abel squeezed her hand affectionately. There was no answering pressure. He drove back more slowly, keeping his talk as polite as on the trip out. Kermit seemed happy. Abel and Nancy seemed a devoted couple, two units in a contented family.

9

Two slaves were shouting drunkenly at each other late that night. Abel got up tiredly and called out the window to the slaves to stop their fighting. It didn't help.

He dressed quickly, having already discovered that dur-

133

ing the Christmas-New Year's season it was best to keep his clothes on the nearest chair, so he could dress without delay in case of trouble. He raced down the hallway, glad to see that his wife's door was closed. It was no time to look at Nancy in her night dress.

Outside, he raced to the slave quarters, almost hitting one of the cisterns in his rush. There was no sign of the overseer, but he did make out a gal's voice along with the men's. She didn't seem to be trying to stop them from a fight. The two bucks were standing ten feet from the battered old church building and threatening each other. Jethro carried a whiskey bottle in one hand, grabbing it by the neck, and raising it as soon as he saw Tuck do the same. Like Tuck, he glowered as he swayed back and forth.

"You an asshole," Tuck was shouting. "I not go near the gal."

"She say you do."

"She lie."

"You call my gal a liar?"

The gal, who stood apart from the two field hands and looked mischievously from one to other, was the pretty youngster, Blossom. She was the first to draw back at Abel's glare. The field hands were too drunk to see him.

"Stop this," Abel ordered.

The slaves turned toward him, saw him, and froze. Tuck made the half-turn to face Abel angrily, but it was Jethro who raised the bottle. It was like looking at a black and muscular (and drunken) copy of himself, with his own thin face dyed dark.

"Put that down or you'll be whipped to within a half-inch of your life," Abel said briskly, and made a point of looking away. After only eight months as master of Fairlawn he knew that showing fear might cost him profits; he refused to think about health or life itself, let alone his family's well-being. "There's to be no fighting here. I want that understood."

Tuck said quietly, "Yes, masta, not fight."

Jethro followed obediently, repeating the same words in

134

almost the same tone of voice. In the darkness, he heard Blossom giggling.

"Blossom, come out here and face me."

The gal did it on the run, as might be expected from the first to obey a direct order and the first to discourage anybody else from doing so. He glared at her briefly, turning his attention to the field hands.

"Get back to your quarters. If either of you is marked up, I'll put both of you on the red tree and whip the daylights out of you."

Tuck was the first to walk away silently. Jethro started to say something, but he glanced at Tuck and hurried off in another direction. Blossom, looking after them, snorted.

"What does that mean, Blossom? Why did you make that sound?"

"I sorry, masta."

"You didn't sound as if you were sorry about anything."

Blossom's eyes probed his. Abel found himself tempted to tell the slave gal to turn around and only talk to him from that position. He wouldn't do that, though, or walk away.

Instead, determined to make her uncomfortable, he asked, "Been having a good time, Blossom?"

"Yes, masta."

"Then you like getting one buck to fight another?"

"Yes, masta."

"Don't you realize how wicked that is?"

"No wicked, masta." But the lips were stretched as if she was on the point of sharing a joke with him. "Jethro my favorite and Tuck is my favorite, too."

She looked up at him wide-eyed. Abel knew that he was expected to say something mildly contemptuous, if he didn't bother to explain that a gal couldn't have more than one favorite. It was the nigra tactic that he had sometimes noticed in his own son: keep the powerful one amused, so you won't be taken seriously, and the powerful one won't become angry. The nigras would lie to keep from being whipped, steal to get a little whiskey to help them forget their situation, pretend to be stupid in order to stay alive.

135

"I don't want this to happen again," he said, looking from the gal's curvy breasts up to the high cheekbones and the dark eyes. "You're to be a good gal and not start any fights, Blossom. Otherwise I'll know what to do about it."

She pouted so attractively that he had to look downwards. The breasts drew his eyes magnetically. The palms of his hands itched. Abel suddenly drew both hands down in front of his crotch. Blossom, seeing the movement, smiled.

"Back to your quarters." No slave gal who wasn't even seventeen years old was going to patronize her own master, not at Fairlawn or anywhere else.

"Yes, masta," Blossom said obediently, but she didn't move.

There was talk going on around him in the darkness, most of it in loud drunken whispers.

"More of that, Obie. That's good stuff to drink."

"You drink too much, you die."

"What for I live, anyhow?"

And a gal whispering more loudly, "Do that again, Shep, and let the others wait for their turn."

"There! That okay?"

"I love that, just love it."

"Have some more, honey."

"Well, one in the front and one from the back. . . . That's the way. And one in the mouth. Hey there, Lije! You open your pants and don't keep that to yourself. I want that in my mouth."

"It's all yours, honey, all yours."

There was silence from those slaves now, except for one sound that Abel recognized. He had to put his hands further in front of himself when he heard it. There seemed to be an acute pain in the exact center of his body from the hips down.

And again, "Ish, you get away from here, you too old for this. You keep doin' this and you die like a dog."

"I die happy, and cheat the masta."

"You don't cheat nobody. You a no-good piece of prop'ty now. You too old."

136

"Who too old? You spread them legs again, honey, and I show you I never gonna be too old. . . . Ohhh, good gal! You sure do know your business!"

Abel took a deep breath and glared at the gal who faced him. "Didn't I tell you, Blossom, to go back to your quarters?"

"Yes, masta."

She was perfectly still.

"Then what are you waiting for?"

She looked down modestly, an obedient slave trying to ask a request from a stern master. "I leave a scarf in the old sugar house, and I hope masta lets Blossom go there for it."

"Go ahead, then. Don't bother me with nonsense."

She said slyly, "It might take me a little time to find it. Very dark in sugar house."

"Don't bother me about that, either."

"Yes, masta."

She walked off slowly, so that he couldn't resist looking after her. There was nothing underneath her dress, and she was almost as good as naked.

She was out of sight at last.

Abel looked over toward the mansion. No lights were on. Nancy was asleep. Well, it had been a long time since his wife had let him make love to her, and there wasn't a nigra on his grounds who wasn't having a good time. Did Nancy expect a man in his twenties to think all the time only about what actions might be good business for him? Did she think she had cast her lot in life with a machine who could be turned on and off whenever milady tilted a fan?

He looked in the direction of the sugar house. By the moon's light he saw that the door was open. He looked back toward the mansion one more time and then raced to the sugar house. His breath was short when he closed the door and leaned against it.

"Blossom?"

"Yes, masta." There was a smudged window, and he could see a hand move slowly by the moon's light.

137

"Is anybody else here?"

"No, masta. We by ourselves."

She stood near the window, but not directly in its light. As he watched, she was reaching her hands down to the hem of her dress to raise it. She lifted the dress over her head. Mahogany breasts shone in the moonlight as she took an instinctive step to the right. Her small dusky nipples seemed to be expanding under his sight. Her stomach was flat and she had a larger bellybutton than he could ever remember seeing on the few women he had known before marriage. The skin color fascinated him. Never had he taken a woman of Blossom's skin color. It would be something to do, just one time in his life.

"You're to keep quiet about this, Blossom, or I'll cut your tongue out before I sell you down the river. Is that clear?"

"Yes, masta."

She leaned over, one hand modestly in front of those beautiful breasts, to put the skimpy dress down on the dirty floor as a cushion for her body. He paused to take off his clothes, rather than have any odor get on them. Instead of dropping them casually, he rested everything on his shoes. He moved swiftly across the squalid floor.

The gal was waiting for him, on her back, one leg raised. She kept her hands behind her back and rested her eyes briefly on her crotch, then looked up smilingly at him. He shook his head, and lay down next to her with his head against her. He wouldn't kiss her on the lips, but couldn't keep from kissing and fondling the beautiful breasts, working his tongue over first one rising nipple and then the other.

Blossom waited, giving nothing but her body.

It was enough. He was over her and then inside her. She gasped almost in spite of herself as he became part of her, and he took her again and yet again. Certainly he had found something he needed, but at the same time he had lost something else he'd hoped he would be able to keep. He would never do anything like this with a Black again,

138

as long as he lived. That was why he took her a third time, so that he'd be able to remember afterwards what it had been like.

Back at the mansion, he woke up one of the house servants and ordered her to prepare a tub for him in the kitchen. He washed and soaped himself thoroughly, especially his private parts. He rinsed his mouth with soap and water. It took an hour before he was satisfied that he had washed himself as thoroughly as possible.

10

"That's not why you're giving me my walking papers," Felix Bygraves said.

The overseer wasn't offended. He stood with arms akimbo and faced Abel Debenker. There was a quixotic look on his firm features.

"I've told you the truth," Abel said.

They were watching a newborn chestnut foal disporting itself weakly in the stableyard. If it grew into a sturdy horse, Abel told himself, he'd ride it—if he stayed at Fairlawn that long.

Inside the stable, a trio of mules could be heard making noises of displeasure. Abel had ordered mules brought in for the wagon work, as they could take more punishment than horses and were much more stubborn. One mule had been beaten to death by an angry slave, Noah, who had been beaten painfully in turn at Abel's orders; but on a Saturday night, so that he could get back to work by Monday.

Bygraves was shaking his head gently. "You don't want me to leave because it's February, and there've been practically two months without major work, Mr. Debenker. Or because I didn't happen to be at the scene of a dust-up between two niggers during Christmas week. Or even be-

139

cause John C. Fremont will probably run for President of the United States on the know-nothing ticket. No, sir, there's a much simpler reason and we both know it."

"Tell me what it is," Abel said easily, his eyes on the chestnut.

"Yes, sir, a new cotton crop gets under way in April, and by that time you want a new overseer on the job who'll be your man, somebody who won't be in a position of power, and who has not been here longer than you, Mr. Debenker. It makes perfect good sense."

Abel turned to one side. "Any explanation that pleases you is just as well."

"How long do you want me on the grounds, Mr. Debenker?"

"The end of March ought to be sufficient."

"Very well, sir." Bygraves turned and walked away, his back rigid.

One of the mules inside the stable was kicking at a partition as the overseer walked back slowly to his cabin.

It was at a tea dance given by Barton Manders and his wife on the first Saturday night in March that Abel Debenker discovered that letting his overseer go was to make him an unexpected enemy. The Manders' home had been decorated beautifully for this affair, the floors shined almost to a mirrorlike perfection and raised platforms holding sofas and divans. A row of chairs around the room had been tied together with sturdy cord.

Abel had escorted Nancy in her dark-red dress to a divan to sit beside Mrs. Tom Holman, when his shoulder was tapped and he turned around to see Giraud Duval. The dandified planter was smiling agreeably as he shook hands with Abel, keeping the contact longer than necessary and giving a smile of mockery at Abel's momentary discomfit.

"I owe you a vote of thanks, my dear friend," he said. "I've just hired your overseer, dear Felix."

"Felix Bygraves, you mean?"

"Yes, a dear boy. He does need the job and he told me

140

that for the addition in salary that I offered he was willing to make some added—ah, accommodations, with me. It will be a pleasure to have him—ah, to have him on my staff."

"He's a satisfactory overseer, by and large. I didn't find any major complaint with his work."

"I'm sure he'll work—ah, harder for me."

Abel said carefully, "Excuse me, please."

"Reluctantly, my dear friend, very reluctantly."

Abel met the other man's eyes and saw obscene laughter in them. Duval made a habit of embarrassing younger men as if he was intimate with them. It didn't amuse Abel at all. Twenty minutes later, having talked with his host and hostess, he walked back to Nancy and bowed from the waist like a stranger, then asked if she would do him the honor of dancing with him.

"A dance with one's own husband isn't the most exciting of pastimes," she said, looking quizzically up at him. "*Are* you letting Mr. Bygraves go, as that horrid creature said?"

"Yes."

"And does that mean you'll be letting the slaves free very soon now?"

"I hope so."

"Do you have any immediate plans for freeing our slaves?"

"Not at this moment; No."

"I see." She gestured to a house servant for a glass of wine and drank it down swiftly.

He glanced away from her when she gestured for another glass, then said, "Mr. Duval can cause considerable mischief when he struts and postures."

"Not to us, O lord and master," Nancy said quietly. "I am at your beck and call, so you have only to speak, and I obey."

Abel snorted and walked off. Duval had sauntered over to a group of men and was talking only to the youngest man in the group. From a distance, Abel recognized the fair-haired Peter Quendale, lawyer Whitcomb's assistant.

141

Whitcomb was in the group and turned to stare piercingly at Duval, who didn't seem to be affected.

He took a few steps back to Nancy, but looked at a point over her head. "I'm going to walk over to Duval and see if I can't de-fang him. He's a damned nuisance."

Nancy said nothing, but raised the cup to her lips.

Duval was still holding the distrait Peter Quendale's right hand in his as Abel approached. Quendale made a sudden move to pull his hand free, but Duval was stronger. As he was about to turn, Duval said, "My dear boy, I hope I haven't done anything to offend you."

The other man looked away awkwardly, as if this was the young man's initiation to some fraternity whose existence they wouldn't publicly acknowledge. Only Whitcomb, to his credit, was offended, but he hesitated to reprove a client or a prospective client. Abel smilingly joined the group, approaching from Duval's side. The smell of hair pomade and other perfumes made him squint his nose briefly. In front of him and to the right, on the ballroom floor, couples were dancing indifferently to the music of a white orchestra brought to the Manders' plantation from New Orleans.

"How are you, Quendale?" Abel said sunnily, not expecting an answer. "And you, Duval?"

"Very well, thank you." Duval turned to this fresh game. "I hope that you two boys aren't secretly fighting for my attentions."

"Not at all," Abel said comfortably, lighting one of the Cuban cigars he had recently become fond of. "Perhaps we can arrange a get-together for tomorrow, you and I."

Duval's eyes were appraising, now. Young Quendale drew back. Vic Jobelin, who had been talking animatedly to Whitcomb, suddenly reared almost like a horse. Except for Abel and Duval, every man in the group was embarrassed.

"Honored, my dear boy." Duval returned Abel's smile. "Perhaps you'll come to my place where I can assure you of privacy."

"Indeed." Abel nodded. "I hope you'll only want me to

do as much as a certain friend of ours did recently, and no more."

The silence in the group of plantation owners was almost a physical presence in the ballroom.

"Honored, my dear boy," Duval said, licking his thin lips fiercely. "I don't know which of our many mutual friends you have in mind——."

Now he looked pointedly at the others, signalling that he wanted to keep talking somewhere else.

"It doesn't matter, Giraud," Abel said placidly. "I've been told that what you want is usually the same sort of thing. I'm willing to oblige, as a token of sincere friendship."

Duval gripped Abel by the arm more strongly than he looked capable of doing, leaned over, and whispered into Abel's ear, "The porch, you fool, out to the porch!"

"That's hardly necessary," Abel drawled, making a point of stepping closer to the man and throwing off his hand at the same time. "Tomorrow at your place at, say, four o'clock, will be fine. And I'll certainly make a point of bringing my horsewhip, although I understand you've got a great many of them at your place."

Duval's grin was rigid. "What are you talking about, you fool?"

"Why, the horsewhip, of course," Abel said, sounding surprised. "I'll be glad to give you ten strokes of the whip, as you like. I understand that you became very ill after you begged for twenty strokes and received them, and I certainly wouldn't want to cause you any illness."

Duval said carefully, "You're absolutely insane!"

"Well, if the horsewhip is too vigorous, Giraud, I can bring a dogwhip. My slave drivers carry them, and I understand the whips have got quite a—ha!—quite a sting in the tail."

There was laughter from the men.

"I can assure you that I'll save the most refined punishments for last. After ten strokes of the dogwhip, you'll whine and plead for more. I'll hold the whip in my hand, wave it over your head, and even crack it. You'll beg to be

143

punished further, but I won't oblige. That is the ultimate in punishment, and much favored in certain New Orleans' bordellos, I'm given to understand."

Giraud Duval's weak mouth was wide open with silent rage. He suddenly stamped his foot twice in furious anger and ran out to the porch, hands over his ears to escape the sound of laughter that followed him. Barton Manders, the host, who always looked crestfallen, came near to brightening up when Tom Holman told him what had just taken place.

"Good work, Abel," Jarvis Whitcomb said, clapping him jovially on the back. "Duval has been a public nuisance because of his private tastes for a long time now, and nobody else ever figured out just how to cope with him. For that alone, you certainly deserve a vote of appreciation."

He had to shake hands with every planter in the group before he could get back to Nancy, flushed with triumph. His wife was holding a filled wine glass, but she wasn't drinking as he approached.

"You've become the hero of the evening, to judge by the gossip I've just heard," she said, reaching out a hand for him. "Sometimes you can be a genuinely decent man, Abel."

"Well, thank you—sometimes."

She reached out her hand towards him invitingly. "I think now that I would like to dance with you."

Abel surprised himself by shaking his head. "Not right now."

Nancy cocked her head. "Is something the matter?"

"You wouldn't understand me if I told you what's wrong."

The mocking smile slid into place on her lips. "Of course not, O my lord and my master."

He walked away and drank a little more than was usual for him that night. On the way home, in the carriage that Ishmael was driving, he sat sullenly with the rear windows open on the warm night air. Nancy peered at her husband from the corners of half-closed eyes.

144

"Now would you care to tell me why you've been so upset about doing a decent thing back at the Manders' place? You put that miserable Duval in his place once and for all, so I should think that you'd be pleased and proud. Why aren't you, Abel?"

He turned toward her, eyes heavy-lidded. "You've been so damned distant for such a long time that I'm surprised you should suddenly care about that."

"I'm curious to know why the man I think I married should be so upset about having done a kindness."

"It's not a kindness to me," Abel pointed out irritably, darting two hands into his pockets. "He's a planter and so am I. Duval and I are in the same line of work, and one of us might need a favor from the other at some time. To make the man a permanent enemy, which I seem to have done, is to rule out a source of some needed favor in the near or far future."

"I see. You might not be able to make a slave trade with him or something as serious as that."

"Never mind, dear." The last word came automatically these days, without meaning. He had spent the last year brushing away insults, forgetting innuendoes, listening to nerve-caused nonsense from the woman he loved. Love means having to turn the other cheek. "We'll be home soon."

It was after midnight when they first saw the darkened mansion through the carriage windows. They stepped out to the stable, where Nancy took off her shoes and put on a pair of boots, for the walk across the dirt to the mansion. Abel did the same. Like his wife, he carried the shoes as he walked. Nancy shook her head when he reached automatically for her button shoes that she favored, and insisted on carrying them over her head. They got to the lighted hallway of the mansion at last. Hester, a pudding-faced house servant, waited until Nancy sat down in a chair, then knelt before her. The slave woman's right hand caressed the top of Nancy's boot, her left hand beneath the toe, touching the dirt. Nancy automatically drew her foot back.

145

The house slave looked alarmed. "You mad at me, Miz Nancy?"

"No, I—no, certainly not, Hester."

The woman hadn't risen from her knees and was looking up pitifully. "You mad at Hester and she don't know why. If you not mad, you let Hester take off dirty old boots, Miz Nancy."

There was a catch in the slave's voice, and she looked uneasily from Abel back to her mistress. Probably she was imagining herself being flogged for some offense she didn't know about or put back into the field or sold down the river. Her eyes were wide with horror at the sights parading before her mind.

Nancy bowed to the inevitable. "Take off my boots, Hester."

Abel took off his own boots and left them on top of eight spread apart double sheets of the *Festin Chronicle*. He walked upstairs with Nancy, arm in arm. Nancy didn't speak until they had reached the top steps. Her breasts were moving in and out almost frantically under the dark-red party dress.

"We don't belong here, either of us."

There was no harm in agreeing tacitly. "We're only out here to earn our fortune."

"I hate to nag and nag at you, Abel. I didn't get married so that I'd have some man whose life I could make unhappy." She looked around and put a finger to her lips, then whispered, "Tonight we'll be dissolute."

"Good."

She slipped away from him as he reached out towards her. "I'll look in on Kermit first, and you go into my bedroom and wait for me, Abel. Please."

He nodded and looked after her as she walked down the hall to their three year old son's door. Then he walked through the dim boudoir, with its smells of glycerine and rose water, wintergreen oil, flowers in bloom, and a tart smell of wine that he didn't like at all. In his wife's bedroom, he lighted the kerosene lamp with a friction match and pulled the rep curtains, then undressed methodically

146

and got into bed, warming it for her and plumped up the pillows. At the last minute he blew out the lamp and opened the curtains once more. It had been such a long time between visits that he had almost forgotten his wife's preferences.

The door opened and closed on Nancy. She had undressed herself in the boudoir and wasn't wearing a stitch of clothes, now. She didn't look any less beautiful than when he had first seen her in the nude, the figure as full, the nipples as large and pink-tipped, the stomach flat, the thighs lean, the rear supple. She didn't seem to have changed at all in any way, and he felt as if the last year had never taken place.

"Hester ran up to see me when I was leaving Kermit's room." Nancy climbed into bed and threw the sheet off so that the moonlight gleamed on her magnificent full figure. "I do declare, she wanted me to tell her again that I wasn't angry at her, and then she kissed my hand when I told her that I wasn't."

"Shh," he said, reaching out a hand toward her right breast and playing with the nipple. It rose satisfactorily, and he put his lips down to the other nipple, using his free hand on her right thigh, and then on the left thigh.

"It's impossible to know what bothers Negroes or why," Nancy said, taking his hand and putting it on her flat stomach. "You'd think that a woman like Hester would know perfectly well—."

"If she's been reassured, then that's all there is to it." He drew a deep breath. "Now let's pleasure ourselves."

Nancy lay back, soothed by her husband's sincerity. "She's a sensitive person and I'd hate to think of her—."

"Nancy, I guess there's only one way I can get your full attention."

He started to move down on her, distracting her from any thoughts other than those about what her husband was doing then, and what he did afterwards.

11

He was on his way back to the stable from his daily inspection of the plantation. Actually, it was a ride that took him no more than three-quarters of an hour, enough time on this day to notice that the March rains hadn't done any damage to the levees or the ground, and that when he was ready to let the timber be felled he would probably earn some good money for it. He was waiting for prices to rise nationwide, but it wasn't going to happen until the cotton crop was processed. He wished it was possible to save more money from a year's work than he had managed to do, but the earnings from another crop or so—not more—would satisfy him.

He had made a wide turn on horseback to avoid the slave quarters when he saw one of the nigras running towards him. It was Shep, a prime hand. Abel drew his horse to a halt.

"Masta, if I can talk to you," the slave began hopefully.

Abel waited, rather than make believe he was busy with important matters. The hawk-nosed, burning-eyed field hand looked as if he couldn't be prevented from saying whatever might be on his mind.

"I—masta, I been paying Masta Lyon so I could be free," the slave began.

"You *what?*"

"Yes, masta, I pay this money every time before crop be put into ground."

"How long has this been going on?"

"Long time. Since I be little."

"Did you have to put your *x* on a piece of paper when you gave your master the money?"

"Oh yes, masta, all the time."

Abel nodded tautly, his suspicions confirmed. It was a

lie, of course. Lyon Debenker would certainly have kept a record of any such business transaction. There wasn't any such record. From a pocket of his pants the slave drew out several wadded bills and gave them to his owner. Abel took them. There couldn't have been more than twenty-five dollars here. The slave had scrimped and even stolen to get together enough money for his freedom, and had invented a story as well. It was almost a joke to think of a prime field hand convinced he could buy his freedom for twenty-five dollars. The slave had stepped back respectfully so that Abel couldn't give the money back, and he didn't want to throw it to him.

"What would you do with freedom?" Abel asked thoughtfully.

"Go far away."

"Could you get out of this section without some slave catcher destroying your freedom papers and selling you somewhere else?"

"I die if that happen," Shep said simply. "The slave catcher, he die, too."

Abel straightened out the money in his hand. There were twenty-three dollars in United States currency, sweat on the five dollar bills, and a yellowish substance on a dollar. All the bills smelled as if they had been kept buried for awhile.

"I be free, masta," Shep said. "One way or other, I be free."

"Don't you think that every slave wants to be free?"

"No, masta. Some boys and gals happy like this. I not happy. Never be happy while I a slave. Want to die if I can't be free. Nobody who's black is gonna be free if he wouldn't die for it, masta. Shep is ready to die if he has to."

"Yes, I see." He looked ruefully down at the money in his hand. "A number of papers would have to be filled out, and I think I'd see to it that you were sent to somebody I know in New York City, who'd notify me if you failed to arrive. From New York City you could go to

149

England, where you'd be safe and free for the rest of your days. Would you be willing to make such a big change in your life?"

"Yes." He didn't use Abel's title. The slave seemed to have straightened where he stood.

Abel made his decision. "It'll need a little time to arrange, but I want you to promise that you won't tell anybody else among the slaves about this—." He raised the hand with the money." —business deal."

"No, masta, I not tell any slave. They gonna think you sold me."

Abel looked down at the few bills that would have been of some aid in starting a new life for a black man with nothing to offer but a willingness to work. To return the pitiful few bills would have been an insult to the man. Abel folded the bills carefully, tucked them into his pants pocket, and rode back to the stable.

12

Abel woke up instantly on that mid-April morning, as he did on most mornings, and then realized that nothing was wrong. For a moment he lay in bed to gather his strength, then got up and dressed. It was half-past five. He walked down to the kitchen and took a cup of black coffee from Hester. The house woman chattered more than usual about nothing at all, putting Abel's nerves on edge without his being able to give a reason for being upset. He stepped out on the porch in time to see the sun finding its place in the morning sky. Everything was wet to the touch even though it hadn't rained, so he guessed he knew why he was tense. For a moment he allowed himself to feel better.

He exchanged a few words with the stable boy, who was getting mule wagons set for the day, then took his dark horse out to the slave quarters. He was aware of silence around him as he moved, and looked to his right and left without seeing anything out of order.

The slaves weren't talking or eating or complaining. They sat or stood around in front of their scanty so-called cabins and looked grim-faced. Jethro was making fists and unmaking them. Sunshine was looking down at her oversized belly, jaw muscles taut. Even the usually placid Elihu was standing with his left foot out and hands up as if he was ready to box.

Abel's newly-hired overseer had been inspecting mule wagons and now he turned around and stood with fists on hips. In this morning weather, with the sun touching his face, he didn't look like a free man with one-sixteenth of black blood as his papers insisted. His nose was thick and his lips large in a strong face whiter in complexion than Abel's. Omar Gray stood with legs apart, whip in one hand.

"You've had your eating time," he called out, looking from one to another of the forty-five field hands. "Into the wagons with you."

Nobody moved.

Abel watched from ten feet off, certain now that he had made an error in hiring this man as overseer. Gray had insisted that he could handle niggers—he had used the term, too—better than most overseers. He might be considered one of them, he said, although he could write and read and his face was pale. But he'd be able to win their trust and get the best out of them. Abel had said he was willing to give Omar Gray a chance for his slaves' sakes. He had imagined that the nigras would all want to make a showing and help somebody who was in part, at least, one of their own. He realized now that he ought to have talked over the new move with another planter who knew nigras better than Abel did.

"I'm not going to stand for this," Gray said crisply with great care, never slurring a word. "You can get away with this nonsense if you've got some other overseer, but not Omar Gray. Not me."

151

He had been looking from one impassive face to another as he spoke. The half a dozen drivers, off to one side, glared at him and then away. The drivers were apparently willing to work reluctantly at supervising small units of field hands. Blossom was whispering to Jethro, who nodded and took a step away from his cabin at the far end of the rows of slave quarters. Abel, looking emotionless in their direction, wondered if they had spent the night together and then decided that he didn't really care about that. Blossom had never looked more attractive on any morning that Abel could remember. Her high cheekbones fairly glowed with recollected pleasure.

"If nobody will go to work," the overseer said swiftly, "I'm going to pick one example and use the whip on him. Who's going to be whipped?"

No response whatever. The overseer might have been talking to a group of statues. Omar Gray uncoiled the bullwhip, its shadow plain on the earth at his feet. He raised it, then, and snapped it in the moist air. There was a cracking sound.

"You!" Gray glared at Elihu, the least likely choice. "Come here, you! Come here and turn your back to me so I can carve my initials on you."

It was Blossom who snapped at Sunshine's husband, "Don't move for this fucker!"

Gray's little eyes narrowed at the sight of Blossom and he took half a dozen steps forward in her direction. Blossom held her place.

That was when Jethro called out, "You touch her and you a dead nigger."

Gray turned so furiously upon his new tormentor that his wide blue hat nearly dropped to the ground. He wore the hat by day no matter where he was, as he had told Abel; no doubt he didn't want his face to develop any color but what nature had given it. At Jethro's side, Blossom looked satisfied.

As Gray raised the whip, ready to assail Jethro, a dozen field hands formed a rough circle around him. Abel knew that the overseer couldn't crack that whip twice if he was

152

able to do it the first time. It was a war of pride now, with Gray unable to spend a second day on this job if he didn't whip Jethro. The other field hands wére determined to strike at the overseer if necessary and risk their very lives by doing it. Abel moved his horse closer to the overseer, aware that the move would be seen by at least a few field hands out of the corners of their eyes.

Blossom called out, "Get 'em both and do it now—you hear? Be men for once in your life, not just boys."

He hadn't seen Blossom calling out, and when he looked towards her he saw that her back was to them all. She was willing to incite the others, but not at the risk of being seen at it in case her plans went wrong. Abel found himself hiding a smile in spite of what was happening around him.

Gray glanced over his shoulder long enough to see Abel and then drew back, apparently planning to protect Abel if that became necessary. He glowered at the drivers, who turned away under his silent scorn. Abel followed his glance and then looked directly at the mule wagons waiting at the end of the slave quarters to take the field hands to work. One of the drivers nodded fearfully and whispered to the others. As Abel watched, the drivers approached various hands and roughly thumbed them into the wagons. Any field hand who hesitated was shown the whip. The hands, who hated Gray because he was part-Negro and overseer, didn't hesitate to do what the drivers told them. Gray had stepped further back, the whip uncoiled. Blossom, at his side, was suddenly tapped by a driver. She hurried over to a mule wagon without sparing a word for Jethro, let alone a glance or a touch.

Jethro was alone now, facing Gray, in sight of Abel and the slaves in the wagons. The slaves were leaning forward, ready to jump out at any movement from Gray. Abel caught the first driver's eye and pushed his left hand outward. The driver nodded. His mule had to be hit several times with the butt end of a dogwhip, but the wagon finally got under way. The second wagon took longer. The third one waited, only half a dozen field hands in it.

"Go to your wagon," Gray snapped.

Jethro glanced to his left long enough to see that Blossom wasn't in sight. When he looked back he had become confused, it seemed to Abel. The whip sang against earth at his feet. Jethro turned slowly and walked to the waiting mule wagon. He climbed in slowly. The wagon started off. Gray turned and walked to where he could talk to his employer without having to raise his voice unnecessarily.

"I knew that my first morning on the job would be a difficult time, Mr. Debenker."

"You were right," Abel said drily. "I can't be with you every minute to make sure that discipline is enforced, Mr. Gray. I'm sure you understand that."

"I'll get the men under control," the overseer muttered.

"Yes, and the women, too."

Abel was thinking swiftly. "You're going out to the field on a horse, Mr. Gray. Stay on that horse and keep the whip in your hand. I'll be at your side for the day."

The overseer looked defiant. "Mr. Debenker, I have to prove myself to them. I have to go out there myself and prove I'm not afraid. Otherwise I'll never be any good to the plantation. You must know that, sir, as well as I do."

"Perhaps," Abel agreed. "But follow my orders in other respects. I don't want you off that horse."

Abel turned around and rode back to the stables, then walked up to his room and changed into clothes that didn't smell of horse sweat. He was downstairs for a light breakfast with his family at half-past eight.

Nancy wore white, and her eyes looked shadowed. Abel tried to arrange breakfast so that Nancy would sit facing the sun, and he could always tell by her first response whether she'd been drinking wine during the previous night. This time Nancy shifted to the left without looking as if she'd been stabbed, so he knew she'd been sober during the night. Kermit was irritable and difficult for Nancy to tolerate on a morning after she'd imbibed too much. The child cried all through the meal, for no cause that Abel could see. Not a word was spoken until breakfast

154

was nearly finished, and then it was Nancy who talked to his back as he was leaving.

"So you really *are* going through with it?" she asked softly. "Another crop, another year of torture for all of us."

He walked out.

At ten-thirty he was riding out to the fields again. There was no sign of Omar Gray near the plow gang, whose members moved sullenly across the land. Work was going slowly. At the other end of the field, the members of a hoe gang were thinning out the cotton and cutting down the grass and weeds that the plows hadn't got to. One of the gals was asking a driver for permission to go back to the cabin and suckle her baby. Gray was nowhere in sight. Abel gestured one of the drivers to the side and talked to him.

"Where's the buckra?"

The driver looked down at his feet. "Omar Gray, you mean?"

Abel understood part of what must have happened. Gray had probably been needled by being called by his first name several times, and had responded with his full name. It didn't encourage him to think that the morning had been worthwhile; with his rough eye for work speeds, he doubted if the slaves would work as much as ten acres of land by sundown. The driver sensed Abel's anger without meeting his eyes.

"He at his cabin, masta," the driver said meekly. "He say he not so good."

Abel looked down to the ground just as the driver glanced up at him. Hoofprints could be seen leading away from the direction of the cabin in a zizzag fashion, indicating that the overseer either hadn't been in control or that he'd been unhorsed. The overseer's cabin, a level above and away from the slave quarters, showed the door left open. Abel rode up and was careful to tie his horse to a tree before looking inside.

Omar Gray was in bed, lying on his back. He wore nothing. His eyes were wide open but unblinking, his

155

hands at his sides. His body was livid with red welts and freshly made scars. A long line went from the navel down into the pubic hair. Every welt had produced blood, and the mattress was red. A swarm of flies had settled on it busily. A fist had crashed one side of his jaw and three even white teeth, stained by red spots, could be seen against his left shoulder. A freshet of blood issued forth from a line beneath the toes of his right foot as Abel looked on wordlessly. The overseer's Negroid lips had been pulled and struck until they seemed mashed. The nose, always thick and squashed-looking, had become a mass of wet red pulp. It wasn't possible to guess how many blows the dead man had received.

As Abel turned away, sick at heart, he became aware of a smell of fecal matter. The overseer's wastes had been emptied from his body after death.

Abel walked out slowly. Dozens of chores had to be done at once. The body had to be removed, and local officials pacified. A new overseer had to be hired. His field hands had to be sold to new and scattered owners and other ones bought, a job that would take awhile, but had to be started right away. Above all, the crop had to be processed in time.

He wouldn't let himself think about anything else, not his faults, not the well-meant mistakes he had made, not the sight of a man with some Negro blood who had been destroyed by Negroes. He would think of nothing except business matters, nothing at all.

13

"And here's the extra special little beauty, my friends," said Elkahan Melville, the slave auctioneer, smiling as it was brought out to the stage. "I promised you an added item of interest, and here it is. Permit me to explain its workings to you."

156

Elkahan Melville moved around the dais as easily as if it was his own living room, rubbing his thick hands together and almost doing small dance steps to keep the attention of the prospective buyers. He had staged a combination slave auction and antique auction to bring the ladies. The affair had been a success from his point of view, but he didn't want to let matters go without selling the equipment that had just been hauled up to the dais.

It seemed to have been constructed like a giant mattress spring, with a metal rod at its base. There was a barrel nearby and what looked like a hollowed-out drum with a wooden ladle sticking out of it. Most of the men in the audience were respectfully silent. Ben Pollard suddenly snorted and then laughed.

"Haven't seen one of those since childhood," he said.

His wife, dark-haired Serena, put a hand on his in order to quiet him. Her eyes left his face at last and met the eyes of Abel Debenker, who was standing less than ten feet away. He had bought six field slaves and was feeling depressed, but now he shrugged and smiled into Serena Pollard's warm eyes. He liked those eyes and the long chin line as well. He liked her figure even more. It wasn't hard to imagine her in bed, legs apart and arms raised to embrace a man.

She may have sensed what he was thinking, as a woman sometimes did. Her smile became warmer, and she looked gratified. A flush started at the base of her jaw and spread upwards.

Ben Pollard, freed of his wife's attentions, called out, "Where does the mash go, Elkahan Melville? Show these city folks how it runs."

"Certainly," Elkahan Melville agreed, rubbing his hands together with a sound like dry twigs crackling underfoot. "The right way to begin is with a twenty-five pound sack of meal, to scald it, and pour it in here." With a foot he tapped the wooden box. "Give the mash time to cool. That's when you put in a peck of ground sprout."

Abel must have looked confused.

157

Ben Pollard, grinning loutishly, said to him, "Malt corn is what he means."

"Ground sprouted malt corn?"

"That's it."

Melville was continuing, "Now you make sure that the box is half full of water. It's time to put in grains of sugar, about—oh, fifty pounds worth. It's best to cover it with a pan to keep prowling chickens or horses out, and you let it sit for ten days."

"Six," Pollard called out, ignoring Serena's whispered objections. "Six days and you've got still beer."

"Six, maybe," Elkahan Melville agreed cautiously. "After six days, it's ready to run. Ten is better, though, or what you get will taste like shoes in a trough."

Abel's head turned toward the auctioneer on that duckboard dais. He had just become sharply interested in the merchandise for sale. He gazed from giant mattress spring to wooden box to carved out drum and then brought his eyes back to the auctioneer.

"If you go through all that," he asked, "how much corn liquor would you make?"

"About three hundred gallons," Elkahan Melville answered promptly.

Ben Pollard waved a hand lazily. "One hundred and fifty to two hundred half gallons is a lot closer to the truth."

"The overall cost for that batch," Abel said, calculating swiftly, "would be from thirty-five to forty dollars at today's prices."

This time there was no contradiction from Pollard. Abel felt himself preening under Serena Pollard's glance. He was much more at ease than during the slave purchases awhile ago.

"Thirty to forty," the auctioneer agreed, rubbing both hands together again. He raised his voice. "As I say, this is the surprise item that I promised you. A historical item of interest that can be used today if you want to taste real old-fashioned whiskey like your folks used to love. I'll open the bidding at one hundred dollars."

Abel suggested quickly, "Try seventy-five instead."

"You can't be serious, sir! Seventy-five dollars for this item would virtually be a giveaway."

"You might as well give it away," Abel pointed out, "because I could probably arrange for some handyman in town to make me another one at half the price. I'm just helping you along to get it off your hands."

There was a ripple of laughter.

Elkahan Melville made one of his all-embracing gestures with his hand, taking in the still and the duckboard dais, the mule carts near Courthouse Square and the plantation owners, many of them with their wives, in the warm October sunlight.

"I'll open the bidding at eighty-five, then, to oblige friend Debenker."

Abel drawled, "What about a closing at eighty-five?"

Elkahan Melville protested dramatically. "The way my business is going, for another eighty-five you can have that, too."

Nobody in sight of him knew why Abel Debenker suddenly winced. His tone deepened, becoming more serious.

"Eighty-five or no deal, Melville. Which is it?"

"Agreed at eighty-five," Melville said quickly, sensing that he had suddenly lost the customer's good will without knowing why. "Delivery to your plantation before sundown, along with the other merchandise."

Melville lowered his right hand to seal the bargain and thanked "the flower of Festin aristocracy" for having attended this auction. Abel started toward the small table at one side, where he'd leave a check for the whiskey still, and a deposit for the slaves, the balance pending the results of medical examinations. He nearly bumped into Ben Pollard's broad back, apologized, and started to walk around him. He was face-to-face with Serena, and he suddenly swallowed air like a small boy confronting the most radiant creature in this world.

Ben Pollard didn't notice. He boomed cordially, "You've been buying and selling prime hands for the last

159

few months, I notice. Ever since that nigger overseer of yours got himself killed."

Abel nodded.

"They'll never work for one of theirs, Debenker. A nigger overseer has got no more chance than a Kansas delegate in the House of Representatives."

He chuckled, remembering the latest news from bleeding Kansas. Serena, who was carrying a copy of *John Halifax, Gentleman,* under one arm, suddenly tapped it impatiently against a well-covered thigh. Abel wondered why such a refined creature chose to stay with a boor like this man, let alone why she could have married him in the first place.

In her soft voice, Serena said pleasantly, "Your good wife hasn't come out to join us."

"She was very sorry about that, but there are dozens of things she has to see to around the mansion. Woman's work is never done."

Serena Pollard nodded so quickly that he wondered if she knew how unhappy his wife was. She looked down, rather than face him, as if she was faintly embarrassed.

"Give my love to your Nancy," she said graciously.

Ben snapped at her, "Yes, yes, I'm sure he will. And I'm sure he'll give *his* love to her, which is more important." This time his laugh was mercifully brief; he had made the same response to his wife's good wishes to other women many a time, Abel knew, and she must have wanted to show him what a boor she had married. He sent his sympathies in silence, and sensed that they had been received.

The business was done quickly. He got into the carriage, and Ishmael drove him back to Fairlawn. The hot summer stillness and damp warmth weren't in the air any longer. He was able to sniff the air, notice the descent of darkness at six-thirty in the evening, and remember the shape of Serena Pollard's lips at one and the same time.

The carriage reached Fairlawn at last, taking the road directly to the mansion. The gin house doors remained open, and he could smell the dry warmth of cotton, the

160

acrid tang of razor-cut hemp, and the sourness of burlap too long in the sun. The gin house needed more tables on which to keep bales and supplies. He made a note of it when he walked into his office at ten minutes to seven, and then hurried upstairs to change for supper. It turned out to be a quiet meal, during which a swaying Nancy hardly talked to him, and Kermit was made nervous by the tension between his parents.

Abel didn't see Nancy at all during the next morning. Three new slaves had been delivered during the night and had taken cabin places of slaves who had been sold awhile ago. The newly arrived whiskey still had been put in the sugar house, where it looked much less impressive than on the dais with Elkahan Melville talking about it as if it had been a magic carpet back to the golden past. He stood with arms akimbo, considering as he looked down at it. He knew very well why he'd bought it and how he hoped to earn a profit, but there didn't seem any possible way he could make the arrangement—.

There was a slurring noise back of him.

He whirled around, automatically looking to left and right for support. He'd been told often enough that he had to be in company with others when he faced nigras, and he mustn't stand for any nonsense from them. Jethro stood in the doorway. The black man's slim features, almost white features in the coal-black face, shone with sweat. He raised a hand to gesture and moved the hand firmly, but no words were coming out. Abel was more relaxed. The black man was almost as unsettled as he had been. Jethro took a step back, keeping one foot behind the other as if he was going to make an about-face and run.

And then Blossom's voice said clearly, "Talk, talk! Tell the masta why you here."

She was standing just behind Jethro and to the right. There was a look of little-girl mischief in her dark eyes. She was breathing quickly.

"Yes, yes, I—masta, I can talk to you."

"Why aren't you at the gin house and working?"

"I just be a little time, masta." But the lips were dry,

161

and he moved them time and again to help get words out.

Abel looked over the slave's shoulder. "Blossom, what does he want to say? You must have egged him on to do it, so you know. Well?"

Jethro stepped into the sugar house and over to one side. Blossom put both hands over her high cheekbones, reaching the ears with the tips of her work-stained fingers as if to shut out the words.

Jethro, stung, spoke too loudly. "You selling off all the prime hands who maybe hurt that nigger!"

"I haven't sold you or Tuck or a few others." He was making changes slowly, but this wasn't the time to say so. "What about it?"

"You will. You sell me, you sell Tuck, and then you sell the gals."

"Are you telling me what I'm going to do?"

"Masta, I—please, masta, I have to say this." He fell silent again.

This time he didn't speak when Abel looked at Blossom, silently ordering her to talk.

"Jethro, he don't want to get sold," Blossom said carefully. "He sure you don't sell him."

"Why is he so sure?"

Jethro got a little of his nerve back. "You sell me, masta, you sell your family."

"I know you've been at Fairlawn all your life," Abel said easily. "I've got no plans to keep you and Blossom apart. That's probably what Blossom is worried about."

He didn't particularly enjoy telling a lie to anybody, white or black, even if some business problem made it necessary. With Blacks, though, it was like telling a lie to some child. It was wrong to think of a grown black person as anything less than a grown person with a dark skin, but he couldn't help it any more. He had seen a year of whining and lying and pretending sickness and petty stealing by his slaves; they were human beings who had turned themselves into fractious children.

Jethro said, "My mammy a slave gal who is sold a little while after I born. My daddy—."

162

It was the pause and the sudden riveting of Blossom's eyes on Abel's face that alerted him. This was going to be a business deal of a type he wasn't used to. His face purposely took on that poker-playing look of his.

"Go on, Jethro," he said softly. "Tell me who your daddy was."

"Lyon Debenker was my daddy," Jethro said after a pause that seemed endless. "The same as your daddy, he my daddy."

Abel had guessed it during the pause, having examined his own small-featured face in black. It was suddenly like looking at himself with burnt cork on his face from the neck up, like somebody in a minstrel show.

Blossom tried to make her voice persuasive. "Some other masta, he might sell Jethro on account of them having the same daddy. Some other masta, he might not want to see Jethro all the time and know what is the truth. But you a good masta, a kind masta. You not hurt Jethro."

Abel hadn't realized how quickly he was thinking.

"If you'll agree to get out of the state and not tell any of the other slaves what we've been talking about, Jethro, I'll give you the papers to set you free."

"And I'll give you enough money to carry you to New York or even further away if you wanted to go there."

"Free?" Jethro looked down at his hard hands as if they had become lucky charms to ward off the devil. "But where I go? What I do? I know nothin' but to pick the cotton and chop the tree. What I do in the North?"

"You fool, you damn fool!" Blossom whispered. "First you get free, then you buy me free, and we together. *I* tell you what you do."

He couldn't help turning to her, "You not be with me when I free. I don't know what I do or where I go. Now I know who I am. Free, I know nothing, I be nothing."

"You nothing now. You a slave. You can be sold or traded or led around by the nose. You can be cut off at the crotch if masta wants to do that, and you can say nothin'. You nothin' yourself, now. You free, you somethin'. You somebody."

163

"But then a white man come along and sell me again, and I not free. I know all about what happens to some free boys. You think Jethro don't know?"

Blossom made a pair of fists and silently beat her thighs with them. Abel had never seen a female in such a state of fury.

Jethro looked at his half-brother the way a dog might have looked at Abel. Masta would attend to it, somehow. Masta would fix it so that a slave boy didn't have any troubles, so that he wouldn't have to make choices like free men did.

He said hesitantly, "I go back to gin house."

"Of course," said Abel Debenker.

His conscience wouldn't let him rest or forget what he had been told. On Thursday of that week, he had to go into Festin for some supplies and to give Elkahan Melville a check for the balance of the money for his recent purchase of slaves. The business with Melville was done quickly enough. He was on his way out of the hotel when he saw Tom Holman taking a brisk walk along Courthouse Square. Abel joined him and put a question discreetly. The tall, whey-faced plantation owner considered it while making long strides.

"I don't think there's a land owner in the South who doesn't have a brother or sister born on the wrong side of the blanket," Holman said as they passed Jarvis Whitcomb's law office. "The thing to do is to get rid of 'em."

"Selling them, you mean? But it's not fair."

"What has being fair got to do with living your life comfortably?"

"But a half-brother or sister is entitled by natural law to some part of what the father has left behind."

"Niggers can't inherit without special provisions of law. The father didn't free that nigger—why should anybody else do it?"

"Because it's right."

"What's right is to see that you don't have somebody on

164

the land who is a constant source of tension, Abel. Sell that nigger and sell him quick. Try to make sure that the new situation is a good one for the nigger, if you feel so strongly about it, but above all, get him or her sold and do it quick."

"Then you won't give him money and set him free."

"Certainly not. You can't set a nigger really free unless every nigger has already been set free by the government, in which case you don't have to do a thing. Very few niggers have got the brains or the will to survive in a country where almost every hand is turned against 'em if they're free. As for sharing your holdings with a nigger, that's no good because the nigger isn't any help at all and only a drain. As for giving a nigger a lot of money, why, you might just as well buy earrings for a baboon."

Abel winced.

"Mind you, I'm not one of those who think that all niggers are worthless, but you have to live in the world as it is and not as you'd like it to be." Tom Holman's pace slowed down for a serious question on his mind. "Do you think that the country is going to make James Buchanan its President next month?"

The new overseer kept him busy on Friday with details for enlarging the gin house. John Platter, a solemn Scots-Irishman, wouldn't stand for the slightest nonsense from Negroes, nor would he use the whip unless there was absolutely no choice. Abel thought that he might work out nicely.

On Saturday afternoon he and Abel spoke to several workmen in town about getting specially made tables with lower compartments and adding "a wing" as Platter humorlessly called it, to the old building. It was decided to go ahead during the last half of January.

On Sunday, Abel told Platter to take a rest, and walked over to the slave church to listen to the sermon, as the law required one white man to do. The Reverend Clack gave his usual sermon about the virtues of humbleness.

165

"The nigger has still got to be humble," he shouted in half singing voice. "The nigger has still got to obey his master . . . ."

Abel happened to be looking at his half-brother's back as the weak "amens" came from the audience. Something suddenly clicked in his mind, and during the rest of the sermon he worked out his plans. As the slaves filed out of church slowly, Abel caught Jethro's eye. Jethro, who had been walking next to Blossom, nodded. Abel stepped outside and waited until Jethro hurried over to him.

"Yes, masta, I here."

Abel nodded. He didn't think twice about his half-brother calling him master, having remembered what happened when he wanted Jethro to call him mister instead of that other odious title. In that sense, he was taking Tom Holman's advice and trying to live in the world as he found it.

"Walk behind me," Abel said.

It was a short walk on this cool afternoon over to the dilapidated and unused sugar house. He pointed to the equipment he had bought from Elkahan Melville.

"Do you know how to make whiskey?"

"No, masta, I not know."

"You will," Abel promised.

Swiftly, and with fewer words than the auctioneer had used, he explained about corn mash and ground sprouted malt corn and sugar and water to make beer or whiskey after a six to ten day waiting period. He took Jethro over the steps again, so that the black man understood what he was being told.

"Jethro, I'm going to see to it that—no, never mind." He couldn't talk about the future to somebody who would never admit that anything mattered except this day. "You're to take this equipment out of the sugar house and put it where it'll be sheltered from rain. You'll get the supplies for a new batch of whiskey from me when I think it's time to make a new batch."

"Yes, masta."

"You're to put the stuff into quart bottles. I'll buy those,

166

too. I know that you and others get money to buy whiskey from traders and I want it stopped."

Jethro looked surprised. "You want we give the lightnin' away, masta?"

"No. If you do that, the stuff won't be worth much to the others. I want you to sell it at—. What's the usual price for a bottle about this big?"

"Two dollar, masta."

"Two dollars, then." A possible gross of three hundred dollars, a possible net of two hundred and fifty. Take away the eighty-five dollars for the basic equipment and perhaps as much as ten dollars more for the bottles, and a quick return of one fifty-five wasn't bad. "I'll know how many bottles are sold because of what I'll be giving you to sell. As soon as it's time for another batch, you collect the used bottles and wash them out and fill them again. I'm going to want all the money you make—."

"Yes, masta." Jethro's face looked as if it had fallen in.

"Except twenty dollars for every batch, which you keep for yourself." He wasn't sure what use a slave might find for money, but there was a lot about slave living that he still didn't know.

"Twenty dollar for me? Thank you, masta."

"Now remember, you bring me the rest," Abel said sternly.

"Yes, masta, I bring."

"And if this works out well, you can do the same thing over and over again."

"Yes, masta." Jethro's eyes were swimming with gratitude. "You the best masta in the world, the best masta there ever is."

Abel looked away. He left Jethro taking the equipment out of the sugar house with some difficulty and walked back to the mansion. Nancy and their small son were waiting in the carriage to go to church, Nancy in a dark, black dress that she probably knew he didn't like. He joined them.

"By the way, I'll be opening up a special account at the Festin National Bank, an account that will be marked in

167

trust to your name. After I die, you're to follow the instructions I'll put into my testament and turn over all that
money to Jethro. Is that clear?"

Nancy looked at him in silence for as much as a minute.
"Yes, it's clear," she said, and turned away.

14

Not until he was four years old, during April '57, did
Kermit have his first direct experience with slavery, and it
probably helped give him opinions that he would hold for
as long as he lived.

As a rule he would go out to play in the morning.
Hester looked after him, generally sitting and watching
him, but more likely she would doze off. Once she took
him over to the slave quarters to look at Sunshine's new
baby, but he generally played with a rubber ball, and by
himself. One time he chased the ball toward the new gin
house, which had become bigger after a few men came
and made a lot of noise in front of it. There was a black
youngster sitting on a turned-up can and peeling potatoes
that he then put into a can that was turned right side up.
The boy must have been a little older than Kermit, but
didn't look nearly as strong in the hands or as full in the
face.

"Who are you?" Kermit asked.

"Obie my name," the boy said.

"Obie what?"

"Obie nothin'. I got the name of an old man what die."

"What are you doing?"

"Peelin' these 'taters."

"Could I do it?"

"Surely."

Kermit was trying to hold the knife until Hester ran
over and saw what was happening. Then she took the
knife out of Kermit's little hand and gave Obie what-for.

She marched Kermit away and back to where she could sit and watch him play by himself. Kermit made a point of sneaking off a couple of days afterwards, and trying to peel potatoes with his new friend. Obie wouldn't let him help, though. When Hester found them together she muttered angrily at Obie, but spoke nice as pie to Kermit. That didn't seem fair. If one kid was wrong, both of them were.

He slept in the early afternoon, but at about five he would be outside again and ready to play by himself. On this one afternoon he heard some boys cheering and he walked over to the slave quarters and looked around. Half a dozen boys were playing with a ball that looked livelier than Kermit's. The fellow with the ball was running, and five other fellows were trying to knock him down. It looked like a lot of fun. As soon as Kermit raised his voice to ask if he could play, the boys ran off to their cabins. The rubber ball was left behind, bouncing along the base of the Bermuda grass.

The next morning, he asked Obie why the others had run away. Obie was peeling potatoes again.

"They run away," he said carefully, "because they got to."

"But I can play ball," Kermit persisted. "I'm as good as they are."

Obie gave him a strange look that was half a smile and half a headshake, but didn't say any more about it.

The next time Kermit walked over to the slave quarters, hoping to find a ball game going on, he saw two of the slave boys fighting each other. A circle of boys and gals was around them and everybody was cheering. Kermit walked over and started to cheer, too, wanting the smaller boy to win. At the sound of his voice, most of the boys turned around and looked at him and then turned back. The cheering was a lot less noisy and less fun when it started up again.

A whole week must have gone by before Kermit saw Obie at the potatoes again, and this time Kermit was upset about what had happened near the slave quarters.

169

Obie said, "I talk to the fellas. It be okay, now on."

"Are you sure?"

"I say so, I sure."

It was true. Two days afterwards Kermit again saw the black boys playing at their ball game. When he appeared they glumly made way for him and let him play. The game wasn't as much fun as he had expected, and he never got the chance to carry the ball so that the others would have to try and get it from him. He was pretty glum after it was finished and the other kids had to go back to some kind of work. He didn't get a chance at the ball during the next game a few days later, either. Worse yet, he didn't get to touch any of the kids who carried the ball, let alone getting it out of their hands. He didn't feel too chipper when that game was finished.

Next time there was a game, Obie kept him busy near the mansion by showing him a few of the jobs he did. Obie was going to become a house servant or bust, he said. Kermit would rather have been playing, but he didn't want to hurt Obie's feelings and say so.

On the April day that he would never quite forget, he woke up early and played a little by himself in the morning. At lunch, Daddy was talking about President James Buchanan, whom he called an idiot; and about the State Disunion Convention, whatever that might have been. Mommy was so upset about somebody named Dred Scott that finally Daddy got a little angry. He said he had to go out and talk to Mr. Platter, the something-seer.

Kermit laughed. "He's not the seer, he's the buckra."

Daddy asked, annoyed, "Where did you hear that word, son?"

Mommy sounded exasperated. "Where do you think he heard it?"

There was a lot of talk between them. Kermit went up to his room and slept, the way he was supposed to. In the afternoon, when he got up and went outside, he was glad to hear the sounds of a game coming from the slave quarters. He hurried over on his short legs. As usual, the boys became quieter when they saw him and everything came to a stop. Obie, who was at the edge of the group, shook his head sadly. Seeing Obie's reaction made Kermit feel more belligerent.

"I want to carry the ball," he said.

"You?" one of the boys started scornfully, but another boy stepped on his foot.

Obie said, "Let him carry it."

Kermit picked up the ball, which felt almost like a big cotton boll, and turned to Obie.

"What are the rules?"

"There are two teams," Obie pointed. "The six on your team are lined up to face the six on the other team—I not play. The one who carry the ball is behind the others. He run. The others on his team try to see he gets where he goes, to keep the others from getting him. Where you carry the ball is over there." He pointed to an area parallel with the cistern between the rows of slave cabins.

"You carry the ball, so you win a point. You win a point, it add to the others."

He looked down and Kermit followed his eyes. There were two rows of toemarks, one row for each team.

"Now you stand there and wait for the ball to get throwed at you."

The ball was thrown lightly. He caught it and started to run, chortling with pleasure. He realized something was wrong before being sure what it was. He suddenly stopped, narrow eyes squinting.

"Why aren't you trying to catch me?" he demanded. "Why don't you try and knock me down like the others?"

The boys stood and stared at him uncomfortably.

"You must try and catch me," Kermit demanded.

He resumed his run. Three boys started after him, but they moved very slowly. He found himself at the point parallel with the cistern and holding the heavy ball. Nobody had tried to come near him.

This time he said angrily, "I'll run with the ball until somebody catches me."

He started running back to the point from which he'd come. Nobody moved.

He taunted them, "You're a bunch of scaredy cats. You don't dare catch me, you don't dare."

That was when he stopped himself and stared from one black face to another. There was no hostility, only resignation. The master's son had wanted the ball and had got it, he wanted to run and he had to be let to run. If he had wanted to punch every one of the boys, Kermit knew with a sinking feeling that he'd have been allowed to do that, too, and nobody would have raised a hand to ward off a punch. Once more he looked at the black faces and then he put the ball down and walked back to the mansion. He never tried to play ball with the black boys again. There would have been no reason for doing so.

15

"You're wonderful," Abel Debenker said, bending over to kiss his wife lightly on the inner left thigh. He raised himself and got out of his wife's bed.

"Very nice," Nancy agreed demurely. She started to raise the sheet over herself, having noted the direction of his eyes. Then she lowered it slightly, instead, displaying shapely legs. "Don't you ever get enough of carnal wickedness?"

"Making love to your wife isn't wicked," Abel said cheerfully. "And when you're—well, when you're in the mood you're wonderful."

"You were going to say that when I'm sober we give each other a good time." Nancy nodded. "I'll try to keep more sober than I've done in the past. Kermit is getting to the age when he notices things."

"Yes."

He was perfectly at ease, but he didn't enjoy being in his wife's bedroom, as such. To his eye, it was jam-packed with ornaments of no use except for a knitting case with

172

needles, beads, and scraps of silk and a Moroccan work bag with scissors and thimbles.

"Have to get dressed," he said. "We're to be at the Pollards by five-thirty."

"Yes, dear, you'll have another chance to give Serena the eye," Nancy said. "But you'll be too tired to do anything about it this time."

"I never have done anything about it," Abel said, turning with fists on hips. "And I'm not aware that I've ever given the lady an eye or anything else but my good wishes."

"Your good wishes for yourself, you mean." Nancy Debenker smiled. "It's almost a joke among the ladies that you've got an eye on Serena Pollard."

"Indeed." Abel walked toward the door, pausing only for his robe and slippers. "Well, I'll be ready in half an hour, dear."

"You won't have to wait for me."

He ordered Hester to fill a bath with well-water and ordered Grover to give him a close shave. He dressed carefully in a dark suit with a white shirt, a dark cravat, and the gold watch and chain that he wore on great occasions. He only had to wait five minutes for his wife to join him, and then she explained that she had only been delayed by saying goodnight to Kermit. She was dressed in dark red, with a daring cut at the neckline. The dress billowed out slightly, showing bright red pumps. Her hair had been tied with a gold ribbon in the back. The sight of her made Abel wish that they could have stopped for several more minutes and gone up to his bedroom, this time. He didn't doubt that she had got dressed so well in order to put Serena Pollard in the shade at her own Thanksgiving Day party. As far as he was concerned, Nancy had succeeded beyond his wildest dreams.

It was almost six o'clock when their carriage topped a rise, and the Pollard mansion was in sight. They had to pass the stable, several dozen feet behind the mansion, and Abel peered into it.

173

"There's only one guest carriage in the stable," he told Nancy. "The Goldthwaits, I think."

Nancy made a face briefly, but covered it. The carriage stopped in front of the mansion to let them off. A black man stared at them.

Abel asked, "Is something wrong inside?"

The house servant opened the door. A smell of warm meat came to them from the hall and so did the sound of tears. Abel and Nancy looked at each other. Abel hurried inside, his wife following as quickly as she could in the long dress.

Serena Pollard was sitting in the reception room on a chair that matched an oak table that had been thrust to one side for the Thanksgiving dinner. Her mouth was in a handkerchief and she sobbed bitterly.

"Why did this happen to me?" she suddenly asked, turning to her companión.

Chad Goldthwait's wife, a small thin woman with suspiciously blonde hair, stroked Serena's arm. Mrs. Goldthwait looked as concerned as she must have felt, but there was placidity in her eyes. Illness, unhappiness, brought out the best in her. She had spent years trying to convince Chad Goldthwait, of all people, that he was delicate and even sickly, so that she could prove to him that she was a competent and devoted wife, even though she had lost a child in '52.

Nancy looked at Lorna Goldthwait. "What happened?"

"Ben Pollard was getting dressed for this party when Serena heard him call out for help. She ran into his room and he was lying on the floor. His face was white and he was breathing very noisily. When she ran to him, he suddenly stopped breathing."

Nancy stared. "Ben Pollard is dead?"

She ran over to Serena's left side and began stroking her other hand. Serena sobbed quietly and persistently.

Abel said, "I'm terribly sorry, Serena."

At his formal condolences, Serena Pollard sobbed more loudly.

174

"Where is Chad? I guess we can make arrangements between us."

"I sent Chad back home in the Passy carriage," Mrs. Goldthwait said. "I didn't want him to stay around here."

"In that case I'll make the arrangements as best I can." He walked outside, where the stricken house slave waited. "Ask the overseer to come here, and hurry."

"Yes, suh."

As the house servant scuttled away to the overseer's cabin, a carriage pulled up in front of the mansion. The black driver got off, opened the door, and let off Victor Jobelin and his wife. The planter's cordial smile faded as he caught sight of Abel hurrying towards him.

"Is anything wrong?" Jobelin asked.

The burial took place on a cloudy Sunday with no rain. The Reverend Mr. MacCubbin officiated calmly, unreeling a string of platitudes with mechanical fervor. The plantation owners, who were honorary pallbearers, walked in front of the slaves who carried the plain wooden coffin to the cemetery plot. Each man scooped up a shovelful of earth in turn, dropped it on top of the coffin, and turned away.

There was a cold collation for the mourners at the Pollard mansion shortly afterwards. Abel left Nancy with a subdued Kermit and found Ben Pollard's study down the hall. It turned out to be no larger than three closets strung together, with paintings of steamboats on each wall and books about navigation on unpainted shelves. There was a ship's pilot wheel at the right side of an oak desk and against the only window. The room told him more about the boorish Ben Pollard than he had known, until this moment when it was totally useless to him. Serena was sitting in the visitor's chair, her face rigid with grief. The Reverend Mr. MacCubbin was watching lawyer Jarvis Whitcomb behind the desk as he leafed through the dead man's papers.

"The land is free and clear, Serena," the lawyer was

175

saying. "No problem in the title, from what I see. A sale ought to be relatively easy to manage."

"I'll cultivate the crop," Serena Pollard said stubbornly, raising her head. "Everything will be just the same as Ben left it."

"You'll find many problems, Serena," the lawyer said, settling back in the chair and stroking his gray hair with a forefinger. "Many problems."

"I won't change anything."

"When you encounter difficulties along the way, Serena, I'm sure you know that you can call on any of us in this room." ·

Serena looked in turn at each man in her late husband's study. Abel wondered afterwards if her gaze had rested longer on him than on the others.

"Thank you," she said softly. "I'll keep that in mind, of course."

He hurried to her home on a wet January afternoon, when she had sent one of the servants to call him. She wore a gray dress so dark that it resembled black to the casual eye, but she was composed.

"I've decided to sell off my acres," Serena said. "I'll keep a few and that will be all, perhaps sixty acres like Jarvis Whitcomb has."

He was thinking swiftly. "Is that a definite decision, Serena? You won't go back on it?"

"Certainly not. Although I don't suppose you can imagine how much I hate cutting myself off from—oh, so many things. A person can't be alone, but it seems as if I'll have to be."

"You've got friends."

"I *had* friends, Abel. Now the married women all think that I'm trying to steal their husbands."

"I'm sure Nancy doesn't think so."

"Are you?"

She gave him a coquettish female look that he wasn't able to interpret. He cleared his throat loudly and talked about the pending sale.

176

"If our land adjoined, I'd buy up whatever you're willing to sell," he said. "As it is, I'd suggest talking to Holman and Duval."

"Will you handle the matter for me?"

"I'm not an attorney."

"Mr. Whitcomb is likely to obtain future business from Tom Holman and Mr. Duval, so he'd be inclined to favor them. Or at least that's the way it seems to me."

"How do you know that I wouldn't favor them also? We're all plantation owners, and men in the same line of work have got a tendency to stick together."

"I think that you're an honest man."

He nodded. They were sitting in Serena's reception room. The oak table had been put back into place, with matching chairs around it. There was a coal-oil lamp and a throw rug in grassy green. The place looked different, and Abel wondered if the river-oriented materials remained in Ben Pollard's study. For Serena's sake, he hoped not.

"Legal papers have to be drawn up, and you'll need an attorney to do that," he said. "I'd suggest you consult one and tell him that I'll be interested in buying land or slaves —I might pick up a few nigras at that, although I'm not sure—so I'll be part of the negotiations and be able to advise you."

She reached out a hand for his, and he took it. "I appreciate this, Abel, more than I can say. It's been two months since I've had a man to advise me."

He knew, then, that she wanted him in her bed. He ought to have realized it all along. He wanted her, too, but didn't know if this was the time. He did know that if he made a suggestion, she would draw back and make believe she had been outraged. Oddly, he didn't have any idea what to say. It had been such a long time since he had tried to make love to any girl but Nancy—he had honestly forgotten the slave girl, Blossom—that he wasn't sure he would know what to say or how to make himself clear.

He found that it wasn't necessary. Serena's soft hand,

177

rising from his, brushed against a pants leg and slowly was drawn back to herself.

"I beg your pardon," she said.

"Not at all."

In dry, hesitating voices, the invitation had been made and accepted. He found himself glancing outside this room and toward the carpeted stairs.

She shook her head once. "I wonder if you would be good enough to close the door. I'm not feeling too well and I wouldn't want the Negroes to see me in distress."

"Of course." Did she plan to make love on the oak table? Spread-eagled on the floor?

She came towards him as he turned. She embraced him, her head warm against his chest. Then she eased herself away from him and turned. He wondered if he had misunderstood her signals. The feeling of illness might have been genuine; symptoms could be taken for what they weren't.

But she said, "Undo the dress." Her voice was soft but commanding.

He did it swiftly, and took his own clothes off as soon as he could. They looked at each other in a state of wonder and pleasure, and then touched again and again in a rush of discovery. The pressure in Abel was building up, and he knew he wouldn't be able to keep part of him contained for another moment. He put a hand down against her crotch and then pushed one leg a little further away from the other. Then he used the second finger of his left hand, drawing it out quickly to insert another part of himself into her. He was in time to help himself, but not her.

The second time he helped her, and she embraced him and kissed his face.

The third time, swaying silently as they did, was pleasanter for both of them than the others had been.

She pulled herself back and away, then looked up at him and reached up both hands to his head and inclined it slightly towards her. Then she kissed the top of his head.

"I've been so long without a man, Abel."

"Yes, I know."

178

"I'm sorry this happened."

"So am I."

"Nancy is such a good woman, such a devoted friend."

"She's a fine wife and a wonderful mother. I wouldn't hurt her for the world."

"We must never do anything like this again."

"Of course not."

There was no smile here, no laughter. It was permissible for a married man to have a fling with another woman, as long as he didn't behave afterwards as if he had enjoyed himself. In that case, pleasure became unforgivable.

16

"He do," Blossom insisted. "He see me, he reach out for me, he touch me here . . ."

Pointing to her breasts.

". . . and here . . ."

The crotch, this time.

". . . and here."

Turning around, pointing a finger at her right buttock through the two-color dress.

At twenty, she was the only slave gal with more than one dress, thanks to the money Jethro had made at selling whiskey. His first batch had been awful, but he'd figured out how to make the stuff and now the slaves paid his price for it or traded knicknacks they had taken from the mansion. Jethro flexed his muscles at the slave who was facing him.

"That the truth," he said, his mind made up.

The other slave nodded affably. "Yes, yes."

Blossom's jaw dropped and then she turned eagerly to Jethro. "You see? He admit what he do."

On this stuffy June night, the slaves were milling tiredly around in front of their quarters. No work had been done on Sunday, as usual. The heat was making everybody grit his teeth. Blossom had seen old Moses walking around with his hands in fists, and that was unusual for the old man.

The slave facing Jethro said, "Yes, yes," again.

Jethro made a pair of fists now and slitted his eyes. "You ask for it, boy, you get it."

There was an interruption. The sullen field hand, Tuck, loomed at Jethro's right and stood between him and the other slave, then moved to the right where he could look from one to the other.

"What you doin'?" he asked Jethro. "What you think you doin'?"

"I show this nigger he no fool around with my gal," Jethro began determinedly.

"How you sure that's what he ever do?"

"Blossom say so."

Tuck shrugged.

"He just say so, too. I see him. I hear him."

Tuck didn't smile often, but he came close to it now. "He say nothin'. He know nothin'."

"He know words."

"He know Yes and nothin' else. Him and the other new boys all supposed to come from Kentucky or Virginia, but—."

"They got writing to say so. I hear masta tell that to the buckra."

"Writing don't matter. These boys come from Africa, where our brothers sell 'em. They come in slave ship, very bad. Amos, here—that his name—he don't know what you say."

"He not fool with my gal," Jethro insisted stubbornly.

"Everybody do it with Blossom, and Blossom do it with everybody," Tuck insisted. "You don't know that much, you stupid."

Jethro looked around. A number of slaves were sitting languidly on the ground in front of their primitive cabins and watching.

Blossom said, "They with you or they don't get the lightnin'. That's all."

180

"You with me or not?" Jethro called out. "I sell you the lightnin', you want more of it so you with me. All of you!"

The faces were without emotion.

"You not with me, I smash the lightnin' machine, and you never get no more except from white trader," Jethro called out. "You with me, you clear a circle and watch me stomp this boy."

Blossom said to Jethro, "Anybody don't move to help, you don't sell no more lightnin'."

"You hear that?" Jethro demanded. "No more if you don't come over here now and get Tuck away."

Amos, the African, looked from Tuck to Jethro and understood that something serious had come up. He watched warily, a gaunt man with whipmarks across his back from the slave ship expedition. The whites of his eyes, by a trick of moonlight, seemed almost as wide as his head and as long as his nose. Jethro, about to move forward, stopped himself and grunted in spite of his anger.

The incident gave Tuck time to shout in turn, "Do you want to see this stupid nigger get his head knock off on account of a no-good gal? If that what you want to see, go with Jethro. You don't want to see that, you stay with me, and you do it now."

Tuck didn't expect anybody to move in either direction, but he hadn't counted on the heat-induced Sunday night edginess. Slowly but menacingly, slaves rose from in front of their quarters and came to stand around Jethro. A few of the others got up and slouched over to stand back of Tuck and on two sides of the bemused African.

Blossom called out exultantly, "We win, Jeth. All the strong niggers are with us."

Her triumphant tones sent a number of gals of all ages and a few youngsters hurrying with one accord to stand with Tuck and the African.

Blossom laughed. "We walk all over you."

Jethro and Tuck looked at each other, each sizing up the potential opponent. There was hesitation in the air at that moment between them.

Blossom said, "You knock the shit outta him, Jethro."

181

"No." Tuck felt his anger rising at Jethro for letting himself be led around, but he tried to control it. "You fight me and everybody else, but you don't fight who we should——."

Jethro didn't hear what was said after the second time Tuck used the word "fight." Blossom suddenly shouted:

"Kill him, Jethro, *now!*"

Jethro's right hand snaked back, but instead of throwing a punch he took two running steps toward his enemy. Tuck landed a right to Jethro's belly under the gray homespun shirt and when he leaned forward cracked a left to the side of his jaw. Jethro kept on his feet and then pulled out both hands to reach around Tuck's neck. Tuck kept on as if there was no barrier to doing what he wanted. He hit his man in the mouth, but didn't neglect Jethro's eyes and stomach. It was the mouth, however, that drew Tuck's fists to it symbolically again and again. Jethro's strong hands put pressure on Tuck's neck and he started to gasp. He brought a foot out, but it did no good. His eyes swam, but he could see and hear what was happening around him. It was ugly, all of it. Men had started to fight other men who had been on the same side of the original argument, women to claw at still other men. Children were punching each other wildly.

As Tuck watched in helplessness, his eyes glazing, he saw a slave suddenly turn and begin to hit a gal across the face with his fists and then to punch her on the breasts. The gal screamed.

Amos, the slave who Tuck had tried to help, came to his aid by getting around back of Jethro and squeezing as much of his neck as possible with his own elbow. Jethro gasped, but didn't let go of Tuck. That was when Blossom started to pound Amos on the back. Amos let out a cry, then released Jethro. He turned and punched Blossom in the stomach, exactly as if she had been a man. Blossom gasped and reeled, falling across a slave who had dropped to the earth when the fighting got under way.

Amos tried to twist Jethro's neck. Jethro hit out uselessly with a bare foot and then with the other. The pres-

182

sure on Tuck's neck had lessened, but he knew that if it
kept on he would die. He punched his enemy in the neck,
but the punches went wide. One punch did hit squarely,
and Jethro released him for a moment, but Tuck was in
such pain that he didn't know it.

Blossom got up from the earth at last and grabbed
Amos by the head to pull it back. The African let out a
bellow of rage and kicked upwards with a leg between
Jethro's feet.

Jethro called out and let Tuck go at last, finally. Tuck
stood absolutely still, trying to get control of the chaos
within him.

He turned in time to see Jethro punch Amos. The
African collapsed, falling across the earth like a slaughtered
animal. His hands and feet were wide apart, and his head
lolled grotesquely like a broken toy.

He heard Sunshine, sensible woman, calling, "Stop this,
stop the crazy thing, stop it!"

The youngster, Obie, having pounded another lad until
he ran off, sat down against a cabin pole and started to
sob. Tuck had to turn away. Jethro jumped up and down
on the fallen Amos. Tuck ran at him and knocked him off.
Jethro gave a bellow of pain, then turned to come directly
at Tuck.

"He not the one," Blossom encouraged him, shouting.
"That fuckin' African nigger, he the one. That bastard
nigger, you get him!"

As Jethro wavered, Tuck hit him solidly in the stomach.
Jethro had to take two steps backward, and then he sat
down in a daze. Blossom was setting herself to stomp on
the back of the fallen Amos.

"Let him alone," Tuck ordered.

"You no tell me what to do," Blossom shouted back. "I
turn him over and I piss in his mouth."

She moved to turn Amos over as Tuck watched stolidly,
then lifted part of her new dress from the back and walked
over to plant her feet on two sides of the unconscious African's face. She squatted, opened his mouth and then
straightened her head.

"You watch, now. You put a finger on me, and I have Jethro kill you. And he do what I tell him."

Tuck went to her, raised her on one of his shoulders, turned around with her, and saw a group of more than a dozen slaves on the• ground frenziedly fighting one another. He took twenty steps carrying Blossom, and dropped her on top of the melee. The round of shouts that rose at his action was almost enough to deafen him. He was the first to hear the crack of a whip in the air. John Platter, the overseer, had run down from his cabin and was using the whip generously to stop the fighting. A round of screams went up that were of greater intensity than any that Tuck had heard a while ago.

"Stop it, all of you," the dour Scotsman shouted. "You're to do a day's work tomorrow, and I'll not have any injuries before that. All of you, stop it!"

The silence came slowly. Tuck looked around him at the swollen eyes and bleeding flesh, the raw-rubbed hands and bruised knuckles, the reddened gums and flecked scattered teeth; and he heard the longdrawn, pain-filled breaths.

"Stupid niggers," he said softly. "We fight each other, and not the white man. Stupid, stupid, stupid."

17

"I believe that everything else is in order," Mr. Emmet said carefully.

"It is," Jarvis Whitcomb agreed, sitting back in the most comfortable chair in his conference room. August sunshine, filtering through the window glass, made his gray hair look almost blond while erasing wrinkles under the eyes and parentheses at the corners of his lips. "All but six acres of the property have already been sold off, from what I've been told."

"Yes, indeed," Mr. Emmet nodded. He was a heavyset

184

attorney with muttonchop whiskers. "Forty-four acres have gone to Giraud Duval and thirty to Thomas Holman. Fifty-nine of the sixty-three slaves were sold at wholesale to Elkahan Melville, the dealer. That leaves four slaves, field hands that my client has agreed to sell."

He looked to his side where Serena Pollard was sitting, in a dark-blue outfit that showed off her pale face under rice powder.

"And my client has agreed to buy," Whitcomb said, nodding at Abel sitting alertly beside him, "if all conditions are met."

"All conditions have been met by Mrs. Pollard, I can assure you."

"Is it clearly understood that no family will be broken up by this sale?" Whitcomb prodded. "Mr. Debenker has insisted upon that."

"Mrs. Pollard has sworn out an affidavit to that effect. I submit that affidavit now."

"Thank you, sir." Whitcomb didn't look at the blue-backed paper. "Now the identifications, please."

Four sets of papers, each set clipped together, were passed across to him.

"Let me see. One, two, three, four. Identification papers all seem to be in order. Yes. Identification. Medical. Dental. The transfer papers are in order. I may tell you that my assistant, Mr. Quendale, searched out the titles to the properties and found no difficulties."

"Of course not, sir," Mr. Emmet said, giving the impression that he had bowed even though he was sitting.

"A moment: do I understand that one of these boys is twenty-six years old?"

"A prime age."

"Certainly, but he doesn't have many prime years left to him."

"Thirty-seven fifty is reasonable for a prime hand, sir," Mr. Emmet said. "My brother recently offered to pay four thousand a piece for two prime niggers, but they went down with the steamship *Pennsylvania*, near Memphis."

"I hope that the final closing hadn't been made for the property," Whitcomb said politely.

"Not yet, fortunately, but the former owner is relying on litigation to steal the money from my brother."

"I'm sure he will be brilliantly defended in court," Whitcomb said, more politely than necessary. "But on the matter of the price for this nig———."

Abel put in quietly, "I've discussed the price with Mrs. Pollard, and I'm satisfied with the price and the condition of the nigras."

Whitcomb bridled, but said nothing. "The ages of the others are suitable, considering the overall price. May be have the signing now?"

"Of course." Emmet reached for the bill of sale papers and marked an *x* at the corner of one dotted line on each sheet. Then he passed them across to Serena Pollard. Serena licked her lips, then took up the quill and signed each sheet. Abel sat with his hands folded, covertly looking at her long lips and the line of her jaw.

Mr. Emmet inspected the signatures, blotted them, and then passed the papers down to the center of the table. Mr. Vance, a fussy and dried-up looking notary public, signed beneath Serena Pollard's name and then inserted each sheet briefly between two rounded edges of a seal. After that, he reached into a box no bigger than what might be used for snuff, and came out with a blob of lukewarm wax. Four times he did that, placing red wax shaped like a bloodstain across part of the bottom of each bill of sale. When he was satisfied, he passed the papers back to Mr. Emmet, who set them down on the table halfway between himself and Whitcomb.

Jarvis Whitcomb glanced at Abel. "May I have the check, please?"

Abel took a check for fifteen thousand dollars out of his pocket and gave it to his attorney. Whitcomb looked at it and pushed his lower lip outward fretfully.

"I'll never understand why you insisted on a certified check, Mr. Emmet, but here it is."

He put it on the table next to the papers. Abel watched

186

his lawyer reach for them while Mr. Emmet took the certified check.

Whitcomb turned to his client. "Not a bad bunch of niggers, Abel, considering the provisos that you insisted upon."

"I'm satisfied."

He heard Mr. Emmet tell Serena, "A generous price, Mrs. Pollard, all things considered."

"Yes, I know."

Emmet suddenly turned to the other lawyer. "I had nearly forgotten about transportation of the property to the buyer's land. I'd suggest that a small added check would cover expenses, with delivery guaranteed by midnight. Ten dollars for each nigger is the standard price, but as this shipment is so small—."

Abel said, "That was taken care of yesterday, Mr. Emmet. Don't forget that Mrs. Pollard has been a neighbor of mine for a while now, and there's a certain amount of trust between us."

"Trust! Humph!"

"I suspect that most people do trust each other, Mr. Emmet, when they aren't in the presence of lawyers."

To his credit, Jarvis Whitcomb laughed.

Abel took Serena to her home, and they made love again in her neatly kept bedroom. In the time since they had become lovers, Serena got into the habit of asking him for advice on all sorts of matters. She wouldn't let a week go by without seeing him. She was a warm and good-natured lover who did anything he wanted, and they were pleased with each other.

She suddenly gripped him around the waist when he was starting to get up, and pulled him to her. He looked at her face inquiringly, then touched her on a full breast. She shook her head. He touched her at the pubic hair and below, but she kept shaking her head.

"All I want right now is to remember how your body feels," she said softly.

187

"I expect you'll refresh your recollection in a few days."

"But I'll have been without a man until that time."

"I can't get away from the plantation very much more often than I do, Serena. I'm sure you recognize that."

"It's lonesome all the time except when we're together."

"Being lonesome is part of being alive."

"Yes, but it was different with Ben. I might have preferred a man of more refinement and as much decency as you've got, but there *was* somebody to talk to or complain to whenever I wanted to. You know what I mean."

"Where are your friends?"

"They see much less of me than they used to. Nancy, for instance. I hardly see her at all, though she's a fine person and we've always liked each other."

"I'll tell her to come out and see you once in a while, if you like."

He would never have expected that a woman with whom he was having an affair might feel badly because she wasn't seeing his wife more often. It seemed bizarre. Twenty-eight years of living hadn't prepared him for the vagaries of attractive women.

"You'll do what you can, dear."

"Of course."

"And here's a little something to remind you of me," she said, and kissed him lightly on the chest and the flat stomach and below. He was more tired than he had expected to be when he left Serena and took the carriage back to Fairlawn.

Nancy agreed to visit Serena during one of her Tuesday visiting days in September, and invited her to dinner on a Friday evening. It was a meal that might have passed awkwardly, but Serena was determined not to appear unhappy.

"Oh, I've bought myself a small dog, which I certainly wouldn't have done if I was still keeping nigras," she said. "You know what they can do to animals by 'accident'."

"I've heard about that sort of thing," Nancy agreed.

188

"Kermit has wanted a dog, but I've been advised not to buy one for him."

Her eyes passed Kermit and moved to her husband. Abel was eating creamed chicken industriously.

"I do declare, Abel Debenker, I have no idea whether you or your son are eating more quickly."

The ladies left him alone very shortly, and Kermit was sent up to his room. Abel remained seated at the round mahogany dining table after the dishes had been cleared. He was reading the *Festin Chronicle* account of a debate between Stephen A. Douglas and Abe Lincoln. Much as he agreed with the Kentucky man's obvious hatred of slavery, he had to concede that Douglas' point of view was the only one that made sense at this time. He certainly wished Abe Lincoln well in what looked like a crusade, but not for a few years yet.

With all this tension around him, it would have been nice if he could have gone off to the Rockies and the big gold rush. He could imagine himself shouting, "Pike's Peak or Bust," along with the youngsters and those who had failed at everything else. It wasn't going to happen, though. The pattern of his life was pretty much settled. A few more crops, maybe only one, and he'd be off to England with his family. They'd live with all the comforts they would ever want, and all that anybody had to give up in exchange was a little time of hard work and sacrifice.

As soon as Hester tiptoed inside the dining room to indicate that Mrs. Pollard wanted to return home, Abel escorted her in a carriage. Moses was driving. Since the old man was almost deaf, he and Serena could talk freely.

"What'll I do?" Serena asked. "I need somebody, and I can't stay alone all the time. I simply can't."

"You might ask a relative to stay for awhile."

"Only as a last resort. If my Cousin Hubert came down from Mississippi, for instance, he'd be fine for a few weeks, and then he'd be at me to sell my holdings and go back to Natchez with him. Festin is where I've lived for a long time, and where I was happy. I want to stay here."

189

"Well, you certainly are going to need somebody to help with the housework. Buy yourself a nigra gal, then."

"I can do all the housework and close off unused rooms. A nigra gal is no company in the world."

"You might want to grow a crop. The money would come in handy, and your interest in life is sure to perk up."

"One nigra would be difficult to keep in line, if you know what I mean, Abel."

"I certainly do, but I tell you what I suggest. I've got a boy I'm planning to sell as soon as possible. What I'd suggest is that I send him over to you by day, beginning in January when it's time to start a new crop."

"If you're planning to sell him, then the nigra must be a troublemaker."

"Not this one. I don't think that Tuck is responsible for the troubles with Jethro. I think it's Jethro's gal who's at the bottom of it, but Jethro is so steamed up by now it hardly makes any difference. At any rate, I'll send Tuck to you by day, and he'll come back to Fairlawn by night. We'll try that arrangement for a month and see if it's good for you."

"That's very generous of you, Abel, but you'll have to let me pay something for the nigra's work." She looked up sharply. "And what about—well, the two of us? We can't do anything when this Tuck is in the house."

"Keep him in the fields, Serena," Abel smiled. "I don't think we'll have any problem."

Abel walked into the reception room of Serena's house on a misty February afternoon, welcomed after a fashion by Serena's dignified bulldog, Prince. Serena, relaxed if not perfectly at ease, put down a copy of *Autocrat of the Breakfast Table* and looked up. She was smiling. For the first time since her husband's death he saw her wearing a bright dress, in this case a pink silk affair, and he smiled, but refrained from telling her what had pleased him.

He hurried to her, expecting that she'd get up to em-

190

brace him. She kept her seat. He stood on a grass-colored throw rug and looked down at her.

"I'd like to talk to you, Abel," she said coolly. "Please sit down."

He did, noticing that a framed wall motto behind her carried the inscription, BLESS THIS HAPPY HOME. He had never seen it in the past, and took its presence as another symbol of recovery from feelings of being alone. He held his white hat in his lap and then set it down on the table near the book.

"I haven't got too much time, Serena," he said. "If you think you'd like to come upstairs, it makes sense to do it now."

"I would, but it doesn't seem right. Not after—well, not after everything."

"Please tell me what you mean."

"Abel, you've been good to me. Very kind. I suspect that you're kind to most people. Even your Negroes think well of you."

"I suppose you asked Tuck about me. Well, he might be lying so as to get on my best side."

"No, Abel. I'm certain that Tuck wouldn't tell me a lie."

There was a catch in Serena Pollard's soft voice that he'd never heard before. He knew everything about the woman physically, but other sides of her character were those of a stranger. Abel pursed his thin lips briefly, wary and annoyed without knowing why. His already narrow eyes looked like slits in the small-featured face.

"What's your point, woman? What is it that you're after?"

"First off, I want you to admit that you trust my judgment."

"Admitted."

"No, I don't want you saying so out of politeness, but because you really feel that way, if you do."

"You're not a fool and you know your own mind, Serena. Now please tell me what outrageous things you want me to do for your pleasure or happiness."

191

"I want you to sell Tuck to me," Serena Pollard said.

Abel ran thumb and forefinger across his slim nostrils, thinking furiously. "If I do that, he may not be as docile as you've found him to date. This way, he knows he's got to reckon with me if his behavior leaves anything to be desired. A much better arrangement like this, Serena."

"You've talked about selling Tuck. This is your chance, Abel. I'm willing to give you the price you want."

"I'm sure we could agree on a reasonable price that would be fair to both of us, Serena. What's beyond me is why in this world or the next you would want one slave to be living here, to be fed here, to sleep here."

He happened to glance up again at the new motto: BLESS THIS HAPPY HOME. When he turned back to Serena, her chin was lifted proudly.

"Have you gone mad?" he asked softly.

"No, sane. I'm saner now than I've been since my husband was taken from me."

"But you can't do this with a black man, Serena."

"I can and I will."

"And you want me to connive at this—this desecration? Is that what you want?"

"It's not easy to talk to a man who's so angry."

"How can I help being angry?"

"You call it a desecration for a woman to be with a Negro, to make love with him. But you men do the same with black women. You men do it all the time."

"Nonsense!"

"Are you going to deny that you've taken advantage of a slave woman, and then come to your wife afterwards?"

"I'm not going to admit anything or deny anything, Serena. But it's fair to say that the men who do that sort of thing don't live with the gal afterwards. Besides, I can assure you that a man isn't as likely to be victimized as a woman in a similar situation."

"I wouldn't be victimized, Abel."

"Tuck will be after you to set him free. If you do that, you'll never see him again."

192

"Then I'll have had good company for another month or two."

"I'm saying that Tuck will walk out on you. He'll leave you, and you'll have brought it upon yourself."

"But if he leaves me when he's free, that'll be his right. I wouldn't want to keep him if he didn't choose to stay with me."

"He might stay long enough to get every penny you own and the land, too." His threat hadn't impressed her. "If you decide against setting him free, he might kill you in your bed."

"In that case, I'll never have to worry about living alone."

"To live alone is one thing, but to—to spread your legs for a nigra is something else altogether, and worse."

"Better for a Negro than for the empty air," Serena said bitterly. "And for whatever it might be worth, Tuck is a decent and gentle person."

He made one last attempt to bring her around. "Don't you realize or care that you'll be an outcast in Feston? You'll be scorned. No decent person would look at you."

"Life isn't much better for a respectable widow who's alone, not much better than that. You can believe me."

She could speak with despair and hope, encouragement and bitterness, all in the same soft tones with their southern inflections and the turns of phrase associated with a gentlewoman. It was maddening.

"Well, I don't agree, Serena." He got to his feet. "The answer to your request is that I must decline it. I'll sell Tuck to Elkahan Melville tomorrow, even though the price won't be nearly what it should be."

"Will you listen?" she demanded, leaning forward. "If you won't agree to my request, I'm prepared to leave with Tuck and go to New York City. We could live as mistress and servant."

"New York City is hell's acres and you know it."

"If anything bad were to happen, then it'll be on your head, Abel Debenker."

193

He said, "All right, then. I'm going to make the best of a bad situation and take it for granted that you can help yourself to a certain extent, at least. I'll tell Jarvis Whitcomb to get in touch with your lawyer, Emmet, and arrange for the sale."

"Thank you, Abel," she murmured. "You've always been very good to me."

He reached for his hat, nearly dislodging the book on the table, and glared down at her. "I've never said this to anybody, Serena, but you're unwelcome at my house from this moment on. You're to have nothing whatever to do with my wife or my small son."

Serena Pollard was looking down at her hands as he walked to the door and his carriage. He didn't look back.

18

Kermit never knew how it happened, but he could remember the start of it. He and Terry Manders had been talking on a July day about something or other. ("This lawyer fellow, Quendale, comes calling on my sister, and it's awful.") Then Frank Jobelin came over to them, and the next thing that any of them knew they had built a raft and were on the river.

Actually, it was a rowboat that they "borrowed" from one of Terry's dad's slaves. Terry became the pilot, and Frank was the captain who tried to sass the pilot. Kermit, at six the youngest by a year, was the crew, and he found himself obeying orders.

"Hold her up to stabbud," Terry shouted.

Frank called, "Let her fall off to labbud."

"I'm the pilot!"

"I'm the captain."

"The captain don't know nothing like what a pilot knows. The pilot *is* the steamboat."

In the course of arguing, Frank lost an oar, and the

194

boat moved swiftly with the current. Kermit, delighted at the start, forced himself to keep tears from forming behind his eyes. Terry, who always looked sad the way his father did, planted himself with both legs apart and grinned.

"I'll get us to port," Terry said.

Frank looked less like a captain and more like a seven year old on a rowboat during a warm July afternoon. "You won't do nothin' if you stand there and make speeches."

Terry passed the other oar across. "Don't let 'er strike and swing, and you be all right, sonny."

Frank nearly raised the oar in anger. "Who are you callin' sonny?"

"You, 'cause you're all of a sudden scared. . . . Ho! Now's the time! Stand by with the buoy!"

"What in tarnation are you talkin' about?"

"Let go the buoy!"

Terry leaped forward, took the oar from Frank's hands and started to row toward shore. He had seen that the current was failing in its power to take them outward, and he did what was necessary. Kermit was tempted to lean over the side and flail with his hands. He tried, but it didn't make any difference.

"Stand by," Terry called, still making believe he was in command of the pilot house of a steamboat.

"Oh, quiet," Frank Jobelin said irritably. "You've got us down to the other side of Natchez by this time, so don't tell us you're a great pilot."

Kermit watched the rowboat come toward an l-shaped landing area built by nature. On the land he saw trees and stumps. There wasn't anything to tell where they were, and he hoped they hadn't all got lost.

Frank, as "captain", was last off the rowboat. The boys stood gazing around them. Kermit, as the "cub", was ordered to ground the boat, which he did with some difficulty. By the time he had finished, and was wiping his brow with his left arm, Terry was waggling a finger urgently in his direction.

"This way."

195

"Why?"

"Me and Frank heard somebody call out while you was a-loafin'."

Kermit walked sullenly behind Terry, then at his side as soon as Terry moved to walk next to Frank. The land hadn't been cultivated and Bermuda grass grew wild.

"This is a road," Terry decided. "We turn here."

"If you can see a road in that dirt," Frank began, and then he looked up.

Kermit had heard it, too. "That's more like a groan. Or somebody wants help."

"I don't believe that." Frank shook his head. "Besides, what tarnation fool would ask *us* for help?"

The answer to that was plain as soon as they reached a clearing. In a rough square that wasn't any longer than thirty feet or wider than twenty, they saw a wooden cage. A black man, stripped to the skin, was sitting disconsolately behind the wooden bars in his own wastes. At sight of the boys he turned slowly because his back had been criss-crossed with welts.

"You he'p," he said weakly. "You he'p poor nigger."

"Yes," Kermit said promptly.

He felt Frank's hard hand gripping his own just before he could start forward.

"What are you going to do? You can't open that box. You haven't got any food to give him. All you can say is that you'll help, but you can't do anything. What good is that? It's worse than useless."

Kermit accused him scornfully, "You don't care 'bout this."

"Well, I don't know what the nigger's done."

Kermit said spitefully, "He ain't done nothin' to deserve that."

"Niggers ain't like we are," Frank insisted. "He don't mind that as much as you would, or me. My daddy says that niggers ain't got proper feelings."

Kermit looked around for some weapon with which to open the cage and set the black man free. Nothing came to hand.

196

"What are you trying to do?" Terry asked.

"I want to get him out of there," Kermit snapped. "He's human, ain't he? He's alive, ain't he?"

Terry said meaningfully, "He is, now."

The boys heard steps in the distance and hid behind a tree, Kermit picking up a rock just before he followed. At the very least, he was determined to bust somebody's head for doing this.

The free nigger, who worked for Rafe Carstairs, came into sight, a burly and unshaven man who carried a red-flecked whip in one hand. The slavebreaker's helper stood briefly with hands on hips.

"Still alive, are you?" He strode over to the cage, where the imprisoned black man cowered. "Well, you won't be for long."

He raised the whip.

Behind the tree, Kermit suddenly felt the rock in his hand taken away by the stronger Frank. He tried to kick out, but Frank punched him with a free hand. He doubled up just as the caged slave started to whine.

The metallic sound of whipcracks and the sight of the whining black man prone against his wastes on the wooden floor of his cage made the boys sick. Terry turned away. Frank, his face green, gasped for breath. Only Kermit stood erect and still, his hands knotted into fists of anger. He looked down at them, wondering idly why he didn't feel the breaking of skin in his palm. The sound of whip against skin kept on and on.

Terry turned back at last, wiping the corners of his lips. Frank leaned against the stunted cypress. The whipcracks halted. Kermit peered out and saw the free nigger turn away with a grunt of satisfaction before moving off. The boys waited until he was out of earshot.

Terry, who hadn't been able to bring himself to look out, asked weakly, "Is he still alive?"

"Yes," Frank said after a moment.

"Poor nigger," Kermit added.

Frank looked back, stung. "We really don't know what he did to get sent up to a slavebreaker. He might 'a hurt

197

somebody. A girl. They say that a lot of niggers do things like that."

Terry spoke before Kermit could argue. "We have to find our way home, and I'm pretty sure how. Rafe Carstairs' place is three miles from the town, and his house faces it. We walk in that direction. When we get back to town, somebody gives us a lift to our homes. How's that, huh? A good pilot always gets you where you want to go."

But the others weren't any longer in a mood to pretend. Frank led the way, keeping clear of the wooden cage. Kermit tried to look back, but it was useless.

They were walking Indian file and keeping to the shelter of scrubby looking trees as much as possible. They suddenly heard a shout from a distance.

"Somebody seen us," Terry said.

The sound of a whipcrack followed.

"No one seen us," Frank reproved his friend.

Kermit put in unhappily, "I wish somebody had."

Terry took his hand sympathetically. The boys walked side by side.

"Another clearing," Frank said.

"Are you going to look?" Kermit asked.

"Sure, if we want to see the house and know which way to walk into town."

"Maybe Rafe Carstairs would give us a lift," Terry suggested.

"I'd kill Rafe Carstairs if I see him," Kermit said convincingly.

Kermit was at Frank's side. He saw Frank's eyes pass over the sight of the wooden cage in this clearing.

"There's the house yonder, down there," Frank said, pointing. "We're in the proper direction for town, so that's all right. And we'd best get away from here before—."

"Look," Kermit said hollowly. "Look inside the cage."

"Now wait a minute," Frank said, his eyes not moving. "I'm sorry this sort of thing has to be done, but I'm no abolitionist."

"Look inside the cage first, and then you can be sorry."

A young girl was in this cage, a girl with whip marks

198

across her face and chest and back. Like the black man in the other cage, she, too, was sitting in her wastes. There was a livid whip welt across the top of her forehead. At the sight of the boys, a pathetic smile crossed her face and she raised a whip-scarred hand to gesture at them. There wasn't a tooth in her mouth, but some of the stumps had recently broken off.

"That gal can't be more than twenty years old," Kermit said. "What did she do, Frank, to get herself thrown into a cage?"

Frank Jobelin turned away. "She's twelve, and one of— one of ours."

Kermit pressed his advantage. "What did she do to deserve this? Did she kill somebody? Did she disturb some white man? What did she do?"

"Leave me alone now. Can't you see I don't feel so good?"

"You walk through Rafe Carstairs' land, and you'll feel a lot worse, Frank. Even you. Now tell me what that gal done so that she's put in a cage and whupped close to death. You tell me that."

Frank was running in the direction of town. Terry didn't have any real choice except to follow. Kermit looked behind him once more, searching for anything that might open the cage, and then realized he couldn't help the gal. He had to run fast so he'd be able to join his friends.

Not a word passed between the three boys as they walked the long distance into town. They were sweaty and hot when they reached Festin's Courthouse Square, and looked around. Nobody they knew well was in sight, and most of the stores were shut up. Through the saddler's window, though, they were seen by Peter Quendale. The young lawyer, who had been paying court to Terry's sister over the last few months, came rushing out and looked inquiringly at Terry.

"We got lost and want to go home," Terry said.

"I'll be glad to take you as soon as I can obtain Mr. Whitcomb's permission," the lawyer said, flushing for some reason to the roots of his blond hair. "And your friends, of course. Please wait for me."

He walked to the law office, and Terry turned to his friends. "He'll drop each of you off first and me last, so he can look like a hero to my sister and hold hands with her."

The other boys didn't make any comment; each of them was lost in thought. The trip didn't take any longer than expected. Just before Frank got out of the carriage, he tapped Kermit on the shoulder.

"I don't like what happens in some places any more than you do," Victor Jobelin's son told him firmly, strengthened in will now that he was so close to home. "But I still am no abolitionist. I don't care what I see, I don't care what you show me. I'm no abolitionist."

"I am," Kermit said for the first time, and watched Frank walk tiredly back to his house.

19

"This is no time to think about the abolition movement or anything else, man," Tom Holman shouted. "Enjoy yourself."

Abel and his wife and son were standing with the Holmans on a corner of Rampart Street in New Orleans and watching the annual February Mardi Gras parade. King Comus and King Rex were on their tinsel-shaped floats waving wooden wands, while men and women screamed themselves hoarse with manufactured pleasure. They were determined to enjoy themselves. The 1860 Mardi Gras parade was a memory-making machine, and infernally noisy as well.

Abel had taken his family to New Orleans, for the first time, to see this event. Nancy had been only mildly curious, but Kermit cared even less than that. The boy had been very restless for some time now and prone to tears.

200

A change of scene, as the Debenkers had been told, would do him more good than all the medicine in the world.

"It's noisy," Abel shouted.

"You bet it is."

"I didn't know there were so many people in the whole world."

"Well, there are," the whey-faced planter assured him. "Don't think about it."

The active Holman had insisted on running the Debenkers ragged, taking them to the picturesque French Quarter with its small houses and large stairways enclosed by colorfully shaped gratings, and then to the French Market on Decatur Street.

"Roo Roy-al," Kermit said, as their carriage passed along that street, trying to pronounce the name in a nasal style that he imagined was proper French.

"Nice work," Tom Holman said approvingly. "And if you're extra good today, your folks will let you see the slave-whipping post."

Kermit looked down sullenly, all his animation gone.

"No niggers are being whipped during Mardi Gras," Holman said, misunderstanding the boy's response. "Well, you might want to look at Bourbon Street instead."

Nancy seemed dubious. "That's an odd name."

"There isn't any whiskey flowing in the gutters, if that's what you mean," Holman laughed. He turned to Abel. "How do you like this city, Debenker?"

"There's a lot more Moorish architecture than I had expected," Abel said, "and a lot less breeze coming into the city off Lake Pontchartrain."

During the colorful parade two hours later, he raised his voice to ask Holman, "Are all these nigras free?"

"Not by any means, but a lot of them are. Hm! Let's see if the view is better from a different spot."

In the early evening, the Holmans and the Debenkers went to a ball being given by a banker friend of theirs. Mr. Quilty had hired a floor of an expensive hotel for the night and was making a point of enjoying himself. Holman disappeared after a few minutes, as usual, and when he came back his right hand was held stiffly at his side and there was a quizzical look on his face.

"I can hardly believe it myself, but I just shook hands with a Jew."

"Was he white?" Mrs. Holman asked, her interest caught. "I've never seen a Jew, but I understand that they're as black as pitch."

"This one was as white as I am myself and as well spoken and with as good manners," Holman marvelled. "He didn't have a beard and he wasn't wearing a skullcap. He wasn't counting money, either. He's not even a usurer, but a businessman here in the city."

Nancy interrupted, turning to Abel. "I think that I'd like to go back to the hotel, dear. I'm very tired."

"And I am, too," Mrs. Holman said cheerfily. She often became tired after trying to follow her energetic husband around.

"Of course, my dear," Holman murmured and looked down at the palm of the hand which had made contact with a Jew. "I'd like to wash my hands first, dear. I'm sure there isn't anything wrong, but it never hurts to be careful."

A carriage took both couples back to the hotel where they were staying, in a quiet neighborhood off Chartres Street. Tom Holman detained Abel.

"Let's have a drink together. It's a festive time after all."

"Of course," Abel agreed promptly, and told his wife, "I'll be up in awhile, dear. Keep your door locked."

"I always do," Nancy said with controlled bitterness. "Or nearly always."

Tom Holman waited until the women were out of earshot.

"Would you like to go to an event of great interest? It rarely happens, but when it does, it's of great interest."

"I suppose you'll look in for a second and then want to run off somewhere else."

"I won't run from the Quadroon Ball," Holman promised.

"Quadroons? People with an eighth Negro blood?"

"Yes, and it's an incredible evening. Are you game for it?"

"Certainly, if just to carry you home in case of need. There must be a considerable number of footpads roaming on a night like this."

Holman shrugged that off and led the way to a cab. The ride wasn't a long one, and their carriage came to a halt around the corner from a church. Several minutes afterwards, Abel Debenker nearly had a bad accident. He gripped Holman's sleeve to keep from falling as they walked into the ballroom. It was fortunate that Holman had slowed his pace, for once.

"Damn slipperiest floor I ever walked on," Abel muttered and looked down. His jaw dropped. "Why it's—it's *transparent*. You can see the ballroom below it."

"It's made of glass, reinforced," Holman chuckled. "Look around you."

People seemed to be enjoying themselves. Attractive women of all ages were strolling idly back and forth, fanning themselves after dancing. Their ballroom gowns were as colorful and well-made as a man was likely to see almost anywhere on earth, with billowing silk and varicolored plumes. There was a sweet cloying smell from spilled liqueurs.

"You must have a waltz with one of these dusky maidens," said Tom Holman. "Indeed, if you'll pardon me, I think I see someone I would like to dance with."

Left alone, Abel turned away and nearly bumped into a young woman walking away from the dance floor. Her skin was nearly as white as his own. She was wearing a pink silk gown with dark plumes, and ruffles at the wrists and throat. She was smiling generously.

"Is anything wrong?" she asked in a soft, warm voice.

"No, I—. Not at all." His own voice seemed higher than usual.

203

Eyes probed him, and he was aware of having been sized up and placed in some perspective. "Yes, I see. You're a white man who's never been to one of these affairs and has come to find a quadroon girl he can carouse with."

There was a rush of impatience in his attitude, but he said nothing.

"Yes, I understand the silence, too. You've never spoken to a girl with Negro blood who is able to form sentences. You probably feel as if a barbary ape had begun to talk."

Denials rushed to his lips, but honesty wouldn't let them be spoken.

"You're not the first and you won't be the last," the girl said, self-possessed. "Now if you'll pardon me—."

"No, I—. Look here, could we speak together? Isn't there someplace we could sit down and talk?"

"I hardly see the point to it." The girl smiled, not pleasantly. "You want to tell me that you've got some slaves, but that you treat them well, and they love you. Isn't that true?"

"No—. Well, I don't know what I want to tell you."

"And after that, you want to suggest that we go off to a private room and make love. I'm sure that's true, isn't it?"

A dark-skinned lad was carrying a tray of cordials. He paused, and a white man took one drink and drew out a palm and rubbed the top of the lad's head for good luck. Abel signalled for a drink. The lad waited, his head down to a point where it could be rubbed for good luck. Abel refrained. The lad looked disappointed. Abel submitted the lad to what would have seemed to him an indignity. The lad was grinning as he walked off.

The young woman said, "You didn't want to rub his head for good luck, but you did it because he expected you to. That shows a certain amount of human feeling."

"Thank you, I suppose."

"Oh now, you mustn't let yourself sound sullen because you've been complimented by a barbary ape."

204

"I demand that you never——. I wish that you wouldn't make fun of me, even if you don't want to talk at all."

"Oh, let's rest, then," the young woman said, bowing coolly. "All I ask in return, aside from good manners, is that I don't hear about your slaves."

"Agreed."

She led him past a series of rooms where men played cards, then over to the balcony. There was a view of the St. Louis cathedral with a trio of spires, and he must have looked from the spires to the young woman and back again. Had his face become red?

"Talking to a girl with Negro blood while you're in sight of a church," she started, "must be very uncomf——."

"Please!"

She smiled and led him along one side of the ballroom and down a staircase. There was a courtyard behind the building. Tables and chairs had been set in the shade of shrubs that looked like ivory hairbrushes. Couples sat and talked quietly.

"All you need to know about me is that my name is Fran," the young woman said coolly. "As for my position in life, I'll add that my parents have been free for several generations and that I hope to be married within two years."

"What sort of work does your family do?" Talk of business was safe ground for him, always.

"My father is putting up some of the financing behind the construction of a machine to bind sheaves of grain. He is currently on a trip to Oregon, now that it has become a state, and hopes to find new opportunities for investment."

"He ought to get involved with a newly established firm," Abel said. "Horsecars, perhaps, or Pullman and his trains for sleeping, or cross-country mail delivery. You may not know this, but it's possible to get mail across the country in less than a month."

"In twenty-five days, to be exact," Fran said drily.

"Money ought to be kept in an enterprise with a future." Was he really talking this way to a girl, let alone a

205

girl with Negro blood? "Almost anything is better than farming or growing cotton."

Fran made a mock, shivering motion.

"Growing cotton is difficult for the grower in lots of ways that somebody who isn't in it can't ever hope to understand," he said thoughtfully. "It gives a gentleman a certain coarseness that doesn't belong to a cultivated man. He puts small value on human life of any type. The Fugitive Slave Act is declared constitutional, and the cotton man is cheerful at this affirmation of property values. The Vicksburg Convention calls for the reopening of the slave trade from Africa, and part of the grower's mind says that it's necessary. John Brown talks about slavery as an evil and tries to correct it and he becomes a lunatic and a madman who would destroy property values and a strong economy. The grower changes in character and becomes casually cruel, which also seems necessary as part of the system."

Fran said sharply, "This is the most amazing foolishness I ever listened to in my life. Do you have the gall to ask me to be sorry for *you?*"

"Don't be sorry for anybody, Fran. Try to understand him, instead."

"I will not allow myself to feel even a speck of pity for a slaveholder."

"All I'm saying to you is that the system doesn't only hurt Negroes, which of course it does. I'm saying that the peculiar institution, slavery, hurts everybody who comes in contact with it, everybody who is close to it, black or white. The white man is a victim, too, and so is his family. He can be an owner, a dealer, a slavebreaker or an overseer; but he's a victim, too. You have to understand that if you ever hope to know anything about slavery or Blacks or whites or the world we live in."

"You're a fool if you think that one degree of hurt is the same as the other. You're wicked if you're trying to convince me while you know better yourself."

"I'm talking about the problems of day to day living under a system that will have to be changed."

206

"If you know that the system is bad, then get out of it. Sell your land and free your slaves."

"I can't do that until——."

Fran had turned her back and started to walk off.

"I can guess what you'd say if I told you," Abel called after her. "Exactly what my wife keeps saying, and it's completely impractical."

Fran spoke without turning to him. "I won't say anything more. Your reasons don't interest me. Or what you think are your reasons. They don't count. Only what you do is what counts, not what you say or what you feel."

She walked up the curved staircase and back to the ballroom. Abel plunged his hands deep into his suit pockets and waited until she was out of sight.

Morosely, he walked to the stairs. Couples were talking vivaciously as he moved toward them and parallel and away: a young man using his hands to drive a point home, a young girl making a sudden move and showing the top of an undergarment beneath a low-cut silk gown. At the age of thirty, he was thinking of other people as young, happy, carefree. His mental age was showing.

He held on to the stair rail with one hand, straightening himself at last when he reached the ballroom. There was no sign of Tom Holman among the swirling couples on the reinforced glass floor. He found the planter getting up from a gambling table, where he had probably played no more than two or three hands of poker. Judging by the man's pinched lips, he had lost to the *cafe au lait* gentleman who was riffling cards. Abel caught his attention. Gratefully, Tom Holman hurried over and dug Abel in the ribs.

"Did you have a good time with that gal? I saw you with her, Debenker. Don't you deny it."

"We talked."

"I bet she did a damn sight more for you than talk."

Abel wondered why he had ever considered Holman taciturn. "Honest Injun, Tom, all we did was talk."

Holman's lips widened in a grin. "Well, you keep saying

that, boy," the planter told him affably. "Don't let anybody change your story."

20

"Come on, Noah," said Amos in his soft slurred English.

Jethro called, "Win it, Zeke."

Other slaves were crowded around the two in the cabin that Amos shared, looking down at a strip of paper that covered part of the earthen floor. A pair of roaches had been set down at one end of the paper, and Jethro was rooting for the roach at the left to get to the other end of the paper before the roach at the right could manage it. He and Amos were now pitted against each other.

"I bet a hundred dollar that Noah win," Amos said. "I get the money."

"I bet a month's supply of whiskey that Zeke win," Jethro insisted. "I give it to you, you sell it."

Blossom, who had been watching, shouted, "Jethro, you fool!"

Jethro shrugged. "It's somethin' to do."

"Take the bet back, Jethro, and do it now."

"No. You always tell me what I should do, but not this time. What I want, I do."

"Then get somebody else to put up money against him for part of the payoff when you lose."

"I don't lose," Jethro insisted, his narrowed eyes snapping. "Go 'way, gal."

Elihu suddenly said, "That's right, we put up money against winnings. I put up two dollar. Blossom right."

"Two dollar is a big help," Jethro chortled.

It didn't take long before sixty dollars had been pledged to Jethro's side. An added forty was pledged to Amos, so that the loss wouldn't weigh heavily on either bettor. The

208

roaches were moving slowly. Jethro's candidate suddenly stopped.

"You stupid fucker," Jethro called, stretching out a hand toward the other end of the sheet of paper. "What do you think this is, a picnic? You get a move on, you lazy nigger!"

Sunshine, who had looked in briefly at what was happening, raised her voice in turn. "Why don't you get a whip, Jethro?"

The men were clustered around and looking down, many peering over other men's shoulders as they called and shouted for the roach they favored to win. Blossom, who usually didn't have any warm feelings for a child-loving woman like Sunshine, looked almost approvingly to one side.

"Men is awful."

Sunshine nodded. "Not good for much."

"Good for some things."

"Not now they no good," Sunshine said, as a groan came up from the men in the slave cabin. "They gamble, they drink now, so they no good."

"They be finished soon."

"No. One of the roaches wins, the boy who backed the other say he won't pay, there be a fight. The fight over, the boys drink together from the whiskey. Next morning they can't work, and the buckra whup 'em both 'till his arm ache. You know it, I know it."

"Yes."

"Now you can't even move Jethro," Sunshine pointed out and shrugged. "Amos has no steady gal. I go to my kids. Baby very troublesome."

She spoke with pride. Blossom snorted, wondering if the other woman really thought that nobody except the whites knew that the pickaninnies weren't really hers.

"You stupid fucker!" Amos' voice rose to a howl. "You roach, you stupid, stupid fucker!"

Jethro and some other boys were laughing. Blossom tried to get away from the sound. On this Sunday afternoon in February, she moved quickly. There was a nice warm smell in the air, but she hardly noticed it. She stopped when she saw the master coming out of the gin house and mounting a chestnut quarter horse that he had recently taken to riding. She coughed lightly to draw attention to herself and then cast her eyes down modestly.

Abel, who had been conducting his first inspection since bringing back his family from New Orleans, looked down at her.

"What do you want, Blossom?"

"I walk, masta."

"What made you attract my attention? You do nothing unless there's a reason."

"To see you smile at me, masta."

"Of course you did! You're secretly in love with the man who has life and death power over you, if he wants to use it."

Blossom hung her head, so that Abel didn't see that she was smiling. She had recognized that nervous tone of his, and turned her head very slightly so that she could look sideways in the direction of the disused sugar house.

"You're very sympathetic to my problems, of course, Blossom. You understand how much I contend with and what a difficult time I have. Of course, yes. You and—well, never mind that. Never mind any of it."

"Yes, masta. I can go now?"

"Do what you damn please!"

"Thank you, masta. I go to sugar house. I leave something there a few days ago, I get it now."

"Oh." A different tone in Abel's voice, now. Nancy and the boy had gone off to church, and he looked thoughtfully toward the sugar house. It didn't seem occupied. The sounds of shouting from the slave cabins made him jump.

"That's only the fight," Blossom explained helpfully. "The boys drink and they fight. You know, masta. Sunday, so they fight."

"I see." Reliable John Platter would attend to that. "I'll go with you to the sugar house, Blossom. Or rather, I'll

210

meet you there as soon as I put the horse back in the stable."

"Oh, yes, masta."

She hurried away, not looking directly at him. Abel saw to it that the horse was fed and watered, then walked toward the sugar house. Sounds of argument from the slave cabin had grown quieter, and he felt sure that John Platter had brought the nigras under control. He tried not to think about it as he walked, putting it out of his mind altogether.

The sugar house door was open. He walked in. There seemed no relief from the hot sun, and he spared a glance at the areas which had once been filled with expensive sugar-refining equipment. Originally the house had been put up to help Lyon Debenker make his fortune, but all he'd ever made in this house was a slave gal or two.

Blossom lay on the floor on top of her dress, a leg raised and ready for him. She was smiling in anticipation. Abel shucked his clothes quickly, ready for her.

"I don't have to talk to you, Blossom," he said softly. "I don't ever have to explain myself to you."

She smiled and spread her legs for him.

He looked down at the black short hair against dark skin and the soft reddish and almost banana-shaped area that had been opened for him. There was a sudden hunger inside his mouth, a thirst at the back of his tongue. He flicked the tongue in and out, in and out. At that moment he knew very well what he wanted to do. Blossom must have known it, too. She took a deep breath, settled back to show her breasts to better advantage and then raised her head and put her hands back of it so that she'd be able to see her master doing what his lusts or his conscience demanded.

Abel shook his head abruptly and lay down so that they were facing each other. He nuzzled her breasts, and they grew larger under his experienced hands. He smiled, ready to enter her, the previous moment's desired degradation now hopefully forgotten.

Blossom drew out a hand from behind her head and put it on the top of his shoulder and applied light pressure.

211

The sudden raging thirst returned to the back of his tongue, and he shook his head fiercely at himself. Her pressure against him became a little more firm. He lowered himself slightly, but stayed in place, licking her stomach just above the navel. She raised herself briefly then, so that the navel was closer to his tongue, then put her hand at the back of his neck and put mild pressure on it to force his head against her and then away, and against her and away. He didn't oppose her will any longer, but lowered himself quickly, kissing her body in a straight downward line. There was a soft chortle far above him as he drew out his tongue and began worshipping his slave.

21

"Welcome," said Barton Manders, a smile wreathing his usually sad face. "This is a great day for me, and you-all honor me by your presence."

Abel said something appropriate. Nancy curtseyed. Kermit only looked uncomfortable, like any seven year old in a suit.

The Manders' home had been decorated for this occasion, mostly with scentless azaleas that seemed to line their way. Nancy was giving Kermit several last minute instructions about behavior as they walked down the sunlit hall with its gleaming polished floors and shiny double windows.

Abel whispered to his wife, "I hope you behave, too, dear, and I don't have to carry you out a section at a time."

"Yes, oh my lord and master," Nancy murmured, drawing a hand up swiftly to her red hair. "Your vassal hears and she obeys."

The large dining room had been banked with proud magnolias along the sides, and dozens of chairs with an aisle forming two rows. A flower-lined altar had been put up at the far end of the room, a piano hauled in so that it was set underneath one window, and November sunlight could illuminate the music sheets on the gleaming metallic rack. The Reverend Mr. MacCubbin, his fair face lightened further by a smile, was talking to Jarvis Whitcomb. The lawyer caught sight of Abel, excused himself, and came over to shake hands.

Abel said, "I understand that you're a high functionary at this affair."

"Best man," the lawyer agreed, throwing his chest back. "After all, Peter has no close friends in town and he's got a good eye towards advancement in the law business."

"Let's hope that the marriage works out."

"It ought to. Clare is a big talker, and Peter hardly opens his mouth except to point out where a case has been won or lost, in his opinion."

Nancy said ruefully, "And he's not a slaveholder, either. That's a great help."

Whitcomb sensed that he was in the presence of husband-wife antagonism, and diverted the subject. "There probably won't be any slave owners for long if Abraham Lincoln has his way."

"Do you really think so?" Nancy, the fool, sounded hopeful.

"I don't believe that," Abel said sharply. "The Crittenden Compromise will carry the issue, in my opinion, and slave states won't be molested if they stay in the Union and no other slave states are admitted."

"Perhaps," Whitcomb said carefully. "I understand you've hired a new overseer."

"A good one, I think." He had to fire dour John Platter, who wanted to send Jethro to the slavebreaker after insubordination that had been witnessed by other slaves after a fight between Jethro and Amos. He hired an experienced man, Dolph Morin, a straggly-mustached fellow who could probably follow orders, but who sometimes had a need to make matters clearer than necessary.

"No corporal punishment is to be applied without my approval," Abel had told the man. "Is that clear?"

213

"Yes, sir." And Morin had repeated, "No corporal punishment is to be applied without your approval."

It was a small irritation, though, and Abel felt pretty sure that Morin would work out well. . . .

Whitcomb suddenly looked up. "I think I may be wanted by my principal in this matter, Abel. We can talk afterwards, at the banquet."

But Abel gripped the old lawyer's sleeve. "Do you really think that Lincoln wants to destroy our means of livelihood overnight?"

"Remember what he said to little Douglass during one of their debates? 'A house divided against itself cannot stand.' " The lawyer forced a smile to his face. "It's best not to think about this, for today at least."

He hurried back toward the double doors, where a young man had gestured to him. Abel looked away, rather than meet his wife's probing eyes.

"Where's Kermit?" he asked irritably.

"Giving encouragement to Terry Manders, I suppose," Nancy told him absently. "Terry is to hold up the bride's train and he doesn't seem to think that life is worth living any more."

"No, I suppose he doesn't." Abel walked off to shake hands with Giraud Duval and then with Charles Passy and with Victor Jobelin. He smiled at the men and made courteous talk to the Passy and Jobelin families. Chad Goldthwait and his Lorna hurried through the door, Chad taking off a knitted scarf that he'd probably was wearing at his wife's insistence in order to protect his throat.

"Looks like the whole community has been invited," he said, giving the scarf angrily to his wife and watching her call one of the house servants over to her. "Except for that damn Serena Pollard."

Mrs. Jobelin said, "She wouldn't be welcome in decent society."

"No, you'd have to invite that buck nigger of hers, too, as a couple." Goldthwait made an ugly face. "I never heard of anything so disgusting."

214

Lorna Goldthwait muttered, "Don't let yourself get too excited, Chad. You know that it isn't good for you."

"My dear, I wonder if you'd be so kind as to fetch me a drink," Goldthwait said formally. "Wine, if you think that would be better for me."

He looked at his wife as she scuttled away, then asked the other planters, "Well, how do you men feel about the election? Are we to stay in the United States or not?"

"Lincoln hasn't taken office yet," Charles Passy pointed out, cradling his wine glass. "In politics, a man often says one thing in order to win and then turns around and does something entirely different."

Giraud Duval wandered away and over towards the porch, where a group of Blacks were waiting quietly to see the wedding. They had obviously been granted permission.

"Abe Lincoln will be President of all the slave owners, too," Jobelin pointed out. "If this country is a democracy, he must appreciate that."

"I don't think that even a hysterical gibbon ape like Lincoln wants to destroy American business," Goldthwait snapped. "He'd have to be a fanatic."

"Personally, I hope that Lincoln can, indeed, get rid of slavery," Abel said sincerely. "But I'd hate for him to do it so quickly that the change becomes impossibly difficult for everybody."

Tom Holman, entering with his wife and two sons, hurried over to join the group and put in, "For my part, if it's a war that Lincoln wants, he'll get one."

"It hasn't come to that yet," Abel pointed out swiftly.

"It will. Frankly, I'm getting ready for it and I think that you should all do the same. And the younger ones among you should expect to enlist."

The Reverend Mr. MacCubbin, who had overheard the last remark, approached them. His hands were raised to cut off further discussion, though.

"Please find your seats, gentlemen. We're almost ready to begin."

Abel saw the ever-active Holman move around and re-

215

peat the message, settling others in hard chairs. The church organist sat down at the piano, her back rigid with pride. Her best dress, which happened to be black, rustled on her thin body, and she was suddenly doing her best to hold off a sneeze.

Giraud Duval, on the porch with the Blacks, was saying, "But you're going to sing afterwards, aren't you? All I'm telling you to do is to sing 'Old Black Joe.' It's a beautiful song."

"Suh," one of the slaves said apologetically, "we never hear it."

"Are you impudent enough to say that you've never heard 'Old Black Joe'?" Duval planted both hands on hips and looked outraged. "What kind of fools are you? It's a nigger song. Everybody knows it."

"Sorry, suh."

Duval threw his head back and sang in a light tenor that "he was coming" and that "his head was bending low" and that "he heard the angel voices calling, Old Black Joe." Then he threw his head forward again.

"*Now* do you know it?"

"I sorry, suh."

"You *still* don't know it? Why, I never heard of such dunderheads." And he turned, weight on his right hip, to Barton Manders coming up urgently back of him. "Barton, you've got the only niggers in the whole world who don't know any spirituals."

Abel, in spite of his worries, had to put up a hand over his lips to keep from laughing. It was an incident that he and Nancy would have talked about for a long time afterwards, and even made the last few words into a catchphrase between them; but he and Nancy hadn't been on such terms since they had left England almost seven years ago.

The pianist finally pulled out a black handkerchief and sneezed into it. One of the youngsters applauded mockingly and then was quieted. At the rear, a door was opened and closed very quickly, indeed. The pianist began to play "O Promise Me."

Again the door at the rear was opened quickly. It remained open. There was a pause. An usher and a bridesmaid appeared, walking solemnly down the impromptu aisle. Three more pairs walked down the aisle and fanned out before the dais. The groom and best man entered. For once, there was a line of sweat on Peter Quendale's brow. His pace didn't seem steady. There was a flush on his cheeks.

"Been drinking," Abel whispered to Nancy.

"Yes," Nancy agreed, and added, "*She's* the one who ought to have been drinking."

The matron of honor, Mrs. Manders, entered shortly afterwards. Baron Manders, his daughter's hand on his, walked more slowly than any of the others. The brides face was veiled, and her white silk must have set Barton back a small fortune. Terry, behind the bride and holding her train to keep it off the floor, certainly looked as if he wished he were dead.

The Reverend Mr. MacCubbin waited until the couple was facing him and then spoke with a carrying quietness. "We are here to unite you, Peter, and you, Clare, in the bonds of matrimony in the sight of God Almighty. About marriage itself, there isn't too much advice to be given. The key to a successful marriage is mutual respect. Marriage can be difficult and wonderful, blessed and accursed, and every marriage is all of those things at different times. To enter into matrimony is to signify to the world that you wish to be part of a relationship that cannot end happily, and is in that sense a sign and symbol of maturity. Is a good marriage worth all the work and difficulty? Yes, it is. You need have no reservations about that."

He paused and added, "We are living in difficult times, perhaps in times of unique difficulties."

There was more to his speech about what he foresaw as hard times for a seceding South, and then the ceremony was completed with the ritual words. Quendale lifted the bride's veil and kissed her. They walked up the aisle, the bride leaning over to whisper shyly to her groom.

After a pause, the party went out to the lawn, where

217

they were served hot chicken or cold, succulent roast beef with corn bread, peas, beets, green beans, carrots, spinach, coffee, and cake with cream icing on it. The Blacks sang well, and were applauded generously. Every white man and woman seemed contented, and it had suddenly become clear that they would all be happy, healthy, wealthy, and wise forever and ever.

Book Three (1865)

1

"We're in a damned difficult situation," Abel reminded the men in Chad Goldthwait's study during the Thursday evening so-called "sociable" in late April of '65. "It's not impossible, though."

"You could have fooled me," Tom Holman said, looking down bitterly at the stump of his left leg lost in the Confederate cause. The whey-faced planter would have been walking around the small study in a churn of movement, otherwise. "The South has had the daylights beaten out of it, and now Lincoln is gone, and we're about to lose everything."

Chad Goldthwait, drinking cheap whiskey that he wouldn't have tolerated in his home before the war, said morosely, "Vic Jobelin and that nancy-boy, Duval, may have been smart to run out and leave their land behind. Who knows?"

"I don't think they were smart." Abel leaned forward, his only white jacket that remained in good condition nearly taking a dollop of whiskey from Charles Passy's filled glass. "I think we can beat this if we work at it."

"I know you aren't a fool," Manders put in, his usual depression almost unnoticeable in the room, "but we've all been plagued by runaways and we've borrowed heavily to see us through the next crop. At three percent—with our lands mortgaged to the hilt at a rate of thirty-five dollars the arable acre—damn it, we've *lost*, and we have to take all the consequences."

"We've got one advantage, though," Abel reminded him and the others, "with the absence of Beast Butler and his Federals in this vicinity."

"We paid enough for the privilege, though not directly to Butler," Manders agreed. "Another notion of yours, as I remember."

Tom Holman was straightening in his chair, a hand around both crutches. "What advantage do you see in that, Abel, aside from the obvious one? There's nobody to work our crops."

There are people to work my crops," Abel said quietly. "I still have fifty-three nigras, of whom twenty-three are prime field hands."

"You'll need to pay them to work your lands," Goldthwait pointed out, both hands on his ample stomach. "You happen to get on well with your niggers so that they might agree to work for you, but you haven't got the money to pay unless you take it out of savings—and you'd be the fool of the world to do that."

"I can't afford to pay them until I've got money for the next crop."

"They won't agree to that. Hang it, Abel, niggers have got no sense of the future. I'd guess you have to pay a free nigger every day, like Rafe Carstairs used to do with his boy until six months or so had gone past."

"In this case, my nigras aren't making the agreement," Abel said quietly, "I've decided to do that for them."

"Dammit!" Chad Goldthwait rapped the top of his desk with chubby knuckles. "What in tarnation are you talkin' about? If you've got an idea to get us all out of this mess, I want to hear what it is."

There was a light knock on the door. It opened on Peter Quendale. The young lawyer, who had taken over Jarvis Whitcomb's practice after Whitcomb's death, smiled tautly as he looked around the room.

Barton Manders, his father-in-law, looked up and asked worriedly, "Clare isn't sick, is she?"

"No, she's fine." Clare Manders Quendale was expecting her third child. "Won't be long now before now before you've got another grandchild."

"You'll have to feed the new one legal papers 'cause there won't be anything else around," Barton Manders grumped.

Abel said quickly, "I hope you'll all hear me out before

220

deciding that we're doomed. This can be licked, but it needs cooperation from everybody in the room."

Quendale looked up alertly. "If it's not legal, whatever it is, I shouldn't know about it."

"It's not legal, but you had better know," Abel said grimly. "We have a lot of work to do in the way of threshing out details. What I plan to do—and what I want you all to do—is to go on exactly as if the war was still being fought."

Chad Goldthwait blinked repeatedly. "Have you taken leave of your senses, sir?"

"Not at all. I suggest that we make contact with the editor of the *Festin Chronicle,* sparse as it is, and firmly suggest that the paper not publish anything to do with the end of the war. Further, I suggest that anyone in this area who doesn't own nigras be firmly warned against advising any Blacks about what has happened."

Chad Goldthwait said, "Somebody has to talk to Ben Pollard's widow. She hasn't got any free niggers on her grounds—I had to get rid of the one that you gave her, Abel—but she's likely to be sympathetic."

Holman said, "There's a cousin of hers from ole Mississip' who's staying with her now. Talk to him, and it'll be all right, I'm sure." He added, "I'll talk to her. She'll sympathize with me for having lost a leg."

"If you have any trouble, let us know," Goldthwait rumbled.

Abel said cuttingly, "You're such a diplomat that you can probably arrange it and get into Serena Pollard's good graces as well."

"I don't want to get into anything of hers," Goldthwait snapped. "Nigger-lover is what that woman is!"

Abel said, "We have to talk to the free Blacks, too."

"I'll get to that nigger preacher, Clack," Charles Passy promised with the confidence of the wealthy. "Rafe Carstairs has got a free nigger working for him, and I don't know what can be done there."

"He'll be paid off as long as we let Carstairs stay in

221

business," Chad Goldthwait pointed out. "Besides, we need Carstairs to frighten the niggers."

"I don't like that idea," Holman said, "but I guess it's necessary."

Goldthwait added, "I think we might get Elkahan Melville to pretend there's a slave auction in town and actually put one on. The niggers ought to be convinced by that."

"Good idea," Passy said.

Abel put in, "One more thing. It's necessary to start a new set of books, and to enter in it each slave's name and a set amount of earnings per working day—I believe that one dollar is fair. Against that, you have to enter every expense that a slave incurs and to deduct those expenses from the earned income. As soon as the crop is sold, you settle up with your slaves and let as many of them stay and work for you as want to."

"That's what *you'll* probably do," Chad Goldthwait remarked. "It'll cost you thousands of dollars."

"What else can anybody do if he's got any decent feelings?"

"My feelings are decent enough," Goldthwait drawled, "but there's a line between decency and suicide, and I'll draw that line. No doubt you'll pardon me."

Abel looked startled and angry. "If I'd known anybody would try to cheat those nigras out of their hard-earned money—."

"You'd have come up with exactly the same idea," Manders snapped. "We're all in this together, Abel, and none of us can afford to forget it. Personally, I have no real hope for this notion of yours, but I'll do my best to go along with it."

Abel looked around the room. "Is anybody else going to cheat those nigras out of perhaps the only stake they'll ever have?"

"I'll pay 'em for next season's work," Charles Passy said mildly, "if this crop is brought in satisfactorily."

Tom Holman shrugged. "I'll do the best I can for my family."

222

"Likewise," Barton Manders said. "Who can be sure that Andy Johnson won't put us all in jail, and my wife will need whatever money she can get her hands on? Who can be sure about that, hey?"

Quendale, who didn't own any land, was silent.

"So everything is arranged," Abel said, "with one exception. Some of you are going to need more money than you expect."

"What does that mean?" Goldthwait was pugnacious.

"I've been putting off the sale of my land, but I've just decided that the next crop due in will be the time to make the deal," Abel said. "All my property will be up for sale in January."

"Sorry to hear that," Charles Passy rumbled. "You've been a conscientious neighbor. Bright, too."

Barton Manders said, "The current prices for arable land are no more than thirty-five dollars the acre. Now you've got about four hundred and fifty acres, so that would amount to—let's see—."

"Four hundred acres, and you've got the price wrong."

"Thirty-five an acre is the latest valuation from the First New Orleans Bank and Trust."

"I want fifty-five the acre and I won't sell for less," Abel snapped. "Land will bounce back in value, as I'm sure we all know. You'll learn the uses of crop rotation, and fifty-five is a bargain. You know it, and so do I."

"With all our additional expenses," Holman said carefully, "I don't see how any of us could manage to buy from you at fifty-five the acre."

"Try." Abel looked down at his former friend sadly. "We've had some pleasant times together, but when everything is said and done you're only a plantation owner. I'm sorry about that, Tom."

Goldthwait put in heavily, "Your suggested price will be considered, Debenker, but you can't ask for more."

"I can ask for agreement. In this situation, I can demand it."

"There's a vulgar word for what you're doing, Debenker."

"No, I'm offering a bargain, and you all know it."

Charles Passy said, "Very well, then. I don't know just how we'll manage to get the money together in these circumstances, but we'll do the best we can."

"Good." Abel, surging to his feet, turned to Quendale. "You'll represent me?"

"Of course, if you like. I'll have the papers drawn up in a few days."

"Very well." He turned back to the others. "I know I'm not likely to be as welcome at your social Thursdays as in the past, Chad, but I think I ought to continue coming to see you. There are plans to be made, and we have to consult each other on progress in getting the crop out."

"Agreed," Goldthwait nodded.

Abel bowed from the waist, mocking a southern tradition of gentlemanly behavior. "And now, if you'll be kind enough to excuse me, I think I'll get home to a little decent society."

2

Abel left his carriage in the lantern-lit stable, after seeing to it that the horse had been fed out of a patched-up old nosebag. There was a nick on the lip of the water bucket that might very well give a horse a splinter or two, but no other was in sight. The stable smelled of warm wood instead of straw, he noticed, almost the way the gin house did.

He let himself inside the mansion a few minutes later without having to worry about chickens that might be scampering around in front of the house; he hadn't given that a thought since a few months after the beginning of the war. The foyer and living room, into which he could look, needed repainting and some new furniture.

Hester came towards him as soon as he appeared, her face showing concern.

"Anything you want from Hester?"

"No, thanks. Get a night's sleep."

Tiredly, he walked upstairs. The door of Nancy's boudoir opened, and his wife peered out anxiously. She straightened up when she saw him. He couldn't help smiling.

"Can I come in?"

"Of course, if you like." The door was held wide open for him. His wife was wearing a robe with silken slashes at the throat, one that he'd bought for her just two months before the insurrection began. Now the silk slashes seemed frayed, and there was a triangle-shaped rip against one thigh.

He sat down tiredly on a chair in front of the miniature model piano, which hadn't played since he-didn't-remember-when. Some of the chintz upholstery were starting to show dark green flecks. There was a stain shaped like a comma against the top drawer of Nancy's writing desk. It seemed impossible that two persons with their savings would be living so badly, even in wartime.

In a low voice she asked, "Was the meeting a pleasant one?"

"It was productive." He was about to fold both hands in his lap, but that was the gesture he remembered seeing Chad Goldthwait make just before turning unpleasant. "Nancy, you're certain to be very angry when I'm finished talking, but I hope you'll control yourself."

"I'll try."

He nodded, gratified.

"There isn't anything more to be angry about, as far as I can see." Was she smiling at a time like this? "The war is over and the slave system is finished. You can't be part of that for even another day."

"I can be. I will be. I am."

"Tell me what you mean."

"All the planters have decided to guard their investments in the next crop by carrying on as if the war was still being fought. That means continuing slavery until the crop is in."

225

"But you can't—you can't do that."

"We have to."

"How can you let yourself be a part of it?"

"My investment in this crop is too big to jeopardize. I've got twenty-five thousand and some odd dollars committed to the next crop, what with loan rates being as high as they are. I don't want us to lose as much money as that."

"We have savings."

"Agreed, but the loss would be substantial."

"Abel, you can't do this!"

"It's not as bad as it sounds, believe me. I'm keeping accounts of slave expenses and putting each one on a salary of a dollar a day. As soon as the crop is in, I'll settle up with them, and they'll have a stake for themselves. From now on, the nigras are on salary."

"But they don't know that!"

"I can't—I won't—take the time from getting a crop ready for market to carry out a major readjustment. I simply can't spare the time or the energy and no one else can, either."

Nancy turned away from him.

"There's something else," he began.

"Whatever it is, I don't want to hear it. You're not welcome in my boudoir, Abel."

"I plan to stay here until I finish speaking, and you're going to hear every word."

"It's not necessary. You want me to shut Kermit's mouth about whatever he may know of the war's end. I'll do that. I have to. Time and again you've discreetly pointed out that I'm helpless without you, and I accept the truth of that. So you can leave now."

"There's something else. I've definitely put up Fairlawn for sale."

"I don't believe that. You'll tell me anything to make sure I'm quiet until the next crop is on its way to New Orleans or Natchez or hell, for that matter. Don't think I've forgotten your having 'tried to sell' the land before this, and not really wanting to sell it."

226

"I've definitely arranged for the sale to take place to a group of the other planters."

Nancy faced him again, wordless.

"I I plan that in January of '65, we're going to take a trip to New York overland, and go from there to Southampton to settle in England."

"Abel, is this really true?"

"Tomorrow I'll be sending away for the tickets."

She shrugged irritably. Presented with that last promise, she had become skeptical again. "And no doubt you'll show them as proof to win my agreement to everything you're doing. Then, as soon as the crop had been paid for, you'll shred the tickets and say that we can't afford to leave just yet for some reason or other."

"We can afford to, Nancy, and that's exactly what we'll be doing in January. You've got my promise on that, my sacred word."

She stood with feet apart, hands behind her back, her body tilted inquiringly to the left. "Why should I believe you this time after the things that have happened?"

"Because I ask you to believe me."

"That's not enough reason."

He shook his head hopelessly rather than talk to her about friends with no decency, good-mannered liars, cheats who were splendid hosts, southern gentlemen who were bent on destroying persons of a different skin color, easygoing tyrants.

"It's time to move on, Nancy, to settle in England. If you don't believe how strongly I feel about it, then suspend judgment until you see for yourself."

"I'm not sure I can do that."

"You have to, or it will be very difficult for us together. And for the boy, too. You understand?"

"For Kermit's sake, I must agree." She threw her shoulders back. "And now I suppose you want to come into my bed."

"I'd like to very much, Nancy, but you wouldn't enjoy my company. I wouldn't want to displease you in such a matter."

"You've always been a considerate man, Abel, even a decent man, except when it comes to——." Her hands were in midair, drawing shapes without substance. "This."

"Except when it comes to earning a living, so that my family will be able to exist in comfort and my son after me won't have to worry about where the next pennies are coming from. Is that an indecency?"

She shuddered and then gave an icy smile he knew only too well. "Very well. My lord and master scorns me in his bed tonight, and I bow to his edict."

The sarcasm would keep her from thinking, from a direct response to pleas and questions, from giving any sympathy. She could then accuse him (without actually saying it) of showing no human feelings.

"I hope we understand each other," he said.

"Yes." This time the smile wasn't for him. "Perhaps, Abel, that is our difficulty."

3

"I can't tell you," Kermit said to his friend.

The two boys were sitting in the Bermuda grass and watching a steamboat move forward at a stately pace along the muddy river water. Kermit would never remember in later life that the river water had been anything but mirror-clean.

"I can guess the thing you can't tell me," Obie said, looking wise. At eight years old to Kermit's seven, he often pretended that he knew things that the white lad was only just discovering. "It ain't hard to guess."

"About the fighting?" Kermit pursued.

"Sure I know. Honest Injun!"

"Well, then, you could be gone away from here."

"I know," Obie nodded. "But what for I do that?"

"You can if you want to."

"Sure, but then I have to go to the fightin'."

228

"The fighting?"

"Sure. They want niggers to help in the fightin'. What for I do that? Why I get killed?"

"But, Obie—."

"Not me. Obie stay home, and let the soldiers fight and get killed. That's what Obie do."

"Obie, I'm not supposed to tell this to anybody, not a living soul, but—."

"No, I get caught by the North, and that's very bad for Obie. Or I get caught by them northern niggers and I lose my hide. Not Obie, uh-uh."

Kermit cleared his throat.

Obie suddenly looked up at the sky. "Oh-oh. Ole sun come out. That means Obie go back or he get his ass whupped."

"But Obie, you don't have to ever—."

It was too late. Obie was running back to the slave quarters.

At a pause in the field work, Sunshine asked the lad, "What does Masta Kermit say?"

"He can't tell me the fighting bad," Obie conjectured. "I could go to fight, but don't want to."

"That's good, boy. Let the whites do the killing and get killed, too." Sunshine started to fuss with the stinking apron that she wore, then shook her head and left it on her body. "The war go on and on. It never stop."

Blossom, sitting down tiredly on a tree stump, looked across at Sunshine and the lad. "You crazy, Sunshine. The war finished, the South is lose. I say it to Jethro, but he scared to think of that."

Sunshine asked levelly, "How you be sure?"

"I sure."

"That not good enough. Blossom sure, so the war is finish."

"More than that." Blossom's dark eyes eyes darted back and forth as if she was looking for proof. "You see boats with wheels. You see no gray men in them boats. You see blue men. Blue is what they wear up North."

Obie looked thoughtful, but didn't interrupt his elders.

"Is that all? Maybe you see blue men, but nobody else see them."

"Nobody else tell," Blossom insisted. "And more; Jethro asks masta to let us grow cotton, and masta not do that. Why not? Why he don't want us to?"

"Maybe he think we steal some of his cotton and try to sell it like it's ours."

"Maybe he not want poor niggers to have anything good. Maybe he know it not matter, and we free."

Sunshine said acidly, "You sure do convince yourself, gal."

Blossom nodded firmly, not having caught the other woman's tone or listened to the last words. "Maybe now things happen, when one person be convinced."

She suddenly turned to her left, startled. Lucas Tinsley, the overseer, was walking among the slaves, his whip poised.

"Back to work, all of you," the overseer shouted, scowling, "or you get a taste of this. Back to work, I say! Do it now."

Blossom found Jethro sitting dully in front of his cabin on the ground, legs outstretched. There was a glazed look in his eyes.

"You talk to masta one more time," she said firmly at the start. "Not 'bout cotton, now. You tell him you know we free. You tell him we know the war over and the South lose. You hear what he says."

Jethro glanced up indifferently at her. "He have me whupped, that what he do."

"Masta don't like to have his niggers whupped 'cause then they don't work." Blossom chuckled. "Now you get busy right away and talk to him."

Jethro sighed. He didn't know just the right way to argue with Blossom. The two of them had been together for a long while now. Blossom ought to have been getting long in the tooth, but she was still good-looking and she certainly knew what to do when she was under a boy. All

230

the same, he wished for awhile that he could be with somebody else.

Slowly he got to his feet. "All right, I try find masta. We see what happen."

Blossom looked after him as he started along the row of slave cabins, hoping that the master would be on the grounds as he sometimes was. He was moving more quickly than usual, which was disturbing.

She knew very well that her man didn't usually agree so quickly to doing what she wanted. As a rule, she had to keep pestering him for awhile before he gave in. Not this time. It was hard not to wonder about that. She was looking at him under the moonlight when she saw his broad back suddenly disappear between two cabins. She cocked her head, listening for words. Nothing. She got up and walked over slowly and looked inside one of the cabins. Empty. She looked inside the other one.

At the far end of it, Jethro was with a gal. He was on top of her and they were grinding into each other. The gal's hands were around Jethro's back, dropping along the edge of his spine. Jethro's face was almost buried in one of the gal's heavy titties. Blossom peered into the cabin for a moment. The gal was Neva, and she hadn't been here before the last crop. A newcomer, a young gal who would take her Jethro away if nothing was done about it.

Blossom acted swiftly. With her hands she pulled out one tent pole of the cabin, sending part of the canvas down to the earth at her feet. She rushed to the next pole and wrenched that one out of the earth as well. From under the canvas she heard a squall of protests in Jethro's deep voice and Neva's high one.

"Now you fuckers," Blossom called, running onto the canvas to where she could see the bulge caused by two bodies. "You go ahead and fuck—nobody stop you!"

And she raised her bare right foot and kicked the body that was trying to raise itself.

"Blossom," Jethro called out, "you keep us here and we die."

"You want to fuck, then fuck," Blossom called back,

231

and she raised herself to stand on the bulge that was thrashing underneath her. "You can get deep into her, now. You fuckers!"

Jethro suddenly raised himself, throwing Blossom briefly off balance. She sobbed and righted herself, fists ready. Jethro worked his way out of the canvas at last, Neva at his side and looking angry as well as frightened.

Jethro said, "You leave Neva alone or I fix you."

"You fix nobody." Blossom drew a deep breath. "All right, I leave her alone, and you talk to masta, like I tell you."

Jethro nodded slowly. "I talk to masta."

Abel was in a reflective mood as he rode the grounds next afternoon. He was approaching the timberlands, which showed stumps and nothing more. Wood had been shipped to the southern forces at the price of one dollar seventy the cord. Other planters, not going to war themselves, had followed Abel's lead in the matter. It had been an act of patriotism, lengthening a useless war so that more young men could die.

It occurred to him as he rode that there was a business opportunity around here. Some smart dealer could set himself up very nicely on a land strip between two plantations and build a two story frame house or use logs from old flat-boats, if that was necessary, to save money. At that location he could establish a store and sell to free Negroes. Business would only be done for cash, of course, and it wouldn't surprise him if a store like that could take in some seventy-five dollars a day. The money would have to pay back initial loans for inventory at the current rate of three percent per month. After the first few months, though, the store would be on its own feet.

The inventory would be cheap, of course, for the Negro trade. Denims and calicoes and cottonades, hats and shoes, and multi-colored head handkerchiefs, tobacco for the men and brass jewelry for the women. Along with that, the storekeeper could stock foods that didn't need preparing, such as cheeses and sardines and candy. Whis-

232

key, too, if the dealer was smart. Water it down by a fourth and give it sting by using pods or red pepper. The prices could be kept reasonable, and the profits remain high.

In a store like that, a man could put his wife and family to work, and maybe hire one black couple to do any extra work. He'd be able to retire in only a few years. If Abel was going to keep the land, he would have tried to interest some northern migrant in taking on the business. He'd build the house, or have it built, and try to offer other help as well. Assuming an eighty-percent profit in day-to-day operations, Abel could certainly take eight percent of that eighty for himself.

Well, it wouldn't happen. He was going to turn his back on the southern United States and go to England with Nancy and their son. His mind was made up, and he knew it wouldn't be changed.

He was aware of a black man running towards him as he turned away from the tree stumps. It was Jethro, and Abel Debenker found himself looking at his own facial features covered by black skin. He tried never to think of Jethro as his half-brother. Jethro stopped and drew his breath in and out, then looked down and waited for the master to speak.

"What is it this time, Jethro?" Best to remind him indirectly about the favor that had been done for him. "Is there any trouble about the whiskey?"

"No, masta, all good. Masta, I hope you tell me—tell me how is the fight."

"The war?" Abel's voice was quieter, now. "It's still going on."

"Not over?"

"No, of course not. The South will fight on until the war is over, and we've won it."

"Do we win?"

"Yes."

"If the war over, and I a free man," Jethro said swiftly after a moment's thought, "I want to work for masta."

233

Abel drew back and actually put up a hand in front of his face as if to ward off evil.

"You a good masta, a kind masta. All the niggers want work for you."

"Thank you, Jethro, I'll remember that." He swallowed air and dust. "Is there anything else you want to tell me?"

"No, masta, nothing more. This nigger had best get back to the fields."

And Jethro ran lightly in the direction of the cotton fields.

Abel watched him briefly and then rode onwards. His face was a deep red under the white hat. After he had stabled the horse and changed his clothes, he went into his office and settled down behind the desk. He knew he could lie well and make deals that brought in a substantial profit even in these bad days, but he couldn't keep Abel Debenker from suddenly hating himself.

4

Mr. Collins, the publisher and editor of the *Festin Chronicle,* was a droopy-mustached man in his fifties. He sat on the desk in his office and looked across at Chad Goldthwait, who stood facing him with arms akimbo. Barton Manders, his lips drooping at the corners, stood at Goldthwait's side.

"You want me to write nothing about the settlement of the war? Nothing at all?"

"That's what I tell you."

Collins looked down sadly at his desk, where he had been working at pencilled notes for a news account of the capture of Jefferson Davis.

"Gentlemen, this is perhaps the saddest day of my life," he said. He tore up the sheet of notes, and his eyes rested on another sheet with notes about a riot between freed Negroes and Union soldiers in Natchez. The Union men

234

had become drunkenly angry and shouted that they'd been forced to fight and many of them to die or be maimed only for what a soldier had called "stupid animal niggers". The news account was certainly likely to prove what ungentlemanly people the Yankees were.

"You've only run four pages an issue since '63, as I recall it," Goldthwait told him. "You can stick to the local news, if you've got enough space for that."

"If you gentlemen insist, then I don't seem to have any choice."

"That's very sensible," Chad Goldthwait nodded. "Your cooperation will be appreciated and rewarded by your advertisers, Mr. Collins."

Collins looked down at his ungainly body. "If I was a younger man I'd tell you both to go to hell."

But he said the words softly, and his visitors were on the way out at the time.

Chad Goldthwait, leading the way to the church, said, "That's the way to handle this matter."

"He may not go along with us," Barton Manders remarked.

"If he doesn't, we'll hang him," Goldthwait said. "Him and anybody else who won't do what we tell 'em. You don't think we're going to let these fools ruin our crops now, do you?"

"You ask me to refrain from mention of the war news so that you can impose slavery for a longer time?" The Reverend Mr. MacCubbin's fair face lengthened in dismay. "How can you make such a suggestion to a man of God?"

"God is practical." The day's efforts had brought cube-shaped sweat drops to Chad Goldthwait's long upper lip and thin forehead, and his heavy body moved angrily in constricting clothes. "This is a matter of business and nothing more."

"But then you'll want to do the same for the next crop and the one after that and so on."

Barton Manders put in briskly, "We're not fools, Rever-

235

end. We know perfectly well that the Federal government would never let us do anything like this again. It's our only real chance to get out a crop this year, when the South is broken in its bones, and we need the resources desperately."

"It's an obscenity."

Manders ran thumb and forefinger across his luxuriant mustaches and said, "I didn't come here to help Mr. Goldthwait discuss morals."

"It's an indecency!"

"It's a matter of business and a necessary one, Mr. MacCubbin, nothing more. No harm will come to the niggers, obviously, because we need 'em to keep working our land for this season. Before the '66 crop is planted, adjustments will have to be made."

"And if I don't give you my word to remain silent in the presence of Negroes, what then?"

"Then you'll pack your clothes, Reverend, assuming that you'll leave Festin for some earthly place."

Reverend Mr. MacCubbin stared at Goldthwait, who had spoken so pointedly. "You wouldn't dare do that."

"No? You talk about destroying a whole area's income, and you think anybody would hesitate to prevent you from doing it? Or to take revenge after it had been done? If that's what you think, then you're a fool! And just because you claim that you have God's ear, don't confuse yourself with Him. You're a human being, you can be hurt, and your shit stinks just like ours does."

There was no further response. Reverend Mr. MacCubbin turned away from them and walked slowly into his church building.

"He'll listen," Goldthwait snapped before Manders could disagree. "Let's get a move on to our next port of call. That one ought to be a rough one."

Serena Pollard's cousin, Hubert, had walked out as soon as the trap appeared on Serena's grounds. He stopped parallel with the horses and looked up at the two

236

strangers, a gray-haired, gray-mustached man with broad shoulders. Goldthwait spoke swiftly and to the point.

"I assume that I wouldn't be welcome in the house, but I've got a message of importance and I can give it to you here."

"Please do, sir." The Mississippian inclined his head.

It took Goldthwait two minutes to make his explanation.

Hubert, having listened carefully, said, "I will be glad to cooperate, sir. You may rest assured of that. As for my cousin, she rarely leaves the house these days and wouldn't discuss the tragedy of the South with anyone, white or nigra."

"All the same, sir, I hope that you will talk to her."

"Trust me to drive the point home. Indeed I shall take very good care to do so as I plan to go back to Natchez soon. It's my home and I ought to be there in its time of trial."

Manders stopped himself from saying wryly that the time of trial had come and gone with the active conflict.

"I shall explain to my cousin," Hubert said carefully, "that slavery cannot be considered illegal in this state until the sovereign legislature passes an ordinance to that effect."

"And explain to her that the white plantation owners are willing to enforce their request for silence," Goldthwait put in. You may ask her to recall what happened to a friend of hers named Tuck, and tell her that she's not immune to similar treatment."

Manders saw Cousin Hubert becoming angry and said quickly, "Not that anybody would ever raise a hand to a southern lady, but in a crisis, sir, it can't hurt to reinforce one's statements."

"Sir, I feel sure that you need have no worries about my cousin's behavior or her sympathies. She is a true woman of the South."

"Thank you, sir. I knew that we could rely upon your discretion."

237

"One more thing, sir." Hubert hesitated. "There is a rumor that the Yankees have captured Jefferson Davis. Would that be the truth?"

"I think so," Manders said. "I've heard it so often that I believe it. Caught in Nashville, on a train, I heard it."

Hubert took a step away from the trap at last. "This is a sad time for us all."

Manders shrugged irritably. The sad time for the southern states had come upon them all long before Jeff Davis had been captured. It had come with the first shipment of illegal slaves from Africa, the first successful crop of cotton, the first horsewhip and dogwhip and pair of chains and manacles. There was no sense in crossing the bar over the top half of the *t*. Hubert whatever-his-name was a southern gentleman who hadn't been brought up to understand about the rights of human beings who weren't under his roof.

As Manders inclined his head in farewell, Serena's cousin suddenly drew himself up and saluted with military correctness. Manders, who was driving the trap, raised and lowered the reins lightly. The horses hurried away.

Reverend Clack lived a mile outside of the town limits of Festin, occupying a small, unpainted house. He had made one effort to paint it several years ago, but a white man had made it clear that only a nigger who didn't know his place would want to fix up his house. It hadn't been repainted and the wooden frame smelled of sweat and decay under the warm sun.

Two children scurried indoors as soon as the trap came into view. There was a pause when Manders settled the horses down. Reverend Clack came out the front door, putting on his silver-rimmed glasses as he hurried toward the white men. Manders was aware of children peering out worriedly from behind dirty windows.

"Mr. Manders, Mr. Goldthwait," Reverend Clack said, nodding respectfully. "What can I do for you?"

Manders quieted Goldthwait with a look. "We want your cooperation, Clack, and we must have it."

238

"Well, gentlemen?"

"There are rumors that the war is over and that the institution of slavery no longer exists in the South."

" 'Rumors'? Do you gentlemen claim that the loss of the war is a rumor?"

"That's what we tell you, boy," Goldthwait rumbled, "and you'd best remember it."

"You've been tending to the spiritual needs of our nigras for a long time now," Manders resumed swiftly. "We want you to keep doing so. Indeed, you'll be paid accordingly."

"I see. Otherwise my life is forfeit. Is that it?"

"Yours, and the pickaninnies in there." Goldthwait pointed to the house. "We mean it, boy, or we wouldn't waste our breath on you."

Clark lowered his eyes. It occurred to Manders that Clark had always been proud of his freedom because it set him apart from other nigras; now they were all free, and his only distinction was gone, all of them were free to be hectored by whites.

"Very well, gentlemen. You've made me exploit my own race before. This won't be the first time."

"You watch your tongue, nigger," Goldthwait said furiously.

"I will, Mr. Goldthwait, I know my place." Clack glanced behind him to the unpainted cabin where he and his family lived. "My kids don't know their places, not yet, but I know mine. I've lived here long enough for that."

"I think we're all set now," Goldthwait remarked as he took the trap reins in hand to drive them back to their plantations.

"I don't know about that, Chad. In my opinion, we ought to go up and down Festin to make sure that every white person understands what's expected."

"You *would* think so," Chad Goldthwait said sourly. "And after it's done you'll doubt if we accomplished anything worth a tinker's damn."

"I doubt if it'll do much good, really," Manders said

239

with his usual pessimism, as Goldthwait had expected. "But we certainly ought to try."

5

Abel set down the cup of weak coffee and reached idly for a gardenia in the vase of cut flowers at the center of the table, then shook his head and glanced at the breast pocket where he used to keep Cuban cigars to be smoked after a meal. He shrugged. Coffee, two eggs, a thin strip of bacon, and a cup of lentile soup hardly amounted to a lunch, except in these postwar days.

Nancy was telling Kermit angrily, "At your age, you should certainly be able to eat with better manners, and you should be able to wipe your own face afterwards."

She started to wipe his face. Kermit winced and then sighed.

Largely to help his son, by diverting Nancy's attention, Abel said, "You might want to resume your prewar schedule of Tuesday visiting."

Nancy looked up without stopping her work on Kermit's face. "Do you have anybody in mind?"

"Serena Pollard. I understand that her cousin has just gone back to Natchez, and he's the one who was keeping her from stopping the paddles in the steamboat, so to speak."

Nancy said quietly, "You want me to warn Serena to be quiet about—."

"You know about what," Abel interrupted harshly, with a glance at the closed door. He softened his voice. "By the way, those Atlantic crossing tickets for January are waiting for us in New York City. I've received definite word about that."

He looked sadly at his wife. Still beautiful, still a good partner in bed, but it would be difficult to talk to her as a friend until they were out of the South. He wondered

240

vaguely if his wife was just simply too civilized for her own good.

Nancy didn't start out until she made sure that Kermit wasn't angry at her for the small scene she had made at lunch. The Debenker carriage, with Moses driving, took her to the Goldthwait place, where she spent half an hour with Lorna Goldthwait in return for a recent visit of hers.

She saw Chad only briefly, and the man of the house snorted at sight of her and rushed out to the fields to supervise the picking. Lorna happened to be in a morose mood about the infant she had lost in childbirth some years ago, computing its present age and tearfully talking about the clothes it would have been wearing.

"I hope that my Chad isn't developing a cold," she suddenly remarked in a lightning-quick change of subject. "He was out late last night for some reason, and if anything happened to my Chad I don't know what I'd do."

It took Nancy another fifteen minutes to get away from the Goldthwait mansion. She felt sorry for Lorna, having to depend on a man as cruel as Chad, but she was delighted to leave.

Serena's house looked oddly calm, as she saw when the carriage topped the knoll above which the simple home was located. She knocked on the plain wooden door, but there was no response. Her hand, dropping, touched the knob and put some pressure on it, partly opening the door. A mistake, she thought, not to keep it locked. Even in Louisiana, a woman living alone couldn't be too careful. On the floor of the reception room, she saw the dignified bulldog, Prince, and put up a hand to her mouth to keep from screaming.

The dog lay on a grass-colored throw rug, dead. Prince had been killed, his throat cut. His body had started to decompose as she could tell after even one horrified look; the eyelashes were already gone. The dog's mouth was wide open as if from unbearable pain. His head was tilted to the side, his legs crouched as if in the throes of kicking out against hellish fate. The smell in this room, with its

241

sturdy table and shelves of books and wall motto, was as ghastly as the worst that she could have imagined.

She hurried out of the house and around to the back, hoping to find Serena. When she did, she wished with all her heart that she hadn't. Serena Pollard, like her freed Negro, Tuck, several years ago, had been hanged from a cypress tree. Before that, she had been stripped. Whip marks, as regular looking as the tines of a fork, had been laid across her back and on the front of her, too. A rosy nipple had been torn, and dollops of blood streaked down her. There was a thick colorless liquid against the hair close to her privates and against her rear and running down one dead leg. Nancy wouldn't let herself look at Serena Pollard's dead face, already guessing at the shame and pain that would be reflected in it.

She turned away and suddenly bent over and started to throw up, remaining in that position as if she knew that she would never be able to stop herself.

6

Abel drove into Festin that Thursday evening to pick up Peter Quendale and take him out to the so-called sociable at Goldthwait's. Young Quendale was in a cheerful mood, his hair disarrayed and a smile on his lips.

"Anthony Barton Quendale is now among us," he said, sitting back in Abel's trap and running a hand through the blond hair which was darkening with time. Abel looked rueful, remembering the lawyer's extreme youth when he had started to work for Jarvis Whitcomb. "An easy delivery, thank God. No doubt your good wife will hear all the details in time."

"No doubt," Abel agreed drily.

"With three sons, by George, the planters who want to get their daughters married off will have to give them dowries. It's a pretty nice old world after all."

Abel said harshly, "Serena Pollard couldn't have thought much of it before she left."

"Yes, that was damnable."

"Did Goldthwait do it?"

"Nobody knows."

"Is it thought that Chad did it?"

Quendale looked away to the dark road.

Vividly, it was possible to remember the screams of Tuck, the former slave, just before being lynched. And there had been the smell of warm rope in the stagnant air, a horse pawing the ground, Chad and his second in command angry at Abel Debenker for trying to stop them from carrying out what seemed to be their duty.

"I'll accept that answer," Abel said quietly to the lawyer, whose face didn't show the slightest expression. "Now what about the papers you're drawing up to sell my land?"

Quendale, relieved by the change of subject, shrugged. "The papers are ready, but I've reason to believe that your price won't be met. Fifty-five dollars an acre isn't unreasonable, you understand, but your neighbors simply claim they can't afford it."

"I'll take thirty-five an acre in cash, and notes for the balance."

"They won't go along with that either, in my opinion. They feel certain that you'll get out at any price, so they'll either let you out for two or three dollars the acre or simply not make any offer and divide the land among your neighbors after you've left."

"In that case, I think I'll surprise them." Abel smiled unpleasantly. "You'll be going to church on Sunday, I suppose? Will you take time to see me at your office afterwards?"

"Of course, if it's necessary."

"Good. I'd rather not go into town tomorrow or Saturday."

Abel stopped in front of the Goldthwait mansion for his passenger to get off. Quendale looked at him curiously.

"Aren't you coming in?"

243

"I think I'd kill Chad with my bare hands if I saw him now."

"You'll have to join us, as you said last time. For the good of all the planters, it's necessary to stay together. For the good of all the whites in Festin, I ought to say."

"Very well," Abel agreed after a pause, and drove his trap to Goldthwait's stable for the horses to be fed and watered.

He and Quendale were led to the study door by an old Negro, who knocked twice and then opened it. Abel only needed one look to realize that another crisis had come up. Sitting in the room's most comfortable chair behind the desk, was Giraud Duval.

The dandyishly dressed planter, who had run from the land as soon as the war situation grew intensely difficult, smiled at the sight of Abel. He was wearing a deep blue suit with wide lapels and a gardenia in a buttonhole. He saluted Abel by raising his hand with a drink in it.

"Ah, Abel Debenker! I've always thought you were the most handsome of my colleagues. Or that you would be, if your face was a little fuller and the eyes just a trifle wider. I do like to see icy blue eyes in a man—always wasted in a woman—because women don't have thrillingly cruel temperaments."

Chad Goldthwait, standing at the right of his desk, with arms akimbo, turned to nod brusquely at the new arrivals. There was nobody else in the room except the four men. Abel wondered if the others were protesting Serena Pollard's violent death by staying away, or at least by arriving late.

"What are you up to, Duval? What do you want?"

"Nothing I'm not entitled to."

Abel drew himself up. "You want your land back."

"Well, it *is* my land."

"It was, Duval, and then you saw that the going was rough for the Confederacy and for all of us, so you cleared out. You turned tail like a rabbit."

"My assessment of the situation was that the next few years would be surpassingly difficult, but that the South

244

would emerge strong after a period of time. I didn't count on ingenuity—Abel's, I understand—that would let you-all make an agreement with Union forces to bypass this area and permit you-all to carry on as if slavery remained a fact of exis———."

"Quiet!" Goldthwait snapped. "You mustn't even say that much when you're here. Somebody in the hall might be listening. You must keep your teeth tight together when thinking about that subject."

"I see." Duval covered his mouth with languid fingers, perhaps only to hide a smile. "Yes, you really have been clever. I understand that my land has been divided among immediate neighbors, but that my niggers are still accessible. That's good. I've missed some of those boys."

"I'll bet you have." Goldthwait snapped. "The planters who've worked your land are entitled to it because they didn't run out. You know it, Duval."

"I'd be only too pleased to pay them back, if I could raise the money."

"Nobody will give up land he's worked over," Abel said. "I'd offer you a chance to buy my own land at fifty-five the acre as I'm pulling up stakes and taking my family to England, but from what you say—."

"I can't afford it," Duval agreed. "And there's no reason why I should have to buy anything when my land is waiting for me."

"You want to come in and hog the profits without having done any work."

"It's unpretty when you put it that way. I can offer this compensation: I'll keep quiet about all our plans, if justice is done."

"You'll destroy everybody's profits if you don't get what you want, then," Abel said, making and unmaking fists as he glared down at the self-satisfied Duval. "I'm opposed to blackmail."

"I don't see that you've got too much of a choice when I hold all the cards in this game."

Two knocks on the door were followed by Barton Manders' entrance. The sad looking planter glanced at his

245

son-in-law and then stood transfixed at sight of Giraud Duval. He closed the door quickly. Duval explained once more what he wanted and why. Manders' expressive face had settled into his usual doleful I-told-you-that-the-worst-would-happen look, but two more knocks sounded at the door before he could speak.

It opened on Tom Holman, and Abel rushed over with Quendale to help the once-active Holman settle himself in a chair. Goldthwait absently prepared a drink while listening to Duval. Abel brought it over to Holman and turned back.

"I was going to talk about the alternative if my demands aren't met," Duval was saying. "But I'm sure there isn't any need for that. You are all southern gentlemen with a strongly developed sense of justice."

"Exactly," Goldthwait rumbled.

". . . so I'm sure there won't be any problem. If there is, I only have to inform the office of General Ulysses Grant about what's happening, or even to raise my voice in this room and say something like, 'The niggers have been fr——'."

He didn't get any further. As the others watched, he suddenly drew a deep breath and closed his eyes and fell forward, his body lying across Chad Goldthwait's sturdy desk. Goldthwait had taken a step away, but now he moved in closely. Abel saw the man's thick right hand close into a fist held sideways against Duval's blood-spattered neck, and then Goldthwait pulled the fist back to his own side. There was a weak spatter of blood from the neck and Goldthwait let out a sigh. He was holding a blood-drenched letter knife.

"Give me a handkerchief, someone!"

Quendale produced it. Goldthwait wiped the letter knife briefly. Stains had developed on the blade and almost to the bottom of the steel hilt. Goldthwait poured a drink into a glass, then upended the contents over his letter knife. The odor of cheap whiskey filled this small office. The letter knife looked as if it had been washed clean.

Abel had been moving swiftly past Goldthwait and

around the desk. He reached for Duval's right hand, touching the wrist with his other free hand. A faint trace of perfume was in his nostrils along with the smell of blood. The thread of pulse snapped as he rested the hand against his own. Abel put down the dead man's hand, then turned.

"Gone."

"You're damn right he is." Goldthwait shrugged, and returned the letter knife to its place on his desk, then glanced at Quendale. "I owe you a handkerchief."

The young lawyer nodded.

Goldthwait smiled. "We all owe you congratulations on the birth of a son. A bonny lad and an easy delivery, I understand."

Abel cut in brusquely, "Is that all you can say after you kill a man?"

"I did what was necessary. And now I'll have to call in my overseer, and the two of us will take the body outside and bury it. All necessary."

"You didn't have to kill him."

"Of course I did, but let's ask the others." Chad glared at Manders. "What do you say to that, Barton? Was it necessary or not?"

Manders said, "I'm not sure if you can hide the body successfully."

"If it's on my grounds, I can hide it. One vote agrees that it was necessary. What about you, Holman? Was it necessary to kill this sissy bastard over here or wasn't it?"

"I don't know what else we could have done." Tom Holman agreed, sipping his drink.

"And you, Quendale? You probably don't agree with that. You probably take Debenker's side."

"A little talk couldn't have done any harm. I think that we could have arrived at a *modus vivendi*."

"I don't know Greek from Latin, but I do know that if somebody has got the power to destroy you and even suggests he might use that power, you had better get rid of him if you ever want to sleep well again."

Quendale said nothing.

247

"And you, Abel, you wanted to talk, too. Figure out an idea. Compromise. Put off what's inevitable, above everything else in this world, put it off."

"Until you've explored every possibility," Abel started.

"The point is that you won't have a restful minute with somebody like that alive and kicking while he talks about the threats he can hold over you. Not one minute, Abel, of peace. You know that as well as I do. Furthermore, there's a certain amount of strength to be gained from the use of violence. If somebody else is tempted to make a threat, he'll think twice about it after this——. Oh yes, and after what me and my overseer did to the Pollard woman. There are going to be plenty of closed mouths as a result, and you know that, too."

Abel didn't agree in so many words, but he had become quiet.

"I think we understand each other better than most people around here, Abel." Goldthwait rubbed his hands together. "Each of us knows who the other is and what the other does. Each of us knows the other's job and why the other is such an asset to the planters of this community."

"Really? What's my 'job', as you call it?"

"You're a thinker, Abel, and you're good at it. You can be sly if that's necessary, and you can be shrewd. You try not to do anybody out of their moral rights. You even try to give your niggers a fair shake, as much as possible. This much I'll say to you, and I wouldn't say it to almost anybody else: for a blackbirder, a man who deals in niggers to make his bread and butter, you've got some decent instincts. I appreciate that, Abel, because I've got damn few decent instincts in me. I've only got the instinct to survive. But you're a thinking blackbirder, a compassionate blackbirder."

"And you, Chad? What's your big asset to the planters of this community?"

"Me? I'm the man you go to when you need somebody to get rid of your garbage; and as a blackbirder you can't survive without me. You might as well get used to the idea, accept it, try to live with it, Abel. It's the way things

248

are in this system, and the sooner you grow to accept it the better off we'll all be around here."

Abel sank down into the nearest chair, shading his eyes with a suddenly shaky hand. He knew that he had provoked Chad Goldthwait into telling him what was close to the exact truth, and he felt sick to his soul.

7

Lucas Tinsley woke up later than usual on the morning of Sunday, the twenty-fourth of June. The overseer turned in bed with difficulty. Then he sat up, looked at his right and reached out a large hand, touching the shoulder of a slave who was lying there.

"I didn't tell you to stay overnight," he growled. "Now you'll have to change the bedding, you dumb bitch! What the hell is your name again? Oh yes, Neva. Change my bedding."

The slave girl was awake instantly and on her guard, "Yes, buckra, I do it. But this be Sunday, and no gal work on a Sunday."

"You do, just to change the bedding. I won't tell God."

He dressed himself in cotton pants, a light shirt, and a jacket that contained his oversized shoulders. There was a half-empty bottle on the bureau, but he shrugged and left the cheap whiskey' in place. Idly, he watched Neva walk around the cabin, noticing the breasts move lightly at her steps, and taking note once more of the flat stomach. He wondered why his fingerprints couldn't be seen all over that beautiful black body and then decided he must have still been drunk.

"Get the sheets and pillowcase off the bed and put 'em in the laundry sack under the window outside and put fresh things on the bed. Tomorrow morning, you can take the laundry over to the mansion and see that it gets done before night. After you get finished in here, come out to church. Walk behind me. After church, come back here. I'll be in the mood for you, then."

She was nodding as she took the white pillowcase and dropped it to the floor. Tinsley walked down the small hill, glancing in at the slave cabins. Nothing that he saw was unexpected or out of line. He walked toward the mansion porch, arriving in front of it only minutes before Mr. Debenker opened the screen door. He was in his best, Sunday, church-going clothes, dark and shiny.

"Is everything all right over there, Tinsley?" he asked, pointing toward the slave quarters.

"Yes, sir." Tinsley's pale eyes blinked rapidly. "Me and the niggers understand each other. They're in control."

"All right, then. I'll admit I've been so edgy these last couple of months that I think twice about going into town for church worship. If I hadn't promised Quendale to see him afterwards—well, all this seems to you like nonsense, I suppose."

"Mr. Debenker, I assume that a man's woman gets him riled up and broody."

"Yes, perhaps. Now let's talk about our real business and the chances of getting a good crop. I've been figuring on a per acre yield of—."

The next ten minutes were spent in business talk. Abel's expectations seemed reasonable. Nancy and Kermit joined him. They all walked to the carriage, circling the house, three of them on their way to the church in town and a little sociability afterwards. Abel turned to his foreman just before climbing into the carriage and asked, "You'll handle the windbag patrol?"

"Of course, sir." It was the private slang for listening to the sermon over at the nigger church. Tinsley expected that the slave gal, Neva, would give him a massage of the proper parts afterwards, and then he'd let her do another job on him. He might call that older, but still good-looking gal, Blossom, over to join Neva.

Abel said, "Stay as near to that nigra reverend as you can. Don't let him talk to any of the others."

"I'll take care of it, Mr. Debenker."

250

Abel's last communication with the overseer was a grim little nod. He climbed into the carriage. Tinsley closed the door respectfully, then smiled at Nancy Debenker and winked at the lad; no response from either.

The carriage started off, and Lucas Tinsley turned and walked to the Negro church at the end of the twin rows of slave cabins.

The Reverend Clack, a worn Bible under his arm, talked without the usual ringing conviction that Tinsley remembered as being an integral part of his sermons. He hesitated and swayed, losing the thread of what he was saying and not picking it up till he was aware of restlessness among his parishioners.

"To be humble and know the place that the Lord has given you," Reverend Clack was saying, "is the highest grace to which a nigger can——."

Tinsley, standing at the rear of the scruffy church, had closed his eyes briefly. He wasn't aware right away of the change in tempo or voice. When he opened his eyes it was too late, and the damage had already been done. Blossom, that quarrelsome nigger bitch, had started to talk over Clack's voice. She wasn't standing up so that she could be identified, but Tinsley knew her voice as well as anybody else in the church.

". . . all lie," she was saying loudly. "You lie, preacher man! You sell niggers like you are and sell 'em down the river with your lies! You tell us we still slaves when that's not true. We free! We niggers are a free people!"

Jethro whispered loudly, "You'll get in trouble."

Reverend Clack looked at Tinsley very briefly and then said carefully, "In our hearts we're free. In our souls we're free. But the Good Lord has made the decision . . . ."

"We free every way," Blossom shouted. "In our hearts and every way. We free, but nobody tell us. The whites don't tell us. The whites keep us slave, and you help 'em."

Clack asked warily, "How could you know that?"

Another gal answered, shrillness in her voice:

"We know, we know."

251

Tinsley, not ready to interfere unless Clack lost control, watched the slave woman, Sunshine, lean over and talk swiftly to her husband. She was keeping a hand on him as if to anchor him where he sat.

Blossom suddenly shouted, "Look at him! Look! The old nigger, don't know what to say! He admit it! We free, all of us! We free, do you hear that, all you niggers?"

Jethro stood up suddenly and glared at Clack. "Is that true, Reverend? Is the fight over? Are the niggers free? Tell your own people if it true. Tell us."

Clack looked at Tinsley again before saying mournfully, "My friends, it isn't given to any of us to judge our own positions in life or to change them. We are in the place where the good Lord, in His wisdom, has seen fit to put us all—."

And then Jethro called out, "You do lie! She right, my Blossom! You lie!"

Lucas Tinsley suddenly shouted, "Be quiet, you jackasses, all of you! Listen to him!"

That was when Amos, who hadn't arrived from Africa too long ago, got to his feet and said with venom, "We not have to listen to anybody!"

There was muttering among the others. Tinsley knew that they'd have to be put in place again and he closed his fingers as if around the whip that no overseer ever brought into church.

"You be at work tomorrow morning, the whole pack of you, or nobody will get any help from God."

He didn't have the nerve to turn his back on a bunch of niggers, but he started to the door and made a point of walking noisily as if angry and disgusted by the behavior of quarrelling children.

It was Blossom, of course, who called out, "Don't let that white fucker out of here!"

Tinsley never knew how it happened, but as he reached the door he suddenly felt himself gripped from behind. He let out a bellow and tried to draw his hands away angrily, but his right hand was pulled up against his back. He

252

lashed out to the rear with a foot, and felt the tip of a gleaming shoe strike flesh. All the same, he felt himself being pulled back toward the center of the scruffy church and being kept from falling over one peeling wooden bench after another.

"I'll have every one of you hanged," he bellowed.

From a distance, it seemed, he heard Reverend Clack's raised voice. "My brothers and sisters, you must not—."

"Shut up, or you get the same!" Was that the soft-spoken Elihu? "You get the same for lying to your own, you scummy nigger!"

There was a shout, and then Tinsley heard Clack praying at the top of his lungs, "Forgive them, Lord, for · they know not what they do."

"We know what we do," Sunshine said grimly. "Oh yes, we know like we didn't know before."

Clack's voice rose in a scream, and then Blossom shouted, "Get a knife, somebody, get a knife and we fix 'em both real good."

Tinsley was kicking out furiously, but to no avail. Somebody punched him on the back of the neck, and he seemed to know nothing except that he was falling to the earthen floor. There was a moment for him to feel astonishment, as if the furniture in his cabin had suddenly turned against him. And then he felt blackness drop across him like a woman's veil.

He never knew how much time went past until he suddenly felt an almost overpowering pain. He gasped and opened his eyes wide. He didn't believe what he saw and yet he knew very well that it was happening to him. For the gal, Neva, the gal with whom he had spent all last night, that mild and obedient gal, was standing over him with a knife in her hand. She suddenly bent over and pulled something with a wrench that made him briefly blind with pain and held it up and turned around and bent a little way over to where he could see it as his sight cleared.

"Look what I cut off, you fucker, you white fucker,"

253

Neva exulted, crooning softly. There was a triangle of cloth from the crotch of his pants in her hand, but she brushed that away. "You never do it again, not never."

Tinsley looked and his eyes widened very briefly and then he felt soggy wetness against his pants and the pounding pain started again. He hardly cared that he had been kicked on the side as well, just as he himself had needed to kick many a fallen Black. He wanted to scream, but the volume wouldn't come and he couldn't lose himself in hysteria. No matter what happened, he wasn't going to call out.

Amos said, "Give me that knife, gal."

Neva resisted. "He mine." .

That was when Tinsley felt a knife puncture go into his body. In the rush of pain, added to the other agony, he couldn't know exactly where. He opened his mouth, but didn't make a sound. Many times in the past it had been drilled into him that he must never show any nigger that he might be afraid, and it didn't seem to matter that his determination might no longer make any difference to his life or death. Only the ritual remained, slogans to comfort him when there was nothing else at all.

"Give me that," Amos said urgently. "Don't kill him by inches."

"Not yet."

There was another puncture, in the lower half of his stomach this time. He felt himself blinded by pain for moments, and above him he heard a brief struggle for the knife. A moment's gratitude flickered in his consciousness. Whichever nigger had stopped the torture would get some appreciation from him after this was over, if it was possible for him to do anything.

"All right, Amos, take it now."

Tinsley wondered if he had sighed aloud. He was certainly surprised. Amos had never seemed to him a peacemaker, but it was impossible to know about a nigger. For the first time, he was realizing that niggers might not be predictable.

254

"Here," Amos said, breathing hard. "I kill the fucker and do it clean."

Tinsley was left only with time for a deep breath, and then the tip of the already bloody knife was plunged against his heart, and he knew no more.

Amos pulled the knife out of the dead body at last. There wasn't any expression on his face, and the prominent whites of his eyes seemed to have narrowed. Around him he could smell blood as if it was part of a lake. He turned to the body of the Reverend Clack. The preacher lay on his back, mouth open in a last scream that had been silenced. Blood had stopped staining his dark suit. One shoe had been pulled off him by another slave, and he was now putting a hand into it as if it were a glove. The slave was chuckling.

Amos looked back at the body of the overseer he had detested. Tinsley's lips were stretched tight, but he had never shown any sign of cowardice even when he must have been certain he wouldn't leave the church building alive.

"Brave fucker," Amos said quietly. "Why such a bastard be a brave fucker?"

"No fucker no more," Neva said, kicking the testicles out of her way as she stepped a few paces from the body.

Jethro said, "Okay, now. We free. We go away from here and be free."

"Where we go?" Blossom asked. "What we do?"

"I don't know."

"What do you say we do?" Sunshine asked Blossom.

"We wait," Blossom said quickly. "Just for awhile we wait."

"For what?"

There was a nasty grin on Blossom's lips. "We wait for the Masta to get home. The Masta, the wife, and the boy. They get home and Blossom give 'em big surprise."

255

8

The conference room of the law office hadn't changed in too many ways over the last few years, Abel noticed as he walked in behind young Quendale. He hadn't been here since buying a number of slaves from Serena Pollard, if he remembered rightly. Jarvis Whitcomb had taken care of that transaction for him, and Quendale hadn't even looked into the room.

Now Peter Quendale sat in Whitcomb's leather chair at the faultlessly shiny conference table. A young man had risen respectfully upon his entrance and closed the door behind him, as Abel was drawing the shades on a view of Festin's Courthouse Square.

"My new assistant," Quendale started, as Abel found a seat that hadn't been warmed by the June sunlight. "One lawyer has to break in another, you know."

"I'll try not to take much time, as each of us has a family waiting at the church sociable," Abel said, crossing his legs carefully. "The situation about the sale of my land seems to be that my price won't be met, from what you tell me. Indeed, my 'friends' will try to get the land for nothing, if that's possible. I want to make sure that they can't get the land from the next owners, however."

"Do you have any idea who the next owners are going to be?"

"Yes. There will be fifty-three owners."

"Fifty-three? What do you mean, Mr. Debenker?"

"I plan to give the land away to my former slaves," Abel said quietly.

Not a flicker of emotion crossed Quendale's face. "Nigras will be coming from all over the county to work on that land. Chad and the others won't be able to get anybody. They'll be ruined."

"I can face that prospect with equanimity," Abel said. "Now what steps have to be taken?"

"Well, I think it's simply to be considered as another land sale. A price has to be agreed upon."

"One dollar for my lands will be sufficient. Go on."

"Another lawyer has to be hired to represent the—ah—purchasers."

"I'll pay the fee for that."

"A search has to be conducted to be certain that you are able to dispose of title to the land as we don't want it to escheat to the state upon your death. A deed of sale has to be drawn up and signed by each of the purchasers at the closing. Everybody has to appear and sign his name."

"If I give identification for each purchaser, and you confirm it, that ought to be sufficient. Now there's one other condition."

"Name it."

"I want the contract to say that the land is to be divided equally among the adults, so that Elihu and Sunshine, who are married, will get two shares, but the children will get none. I also want the contract to say that each purchaser agrees to stay on the land for five years and to work it, or the contract is voided as far as that purchaser is concerned. Furthermore, in case of a resale, six Blacks have to approve the new purchaser."

"Very well." Quendale hesitated. "One question, if I might. I assume that you expect me to tell the other planters what you have in mind, so that they'll raise the offer and meet your price. Is that true?"

Looking reflectively down at the lighted cigar between the first two fingers of his right hand, Abel seemed lost in thought.

"I think it was true when I first decided on asking you to draw up the papers."

"But isn't it true now?"

"I don't think so, No. In fact, I'm sure it isn't."

"Why do you sincerely plan to go through with it?"

"Because—well, to answer you would mean that I'd

257

have to explain my feelings and the reasons for them. Is that what you want to hear?"

"I'd like to hear a chain of reasoning for this action of yours. My father-in-law will ask me why you did it, and probably my wife as well. I'm asking you what to say to them. Perhaps you can offer me a guideline."

"I'll try if you like, but don't be surprised if it sounds different from what you might expect. Look, I'm not really a soft touch. In the situation as it's existed, I've been as decent to the Blacks on my plantation as any man could be. I've accepted the slavery system out of necessity, yes, but I've tried to make up for that in many ways."

"If you think that the slave system is an iniquity, you couldn't compensate for being part of an evil."

"I've compromised in small but important ways, trying to make the Blacks' lot easier. I've tried to give them respect and an acknowledgment that they've worked hard. I've certainly refrained from having them beaten for minor offenses, and I've done other small things as well. Postulating a vile system, I can say that I've been a good master."

" 'A vile system'? If that's what you think of slavery, you should never have accepted any role in the system."

"It was necessary to do that. A man has to earn a living for his wife and family. I must say to you that from the start of my taking over at Fairlawn I had planned to raise enough money so that my family and I would be able to live in comfort, away from slavery, for the rest of our lives. And my son's children as well."

"But you didn't scruple about using slave labor in order to accomplish that goal."

"If I hadn't used it, somebody else would have."

"Perhaps. But you did use it."

"Yes, counsellor, I used it and lightened many lives in doing just that."

"And now you plan to set them up with your own land as a *mea culpa*. Isn't that right?"

"Perhaps it is. I want the Blacks who worked loyally for

258

me to have a chance to improve their own lot in life and that of their children. Why shouldn't a black man earn enough to send his children to school so that they could become doctors or scientists or even lawyers?"

"A black lawyer?" Quendale cocked his head to one side. "You're trying to get a rise out of me."

"Is it impossible for a black man to apply himself and become a lawyer? Or to go into any of the other professions? They might have to fight against prejudice for large parts of their lives, but the white world will have to come to terms with their existence and with such proficiency as they might develop."

"Do you think they want an education?"

"I don't know, or care about that, frankly. I think that a black man or even a black woman who wants an education should be entitled to one and to get the benefits out of it. Anybody who wants to do a day's work for a day's pay should be treated like anybody else."

"An extraordinary statement from a slave owner," the lawyer said.

"Who is to say that a black man or woman might not discover the cure for heart sickness, or for wasting away like Jarvis Whitcomb did? Or for the common cold. Who is there that can rule it out?"

"My father-in-law's Blacks won't discover any of those things."

"No, but their children or grandchildren might. Haven't you ever run across a black person and thought that if he or she had been born white, then a fresh mark might have been made on the world?"

Quendale nodded slowly, then shrugged.

"So your reason is that you want to compensate for what you felt was a great wrong all the time you were taking part in it. That is correct, isn't it? Taking away all the verbiage, all the philosophy, all the trimmings, you hope to compensate for what you think was an unspeakable wrong. And yet if the war had gone differently, or was still being fought, or hadn't taken place at all, I think that you

259

would still be running the plantation and putting aside some money and hoping to get out of blackbirding someday. Isn't that correct?"

Abel said frankly, "I don't know."

"You come before the court with tarnished hands, but a clean soul."

Abel was brisk. "You are not a court, but a retainer of mine. You ask for my reasoning, and I offer you as much as I can, but you try to make it smaller. You say that I am guilty of a great wrong, and the fact that I know it isn't a mitigating circumstance. I think that it is. Chad Goldthwait, Holman, Passy, your father-in-law, will go to their graves certain that slavery was an excellent system, and that its injustices may have been unfortunate, but couldn't be avoided. That is a wicked point of view."

" 'Wicked'? Are we back in Salem and the witchcraft trials?"

"Aren't we? Do you think that wickedness as such doesn't exist? Do you think that evil doesn't exist?"

"I don't believe in the devil," Quendale said sharply.

"Ah, then you haven't seen the slave system at work, counsellor." Abel held up a hand to forestall an interruption. "I don't think we'll ever agree. You say that with my antislavery feelings I should never have been part of the system. That might be true. It's a young man's attitude that there should be no compromise. You're about ten years younger than I am, I believe."

"I'm twenty-six."

"Nine years, then. My argument is that I felt I could provide better for my family if I participated and tried to mitigate as much of the evil as I could. As a man with a family, Peter, I don't think you can fail to disagree."

Quendale shook his head furiously. Then he laughed. "It isn't my chore to pass judgment on you, as you've pointed out. I'm willing to call the discussion a draw."

Abel put out his cigar and decided that he couldn't wait to reach England, if only to be able to get made-in-Havana cigars at last.

260

"And I, counsellor," he said, rising, "am willing to call it a discussion."

He led the way out of the conference room and into the empty waiting room with its chairs for more people than would ever be here at one time. "You'll have those papers for me to sign, will you?"

"In two weeks, if you like."

Abel said carefully, "No, we'll wait until the crop is in, by late December. Then all of those who are involved will attend the ceremony very shortly before the transfer."

Quendale laughed briefly. "Sensible of you. Otherwise you might be murdered in your bed."

"Agreed. But what I will do in the meantime, is to write and sign a letter of intent. I think it'll keep Chad and his overseer from trying to—ah, change my mind. I'll send one copy to you and the other to a business contact of mine in New York City, so that it won't be accidentally destroyed."

"A very sensible precaution," Quendale acknowledged. "I'd suggest that you get to work on it quickly."

"I'll do it this afternoon," Abel said, opening the door to the stairway, "as soon as I return home."

9

The stable boy helped Amos to hitch the mules up to the wagon, and Amos put in the twenty-five bottles of Jethro's plantation-made whiskey. Then Amos got into the small wagon and the mules were outside and on the way.

The mules needed steering, but not much. These were the same two who made the whiskey run whenever Jethro prepared a batch of the stuff. Nobody had told the masta —the white man—that Jethro was cutting the whiskey even further so as to be able to sell another twenty-five bottles to one of Chad Goldthwait's boys. It was Amos who made the trip in return for half of the money. Jethro usually said he was too tired to do it, and this time he'd been very anxious to stay back at Fairlawn.

There was a ring of trees covered by Spanish moss that seemed to cling wetly whether or not it had rained. Amos halted, got out of the wagon, and patted the mules encouragingly. There was motion to his right. Chad Goldthwait's house boy, Sam, walked between two trees. He stopped as soon as he saw Amos, then walked ahead more slowly.

"Everything all right?" he demanded.

"Better than it ever has been."

Sam looked into the wagon and saw the bottles. "Help me take 'em out."

Amos said calmly, "You want 'em, so you take 'em out."

"Nigger trash," Sam said equably, and did the job. He counted four batches of six bottles each and an extra one besides, which was the way he always did it. As soon as the bottles were outside the wagon, he gave Amos a group of much-folded and dirty bills. Amos, who couldn't count either, made a point of looking at each one and then put them into a pants pocket.

"Now I bury the bottles right here," Sam said, tapping the earth with a bare foot. "You can go."

"No need to bury 'em."

"Are you stupid as well as lazy? The masta see this and I get whupped to an inch of my life."

"Well if he try to do that, you whup him right back."

Sam blinked. "You must be very stupid as well as lazy. I never know that until now."

"No, you don't understand. We—."

"It's been a bad day, with the masta in a bad mood. And on top of everything else, Reverend Clack don't come along to give his speech like he always does on Sunday. Where the Reverend?"

"At Fairlawn. He die."

"What happen to him?"

"One of the niggers stick a knife in him."

"Why do you kill the reverend?"

"Because he always a liar. He don't tell us the truth until just before he die."

"What do you mean?"

"Then he tell us we free. All of us are free. The fight is over. The South is lost. Slavery is finish."

"How come you so—. He say so? Reverend Clack say so?"

"That's right. He say it just before he die. And then we kill the buckra."

"Your buckra dies? Then all of you die."

"Listen to me, you fool! The whites around here keep you and me all the other niggers in slavery when there is no slavery any more. You understand that?"

"All of them? Even your masta, who is such a good masta from what everybody say."

"He no better than the others. You try to take a nigger away from him, and you find out what a good masta he is."

"What say your masta, now?"

"He go to church, like yours do—to church, mind!—and when he come back he get a surprise."

Sam nodded in understanding and sympathy. "We tell every nigger 'bout this, and when masta come back from church, he get a surprise, too. He get a *big* surprise."

The two slaves had never liked each other, but now they shook hands. Amos climbed into the wagon and turned his head as soon as Sam called his name.

"What is it?"

"Are you sure we free?"

"Yes."

Sam looked down at himself. "Thirty year too late. At least I think it's thirty year."

Amos drove off.

"You hear 'bout Fairlawn?" asked the first slave. "The niggers up in Fairlawn, they kill their buckra and are set to kill the masta, too."

"Why, they get sold downriver if they do that."

"No, it can't be. There no more downriver for niggers. No more upriver."

"What do you say?"

"There no more slavery. We free. We been free a long time now, but the white fuckers wouldn't let us go."

"Free? We can do what we want?"

"Yes."

"I want to kill the masta, kill the buckra or any other white fucker."

"You do that."

"And then I go away and never do any work again."

The first slave laughed bitterly, and the second one never knew why. . . .

"Free?"

"Free. And the whites don't let us go."

"They let us go. We kill 'em all, every one."

"Every white man and woman and child must die. There has to be no exception. What they do to us, they have to pay for, and pay in blood."

10

Mr. and Mrs. Barton Manders returned from church and walked into the mansion. It was unusually quiet, Manders thought. Not a nigra in sight, either.

"Clare does look beautiful," Mrs. Manders was saying blissfully. "There's no doubt that giving birth to a child does wonders for a woman's complexion. Remember how I looked after I gave birth to Clare and to Terry?"

Terry, the Manders' young son, hurried into his room so that he could change before going out to play. Manders, stroking his luxuriant mustaches, was silent. There was no reason to get his wife excited about what was worrying him, and she always said that he looked on the worst side of everything.

Most people said that Bart Manders was a pessimist. All the same, a man couldn't be unreasonably cheerful if he had lived in the South at a time when a Freedmen's Bureau for nigras had come into being, when nigras were called to duty to fight for the Confederacy. In his own time, during the last few months, the capital of the Confederacy had been evacuated and cotton had been burned on the docks of New Orleans, Lee had surrendered, and a victorious Abe Lincoln had been shot and killed. And now Jeff Davis had been captured by the northern troops, and there would probably never be an end of blood and death.

Manders went into his room to change. Suddenly he raised his head and sniffed. No doubt of it, something was burning. He walked briskly into his wife's room, surprising his lady in the act of raising her dress. Mrs. Manders blushed like a bride and reached out a hand for him.

"There's no time for that now," Barton Manders said irritably, his eyes smarting as they usually did from the bright colors of Mrs. Manders' bedroom furnishings. "Something's on fire."

"Oh, Bart, you must be dreaming." Mrs. Manders looked annoyed. "Haven't you any idea how difficult it is to live with somebody who's always wearing crepe?"

"Look down."

Mrs. Manders did as she was told. From a space between the northwest end of the vivid carpet and the joining of floor and wall, wisps of gray-black smoke were drifting upwards.

Mrs. Manders smoothed her vivid dress and said, "It might be something left cooking."

"The kitchen isn't underneath us, dear. More likely, the niggers waited till we got home and then set fire to the mansion. We'll go into the hall first and you get Terry."

She ran instantly, Manders following. A last look behind him and out the window showed his carriage being driven out to the stables at a furious pace.

His wife was calling the boy's name as she and her husband ran out to the hall to be met by a curtain of billowing black smoke.

"Help!" Manders called out as he felt sure he'd heard footsteps creak on wood below. "We're up here. The master and mistress are up here."

265

A laugh could be heard from below. "Masta of nothin'. Mistress of shit."

That was the moment Manders knew that the worst had happened; part of him had kept from believing it until now. As his wife and their frightened son hurried out of the boy's room, Manders ducked into his own room and came out with a gleaming gilt Tranter five-shot percussion revolver. Stubby-edged bullets were lodged in the double cavity bullet mold, he saw to his satisfaction.

"Down the stairs," he called to his family. "I'll show the way."

As soon as he took his first steps down, he was aware of a rush of barefoot steps on the way up as if to meet him. He turned and signalled urgently to his wife without speaking: take the back stairs; save your life and go by the back; take the boy with you; God bless you; I love you.

And in the moments of peace that were left to him, Manders saw that vain and silly wife of his suddenly turn and gesture her son to use the other stairs. Terry, his face puckered silently, started to shake his head. Mrs. Manders slapped him. Terry ran, looking behind him as Mrs. Manders proudly walked down to the same step on which her husband stood.

The little band of half-naked ragged Blacks paused and glared up at them. One of the men, seeing the self-possessed Mrs. Manders, smiled with a meaning that couldn't be mistaken. Barton Manders turned towards his wife, the pistol raised in one steady hand.

"I love you, dear," he said, and shot her between the eyes.

As the body hit the stairs and rolled toward the Blacks, Barton Manders looked behind him to see if there was an escape path in that direction. There wasn't. Two burly house servants who had always been well-treated were coming down towards him. Barton Manders charged forward, firing until no more bullets were left in his pistol. It gave him a moment's grim satisfaction to know that three Blacks were lying beside his wife at the bottom of the staircase when he was captured.

He lived for three-quarters of an hour.

The last sounds he ever heard were those of a lad screaming in terror, and he didn't lie to himself about the origin of those sounds. They were ringing in his ears when he died.

11

Tom Holman and his family reached their grounds less than an hour after the church sociable was over. Mrs. Holman got out to help Tom, and so did his older son. The planter, who had always insisted that he didn't want or need any help, shrugged bitterly. There was no reason for lying to his wife or sons.

As he let himself be helped out of the carriage, he felt his oldest boy suddenly become rigid. The boy's face, the same whey color as Tom's, was almost green, now. Holman turned his head. Two of his field hands had approached, and a dozen black men and women stood behind them. Holman's oldest boy looked inquiringly at his father.

It was Tom's wife who asked, "What do you want?"

"You," said one of the Blacks, and moved towards her.

Tom Holman turned to his sons. "Get away from here and call for help. Do what you're told!"

There was no time for the boys to move. They were suddenly held securely by a pair of Blacks. A third one took Holman's crutches away from him, though not without a brief and useless struggle. Holman fell to the ground, sitting up in time to see his sons die by strangulation. The bodies were thrown against him on the earth and the men turned to Mrs. Holman. Twice his wife screamed for him and after that the screams were muffled. Her dress was torn and the undergarments shredded and she was knocked down.

"Spread yo' legs, white bitch . . . open yo' mouth . . .

267

get to one side so I go in by the other . . . now we take turns . . . she do a job on you all right . . ."

He saw the actions and heard the words, but it was as if he wasn't really there. Another man seemed to hear what was being said and done as everything was destroyed in front of him. His woman's muffled screams would be in his ears forever, but they suddenly stopped as he crawled along the earth in hopes of reaching her, using his hands for locomotion and his own foot for leverage and to keep himself from losing his balance. The Blacks got up and away from the stunned woman and one of them drew out a knife. He chuckled while he cut her throat.

Holman, stopping as he gasped, saw the Black turn to him. He nodded, understanding. He welcomed death, now.

The black man, having seen the look in Holman's eyes, suddenly reached for one of Tom Holman's crutches. He broke it in half over a sturdy knee. Then he took the other crutch over his knee and broke that one. Holman watched as the black field hand suddenly raised the four halves of the crutches and threw them contemptuously toward his former owner.

"Stay alive, you fucker," he said tonelessly. "Stay alive and remember."

The Blacks turned away, leaving their former master to a fate worse than death.

12

Abel Debenker sat with his wife and twelve year old son in the carriage. They were returning far later than almost anybody else from the church sociable because of Abel's Sunday consultation with the lawyer, Peter Quendale.

He watched the warm brown southern land passing before his eyes out the window. It was beautiful land, soft to the touch and warm to the eyes. Perhaps he had got to the

South too early. In a few years it would be great again, and with more than one crop.

"Cotton isn't king any more," he said a little sadly, "but I really think that's good for the South."

Nancy looked at him directly, as he saw through a reflection in the window glass. He turned to see a sparkle that he remembered from years ago in her eyes, now.

"Abel," she said quietly, "it suddenly occurs to me that I believe you."

"About wh- —? Oh, about leaving. Well, my mind is made up. Come hell or high water or both, my dear, we leave in January."

As he took her hand he heard his son draw in a deep breath. Kermit's eyes, usually as small as Abel's, had suddenly become round as cotton bolls, and almost as white. Abel turned, following his eyes. They were passing an estate, of course, but the cotton gin looked recently painted. The stable was large. The mansion, also freshly-painted, was certainly the largest near Festin. Charles Passy's estate. For a moment, Abel didn't understand what had upset his son. Then he saw the trap with two horses running around by the stable. Nobody was in the trap.

"Some of those nigras are too damned careless for their own good," Abel said, and sat back.

Kermit was pointing, now. "Look at the house. The mansion."

Abel had to narrow his eyes more tightly than even nature had intended before he could see the wispy gray smoke coming out of a window on the second story. There was smoke from another window as well. He nodded tensely, then rolled the carriage window down and stuck his head out briefly.

"Moses, stop the carriage! Stop it, do you hear?"

The carriage came to a halt, the horses panting.

Nancy asked quietly, but with tenseness, "What are you going to do?"

He was used to thinking swiftly, even as he moved. "I'll help over here as much as I can."

"We'll wait."

269

"No. You two get back to town and call out the fire department." Such as it is, he added under his breath. Two trucks and eighteen volunteers didn't amount to much.

Nancy said automatically, "Be careful."

"Don't waste time," he snapped.

As he started running toward the mansion, he found himself looking back at his wife and son as the carriage turned. He saw Kermit's red head below Nancy's flowing red hair. It occurred to him that there wasn't anybody he loved as much or hated as much as his wife, and he supposed that meant he had a successful and happy marriage. As he watched, almost against his will, Nancy drew up a hand to wave at him. Her other hand nudged Kermit several times. Kermit put up a hand in greeting as well, but his small face with Abel's own features remained frozen in distaste.

He turned his attention to what was happening in front of him.

At that moment his eyes rested on the trap. It had been painted gold, which didn't surprise him. It was in motion, the horses moving it around and around the stable, uselessly. Abel waited until they were close to him, then slapped both chestnuts across the rump and reached for their wet bits. He pulled hard. The horses whickered in complaint, but came to a stop. There was a post at each side of the stable, outdoors. Abel led the horses to it and hitched them while they were still tied to the trap. He ran inside, looking for water to give the beasts, but didn't see buckets or feed bags. He didn't see any other horses, either.

Outside again he looked warily across the large clearing and over to the mansion. It seemed that the fire, unchecked, was spreading. He started running in that direction at last, wondering why he didn't hear any Blacks or an overseer calling out directions. Surely this was the time for a bucket brigade. He couldn't underst- —.

He nearly tripped, but righted himself, and looked down to see what could have caused him to almost fall on this well-barbared land. Then he stopped.

270

The Passys, both of them, lay head to head on their stomachs in the dirt. The clothes of each had been torn up the back. The faces, as nearly as he could tell, had been beaten and stomped on. The earth below them was red with blood and white with teeth. Abel touched their wrists and then let their hands drop, and got up. The absurdly patriotic wealthy man and his affably patronizing wife had died horribly.

An insurrection had certainly caused all this, and the fire as well. It was a warm afternoon, but Abel was shivering as he appreciated by how thin a thread his own life had hung during the slavery years. He couldn't do anything about the fire, not by himself. What he'd have to do was get back to Fairlawn and try to keep the fire from spreading to his land. He ran back to the stable, untied the horses, and then got into the trap and set off.

13

The coal-black young slave, Neva, was coming out of her canvas-topped cabin when she saw Blossom, her face with its high cheekbones was angry and a tic was on the older slave's temples. Blossom glared, standing with head up high so that any neck wrinkles wouldn't show.

"While we wait for the masta, I take care of my own business," Blossom said grimly. "We not slaves any more, so we not worth money so it don't matter."

"What you want?"

"I fix it so you never fuck my Jethro again."

Neva sniffed and started to walk past the other girl, but Blossom made a pair of fists. Neva was ready for a hair pulling if that was what Blossom wanted, but didn't expect the whole world to suddenly blow up at the punch of a fist. The earth and sky swayed in front of her, and the floor punched her back as she fell down. Hate boiled inside her as she rolled on the earth, just as the older gal

271

tried to jump on top of her. Fist and weapon blows thundered against Neva's body. There was a sudden snapping and a silence, but it didn't last long enough.

Neva was lying on the earth and feeling wet clear through when she opened her eyes slowly. Blossom, towering above her, was holding an empty basin. As soon as she realized Neva was conscious again, Blossom let the basin fall out of her hands. Neva had already been doused with the muddy water it had held.

"Okay, nigger bitch, here's more!"

Deftly she wrapped a piece of iron around a wide towel and set the towel in place with five fingers. She raised it a short distance, then tapped it lightly against her opened palm. Neva knew that the damn thing would hurt like hell, and it might be used against her head without leaving a mark. Body bruises could be explained, if that was necessary, by saying that Neva had fallen down.

Neva felt too weak to stand and too angry to lie down and take whatever Blossom wanted to do to her. Her hands were free. She swore under her breath and rolled herself across the earth. Blossom chuckled, then took half a dozen long steps. That towel-draped club landed against Neva's right arm and for the moment turned it into wet pulp. The club crashed into the side of her head and she slipped away into blackness. Again she was revived with cold water, so that she would be able to feel the club on her arm and body.

Neva had almost stopped caring about the pain or trying to dodge it. But a cold core around the belly told the young black girl that she wouldn't stop caring about the hatred inside her. The hatred remained, even though she knew she was losing touch again. This time the darkness was stronger and she liked it so much she stayed inside it.

Amos came running and looked down at Neva. Her eyes were closed. Sweat rushed over her face. Every breath she took was requiring a great effort. He turned to Blossom, who stood swaying. The weapon in her hand was pointed straight down and she was staring at it as if it had gripped her.

Tautly Amos asked, "What you do?"

"She try to hurt me. I hurt her first."

Amos looked down. Neva's left leg was thrust out woodenly, and a red stain seeped down the left thigh.

"You hurt her all right." He gritted his teeth. Blossom called out, then gasped and covered her mouth and took the hand away and tried to talk sensibly.

"Blossom has to take care 'a Blossom."

Amos heard Neva's muffled groans. He looked down at his hands, folding and flattening them. And then the fingers seemed to come up as if of their own free will.

"Neva my gal. Mine, and mine only."

Blossom's eyes widened, but she said, "I couldn't know that."

Her face was almost the shade that sunburn might have made it. She'd have given every penny to strike Amos in his black African face. But she knew that she might give up her life for that as well. She supposed he'd hit out at her, and it was perfectly possible that she'd be lucky if he didn't stamp on her. She knew some awful stories about the way a buckra would treat a nigger he didn't like.

Hatred was in Amos' face and in his mind. A chorus of anger welled up in every part of him, and he knew that he wouldn't walk away from Blossom without hurting her. Part of him actually hoped he wouldn't hurt her too bad. It was almost impossible for him to focus. He knew he wasn't going to walk away as if from a funeral.

Was Neva really finished? Neva and Amos had been good for each other more than once, and to be without her was to feel like part of himself had been chopped away. Wasn't there a chance that they'd be together again?

Amos hadn't often seen Blossom looking better, the figure that had become a little blockier over the last few years almost hidden by a purple dress, the usually spiky hair having been allowed to grow out a little so that it almost gleamed. Pretty as she was, he knew that he wouldn't have spit on her if she caught fire, nigra or not. She was

273

dangerous when she had any sense of direction. She wasn't one of those nigger gals who liked to come and talk about the day when she'd get revenge on whites and she herself would have white slaves; those niggers talked a lot, but never did anything. They couldn't, until now.

To his surprise, the hands moved with their own life. The hands reached for that soft dark neck and then squeezed.

Blossom's eyes grew wide. A burst of spittle rose to her thick lips. . . .

When he released her and she fell to the earth, he knew she was dead.

"Just a nigger gal," he said softly. "Not worth nothin' to nobody, now she ain't a slave."

As he hurried to Neva and raised her in his arms, she expired. He put her down gently and crossed her arms, not knowing what made him do that. A shadow fell across Neva's body as he was holding her. Amos turned around to see the huge Jethro.

"What you do?"

"Your gal kill mine, so I kill her."

Jethro's face settled into lines of anger and he took a step forward. At that moment Elihu called out:

"He come."

Jethro turned toward the road. Abel Debenker, in a borrowed trap, was proceeding up toward the stables. As the slaves watched impassively, he got out of the trap and shouted to the nigger he supposed was inside, then hurried over to the slave quarters.

Jethro walked stolidly to meet him.

14

Abel knew that there was trouble from the moment his black half-brother loomed in front of him in the clearing surrounded by badly-tended pecan trees. The two men

274

faced each other, one in his dark Sunday best and the other in rags. Neither man drew back.

Nevertheless, Abel made his voice businesslike. Better not to let Jethro know he was aware of danger.

"Where's the buckra?"

And Jethro said calmly, "He die."

That was when Abel guessed what had happened without asking further, but he knew he had to ask all the same.

"How did he die?"

Jethro raised a hand, the forefinger extended. He drew the forefinger against his rib cage.

Abel swayed back and forth. He had seen Lucas Tinsley larger than life, and it wasn't easy to accept the notion of such a lively and vital man, bastard and good overseer, dead.

There seemed to have been so much death during these last few years, all of it by violence. Death and cotton were the Southland's crops. "Each man's death diminishes me," a poet had once written. Was that true whether the man was white or black? Was death more important than hatred? Did it cancel out hatred? Had the burly black man in front of him already forgiven the dead for injuries received, for wounds inflicted?

"Did you do it?"

"No."

"Who did?"

"It don't matter."

That was true, but Abel couldn't acknowledge it. He had been living a series of lies for such a long time that one brush with the truth would make the whole structure of his enterprise fall to dust. He was superior; the South was winning its war; all slaves would be attended to as long as they were obedient.

"It does matter."

Jethro shrugged. "You not the masta anymore. No black man has any masta, now."

"What makes you think that?"

"We know."

"Is that the sort of thing Blossom tells you? Haven't

275

you had enough of her talking to you so that you get in trouble and she doesn't?"

"Blossom was telling the truth. Not now. She tell nothing any more."

"Is she dead, too?"

"Amos kill her."

The loss didn't make Abel richer or poorer, not any more. He had used her a few times, and didn't doubt that Blossom had used him. A troublemaker, though, and her death was sure to make this talk easier for him.

"If what you're saying is true and there's no more slavery, then you're on my land and you haven't got any reason to be here. Pack up and go."

Jethro shook his head slowly.

Abel, watching in near-disbelief, tried to guess how much it cost his half-brother to pit his will against Abel Debenker's, even now. Wasn't the habit of slavery ingrained in him, built into his soul and nerves and the fibers of his being? All the same, Jethro was not only opposing his master's will, but looking directly into his eyes at a time of tension.

"No place else to go. We stay here."

"If you're free, then I only have to call the police for all of you to be arrested. I'm no longer responsible for any of you."

"We stay here."

"If you're free, you leave. Is that clear?"

Those tones had always brought white overseers around. It didn't work with his half-brother.

"You keep us as slaves, now you help us as free men and women."

"You'll be off my land by nightfall, the whole pack of you."

"No." Were Jethro's lips twitching in the start of a smile? "Nobody grow the cotton for you. Nobody get it to the boat for N'Orleans. You need us. We need you."

Abel took a step back. "Are you suggesting that we make some sort of a deal?"

"Yes." Jethro shrugged massively. "You teach me how

276

to make the whiskey and sell that, so I able to make different deals."

It was Abel's turn to keep a smile back. Lyon Debenker's heritage was part of Jethro, too. For a moment Abel wondered how Jethro might have turned out if he had been born white and then educated.

"Can you keep the others in line?"

"I can."

"How?"

"I talk to 'em." He raised strong black fists. "I use this, if they won't let me talk."

"Can you do that with women, too?"

"Sure. Not all gals like Blossom."

"Maybe so. I'm not saying anything one way or the other until I know exactly where you're getting at. What's your proposition?"

"You pay us, each of us, two dollar the day."

Abel shook his head promptly, a good negotiating tactic. "I haven't got the money for that, and there isn't any bank business to be done at the moment. There won't be, for awhile."

"You find a way to get the money."

"I'm not sure I can do that, but I might." He could make payments in Confederate bills and then make restitution as soon as the crop had been marketed. "Well, I might."

"You pay at sundown."

"Every day? It would certainly be easier if you took payment by the week."

"How can I tell what happen by the end of the week?"

"Well, I'd have to hire somebody to keep figures in a book as to what you spend from the estate. Food, clothes, living space, all of those items cost money."

"We pay. You keep it honest, and we pay."

"I'm not sure it could work out very well."

Jethro said, "And you pay me two dollar extra every week as I keep the boys and gals in line."

"In other words, you'll be my overseer. I never guessed that freedom would turn you into a buckra."

277

Jethro looked away from him, but not down to the warm earth.

"If we're not slave and master anymore, then I want you to destroy your still. It's on my property and I won't have any overseer of mine taking time from his work."

"All right."

"I'll inspect the distillery in a day or so to make sure you've done what you're being told to do."

Jethro nodded.

"Now I've got certain privileges I never had in the past. Rights, if you want to put it that way—no, I'm not making a joke at your expense. Hear me out."

"Yes."

"If I pay for every day's work, then I don't pay somebody who doesn't put in that day's work. For instance, if you've been drinking and helling around the night before and you're too tired to do a day's work, you lose the two dollars for that day. You or anybody else."

"Yes."

"If the work is sloppy for a few days or so, I can send whoever does bad work away from my land. I'm not responsible for that person any longer if that person doesn't carry out his or her responsibilities to me. That's clear, isn't it?"

"Yes."

"If more boys and gals go away of their own free will, then you're responsible until new workers are found. I'll take that out of your extra two dollars a week at the rate of, say, ten cents for each prime field hand who goes."

"But if you tell 'em to go, I not have to pay."

"That's right."

Abel relaxed enough to put both hands into his pockets, and found himself considering that he could get that last crop to market at a small profit. Furthermore he wouldn't have to put up with near-rebellion any longer. The new conditions, as he'd told other slave owners during the course of the war, might work out as an improvement, all things considered.

278

Jethro suddenly said, "You didn't do right when you lie about the end of the war. That's wrong."

"I suppose so, but I'd hoped to make up for it. After the crop was brought in, I'd hoped to pay each of you separately for the work. I've been keeping records."

Jethro couldn't have known what that last word meant, but he nodded intelligently just the same. Come to think of it, his half-brother had been speaking in the past tense as well as in the present. Abel had never heard him do that as a slave, and it was obscurely unsettling.

"You done wrong and Clack done wrong. We bury Clack."

"He's been killed, too?"

"Yes. He lie to his brothers and sisters, so he die for that."

It occurred to Abel that he was a brother of Jethro's as well, and that he had lied, too, in his time. He shook his head fiercely, brushing the thought to one side.

"All right, then, I think we understand each other. We've got a deal."

His palm was itching, and he felt a fierce and unreasoning instinct to stretch out a hand to seal the agreement. He knew that Jethro would be too startled to take the hand. The other slaves, who must have been watching from out of sight, (ex-slaves, he remembered) wouldn't know what to make of it, either. Certainly it was more polite to keep a distance.

That was when he realized that the few months offered him a chance to make the land turnover easier.

"There's something else I'm going to do, and it's a favor to you," he said. "I'm going to show you as much as I can about what the business side of cotton growing is like. I can't show you figures and haven't got the time to teach you reading or writing, but I think I can show you enough so that you won't be taken advantage of."

Jethro didn't thank his half-brother or nod in acknowledgment or even look curious. Abel wished that the black man wouldn't behave as if he was owed kindness and decency and help of every sort.

279

"There's a reason for this, and I might as well let you know right now just what it is. I plan to take my family to England in January and to stay there. My mind is made up about that."

Jethro didn't break his silence, but he looked to his right and left.

"As for what's going to happen to Fairlawn, I've made arrangements with a lawyer about that. I haven't signed papers yet so that it isn't official, but I'm planning to give Fairlawn to my ex-slaves. All of it."

Jethro didn't look surprised or even pleased. He bit his lower lip and then made and unmade a pair of fists. It seemed almost impossible to believe, but Abel thought that his half-brother was angry.

"You give the land to niggers and that makes up for everything that happens. Everything all right."

"There's nothing I can do about what happened in the past.

"What make you think we want white man's land? How do you think we can live here, with the other whites hating us? All you do is you destroy us. You don't give us the chance to work for the land, but you dump it on us."

"I thought I was doing the right thing," Abel said stiffly. "If you don't want Fairlawn, I'm sure that other arrangements can be made."

"We not want gifts from white 'masta'." At the last word, Jethro took a reflexively angry step toward Abel.

The hatred he had felt for years was erupting now and only because of an act of generosity, it seemed. If Abel was harmed in the next few minutes, it would have been brought on by his own willingness to make amends as best he could.

"We want nothin'," Jethro had raised his voice. "We have to work, we do. We free. We want *nothin'* from you. Nothin' you can give us is enough for what you already done to us."

Abel said briskly, "If you want nothing, then that's what you can have."

Jethro was beyond reason now, his fingers moving, eyes widening, lips open and closing and opening. This was the unreasoning anger of a slave owner, but it had been transposed. Abel was far from shocked, knowing that he had to appeal to reason and a sense of business. There was nothing else to be done.

"I think we can get along and——."

"Now we can get along. Now the niggers are free, you want to get along."

"How often will I have to say that I can't undo what's happened in the last few years? I can't perform magic and cause the past not to have taken place. I can only go forward from what has already happened, and so can you and all the other Blacks."

"We don't want nothin' to do with you." But he was moving toward Abel. Webs of spittle had formed on the corners of his lips.

"Listen to me, Jethro—and don't tell me you haven't got to listen. There are two choices; either we work together or we don't work at all. Either we build together or nothing gets built. The choice is as much yours as it is mine. I choose to try and work together. There's nothing else for either of us, not if we want a chance to——."

"I don't want nothin'," Jethro shouted almost in his half-brother's ear. "I die before I take anything from you. I die, but I kill you first."

"Then that's the way it'll be," Abel said calmly and unbelievingly. "I can't make the choices alone."

He turned his back, which was a mistake. Jethro moved forward. It was too late to protect himself. Jethro's huge dark fingers had circled his throat and were squeezing hard. Abel's own action was a reflex, his hands raised as his fingers circled the black throat. The half-brothers swayed back and forth in their dance of death.

A red river was swimming in front of Abel, his eyes darkening. Salt and bile were in his throat as the fingers squeezed. His own strength had faded everywhere except in his fingers. He couldn't see, he could hardly breathe, and there was hell's own roar in his ears. It was the end, but his fingers suddenly seemed stronger than ever.

His balance was gone. He was falling. His eyes closed in spite of himself. He knew it was over, that he had tried and lost everything. He knew that for a moment, and then he knew nothing.

Amos had watched Obie suddenly run off, then shrugged and decided against trying to catch him. He walked away from the slave quarters and over to the clearing where Jethro and the m———, the white man, had been talking for a long time.

He heard nothing, and looked past the line of trees. He found them. They had fallen to the earth. Jethro's fingers had made grooves in the other's neck and drawn blood dollops as long as the heart had been pumping blood. Jethro's eyes were wide open in fury, and the white man's eyes closed as if to avoid that look. Jethro had stepped away, fallen and cracked his head on a stone. Perhaps he'd been too weary to care.

Amos stared down at the white and black man in death's embrace, and though he himself had been illegally sold and brought from far away to be used in slavery, he found that it was possible to feel sorry for both of them.

15

Obie ran for a few hours and then slept and then walked slowly. He was hungry, but didn't try to ask for food. At the border of Festin, he made up his mind to walk around it. Never had he seen so many whites in his life. They milled through a section with houses on every side, looking scared and worried.

It was no place for a black lad of thirteen. He had turned and started to skirt the area when he heard his

282

name called in a high voice only a little more youthful than his own.

"What are you doing here?" Kermit Debenker asked, and then walked up to him and shook his hand like one white to another.

"On my way," Obie said.

"But where can you go?"

"Anyplace as isn't here."

Kermit's mother's voice called, "Kermit, where are y—, oh, there!" Nancy, in black, came rushing over to him and looked down at the boy by her son's side. She recognized one of the youngsters from Fairlawn, and then realized that it was her task to speak first.

"You look hungry."

Obie shook his head fiercely. "I be all right."

"You go around to the bar and to the rear entrance," Nancy said. "Go with Kermit, and tell the bar people I'll pay for whatever you want, and then come back with Kermit. I'll be in the hotel lobby."

Nancy walked slowly, as if she was asleep. In the underfurnished lobby she heard her name called and then felt herself embraced by a weepy Lorna Goldthwait.

"I'm so sorry about what happened," she said. "You can't trust a-one of them nigras, believe me. Chad and I, my dear, were very fortunate. Chad got the upper hand as soon as trouble started."

Nancy was astonished. Chad Goldthwait, who had always treated his slaves like dirt, had survived this mass outbreak.

"I understand that Bart Manders and his family are dead, that the Passys were killed, and that Tom Holman's family is dead, too. I know that Rafe Carstairs, the slave-breaker, and the nigra who worked for him, both had their throats cut. It's been a horrible time for us all, and we can only hope that something better will come out of it."

"Haven't you heard?" Nancy asked softly. "Things don't work out that way."

283

"Do you have any plans, my dear?"

"Only to see to it that my husband is buried, and then take my son and go back to England with him."

"What about Fairlawn itself? You'll have to sell it out, now."

"I don't care what happens to it."

"Well, that seems like a very strange point of view." Lorna looked up, then turned back absently. "You'll excuse me if I go over to see how my husband is faring. I don't want him to take sick after everything he's been through."

"Of course not."

"You know the way my Chad works himself to the bone. Excuse me, dear, and God bless you."

Nancy watched her cross the lobby to join her husband, then heard Goldthwait's booming voice.

". . . vigilant group to patrol the plantations," Goldthwait was saying loudly. "The nigras will have to lay low if they don't all want to be strung up."

"What about the rumor that Union soldiers are coming into this area?"

"We'll make the best of it, if we have to," Goldthwait answered. "But we're not gonna have any Yankees telling us how to handle our niggers."

She felt almost physically sick, and walked out to the square. Men and women moved back and forth, whispering urgently. There weren't any mule carts over to one side and past the end of the square. She could look out along the corner to the section where slave auctions had been held, but there was no sign of life beyond Courthouse Square. The crowd seemed too much for her and she closed her eyes.

Somebody tugged at her right hand. Nancy opened her eyes to see her rawboned and gangly red-headed son. Kermit, at only twelve, looked as if he'd soon be as tall as she herself.

"Mother, we want to stay," he said.

"What?"

284

"Me and Obie, we want to go back to Fairlawn and stay there."

"*You* can't. Obie. I'm sure, can if he wants to."

"Listen, mother, slavery is against the law these days. Slavery is mainly what you didn't like and me, too. But it won't happen any more."

"How can you bring yourself to want to stay in a place where something so terrible happened to your father? Last night, when we heard the news, you wanted to leave as quickly as possible."

"Yes, but I think it's different now. This is where I live and where my friends are."

"In a few minutes you'll be telling me that there's a good profit to be made," Nancy snapped. "You'll be sounding more and more like your father. I don't want to hear any more of this."

"Well, I'll have to work at something, and I might as well do what I'd like where I'd like to be doing it."

"But the Blacks are going to make a lot of trouble and be very resentful over the things that have happened. I'm sure they can't help it. That's only human nature."

Obie said carefully, "Yes, for awhile. But them Blacks will get old and die and then there'll be others, and the land will be there and the cotton to grow."

Nancy looked directly at her son. "Your father didn't want you to be here."

"No," and his father didn't want him to be here, but he came and he stayed."

"And he died horribly."

"But people are going to have to grow their crops and sell them and keep going. Things have got to change."

Ten feet away, a group of youngsters were singing lustily, "We'll hang Jeff Davis to a sour apple tree."

"If you want me to go to England, I'll come back as soon as I can. If you sell this land, I'll buy it back as soon as I can. I want to stay here in spite of everything that's happened to all of us. I want to grow up and get married and have my kids and die here in the South. And Obie

285

wants to stay, too, and so do a lot of us. You have to give us a chance, mother, you have to."

Nancy Debenker nodded slowly and knew that she would return to Fairlawn and stay. She looked at her son as if she had never seen him until now. And she realized that in spite of everything that had been done to them, people like Obie and her son would never feel lasting hatred. It was possible that the relatively brief duration of hatred was really the hope of the world, the promise of the future. A slim hope, a fragile thread, but there wasn't any other.

www.ingramcontent.com/pod-product-compliance
Lightning Source LLC
Chambersburg PA
CBHW020606260626
47157CB00003B/895